Rise of a Legend

Guardian of Scotland Series ~ Book One

by

Amy Jarecki

Rapture Books

Jarecki, Amy
Rise of a Legend

ISBN: 9781517462628
First Release: November, 2015

Book Cover Design by: Amy Jarecki
Edited by: Scott Moreland

To Anna for believing in this saga. Without her encouragement, it may not have been published!

Foreword

The death of King Alexander III in the year of our Lord 1286 was the catalyst for England's invasion of Scotland. After Alexander was found dead on the shore at the bottom of a stony outcropping, the kingdom spiraled into a time of dark treachery.

With no forthright heir to the throne of Scotland, the ruling Guardians quickly undertook an investigation of the royal ancestry and found two men with the most legitimate claim to the succession: John Balliol, Lord of Galloway and Robert Bruce, Lord of Annandale—grandfather of the future King Robert the Bruce.

These two men now readied themselves to battle for their rightful place as king. Aye, these were brutal times, and civil war in Scotland seemed imminent.

In an attempt to maintain peace, Bishop Fraser of St. Andrew's wrote to King Edward in England, asking for his intervention. After all, Edward had been Alexander's brother-in-law, and Scotland *had been* at relative peace with England.

Seizing an opportunity he couldn't refuse, The King of England arrived and immediately claimed he was the rightful suzerain—or overlord—of Scotland. After much deliberating, he appointed John Balliol to the Scottish throne. Balliol was considered the least likely to pose a threat to England, especially when compared to the powerful, and power hungry Bruces.

Almost immediately, Edward began his humiliation of Balliol, issuing personal insults and demanding public demonstrations of fealty. Worse, the Scots were used like pawns and forced to fight England's battles. Balliol tried to humor Edward until he was pushed too far and the Scottish king formed an alliance with France.

At this point in history, the English army was the greatest fighting machine in Christendom. And when news of Balliol's defection arrived, Edward sent his army to sack Berwick on 30th March, 1296. No mercy was shown. No prisoners were taken.

The slaughter continued for three days. It is said Edward only called a halt when he saw one of his soldiers butchering a woman in the act of childbirth.

The atrocity of Edward's barbarism is still remembered to this day.

Facing the possibility of annihilation, Balliol had no other choice but to abdicate. Edward imprisoned him in the Tower of London and later sent the "puppet king" to France.

Though many of Scotland's nobles possessed property on both sides of the border, the common majority were outraged that their king had been humiliated and wrongfully imprisoned by a tyrant overlord.

Then a warrior of epic repute came on the scene and united a broken nation.

His name was William Wallace.

Chapter One

Eva sat up gasping. Sweat steamed from her brow as she panted, catching her breath and willing her thundering heartbeat to slow. She fumbled for her smartphone while eerie shadows shone through the slats of the caravan's blinds. Shoving her fingers in the crease between the mattress and the wall, she found it. *Four-forty-four.* She shuddered. Why did the nightmares wake her at the same time every night?

Mercy, she'd returned to Scotland fleeing from the terrors of New York—joined the Loudoun Hill dig team. Yeah, hard work and discovering ancient artifacts was supposed to be exciting—supposed to be an auto-reset for her life.

But no one could run from their mind.

She pressed against her eyes and saw the knife again. Drawing in a sharp gasp, she jerked her hands away. Then shook her head. The weapon had always been hewn of blue steel—a bowie knife meant for hunting—or killing. But she'd just pictured an old blade like a dagger or a dirk, maybe even a sword.

Dammit, I'm turning into a nutcase—Eva MacKay, the raving reporter.

She plopped back to her pillow and stared at the ceiling—for about ten seconds. Nope. This time there'd be no going back to sleep. Besides, the team would be stirring soon. In the past two weeks, Professor Tennant had made it eminently clear he liked to start early.

Eva quietly hopped down from her bunk so not to wake her roommates, Linsey and Chrissy. She slid into her skinny jeans, pulled a sweatshirt over her head and shoved her feet into her hiking boots. Reaching for her toiletry bag and a clean pair of undies, she headed for the women's washroom.

Standing under the pressure-less stream of water, Eva poured a dollop of shampoo into her palm and did her best to scrub up a lather. In the fortnight she'd been working with the dig team, she missed two things from her former lifestyle—whirlpool baths and massages. She wouldn't mind if the showers at the caravan park had an iota of pressure, but showering under the pathetic stream of tepid water took a good five minutes to just rinse the shampoo from her thick red hair.

Still jittery from the remnants of her nightmare, she hurried with the conditioner and toweled off. Teeth hastily brushed and hair pulled into a ponytail, she opted to forgo makeup, hoping to slip to the dig site for some alone time before the others arrived.

After she grabbed a takeaway cup of coffee and a scone from the Quiet Harpy, she headed for her car—a red Fiat—her indulgence, purchased on the same day her plane landed in Edinburgh. Once sitting in the driver's seat, the rev of a new engine proved to be far better therapy than a shrink's couch. With a surge of reassurance, she put the Fiat in gear and headed off.

Eva had no idea what prompted her to slow when she approached the turn for the town of Fail. She not only braked, she drove the car onto an unmarked road and drove as if she knew where she was heading. Nonetheless, the road led east. How lost could she get in Ayrshire? Besides, her phone had a GPS. Perhaps today would bring a new adventure. And driving down the single-track road *felt* right.

Just around the bend, a ruin caught her eye and she pulled the Fiat off the road. A ray of light from the rising sun illuminated what looked like the remains of an old church. Amber hues flickered golden over the mossy stone. She stepped out of the car and watched the sunbeam gradually travel over the roofless relic.

Pulling her phone from her pocket, she snapped a photo.

Perfect.

When Eva looked up, the sunglow continued to move to the field beyond, leaving the ruin in the shadows of an enormous ash tree.

A sense of calm spread from her chest and through her limbs, as if the sun's ray had been transported from the church into her body. Blinking, Eva had no idea what had come over her, but at least the jitters from her nightmare finally faded into oblivion.

After one last cursory glance, filled with calm, she climbed back into the Fiat and headed for Loudoun Hill.

***

The tires skidded through the gravel when she pulled into a parking spot above the way-too-modern looking monument erected in honor of William Wallace—not Robert the Bruce. She sniggered at the irony. The dig was sponsored by the NTS to unearth relics from Robert the Bruce's battle. And according to Professor Tennant, Wallace's fight waged on this very ground could only be conjecture since it hadn't made it into historical documents.

Right. That's why Wallace's monument is here—not Bruce's. She sniggered again.

Eva stepped out of her Fiat and grabbed her gear.

Tools in hand, she headed to the trench with a determined hitch in her stride, making a beeline to the same place she'd been working yesterday. Her shoulders again tensed, forgetting the sense of calm she'd experienced at the ruins a few moments ago. The day before, she'd uncovered a boulder that wouldn't budge. They had a backhoe onsite, but by the time she'd brushed the dirt from the top of the rock, no one was there who knew how to use it. A historical journalist brought up in the city, Eva wasn't even about to try.

Maybe because she didn't want to use a backhoe.

Maybe she could carefully chisel around the rock and dislodge the thing herself?

Her gut clenched. As a matter of fact, she needed to, absolutely must, dislodge it herself.

The caffeine from her coffee kicked in to high gear and she started running with pick, trowel and brush in hand. Jumping into the trench, she eyed the offending rock. She set her tools on the shoulder-level ground and pushed up her sleeves—ready for battle. A quick reach for her pick and Eva sauntered toward the piece of granite.

"You're not going to stop me today."

She used the point to dig around the stone as she'd been taught, carefully chipping away pebbles and dark soil as she worked. After clearing a good two inches from the top of the rock, she tugged up her gloves and gave it a good downward shove. The boulder didn't budge. Putting her weight into it, she tried to work the rock from side to side. When it refused to move, she bore down, pushing so hard her feet lifted off the ground. Nothing.

Losing is not an option. Not today.

She braced both hands on top of the stone. "You're going down."

Straining with every ounce of strength, gnashing her teeth, a bead of sweat rolled from her forehead into her eye. With a huff, she released her grip and took in a deep breath. "Double dammit."

She wiped her forehead with the crook of her arm. "You will not get the better of me. I've had enough roadblocks in the past year to last a lifetime." God, she hated anything that stood in her way. Eva worked the pick more vigorously into the dirt at one side of the boulder, and then the other—heck, a backhoe would do a lot more damage than her wee pick.

Eva's palms slipped inside her gloves, but she refused to stop. A goddamned piece of rock could be moved, even by her. For goodness sakes, at five-eleven she was no delicate rose. She'd played basketball for NYU. Well, yeah, she may have graduated five years ago, but she still had "it".

With each stab at the earth, she became more determined. This piece of granite epitomized all the debilitating quicksand in her life—the grief, the fear, the loneliness, and failure, the suffocation of being beaten and crushed by the entire world. And today she would not allow the boulder to win.

She raised the pick over her head and shook it at the sky. "Steve is dead!" she screamed.

Again and again, Eva clawed and brushed earth away from the boulder that seemed to increase in size with her every effort. Conquering this blasted rock served as a symbol of redemption. She *had* to dislodge the boulder. Her life depended on it.

A tear streamed down her face. Finally, months of pent-up grief released through her arms as she tore into the earth with all her strength and more. She would dislodge the beast and prove to the world she could move on.

Prove to myself.

"I will show you, the world, and every murderer out there. I will not be afraid. I will not be intimidated for the rest of my life. Take your knives and bury them beneath this rock!"

With one more stretching blow, she drove the pick behind the boulder. The enormous thing shifted down with a groan from the earth. It stuck there, precariously jammed in the crevice. Eva skittered backward.

Holy shit.

She could have been crushed. The rock had to be at least three feet in diameter.

She climbed out of the trench and stood above her giant boulder. Dropping to her knees, she gave it a forceful shove.

"It's my turn to win, you bastard!"

The slab of granite dislodged and dropped to the ground with a dull thud, debris and stones showering behind it. Now they'd definitely need the backhoe to pull the darned thing out of the trench.

Eva rocked back onto her haunches and chuckled. "That's right. No stone will stop me. You might drag me through hell, but you will *not* take my spirit." She shook her fist and laughed out loud. "I will be victorious."

Jeez, it felt good to blow off steam, and thank God no one was around to tell her she'd lost her mind. She reveled in her victory. As the boulder dropped from its hold, a burden had lifted from her chest like a gateway had finally opened. Eva stood with her fists on her hips and took in deep, reviving breaths, each one filling her limbs with renewed energy.

After she slid back into the trench, she stuck her head inside the gaping hole. She removed her gloves and ran her hand over the jagged surface. Stones had come loose and scattered with the dirt. The tip of her finger hit something hard—almost harder than stone, but with a rounded edge. She froze.

Is it manmade?

Eva's heart skipped a beat as she dug in her pocket for her penlight and shined it on the curious item. *Iron, maybe?*

Holding the light with her left hand, she reached in with her brush and cleared away the dirt from the rusty piece. Certain she'd found something of interest, Eva used the tip of her finger to gently push, testing to see if it was loose. The thing tipped sideways with a clink.

She gasped.

Fingers trembling, she plucked the item from its tomb and pulled it out, resting it in her palm. Carefully, Eva smoothed away the dirt, then angled it toward the sunlight. A faint imprint of an archer embossed the middle. She blew on

the flat side, clearing enough dirt to study the inscription.
sialaW inalA suiliF

Could it be a document seal?

Oh yeah. A stamp would be written backward.

She decoded it in her mind. *Filius Alani Walais.* Her heartbeat sped. She was not just a William Wallace buff, Eva considered herself a diehard super-fan of Scotland's greatest hero. Had she unearthed the man's seal?

"What have you got there?" a deep voice asked.

Eva jolted. She hadn't heard anyone approach, but sure thing, Professor Walter Tennant stood on the embankment right behind.

"I-I think this might be William Wallace's seal." Her hand trembled as she held it up. "Um…you might recall I submitted a series of articles on Wallace I wrote for the *New York Times.* I-I hoped that's what earned me a place on this dig."

The professor nodded. "I remember very well, indeed."

Eva bit her bottom lip and pointed. "See the embossing?"

Walter put on a pair of white cotton gloves, took the brittle stamp and turned it over his hand. "By God." He sat on the edge of the trench with his legs dangling. "If this is genuine, it could very well be the find of the entire summer."

Her heart performed a backflip as Eva pointed to the boulder. "Something drove me to dig out that big rock. I thought I needed to prove to myself I could do it, not that there would be a relic wedged beneath."

Walter blew on the artifact and held it so close to his face, he looked cross-eyed through his coke-bottle lenses.

She stepped toward him. "What do you think?"

"Priceless," he whispered.

Eva pulled out her phone and snapped a picture, then held the camera out. "Will you take one of me with the seal?"

"Hold your palm flat."

She did as he asked and he carefully let the artifact slide into Eva's hand. Raising it as if it were as precious as the Hope Diamond, she cradled the seal to her cheek with the inscription facing the camera—Walter didn't need to tell her to smile. She couldn't wipe the grin off her face if she'd wanted to.

After he returned the phone, he pulled a plastic bag from his pocket and held it out. "This is quite a find."

She tilted her hand and let the seal slip inside. "Are you going to notify the NTS?"

"I'll ring them in a minute and then do some field testing. But this is as authentic as they come, mark me." He peered at Eva with a pointed look. "You ken there are volumes about Wallace's life no one knows. So much was left unrecorded."

She climbed up and sat on the side of the trench beside Walter. "It's a damned shame if you ask me. Blind Harry said Wallace was the son of Malcolm, but the seal—*that seal*—clearly states he's the son of Alan. Even Andrew Fisher agreed the evidence pointed to Alan as William Wallace's father."

Walter chuckled. "Your analysis of Fisher's writings in your article impressed even me."

"Thank you." Eva could have floated right to the top of Loudoun Hill—her editor hadn't been nearly as enthusiastic. "Some say he's done the most thorough research on Wallace."

"Some do." Tennant cleared his throat with a deep rumble. "I wouldn't discount Blind Harry's fifteenth century verse. He recounted stories that had been retold for a hundred and fifty years. There might be a modicum of truth in every chapter."

"But you shot me down when you gave your presentation—said 'we're not chasing after a poet's fairytale' or something like that." Eva thought her imitation of the professor's rolling burr was pretty good.

"I was presenting facts, not conjecture. However when it comes to Blind Harry, people want to believe rather than question."

"Interesting—but all oral stories change every time they're retold." Eva drummed her fingers against her lips. "Regardless of what a fifteenth century poet deemed the gospel, why wouldn't people want to know the truth? That's the very reason I went into journalism. I want to report the truth to the world."

"Quite an ambition." He held the seal up and peered through the plastic. "But isn't one man's truth another man's lie?"

Her shoulders tensed as if he'd issued a slap. "I don't think so. It's the job of the journalist to give an unbiased account of the facts. That's where history errs—too many reporters skewing the truth." She could have debated Walter's statement for the rest of the day, but instead she pointed to the seal. "How do you think that got here?"

"Not sure. Wallace could have lost it himself, or it could have been a keepsake carried by one of Bruce's men."

"Wouldn't it be cool if it was held by Sir Robert Boyd? If my facts are right, he rode with Wallace and then with Robert the Bruce."

Walter's eyes bulged behind his comical glasses. "You do ken your history."

Eva glanced longingly at the stamp. "I wish I knew more."

***

On her way to the dig site the next morning, Eva's car again turned right onto the unmarked road to Fail. She could have sworn the Fiat turned on its own but that would have been absurd. Regardless, the detour wouldn't cause much of a delay. Giving in to *her* intuition, she drove straight to the church ruin she'd found the day before.

The sky violet above, magenta and orange hues illuminated the eastern horizon as she parked beside the old ruin. *Good, I'm in time to see the sunrise.*

As usual, the morning air was cooler than she liked, and she covered her pink NYU sweatshirt with a blue, down-filled vest. The grass a bit boggy, water bubbled beneath her hiking boots with every step. Ever since arriving at the dig she'd been thankful she'd had the wherewithal to purchase a sturdy pair of waterproof boots—red ones.

She stepped across a threshold where the door once would have been. Rectangular quarried blocks covered with moss lay scattered amid the grass, shaded by a canopy of birch and an inordinately tall ash tree. Eva stood for a moment. Tingles spread over her shoulders as if someone had just blown on her neck.

She glanced behind. Nope, she was still alone.

To the east, the oranges and violets of the sunrise pulled Eva toward the old church. She moved into the center of the ruin and faced the sun. Just as the master mason would have planned it in medieval times, rays gradually climbed the lone east-facing wall of the sanctuary. Luminous light sparkled around on the outer corners of the only remaining wall. Somehow it survived the ravages of time.

Her breath caught when a ray streaked down from the wheel-shaped window, as if an angel shone a beam of light straight onto Eva's face. She squinted.

Goosebumps rose across her skin. Gripped by the sudden urge to sing a refrain from the Hallelujah Chorus, Eva opened her mouth but couldn't make her voice work. The air around her levitated as the sun centered itself inside the circular window atop the crumbling wall. In fact, her body became weightless. If it weren't for the angle of her foot awkwardly resting on a stone, Eva would have sworn she was floating.

Continuing up the wall, the sun's light had nearly passed over the window when a flock of mourning doves took flight from the canopy made by the enormous ash. For the second day, the sensation of weightlessness made the woes lift from her shoulders and her mind soar with the birds.

She stared at the wall, not wanting to move. Her mind clear, her fears gone, Eva found her place of calm serenity.

"This church is magical, isn't it?" Walter Tennant's voice whispered directly behind her.

But Eva didn't jolt this time. Her gaze remained fixed on the window, as if she expected the professor to appear. A dove landed on the sill and stared at her.

Taking a deep breath, Eva turned, faced the archaeologist and pointed. "The sunrise. It lined up perfectly with the wheel window. When I drove past yesterday, I thought it might, but wanted to see for myself."

Now that the ethereal moment had passed, she studied him with puzzlement. "What…Why…How did you know I'd be here?" Her fists flew to her hips. "And why did you happen by this place at this very moment?"

He chuckled, cupping his chin between his thumb and pointer finger. "No reason, really. I've often driven past these ruins."

"Honestly?"

"Aye." Walter took a seat on the remains of the wall and patted the spot beside him. "This once was Fail Monastery. It was established in the Trinitarian Order by John de Graham in twelve fifty-two."

"Trinitarian?" Eva didn't recall the order from her studies. "That's unusual, isn't it?"

"Nay, not in those times. They had friaries all over—wore white vestments with a large red-and-blue cross." Walter drew a cross on his chest with his finger.

Eva scrutinized the surroundings—pastoral land sparse with trees, but no other signs of ruins. "If this was a monastery, there would have been a lot more to the grounds than just this nave. What happened? Did it fall victim to The Reformation?"

"Not entirely. And it wasn't a well-to-do sect. The Trinitarian monks were charged with the duty of rescuing Christian captives from slavery." Walter crossed his ankles and looked down in thought. "I reckon they were the most Christian-like of all the orders. They never had much—couldn't compete with wealthier orders because of their generous philanthropy."

Eva smoothed her hand across the stone at her side. "I think it's a shame so many great castles and churches have fallen into ruin."

"I agree. You ken William Wallace could have spent a great deal of time right here. After all, he had an interest in the priesthood."

She let Walter's words sink in for a moment while a hundred questions swarmed about her head, but one stood out. "So, since we know Wallace studied to be a priest, was Blind Harry incorrect when he wrote William was married to Marion Braidfute?"

"Ah yes, the master sixteenth-century poet. As I said before, you must read between the lines of Harry's writings—there are nuggets of truth betwixt the babble." Walter's bottom lip jutted out with his shrug. "But no one knows if William was married. Given his education, it doesn't stand to reason, though. And there's no record that Marion existed."

"True, but at that point in time it wasn't unusual for female births to go unrecorded." Eva stood and looked at the window again. "I wish I could travel into the past and write his true story."

"Och aye, me as well, but I wouldn't be able to sit back and allow history to run its course."

She faced him. "Oh, I could. That's the essence of being a journalist—to be impartial and report the facts as they truly occur."

He rocked back. "Very interesting point of view, indeed. I'm afraid I'd try to intervene. Then Scotland might end up without the greatest hero and martyr who ever lived." Walter spread his arms wide. "Wallace's legacy is epic, legendary, larger than life. It has defined Scotland's sense of pride for over seven hundred years. I'd be mortified if I did anything to jeopardize that."

She tapped a piece of flagstone with her toe. "I have to agree with you there. I think he was exactly what the country needed."

"You'd best believe it, lassie."

She sighed. "If only we knew more about him…I mean *really* knew."

The professor stood and stretched. "And that is up to archaeologists and historical journalists like us to uncover and report—maybe we'll find more clues right here."

Eva expected him to head to his car, but Walter moved to the very place she'd watched the sun shine through the window. "No one can change the past." His voice grew ominous. "That is the only rule."

She gave him a quirky look. He certainly was odd—even for a professor. Though he had an endearing air, sort of like a grandfather—someone she felt comfortable talking with. "May I ask you a question?"

"Depends." Walter rolled his hand through the air.

"Have you ever lost someone close to you—someone who wasn't supposed to die?"

Walter removed a large coin from his pocket and smoothed his thumb over the surface. "Aye." His hand trembled a bit. "Lost my twin sister when we were but in primary school."

Eva drew in a quick breath. "I'm sorry."

He opened his palm and looked at the coin. Eva peered a little closer, realizing the piece was very old and had a metal loop as if it might be a medallion worn around the neck.

"Now it's my turn to ask you something," he said, closing his fingers.

Eva pulled back—she shouldn't have been so nosy. "All right."

"You seem to be born with a silver spoon—you're smart, beautiful, wealthy. Why did you volunteer for this dig?"

That was easy enough. "I'm a historical journalist with a deep love of Scottish history." She stuffed her hands in the pockets of her down vest. "Anyone with my background would be thrilled to be here, regardless."

"Aye?" The look on his face reminded Eva of her father's expression whenever he caught her in a lie. "I think the reason goes far deeper."

She swallowed.

"You were a favorite at the *Times*, a darling Scottish rose." He wasn't going to let up. "Had a stellar career in the making. But you walked away."

Heat flared up the back of her neck. The last thing she needed to hear was a lecture. "How do know so much about my life?"

He gave her a disbelieving smirk. "You're a top-notch journalist and you're asking me?"

Eva folded her arms. Maybe the lecture wasn't coming, but Walter sure knew how to push her buttons, and she wasn't going to let it slide. "You said you lost your sister. Well, I lost my *husband.* A man I was planning to have a family with, a man who meant *everything* to me."

Walter tossed the medallion in the air and caught it. "Och aye, I understand your loss well enough. And I feel for you, lass. I really do. But what I want to know is when will you decide to break down that wall you've built around yourself and get on with your life?"

She didn't want to answer—didn't want to have this conversation, but something in Walter's stance demanded she reply. *Damn him.* "When the pain in my heart stops," she whispered.

"That will come with time." He positioned the artifact in his palm and smoothed his pointer finger around it. Then his enormous eyes met hers in challenge. "If you could do anything in the world, achieve any level of success, what would it be?"

"Aside from winning a Pulitzer?" She threw her head back with a rueful laugh, relieved the conversation had turned to something easier to discuss. "For me, it's not about earning recognition. Not really. It's about telling the story." She took in a deep breath and met Walter's pointed gaze, then stepped closer and squared her shoulders. By God, no one could change her mind about her single remaining passion. "I want to find something so intriguing…"

"Go on," he said.

"…So intriguing, the entire world says *wow.*"

Walter smiled. "A worthy ambition." He pulled a leather thong from his pocket and threaded it through the pendant's loop. "I want you to keep this for me over the summer. It is said this medallion has powers that will direct you toward the path you are to travel."

"You don't believe in magic, do you, Professor?" she teased.

He tied both ends and slipped it over her head. "Aye, lassie." He inclined his chin toward the wall. "A wee bit o' magic happens every time the sun shines through that window up there."

She grasped the medallion and read the inscription. *Verum est quasi malis navis in nocte.*

"It means: *truth is like a beacon.*" Walter reached in and turned it over. "And on the reverse it reads: *but few choose to follow.*"

With a couple years of college Latin under her belt, Eva read the inscription on the back. *Sed pauci volunt sequi.* "If you believe this, then yesterday why did you say one man's truth is another man's lie?"

Walter shrugged. "I wanted to see how you'd respond. You see, I believe we need someone who has a fervent hunger for the truth—someone who's willing to allow history to unravel so she can share her unfettered story with the world—the one that just might make people say *wow*."

Not quite sure what to say, Eva looked down at the bronze disk while another breeze tickled the back of her neck bringing on a swarm of tingling goosebumps. "Well, thank you. I'm honored you trust me with such a keepsake."

"Let us hope your sentiments don't change after…"

"After?"

He glanced up at the window and stroked his chin. "The summer's end."

She wrapped her fingers around the medallion, surprised that it felt warm after having been suspended in the cool air. "Where did you find this piece?"

"A young monk gave it to me right before I tried to alter the past." Walter made no sense at all.

"What?" Eva asked.

The professor batted his hand in front of his nose. "Never mind. That story's for another time and I must be on my way. After your momentous find, there'll be more reporters at the dig site today, mark me."

Eva started to follow him, but he stopped and held up his palm. "Stay here for a while. I wouldn't want you to miss the serenity Fail Monastery brings to those who allow these crumbled walls to speak. I interrupted your moment of solace. Carry on."

Watching Walter head to his car, Eva puzzled. *He's a bit cryptic that one.*

After he drove off, the trees rustled above and a welcomed, woodsy scent fragranced the sanctuary. Suddenly heavy-lidded, Eva sat cross-legged and looked up at the window. "What have you seen in all the centuries you've stood there? Happy times and unfathomable desolation, I'd bet. You most certainly were built in a time of brutality—a time when human life was not valued as highly as it is today."

"*You must not change the past,*" Walter's voice echoed in her head. But those hadn't been his exact words. Regardless, Eva was too tired to rationalize any of the professor's mysterious prattle.

Placing her elbow on a fallen stone, she yawned. Overcome with sleepiness, she rested her head in the crook of her arm and closed her eyes.

I want to find my wow.

Chapter Two

Scottish borders, 1st May, the year of our Lord, 1297

William Wallace galloped his warhorse toward the village of Lochmaben, a score of men following in his wake. Unable to reach the town fast enough, he could not pull his gaze away from the black smoke billowing ahead—a sure sign the messenger had been right.

He'd never prayed so hard for a man to be wrong.

Sour bile churned in his stomach.

Dear Lord, I cannot be too late.

But his gut told him differently. Approaching the cottages near the English fort, the smoke grew thick as fog. Not a woman wept or infant cried. An eerie quiet wafted through the air with the billowing blackness. William drove his horse forward and pulled his mantle across his nose, his eyes tearing at the sting.

Father John Blair rode in beside him. "My God."

Though the butchering had become a common scene, William would never grow accustomed to it. Scots men, women and children lay face down in the mud, their blood turning the puddles to a sickly maroon. Others hung by the neck, suspended from ropes affixed to the lintel of the burning barn. The ropes creaked on the wood, swinging back and forth in a demanding rhythm, screaming outrage as their lifeless bodies swayed.

"Cut them down," William growled.

Riding further into the war-torn border village, William's throat thickened. None of this made sense. A madman had invaded his beloved Scotland and his countrymen paid in blood with these nonsensical raids.

Since Edward Plantagenet sacked Berwick and Dunbar one year past, William had formed a secret militia of a score and ten men. But his efforts were not enough. Worse, the Scottish nobles had been hogtied—any insurrection on their part and the upper class would face ruination. The nobility could lose not only their lands, but indeed their families could end up ruined by the same murderous tyranny William and his men witnessed this day. Forced to sign an oath of fealty, none of the great men in Scotland could stand against the mightiest army in Christendom.

Not unless they are united.

But the day of emancipation seemed a passing dream. Edward had imprisoned the King of the Scots, John Balliol in the Tower of London. English raids grew ever worse. And now the bastards had lured William's father and other influential men into their clutches.

Many faces of the fallen were familiar.

A gust of wind cleared the smoke a bit. Gulping back a heave, William wished it hadn't.

Dread iced through his veins as he inched his horse through the boggy street.

Though the man lay flat on his face, there was no mistaking Wallace gazed upon the remains of his father. All shreds of hope dissolved. The back of Da's legs had been deeply cut, as if the bastards sliced through his sinews to take the big man to his knees. And by the wounds encrusted with blood, they'd attacked his body with spears and knives.

Disbelief clutched William's heart into a tight ball. He'd experienced hate before, but never an all-consuming malignity that seeped from his skin like a sickly plague. Sucking in gasping breaths, his chest heaved. His gaze shifted left then right. *The cowards have fled?* "They'd best not sleep." His voice tremored. "For I will hunt down each of these murderers and watch the life flee from their eyes as they suffer the cold iron of my sword."

"The blackguards' tracks lead north." Blair stepped beside him, his voice sounding like the toll from a lone church bell announcing a funeral.

William wiped his eyes. Gritting his teeth, he dismounted and staggered to his father's side. His tears were no longer caused by the smoke. They represented the anguish spreading through his limbs—his bleeding heart, stunned to the point where every beat pained him. Longshanks had taken his lust for power too far. William had seen annihilation by the English, carried out in the name of their bloodthirsty king, but never had Longshanks' sword struck kin. William's knees turned boneless as he dropped beside his father.

Rage, despair, agony, disbelief all gripped ahold of his heart at once. His hands shook violently as he reached out. His throat thickened and choked him.

Gathering Da into his arms, William clutched the still-warm body to his chest. Rocking back and forth, his every muscle tensed to the point of ferocious tremors. *God in heaven, is this a nightmare from which I will never wake?*

A chasm spread through his chest and boiled until it erupted from his throat with an earth-shattering bellow, "Nooooooooooooooo!"

His mind consumed by burning fury, bloodlust ate his gut. William would never forget the sight of his father slaughtered, Da's blood staining the muddy ground.

The past year of tyranny had taken its toll on Scotland's countrymen. But William would sooner die than lay down his sword and submit. He hadn't signed over his fealty on Longshanks' Ragman Roll. He vowed before God he would never bend to the yoke of tyranny. Yes, Longshanks had humiliated and imprisoned Scotland's true king. The English monarch continued to threaten the nobles and impose insurmountable taxes. And now that he had the ruling class in his grasp, the usurper had taken to raiding small villages and churches—inviting landowners to meetings and slaughtering them, just as he had done this very day.

The bloody English think themselves superior? They're the most heinous barbarians who ever walked through Christendom.

William's jaw set firm as he recalled the verse drilled into him by Brother MacRae, a fierce teacher, knight and monk, "Freedom is best, I tell thee true. Of all things to be won, then never live within the bond of slavery, my son."

"Amen," Blair said behind him. The priest had witnessed the same lesson alongside Wallace when they studied to be Templar monks at Dundee.

William closed his eyes and clutched his father tighter. The lifeless man in his arms had done nothing to incite the ire of the English. A tenant farmer to their landowning uncle, big Alan Wallace had led a peaceful life, raising his family, practicing piety and humility. He'd been a father, a husband, a hard worker—a man any son could look up to with respect. No, Da did not deserve this end—cut down like a criminal.

The men who did this were the unlawful curs, an abomination to all humanity.

"In the name of Christ our Lord," William growled through clenched teeth. "I will spend the rest of my days fighting for Scotland's freedom."

Hoofbeats thundered from the west.

A single horse pulled to a halt beside them.

"The English are headed north into Ayrshire," said Edward Little. "Hell bent on murder, they are."

Blair slammed the blunt end of his pike into the ground. "Good God, ye mean the bastards havena shed enough blood for one day?"

"There can be no rest." William pressed his lips to his father's forehead. "John," he called to his younger brother.

"Take Da's body to our mother." He gently lay Da down and chanced one last glance at the mutilated corpses of his fallen countrymen.

The smallest and fairest of the three brothers, John had seen far too much death and destruction for a man of one and twenty. "Ye mean ye're not going with us?"

William swiped his hands over his face and stood. He'd said farewell to his father. Now he needed to look after the living. "We ride."

Malcolm gestured to the dead. "Will we not bury them first?" A good man, Willy's elder brother was no warrior. He had too gentle a heart like their father.

But William had a heart hewn from granite.

He pointed to his squire, Robbie Boyd, then to Blair and two of the younger men in his army. "Stay behind and give them a Christian burial."

"But," Robbie objected. The lad's father had been hanged by the English when Edward first tried to force the nobles to sign his godforsaken roll of fealty. The murder of the venerated Boyd knight had been a successful tool used by the English king to strike fear in the hearts of the gentry.

Now an orphan, William had agreed to foster Robbie until he reached his majority. Their union would serve two purposes, first to hide the boy from English talons, and secondly, William would turn the lad into a man—a warrior. "I'll not hear a word of complaint."

John led his horse beside their father's corpse. "Uncle Reginald willna approve if we cause a stir in Ayr."

William couldn't believe such dull-witted words had just been uttered by his brother. He clutched the errant jester by the throat. "Those are the words of a coward," he seethed through clenched teeth. "Ye'd sit idle and allow those murderers to run free? Whose village will they pillage next? Will they rape and murder women until there are none left to wed Scotland's sons?" William shoved John away. "Are ye willing to stand by and watch the tyranny unfold, just as it has this verra day so near our own home?"

He turned and mounted his black steed, not waiting for John's reply.

"After them!"

Chapter Three

The screeching sound of steel echoed with chilling scrapes and clangs. Men grunted and bellowed. Someone shrieked in pain.

Eva opened her eyes.

Metal flashed.

Panic shot through her veins.

Her heartbeat raced—as if in the midst of a nightmare.

Jerking up, her head struck something hard—a wooden bench.

Where am I?

Eva blinked, her mind racing. She clapped her hand to her throbbing head.

I was on the ground, but this floor is stone.

The bench above her scraped and teetered.

Eva jolted, clutching her fists to her chest.

Unable to breathe, she stared into the eyes of a madman, brandishing a gory sword dripping with blood.

"P-please, don't kill me," she cried, frozen in place, heart hammering.

He sauntered forward, chuckling with a black-toothed grin. Wearing a red surcoat with three rampant lions embroidered on his chest, he looked like something out of a historical reenactment—but way more realistic—smelled like a sewer, too.

Trying to gain her bearings, Eva scooted from his disgusting pall and wedged herself under the bench. "Y-you're s-scaring me."

"Ye miserable Scots speak nary a bit o' sense." With an evil sneer, the man jerked his sword over his head.

Her heart nearly bursting from her chest, Eva fled on hands and knees. The bench caught on her back and scraped the floor.

The sword hissed.

From the corner of her eye, the blade glistened, just like in her dreams. But Eva didn't recall the sound before.

Gasping, she dropped to her stomach and rolled away from the weapon's arc.

God, this was the worst nightmare she'd had yet.

The lunatic smashed his sword into Eva's bench. Splinters of wood shot through the air.

Screaming, she sprang to her feet and ran. Everywhere she looked, men in red surcoats fought monks dressed in white. Blood splattered everywhere.

Stay alive.

She dashed for an altar below a bronze cross. Diving beneath, she crouched into a ball, praying the maniac would find something else to destroy with his bloody sword.

With a whooshing boom, the door burst from its hinges and clattered to the floor.

Lips trembling, Eva peered out from beneath the table vestments. An enormous behemoth of a man barreled into the sanctuary, baring his teeth, swinging a two-handed sword. A mob of bellowing warriors raced in behind him. Each man armed with medieval swords and battleaxes, they charged into the thick of the fight.

With a resounding thud, the altar tottered.

Eva shrieked.

The murderous freak from the pew cackled with a deranged laugh.

She scooted against the wall clutching her arms tight to her shaking body. "Go fight with the other wackos. I'm not a part of your reenactment!"

"I'll skewer your liver, ye mongrel dog!" The man sliced his weapon beneath the table.

Eva screamed as the blade skimmed inches from her face. "Get the fuck away from me," she shouted. "I'm terrified of sharp objects. Take it away. Now!"

The lunatic roared, trying to shove the altar over.

The sturdy table tottered then rocked back into place.

Eva forced her body flush against the wall. "Jesus Christ. I am *not* playing your game."

Something whizzed through the air.

The smelly creep dropped to the floor, his throat cut, his eyes stunned. Blood oozed over the flagstone, spreading rapidly. The metallic stench of blood mixed with dirt. Eva crouched on her toes, clenching her fists so tightly, her fingernails dug into her palms.

Holy shit. Wake up, Eva.

The cloth lifted and the enormous man from the door peered at her. Christ, his dark eyes bore through her with the intensity of a devil. "We killit all the Inglisch, lad—least thoos who didna touk tal an' flee."

Eva couldn't move. *What the hell did he say?* She pointed a shaking finger at the dead man. "Y-y-you *murdered* him," she whispered.

"Aye, afore the bastart cuid run ye thro."

Eva pushed her back against the stone wall and stared. Something clicked in her head.

He's speaking in Auld Scots.

Then her gaze dropped to the corpse. The only time she'd ever seen a dead man was at the morgue when she'd identified Steve's body.

God, stop freaking me out.

She couldn't take it.

Only seconds ago, the man was alive—trying to kill her. She clapped a hand over her mouth before she coughed up her miserable scone and coffee breakfast.

The behemoth held out his hand. "Come afore Inglisch spies se us. Ye dunna want to be found here."

I can wake any time now.

"Haste ye," A man in a black habit called from the doorway. "We nede ta be heding avay."

The big man shook his extended palm at her with a deranged intensity in his glare. "Now, laddie."

She wanted to flee, but her legs wouldn't move, completely frozen in a crouch. Eva clenched her teeth against her stomach's involuntary heave. All color had drained from the dead man's face. Her foot slid forward. The tip of her boot met with dark red blood.

Red.

This dream grew freakier by the second.

Steeling her grit, she placed her hand in the man's outstretched palm. Warm and calloused fingers closed tightly around hers. "Good lad." His speech became clearer. "We must make haste. Once I ken we've not been followed, I'll see ye home."

He pulled her out.

The fighting had stopped.

Light streaked above from a wheel window shaped like the one at the ruin.

Numb, she let the big man lead her outside at a run. Lord, he was more than a head taller.

Rays of sunlight peeked through brilliant green leaves. She blinked at the pain of sudden brightness.

This dream is way too vivid.

They stopped beside an enormous horse, the saddle high in the front and back, skirted by blue felt, looked like nothing Eva had seen before—not that she'd ever ridden a horse.

The man pulled a scabbard from beneath his saddle blanket and sheathed his sword, then strapped it to his back. "Ye'll have to ride with me, laddie."

Me?

She turned full circle, half expecting to see the Fiat.

Now I know I'm dreaming.

"Ye're not one for words, are ye?" He gave her a quizzical look and gestured to the steed. "Up with ye."

She shrugged. *May as well go with it.*

Eva slipped her foot into the stirrup and launched herself into the saddle. She gave the man a nod, finally able to take a deep breath. His face turned up to the sky, his eyes practically pierced through her—the color of blue crystal, they made her heart flutter clear up to her throat. He wore a full beard just like the others. And though he had shoulder-length brown hair curling from beneath his helm, his beard was uniquely auburn.

His eyebrows drew together at an angle. "G'on, scoot behind. There's nary enough room for us both in my wee saddle."

Licking her lips she blinked and studied it. With a cringe, she leaned forward, and inched her behind up and over the back and landed askew. The horse jolted aside. Eva tightened her grip and gasped. Sitting this massive beast was almost as terrifying as being attacked by the reenactment madman.

Reins in his fist, the big man climbed up like he was ascending to his easy chair. "Bloody oath, ye act as if ye've never been on a horse afore."

Eva's throat was so tight, she couldn't utter a word. She would have told him she preferred to drive her car. Right. If only it were part of this nightmare, she'd speed away.

With a grunt, the behemoth dug in his spurs. The horse lurched and jolted, racing away with such bumpiness, Eva threw her arms around the guy just to stay on. Her entire body tensed as she dug her fingers into the man's mail-clad waist. Something pricked her finger.

The horse snorted and stutter stepped. "Ease up your arse, else we'll both end up on our backsides," he growled like a gruff sailor.

Taking in a deep breath, Eva relaxed her thigh muscles. Immediately, the horse settled into a smooth gait. She pulled her hand away and looked at her finger. A droplet of blood streamed and dripped onto her jeans. She put it in her mouth. The bitter taste of iron oozed across her tongue.

With a gasp, heat flared up the back of her neck. *Taste?* The horse smelled like the barn animals at the county fair. The man in front of her had a strong scent as well—definitely masculine—spicy—musky—*kinda nice.*

As a wisp of his hair brushed her nose, the burning sensation from her neck spread throughout her entire body.

Oh my God. This is real.

Chapter Four

After riding away from the church, the sky turned to dusk, and then dark. In an attempt to regain her sanity, Eva closed her eyes and forced herself to take in consecutive calming breaths.

Who were these men and what did they plan to do with her? And why the hell had she just climbed onto the horse without asking questions?

But, holy hell, she'd been scared out of her wits. What else could she have done? Take on an armored man wielding an enormous sword?

She could have run.

And run to where?

The man had said he'd take her home once they were sure they were not being followed. When would that be and where were they heading now? And who would be following—bad guys or good?

Eva squeezed her eyes shut and tried to think. How had she ended up in a church in the middle of nowhere? What happened to her car? Thus far, she hadn't seen a single road, no houses—nothing but trees. The Ayrshire Eva knew undulated with rolling pastureland—not forest.

How did I end up here?

The sun had set behind them, so they must be heading east.

East to where?

She slipped a hand into her pocket and wrapped her fingers around her smartphone. Before she pulled it out, Eva glanced back over her shoulder.

You must not change the past, Walter's voice resounded in her head. "What in God's name did he mean by that?" she grumbled under her breath.

Just to be cautious, Eva unzipped her vest enough to slip the phone inside to hide the light. Then she pushed the "on" button. Her screen lit up and she slid her finger across to unlock it, just like she always did.

Shit. No service. She tapped the GPS, only to receive an offline message. *Damn, damn, damn.*

About to put the phone back in her pocket, her gaze strayed to the upper right corner of the screen. Eight forty-five Wednesday, 1st May, 1297. Eva blinked and looked closer. There had to be some sort of explanation. She pushed the "off" button and slipped it into her pocket.

Had Walter played a trick on her? The professor didn't seem like the type who would—and how could he get her phone to read May, 1297?

Presently, the problem with the date didn't matter. It was dark and Eva didn't have her bearings. The men she traveled with had killed people in a church—who were also killing people—had even tried to kill her, an innocent bystander.

They'd been riding so long, they had to reach a town soon. Once Eva found *normal* people, she'd cry for help, but until then, she had no choice but to ride along with this band of medieval freaks.

Her stomach growled. Jeez, she was hungry. Surely they'd stop for food soon.

Please. She rummaged in her pocket. At least her three two-pound coins were still there. She'd be able to buy a toasty if they *ever* passed a café.

They traveled about another mile through even thicker forest when the trees opened to a clearing.

"Brother Bartholomew," called the ginormous man in front of her. "Have ye some food for us?"

Eva's mouth watered.

A little, brown-haired monk emerged from the darkness, holding a flaming torch. "Aye. I've been worried the English caught ye this time."

Do they ever let up with the show?

The warrior man dismounted. "Come, lad." He patted the horse's shoulder. "The big fella's put in a hard day. 'Tis time to turn him out to pasture."

Eva held out her hands for help, but the man brushed past and headed behind the bushes with the others. Clothing rustled. Water hit the ground. Eva didn't need to look to know what they were doing. She needed to pee herself.

Lord, the ground seemed so far away. Clamping her fingers onto the rear of the saddle, she reached her foot forward and caught the stirrup. Taking her weight, she wobbled a bit, clutching the saddle for dear life.

The horse snorted.

With a rush of courage, Eva slid her leg over the steed's butt and managed to lower herself to the ground, only stumbling a little bit. Her gaze shot to the men, hoping no one noticed.

The leader adjusted himself and stepped from behind the brush. "Dunna be shy, lad, else ye'll be freezing your cods out here in the wee hours."

Eva nodded and headed behind a bush on the other side of the clearing, well away from the men. Squatting, she peered around the scrub and watched them head into the hazy glow radiating from the cave's entrance. Oh, no. They weren't going to leave her alone in the middle of nowhere.

"Wait," she yelled, finishing and yanking up her panties and skinny jeans together.

Her riding partner stopped and turned with his fists on his hips. "Ye're awfully tall for a lad whose voice hasn't yet changed."

She buttoned and zipped. "You're the one who keeps calling me a lad—with hips like mine, no one ever confuses my gender."

Though darkness veiled his face, the whites of his eyes grew round. "Bloody hell, ye mean to say ye're a woman?"

Eva glanced down at her breasts. Concealed beneath the down vest, she could forgive him for not noticing those, but honestly. Did she look that bad?

He took a step toward her.

She scooted back. "Am I in danger?"

"What tongue do ye speak?" His eyes narrowed. "Are ye an English spy?"

"Of course not. I'm a Scot. Born in Edinburgh."

He folded his arms and tipped his chin up. "Nay, ye speak like no Scot I've ever heard."

"I-I studied abroad."

"Och aye? Ye're full of drivel. A woman who studied abroad? Now I ken ye're a spy," he growled, sauntering forward and wrapping his fingers around the hilt of the dirk sheathed in his belt. "I ought to cut out your tongue for telling tall tales."

"No!" Eva waved her hands in front of her face. "Y-you cannot tell my nationality by the way I talk. My father is…" She faltered, recalling the date on her phone. "…*was* an ambassador. I've spent most of my life overseas." Screaming sirens in the back of her mind told her not to divulge too much. First she needed some answers of her own.

"What were ye doing at Fail Monastery?" The moonlit shadows intensified his glower.

"That was—" She stopped herself from repeating the word Fail and sounding like a complete idiot. *Oh my God. It couldn't be.* "I—ah—what is the date?"

"The first of May, but ye havena answered—"

"The year!" She stamped her foot. "I need to know the year."

"The year of our Lord twelve ninety-seven." The man drew his dirk and took another step toward her, his white teeth flashing with his sneer. For the love of God, he was huge. "But ye best start making some sense, else I'll not only cut out your tongue, I'll carve up your liver and feed it to the pigs."

Squealing, she squeezed her arms into her chest and scooted away until the brush poked her behind. The steel of the knife flickered. "Gah! Does everyone have to threaten me with inordinately sharp objects? I'm telling the truth. Surely you can deduce I don't speak anything like a bloody English subject. I'm as Scottish as you are, you big brute." Eva shoved his shoulder—God only knew what prompted her to do that. The giant asshole could kill her with one swipe of the oversized knife he brandished.

Keep your hands to yourself. An involuntary shudder coursed through her entire body as she cringed at the weapon. *It's a freaking dirk—very sharp and deadly.*

"Och, ye should be afraid of my wee blade." He latched on to her shoulder with fingers hewn of iron, his dirk angling toward her neck. "Answer me. Why were ye at Fail?"

"I—I…" *Jesus Christ, what should I say?* "I was lost. The Trinitarians took me in. I still cannot remember the past few days. One minute I was sitting alone and-and the next, I awoke to someone trying to kill me." She inched her head away from the knife, her voice growing shrill. "Just like you are now." She told most of the truth, at least the part that wouldn't get her burned at the stake.

"Why didna ye say ye were lost?" Narrowing his eyes, the man lowered his blade. "What are ye called?"

"Eva—Eva MacKay." Taking in a gulp of air, she squared her shoulders, eyeing the damned dirk as he sheathed it.

Something told her not to trifle with this man. He was the type who'd respect others more if they didn't cower. She glanced up at his eyes—piercing like arrows. She took a nerve-steeling breath. Backing down now might just get her throat cut and her liver carved out.

Oh, Lord, help.

"I doubt you want me to call you *Beast* for the duration of our association—which I hope will not be long." She cringed—maybe she'd been a little too confident with the Beast comment.

"William."

Then again, maybe not.

"I wish I could say it's been a pleasure making your acquaintance." She inclined her head toward the dim light. "Did you mention there's something to eat in that cave?" The thought of wandering inside with a man a good nine inches taller and ninety pounds heavier, *and* confronting his band of upstarts made shivers skitter up her spine. But Eva didn't care for the alternative either. If she indeed had landed in the thirteenth century, fending for herself in the dead of night in God knew where wasn't an option either—especially without food.

Once she had a chance to think, she'd figure a way out of this mess, but for now, she needed this William on her side.

"Aye, we've food aplenty." He gestured forward. "But tell me, why are ye dressed like a lad?"

Eva had no reply that would make a bit of sense, so she just shrugged. "I wish I knew."

"Ye must have suffered a nasty blow to the head." William grasped her elbow with a surprisingly gentle hand and led her inside. A golden glow flickered on the cave's walls, a hum of deep voices echoed from within. Inside a narrow passageway, he stopped and clamped those powerful fingers on her shoulder. "If ye do anything to cross me, ye'll not live to tell about it."

"Jeez." Eva sucked in a gasp. "You're not only a brute, you're paranoid."

He shoved her against the wall. "What language are ye speaking now? Attempting to pull a veil over my eyes are ye?"

"No, no, no." Eva gulped. She must choose her words carefully—paranoid was definitely too modern. "I meant to say—ah—if I wanted to kill you, I'd have done it whilst I was riding double on your horse. You had your back to me for hours." She quaked inside, praying she'd used the right tact. Lord, the barbarian could turn hostile before she had a chance to blink.

"All right, then," he whispered, leaning a bit too close and smelling like a pine forest. "I think it best if the men believe ye a lad. That way I'll not have to stand guard over ye all night. Then I'll see to it ye'll be on your way on the morrow."

"All right." Eva placed a hand on the wall to steady her dizziness. Maybe something did hit her head.

They rounded a bend and the cave opened into a large cavern. Smoke from the coals made the air hazy, but Eva could see well enough. The entire retinue reclined on furs. A man skewered a slab of meat with a knife and tore off a bite with his teeth while juice dribbled into his beard. Beside him, the holy man in the black robes who'd ridden with them assessed her with a dour frown.

Eva shoved her hands in her pockets.

Across the fire William gestured to a lad who couldn't have been more than twelve or thirteen. "Sit with Robbie. He willna cause ye any mischief—if ye ken my meaning."

Surrounded by a mob of unwashed heathens? Eva knew exactly what William meant.

"Fetch him a portion of meat and a pint of ale," William ordered.

Robbie jumped up. "Straight away."

Eva sat on a pile of furs clumped between the rocks. "Thank you."

"Eat your fill, then sleep." William threw his thumb over his shoulder. "We'll be riding early come matins."

She watched him make his way toward the priest. Dumbfounded, she couldn't tear her gaze from his powerful legs. Wrapped with wool chausses, his muscles flexed with his every step. A broad, powerful frame devoid of fat supported his mail. William stopped beside the holy man, removed his helm and combed his fingers through thick, wavy hair. Then he glanced her way. Damn. The devil had to look like Adonis incarnate.

Robbie tottered back and set a wooden trencher in front of her. An unappetizing lump of meat dribbled juice over the side while the lad passed down a pint of ale. "This'll see ye fixed right up."

"Ta." Eva could have eaten a chunk of cardboard if forced. She sipped the ale and coughed. And she thought an IPA was bitter? This stuff tasted worse than pure quinine. She took another sip. Yep. It was awful.

With her pincer fingers, she lifted the well-cooked meat, then leaned down and clipped a bit with her teeth and swirled it in her mouth. *No too bad, but at least it's not rancid.*

"Where's your eating knife?" Robbie asked, plopping back onto his seat.

Eva bit her bottom lip. "Must have lost it."

The lad pulled a blade from his sleeve, tugged off the leather sheath and held it out. "Use mine. We can see about finding ye one on the morrow."

Her fingers trembled when she took the knife. With a wooden handle, a double sided blade, and a little larger than the steak knives she had in storage, it could have passed for tableware at an upscale restaurant. *At least it has no resemblance to a Bowie knife.*

Eva shuddered.

"Are ye ill or something?"

"No, just not fond of knives."

The boy shook his cap of sandy hair. Jeez, he was adorable with dark blue eyes and a splay of freckles across his nose. "My oath, the more ye talk, the odder ye become. A man's good as dead if he doesn't carry a few blades on his person."

Eva cut off a piece of venison and popped it into her mouth. "Mm." The first full bite of food she'd had since breakfast sent her taste buds into overdrive, even without seasoning. She gave the lad a once-over. "You seem awfully young to be hanging with this band of renegades. Why aren't you home with your parents?"

"Ma died giving me birth. And King Edward…" Robbie spat as if he'd uttered a curse. "…well, he hung my da when he refused to pledge fealty."

"God." Eva gulped against her thickening throat. "You poor boy."

The lad's bottom lip jutted out as he kicked at a rock with the tip of his boot. "Ye asked why I'm not sitting in front of my da's hearth. This war has made a lot of orphans—not just me."

Swirling a bit of the bitter ale in in her mouth to wash down her revulsion, Eva fixated on cutting another piece of meat. What could she do to help this lad? Living in a cave with a mob of heathens was definitely no place for him.

"Besides, I'm two and ten." He puffed out his chest. "Almost a man."

"I'll say." Eva smiled and mussed his hair. "You've no choice but to be." She shoved a bite in her mouth. *Maybe I should take him with me to find a town?*

Across the coals, the priest with the glaring eyes watched her, fingering a dirk tucked inside his rope belt. She pointed. "Who's the friar talking to William?"

"Father John Blair?" Robbie asked.

Eva stopped mid-chew. Was it a coincidence? *So many familiar names.* "Just a minute. What is your full name, Robbie?"

The lad thumped his chest. "I'm Robert Dominus Boyd, squire to William Wallace, leader of the resistance—but dunna tell a soul. This is a secret army. Not even Willy's uncle kens about us."

"Holy shit." The knife slipped from her grasp while her stomach flipped.

"Pardon?" The boy's mouth twisted.

Eva cleared her throat and clutched at her pounding heart. "Is William's uncle Reginald Crawford?"

"Aye, Sheriff of Ayr." Robbie ran his thumb over the pommel of his dirk and narrowed his eyes. "Ye're not an English spy are ye?"

If she said yes, she had no doubt the lad would kill her without an iota of remorse. "No." Eva watched the boy's hand as she made a pretense of calmly taking a sip of ale. "Just a las—uh—lad who's lost his way."

Robbie moved his hand and smoothed his fingers along the fur beneath him. "Ye sure do talk peculiar."

"Aye? Well, my father was an ambassador in the…um…Holy Land. I was away for years and years." A wee fib to Robert Boyd, the future First Baron of Kilmarnock couldn't hurt, *could it?* Eva swiped her hand over her mouth and regarded him. He had no idea he would one day be a favored knight of the forthcoming King Robert the Bruce.

Then her stomach turned upside down as she regarded the legend sitting across the fire, chatting with his personal chaplain, Father John Blair. Deep concern, perhaps even pain, etched lines in his face. In the blink of an eye, Eva's prior contempt for the man turned into awe. No wonder he was so brusque with her—he had every right to believe her a spy. And tomorrow he planned to be rid of her.

I have to ensure that doesn't happen.

She patted her down vest. Good, her notepad was where she always kept it. Then her finger tapped the medallion. *Is this what transported me here? How do I return? Blast Professor Tennant! Why didn't he tell me this would happen?*

William leaned forward and cradled his face in his hands as he shook his head.

Too familiar with that woeful gesture, Eva nudged Robbie with her elbow. "Is something wrong with him?"

"Bloody oath there is." The lad's jaw squared as if he were a grown man who'd seen his share of hardship. "His da was murdered with a number of other landowners in Lochmaben this day."

The date from her mobile phone flashed through her mind. *First May, 1297.* Wallace would kill the Sheriff of Lanark sometime this month. "Does William know who did it?"

"They thought they followed the murderers to Fail Monastery, but it wasn't the same mob of English bastards."

Footsteps echoed from the cave's entrance and every man reached for his weapon.

"'Tis just me, lads," boomed a deep voice. A stout warrior wearing a hauberk and helm stepped inside and strode straight to William.

"Who's that?" Eva asked.

"Eddy Little."

Edward Little? William's cousin. My word, this is like a convention for Wallace fanatics.

"There was a survivor," Eddy said. "An old woman. She said the murderers were Heselrig and his retinue of English thugs from Lanark. It doesn't surprise me. That man's cruelty surpasses Edward Plantagenet himself."

"He's a vassal of the bastard." William stood and the two men grasped elbows—something more personal than a handshake. "His actions are in the name of the English king."

"Aye," Eddy agreed. "But word has it he's headed north for a meeting in Glasgow. I say we ambush—"

Looking directly at Eva, William sliced his hand through the air to cut Eddy off. "We'll bury my father on the morrow, then we'll set our ambush."

Loudoun Hill? Eva wanted to ask, but if she dared speak out, they'd peg her as a spy. Then William would make good on his promise. She clamped her lips tight.

Lord, what the hell am I doing here?

Chapter Five

As usual, William woke before his men. This morrow he wanted to ensure he spirited the woman outside before the encampment roused for the day. The last thing they needed was a female amongst their ranks, especially one as lovely as Eva. And aye, even in the dark, her beauty had not gone completely unnoticed.

Though dressed in men's clothing, it wouldn't be long before the men figured out her gender—even with tresses shorn like a man's. Why any woman would cut her hair to her shoulders, William couldn't fathom. Tresses, especially fiery red locks such as hers should be allowed to grow and blow free in the wind. Och, he maintained an errant affinity for ginger-haired lasses for certain.

After collecting a loaf of bread, he stood over Eva for a moment. She slept curled into the deer hide like a wee bairn. Her arms encircled her knees, but did not hide her long, slender legs. William was an inordinately tall man—taller than anyone he'd ever met. Last eve, Eva had stood but two hands shorter than he. Rarely had William encountered a man who could come close to peering over his shoulder, let alone a woman.

Gingerly, he placed his palm on the lassie's arm and roused her. She jolted awake, and sat up looking at him with terror in her green eyes, as if afraid he'd run her through.

Thank the stars she didn't scream. He put his finger to his lips indicating quiet. "Come," he whispered.

She nodded her understanding and followed him outside. "Aren't you going to wake the others?"

"I thought ye might want to take care of your—ah—needs first."

Once in the dawning sunlight, he could see her face clearly for the first time. Her eyes shimmered—as green as the rolling hills of Scotland. Bless it, fanned by red lashes, those eyes could melt the most hardened of hearts.

A pink blush blossomed in her creamy-white cheeks. "Thank you." The feminine softness of her voice, combined with the breeze tossing wisps of her red tresses made his tongue slip out and tap his upper lip. Would those wild curls be silken if he ran his fingers through them? Heaven help him, he forced himself to clench his fists against such an improper urge.

William shifted his feet while he watched her head behind a clump of yellow gorse. God's teeth, her long legs stretched upward to the most alluring heart-shaped buttocks he'd ever seen in his life. He swiped a hand across his mouth. "I-I'll just stand guard over here," his voice rasped.

"Okay."

But, Lord, her speech was odd. *Though I can understand her for the most part. As she said, she doesn't sound English, but did she speak true about hailing from Edinburgh?*

William had tried to ignore her last eve, but he'd been aware of the woman's every movement sitting beside his squire. Robbie ran at the mouth as if he'd been seated with kin. William almost put an end to their chattering, until he'd been distracted by Eddy Little's message.

The news grew worse with every murderous report of English hostilities against his countrymen.

Nearly a year ago, William had cast aside his ambitions to enter the priesthood and took up the sword in the name of

King John Balliol. Leading his small band of rebels, one blunder after another hit him between the eyes. *If we had been a half-day earlier, Da would still be alive. All those ill-fated victims would still be alive.*

Thunder pounded in his ears while his gut twisted. If only he had forty-thousand men, he could drive the vermin out of Scotland and build a wall across her border like the Romans had done—but this time to keep the English barbarians out. If only. Fortunately for William, years of training to be a Templar had deeply seated the most important lesson: *In war there is no greater virtue than patience. Ponder and deliberate before making a move.*

William slammed his fist into his palm. *I will discover who wielded the sword and avenge my father's death. The time of action is neigh regardless of our numbers.*

It didn't matter that he'd been fifty miles northwest when news came of the English raid, William felt responsible. He needed more scouts. That his father was one of the slain made his guilt sink to new lows. He and his men carried the torch of freedom because they had sworn no fealty to the oppressor. He would see his king reinstated on the throne or die in the process. That is what united this band of warriors—brothers in a common fight to preserve the identity of a nation.

Eva emerged from the clump of gorse. The sun shimmered across her ginger hair and highlighted the smooth creaminess of her skin. Had he seen her in full light before, he never would have mistaken her for a lad, even though her height was unusual. William slid his gaze down her long legs and his nether parts stirred. "No woman should be clad thus," he growled, unable to pull his gaze away.

Though she wore a thick doublet hiding her upper body, her slender legs were scandalous. *There is a reason women wear layers of skirts. If even half are as well formed as Eva, no man could engage in an honest day's labor when faced with lasses clad in tight-fitting chausses.*

Worse, a woman had no place amongst his band of rebels. Rebel—that's what many of his countrymen believed him to be. But William saw himself as a Samaritan to Scotland's common man—a patriot.

He inclined his head toward a fallen log. "Come. Let us break our fast."

She pushed the heels of her hands against her temples as if she had an ache in her head. "I need a cup of coffee."

William sat on a log. "What is this ye say…coffee?"

She looked at him and arched one brow as if she considered him daft. "It's a hot drink that helps me wake up in the morning."

"But ye are already awake." He broke off a chunk of bread and handed it to her.

Taking it, she nibbled. A crease etched between her eyebrows like she definitely had a sore head.

William always felt his best come morn. *Mayhap she did suffer a severe blow to her skull.* "Do ye have any knots on your head?"

"I beg your pardon?"

"Because of your forgetfulness. If ye were knocked atop your head, ye might have a tender spot."

She clamped the piece of bread between her teeth and ran her hands over her silken red tresses. "The whole thing hurts—I think because I still have no idea how I ended up—ah—at Fail Monastery."

Eva repeated "Fail Monastery" like it was a question, as if she didn't believe that's where she truly had been when he found her cowering beneath the altar.

William tore a bite of bread with his teeth. "I assure ye. There is no doubt in my mind where ye were when we happened upon the monastery. And I'd venture to say, ye'd not be alive had my men and I not arrived when we did."

She stopped chewing and regarded him. Bloody oath, she could melt the most hardened of hearts with that green-eyed stare. “I haven’t thanked you yet. Please forgive me.”

He looked away and swiped his hand through the air. God’s teeth, he needed to find her kin and be rid of such a distraction. “’Twas nothing. At least we were able to save one life.” William gulped down his bread, thickness swelling in his throat. He glanced away while the fire of rage ignited in his chest.

I’ll not be thinking of bonny eyes whilst my father’s body is still warm.

When she placed her palm on his hand, William took in a sharp breath. Her lithe fingers, soft as rose petals, soothed ever so much. Damnation, he should have pulled away, but the warmth of her touch and the kindness of her gesture drew him inexplicably. It had been too long since he’d been shown tenderness.

Mayhap a moment of respite.

Eva must have sensed the tension in his body ease, because she slowly rubbed her fingers back and forth atop his hand.

“I’m sorry about your father,” she said so softly, he barely made out the words.

William closed his eyes and swallowed. “He was a good man.”

“And you will carry his honor in your heart.”

“Aye. That I will.” He forced himself to snatch his hand away. “But ’tis none of your concern.”

A pained expression flashed in her eyes, then she averted her face and took another bite of bread. William didn’t doubt she’d seen trauma and pain beyond her years. Who hadn’t in these trying times?

His gaze drifted down to her boots and he stared. “Where the devil did ye find such craftsmanship?” He leaned forward for a better look. “I’ve never seen the like.”

She crossed her ankles and tucked her feet taut against the log. "They're functional—keep my feet dry in the wet."

His eyes strayed up those damned tight-fitting chausses again. "Mayhap we can find ye some proper clothing. I hate to think what the townsfolk will say when they see ye." He pinched her peculiar doublet between his fingers. "Your costume will draw consternation for certain."

Biting her bottom lip, she smoothed her hands down the overstuffed quilting. "Do you have a mantle I can borrow?"

"Dunna worry about that. 'Tis best to pass ye off as a lad until ye can be properly dressed. Ye wouldna want the old crows to think ye a witch."

She shuddered. "Surely they wouldn't. I possess no magical powers whatsoever."

Footsteps resounding from the cave drew William's attention.

"There ye are," Blair said, heading toward the brush. "We'll need to be away soon."

William shoved the remaining bit of bread in his mouth. "Och, aye. The sooner the better." He turned to Eva. "Since we'll be riding out of the forest in daylight, I'll have to blindfold ye."

Mayhap the woman looked bonnier than a posy of heather, but he still couldn't trust her—couldn't trust anyone outside his inner circle of men.

***

Thrust into hell and then blindfolded?

Unable to see a thing, Eva stood near a tree. Dammit, she needed her sight to write this story. Not to mention William had been right that her attire would bring her a world of trouble. In medieval times, her present state of dress would be enough to see her locked in the stocks or worse. What a predicament she'd literally fallen into.

Should she fear for her life or be elated?

Grave danger lay ahead for certain.

Excitement, too?

Possibly.

If only she could find a way to allay William's suspicions about her character. Nonetheless, his distrust did nothing to quash the electricity firing across her skin. Talk about the story of a lifetime. If she could figure out how to get back home, she already had enough material to write one helluva tale.

The blindfold was so tight, it made her headache throb. To top it off, caffeine withdrawals grew more torturous by the moment. Standing completely sightless, she tugged the coarse cloth in an attempt to loosen it enough not to hurt. "Where are we heading?"

"Ellerslie," William's deep voice rumbled.

Her stomach flipped. Though she'd tried to refrain from asking too many questions, she couldn't let this one slip past, "Do you mean Elderslie in Renfrewshire?"

"No."

Damn. But it's still a clue.

He grasped her arm and pulled her forward. "Come."

The unmistakable scent of horse neared as she scooted her feet over the uneven ground. Eva would never forget last night riding on the back of Wallace's enormous warhorse. Every time the animal's movement jerked, her heart nearly burst out of her chest.

"I'll give ye a leg up," William said, placing his hands on her knee.

Her stomach lurched. "What?"

"Bend your knee, ye daft woman."

Eva complied, and before she could brace herself, he hefted her straddling on to the back of the horse. She reached forward—yep, the saddle was right in front of her.

William gave her thigh a slap. "I'd think a lass as well traveled as ye would be a mite more comfortable on the back of a horse."

An image of the red Fiat flashed through Eva's mind. "Well…" She grimaced. "You've either seen me frightened because I'd nearly been killed by a madman or blindfolded. I don't think you have grounds upon which to judge."

The horse jostled while the saddle creaked under William's weight. With a squeal, Eva threw her arms around him. Her cheek smashed into steel. Nothing quite as unromantic as grabbing a man wrapped in mail.

He chuckled. "Ye see what I mean. Ye're no horsewoman."

I never claimed to be. Chewing the inside of her cheek, hundreds of thoughts warred in her head, the first being her sore butt. Straddling the horse stretched her inner thighs, aching from spending so much time on the back of the gelding the day before. It would kill her to ride the entire day. "How long will it take to get to Ellerslie?"

"We'll be there by midday."

The cloth encircling her head itched. "How long do I have to wear this blindfold?"

"Until I say."

Eva closed her eyes and listened to the sounds. Twigs snapped behind and leaves rustled above.

"Do ye have kin in Edinburgh?" he asked.

"N-no."

"Where are they?"

"Dead." What else could she say? Her parents wouldn't be born for about six hundred and sixty years.

William didn't respond right away. "Do ye have any recollection of how ye ended up in the monastery?"

"I wish I did." Eva unzipped her vest and clasped her fingers around the medallion. *It must have had something to do with Walter Tennant and this piece of bronze. But how do I explain that? I fell seven hundred years through some sort of wormhole and here I am? Right. Might as well tell him to stop the horse and string me up in the nearest tree.*

"What was the last thing ye remember?" His deep voice rolled—sexier than…

Damn, she needed to think. She'd said she was born in Edinburgh—told Robbie she'd traveled to the Holy Land. Thank God she and Steve had toured the Mediterranean with her folks a few years back. She pulled her pen and notebook from the inside of her vest and started writing blind. *The only way to keep my facts straight is to write them down.*

"What are ye doing?" William asked.

"Trying to remember." Writing without sight was near impossible, but it helped her think. She scribbled as best as she could:

In May of 1297, a common woman could hope for little more than to be a servant—if that. One year prior, the towns of Berwick and Dunbar were savagely attacked by the English. Since then, King Edward has wasted no time besieging castles, instilling his tyrannical government and ensuring the Scottish nobles and landowners paid him fealty. Everyone is scared. Many nobles sided with Edward to retain their lands.

She stilled her pen for a moment, biting her bottom lip, then finished her entry:

These are among the most barbaric times in the history of Scotland.

Too many sharp objects!

Eva rubbed her thumb over the medallion as ice pulsed through her veins. *I may not survive the next twenty-four hours, let alone make it home to tell my story.*

She took a deep breath to steady her nerves. "Ma died giving me birth." She stole that line from Robbie. "Da fought with the Knights Hospitallers and was killed by the Mamluks in Egypt." She'd learned that tidbit from her vacation. "After I returned to Edinburgh, I found employment as a chambermaid for Lady Comyn and moved to Dunbar…and you know what happened there." Thank God she'd studied history in college.

William's saddle creaked with the sway of the horse's gait. "Aye, but that doesna explain why ye were on the other side of the country in Fail."

Eva guessed the distance between Dunbar and Fail to be about ninety miles—not too far a distance to travel on foot over a year. "After the English attack, I wandered. Times are lean and there's not much work for the daughter of a knight. Though I can read and write, it is heresy for a female to be a cleric."

"So, ye became a tinker…"

"Aye." Eva scribbled the word, synonymous for a Scottish Gypsy. She couldn't have said it any better. "I was set upon by outlaws and that's the last thing I remember."

"Ye're lucky to be alive."

Eva groped to slide her notebook and pen into her inside pocket. "I surely am." She let out a long sigh, satisfied that she'd woven a believable story—at least one that a thirteenth century Scotsman could believe. On the other hand, she hated lying. She wanted to be the journalist who always reported the truth and to do that she must live by a code of ethics with honesty at the top.

Perhaps she'd be able to reveal the truth in time. Today, however, she set her priorities for this quest: first, stay alive, and then somehow weave her way into Wallace's confidence.

Chapter Six

A good hour after William allowed Eva to remove her blindfold, they neared a stone longhouse. To the east, the smell of hay wafted from a stable. Beyond, tilled fields sprouted shoots promising good crops. As they rode closer, the sound of a woman's wail sent a woeful knell cutting through the breeze.

Her stomach clenched. Lord knew she was familiar with the sound of a widow's lament.

The tension emanating from William's back demanded that Eva remain quiet. This was a time of mourning. Any questions she might have must wait.

William dismounted and reached his hands up to her.

She peered out the corner of her eye to see if anyone was looking. He'd become more gentlemanly now he knew her gender. Ignoring his gesture, she slid her foot forward into the stirrup and grasped the saddle like she'd done the day before. "I can do it."

At least that's what she thought. When she leaned forward to dismount, her heel dug into the horse's flank. The animal swung his hindquarters aside and reared. Shrieking, Eva flew backward and landed on her backside. "Ow."

"Ye should have let me help." Wallace pulled her up. "If my men didn't ken ye were a lass, they do now."

Eva caught John Blair's stunned expression—then Robbie's wide-eyed, gaped-mouthed stare. "Sorry," she apologized, trying to shrink.

Robbie scratched his head. "Why didna ye say ye were a lass?"

"Wheesht," William said over his shoulder, then led Eva toward the cottage. "I've a great many things to do, the first to see to my mother. I'll have Wynda find ye something suitable to wear. I'd ask Ma to help ye gain employment, but I cannot lumber her with such a task when she's in mourning."

Eva hurried to keep up with his long strides. "You don't need to worry about me. I'm…I'm a very helpful person. I could ride along with you and your men. You know—be your chronicler. Yep. That would be the perfect employment for me."

He stopped and grasped her shoulders. "The last thing ye are cut out for is to ride with a mob of patriots. I'll make some inquiries on your behalf and that's all I the assistance I can offer ye."

He didn't understand. With her training in journalism, she could record events as they happened like no one else. A little rejection? Oh no. She couldn't back down. "But—"

"Keep quiet and mind yourself." William opened the door.

Eva followed, pushing her agenda aside—but by no means letting it go.

"Wynda," he called, leading Eva across the threshold into a dimly lit room. A hearth with blackened iron pots filled the far wall, but Eva's gaze immediately snapped to a body wrapped in linen, lying atop the rectangular table. A woman sat in a chair, her head bent toward the deceased while she dabbed her eyes with a kerchief.

Before Eva could observe more, another woman dressed in a roughhewn blue dress with a linen apron bustled forward.

She curtseyed and bowed her head, topped with a servant's coif. "Aye, Mr. Willy?"

"This is Eva. She's lost—suffered a blow to the head. Please find her something more suitable to wear."

The woman gaped at Eva's legs. "Ye've brought a wayward tinker to your father's house when we're all overcome with grief?"

William placed his hand on the woman's shoulder. "The lass barely escaped an English sword yesterday. I couldna stand by whilst he slit her throat. Now be a good matron and find her a gown."

And a bath and a toothbrush…and a cup of coffee. Eva bowed her head to Wallace. "Thank you for your generosity."

Wynda rolled her eyes. "Ye not only bring a tinker into the cottage, ye bring a foreign heathen." She grabbed Eva by the arm, none too gently. "What are ye thinking, ye fool-born lad?"

William flicked his wrist as if to shoo them away. "Just see to her needs whilst I comfort Ma."

Wynda pulled Eva down a narrow passageway and into a room with a pallet and three trunks lining the walls. "Ye're fortunate the Wallace's are a charitable lot. If it were up to me, I'd send ye on your way."

Eva's face burned. "I apologize for the intrusion. Unfortunately, I've found myself in a very awkward situation."

"I'll say. The gall to be running around the countryside dressed in chausses." The woman huffed at Eva's skinny jeans. "Ye ought to be taken out back and have the hide beat out of ye."

Eva opened her mouth to argue, but decided against it. Breaking sumptuary laws in medieval times was a serious offense. She let out a whoosh of air and clasped her hands under her chin. "Is there anything I can do to help?"

"Aye, ye'll earn your keep as long as ye are under the Wallace's roof." Wynda pulled a wrinkled blue dress from one of the trunks and held it up. "This ought to cover ye at least, though I've never seen a woman so tall." She shook her finger. "And dunna be asking me to take out the hem for ye. I've nay enough time for that."

Eva reached for the musty smelling garment. "This will be fine. I can manage from here, thank you." If Wynda got a peek at Eva's bra and panties, she'd probably have a heart attack.

The old crow frowned and held out a linen apron. "Have ye anything to cover your head?"

Eva ran her hands over her hair and grimaced. "I'm afraid not." *Darn.* The shoulder-length cut would also make her stand out—not only as a lowlife, but people would be suspicious that she'd received public punishment for some misdeed.

"How did your tresses end up shorn?" the servant asked.

Eva thought fast. "English soldiers took a knife to my hair in Dunbar. After serving Lady Comyn, I barely escaped with my life."

"You attended Lady Comyn, the Countess of March?" she asked with a bit more respect in her tone.

"Aye," Eva dabbed the corner of her eye for added effect. "After my father was killed fighting with the Hospitallers."

Wynda patted her chest. "My heavens, why didna Willy tell me your da was a knight?" The serving maid grasped Eva by the elbow and led her to a rickety wooden chair. "It seems ye have been hard torn for luck, lass. Forgive me for being gruff. The news of Master…" Her eyes rimmed with tears.

Eva patted the maid's hand, her stomach twisting from the lines of lies spewing from her mouth. "I know. I am so sorry to burden you at such a difficult time."

Wynda shook her head and fanned her face. "'Tis to be endured." She dug in the trunk and pulled out a blue linen veil and a cord. "This will hide your hair."

Eva accepted it and sat. "Thank you ever so much. I cannot express how much I appreciate your kindness."

"We'll see ye set to rights." She drew a white linen garment from one of the other trunks. "Ye'll need a shift as well."

"I suppose I will." Leaning forward, Eva cradled her forehead in her hand. "I've no idea where I am."

"Ye're at Ellerslie, the family croft." Wynda shook the shift like a rag rug.

Eva snapped upright. "The farm's named Ellerslie?"

"Aye."

That explains Blind Harry's account. They hadn't even ridden through a village—at least none she'd seen. "What's the nearest town?"

"Kilmarnock is up the road and a bit to the east."

Oh my goodness, that's just north of Fail Monastery.

Wynda gave her the shift and patted her shoulder. "This isn't much but it will see ye looking presentable."

Eva looked at the bundle of clothing in her lap and tapped her foot. "Thank you for helping me."

"'Tis no bother, lass." Wynda walked toward the door. "Be mindful of the melancholy this day. The funeral will begin soon."

Offering a thoughtful nod, Eva watched the woman leave.

Immediately, she dug into her inner vest pocket, pulled out her journal and recorded her conversation with the servant. Then she stared at the stone wall. This being the first time Eva had been alone since awaking to a madman with a sword, she breathed a heavy sigh. She'd just survived a night surrounded by men with swords. Come to think of it, she'd even slept soundly.

How did I get here?

A tingling sensation jittered inside her chest.

How do I get home?

She unzipped her vest and pulled out the medallion. *Truth is like a beacon…but few choose to follow. What is Walter up to? Did he know I would meet Wallace? Probably. He'd even commented on the magic of the crumbling walls. Is this why he selected me for the dig team?*

She shuddered. Lord knew how much she feared sharp objects. Undeniably, everyone in this century armed themselves to the teeth. But she wanted to stay—absolutely had to discover more. *This is one chance in a billion.* She looked closer at the medallion, hoping for some fine print with instructions on how to transport herself back to the twenty-first century.

Finding nothing, she groaned. Fail Monastery was her only clue. She must make it back there soon.

Right?

In a fluttering heartbeat, she stood and shook out the dress. *I'm going to face my fears and stay. And this story's too good to worry about how I'll get home—yet. Besides, I can only agonize over one thing at a time.*

Reluctantly, she removed her NYU sweatshirt and donned the linen shift. True to its era, the underdress was no more than a loose-fitting smock with a corded tie to close the scooped neck. And as Wynda said, the gown fit well enough. A bit baggy, Eva was grateful for the loose fit rather than tight—and doubly grateful stays weren't in style yet. She put on the apron and tied it around her waist. Not sexy, but at least it gave the dress a bit of shape.

She pointed her booted toe to the side. The gown hung about ten inches too short. With unknown danger lurking at every turn, Eva wasn't about to discard her jeans. Besides, Wynda hadn't offered any woolen stockings. *Thank God.* Wearing wool directly against her skin gave Eva a rash.

Without a mirror, she did her best to secure the veil atop her head. Though she could live without her NYU sweatshirt, she needed her vest with its pockets. Maybe she could find an old satchel in which to keep her things. She lifted the lid to one of the trunks and rummaged inside. *No bag of any sort.* Well, the vest would have to remain zipped atop her gown.

She stood in the middle of the room, smoothing her hands over the garments to ensure everything was in place. Lord, the musty smell hadn't improved, and rather than feeling refreshed, her skin crawled. She even checked the weave for fleas.

Gross.

Sucking it up, Eva shook off her dread. Yes, she'd jump at her first opportunity to bathe, but if she wanted to stay—to get her story, she had to fit in.

Cementing her resolve, she opened the door and listened. Hushed voices came from the main chamber. Uneasy, as if she were crashing a funeral, she crept down the passageway and waited at the edge of the passageway.

Facing her, William kneeled over the body of his father with his head bowed and his eyes closed. Clutching a black book, his lips moved in silent prayer. A few other men encircled the table, but Eva studied only one. The anguish etched on Wallace's rugged face was undeniable. Over the past year, she'd looked in the mirror enough times to be all too familiar with the pinch between the brows, the drawn mouth—a face in the depths of grief.

I should leave the family alone.

Eva tiptoed to the door. William looked up before she reached for the latch. Never in her life had she seen eyes so expressive. Yes, the misery she'd read in his features was there, but his eyes bore something far deeper. Honor, pride, courage were all conveyed in a look. The most alarming? Deadly determination.

Eva didn't even want to consider what William Wallace was capable of. Goosebumps rose across her skin as she took in a stuttered breath. She bowed her head, curtseyed and hastened out the door.

***

As the mass ended, black clouds moved in from the west—just like the black mood hanging over the gathering of mourners at Da's gravesite. William could have sworn iron rods drilled between his shoulders while he listened to his mother weep during Blair's chanting of the Latin funeral mass. With his mother's every tear, William's gut twisted tighter. Blaming himself for his father's death would never bring back Da, but he was to blame nonetheless. He hadn't arrived in time, but by God he'd ensure the murderers would be punished. On that he made his silent vow.

William scooped a handful of earth into his palm and sprinkled it over Da's white death linens. "I will vindicate your murder if it is the last thing I do on this earth." Sloppy droplets of rain wet the newly turned soil as if the angels wept with him.

Uncle Reginald Crawford, the Sheriff of Ayr gave him a stern look as the funeral procession headed back down the hill. "You'd best leave it be, lad."

It was a good thing William's sword had been left with his saddle. In the past year, his uncle's show of support for King Edward's cause grew thin. To maintain his appointment as sheriff, Reginald needed to pay fealty to Edward, though William suspected the sheriff turned a blind eye to his small group of rebels. As long as William didn't cause too much of a stir, his uncle demonstrated his true loyalty by keeping silent.

But now the English dog had dealt a blow directly to family. William stopped and glared down into his uncle's face. "I will not kiss an English king's arse. 'Tis time to make a stand."

The rain pelted harder.

Uncle Reginald affected a cautionary arch to his brow. "Be mindful of your words. Men—Scottish lads have been hung for treason speaking as ye do."

"How can it be treason to speak out against a foreign king?" William's stomach clamped into a knot. "Do ye intend to turn your back to the tyranny spreading around us?"

Uncle's eyes shifted. "A man must ken when to pick his battles, lad."

William leaned in. "A man must also ken when 'tis time to strap on his sword and fight for freedom."

"With talk like that..." Uncle held up a finger. "I'm afraid ye will end up in a grave beside your da."

Wallace narrowed his gaze. "My death is an absolute certainty. The only question is when." It was all William could do not to wrap his fingers around the sheriff's neck—even if he was kin.

"But—"

"No. There will be no more talk. Now is a time for action." William turned to leave, but first regarded his uncle over his shoulder. "Do what ye must to protect your lands. I'll not take an honest living away from any man." Then he strode away.

By the time William made it down the hill, the squall had passed, dusk had settled and his men had set to turning a pig on a spit.

Blair handed him a tankard. "A bit of whisky ought to take that scowl off your face."

Grasping the handle, William held it up, the amber liquid sloshing in the bottom of the cup. "My thanks, though I doubt my spirits would rise even if I drowned myself in a barrel full."

Together they sat against a log near the fire—something they'd done often in happier times.

"Ye'll feel a bit better once we've found the culprits who did this." Blair sipped from his own tankard. "I ken *I* will."

William joined him, the fiery spirit warming his insides. When he looked up, he met Eva's stare from across the fire. The burning from whisky on an empty stomach kindled a raging fire that spread through his chest. Now she'd donned a proper dress, she looked ever so bonny.

"I kent that lad was a lass," Blair said.

Willy took a longer draw from his cup. "'Tis a shame ye've taken up the cloth and I've this miserable band of patriots to lead. Someone should court such a delectable morsel."

"Bah." Blair swiped his hand through the air. "Women only bring misery. We're both better off without them—or her, bonny or nay."

William licked lips and smirked. "Ever the practical one."

"Ye'd best believe it. I wouldna have taken my sacred vows had I wanted a wife. And after we've driven the English out of Scotland, I suggest ye return to Dundee and take yours."

"Perhaps I will." William sipped, watching Eva over the rim of his tankard. *But this bloody war may never end.*

Sitting beside Robbie Boyd, Eva easily chatted with the lad. Robbie's face was aglow as he spread his arms wide, spinning some ridiculous yarn, no doubt. How a lad of two and ten could enrapture a grown woman, William had no idea. He himself had never been particularly comfortable around lassies. They were inordinately frail creatures and always looked at him as if he were some sort of monstrous Goliath.

Eva listened to the lad intently like she set his every word to memory. William picked up a stick and threw it into the fire. *Ballocks, the wet-eared lad will be proposing marriage by the eve's end.*

Having the woman consorting with his men went against William's every grain. He hadn't ruled out the possibility that she could be a spy. Bloody oath, in the blink of an eye, she could turn backstabber.

Narrowing his eyes, William studied her. How could a woman concoct such an outlandish tale as hers? And her speech was nothing like he'd ever heard.

William was a stalwart representative of the common good. He may not have taken up the cloth like Blair, but he would protect every living Scottish soul and fight for their liberty. Born to hearty, common stock, God had given William gifts most men only hoped for. Educated in languages and the art of war, he aimed to use everything in his power to help unshackle the commoners—the people who comprised the heartbeat of a nation.

If Eva, with her broad tongue, truly was Scottish born, then he would care for her just as he would any other subject of the Scottish crown. That she honored William's father by attending the funeral and remained prayerful whilst standing at a respectful distance spoke volumes about her character.

I doubt she's a spy.

Perhaps she could remain at Ellerslie whilst she awaited suitable employment? He might even see the lass from time to time. She certainly was pleasant to look upon. With Ellerslie under Uncle Reginald's watch, she would be as safe there as anywhere.

Robbie draped his arm around Eva's shoulders and leaned in to her with a hearty laugh.

William sprang to his feet, marched around the fire pit and glared at the lad. "Go fashion a pallet in a horse stall for Miss Eva and find her some bedclothes." He panned his gaze across the faces of his men. "The lass is under my protection. If anyone dare lay a hand on her, he'll answer to me."

She looked up at him, her eyes sparkling with firelight—yet they expressed undue sadness—the same grief clamping his heart like a vise. "Thank you."

Blast it. *Why does she have to be so damned bonny?* "Ye should have gone on posing as a lad. Now ye'll have half the men wanting to court ye."

She brushed her hands over her skirts. "As I recall, it was you who insisted I don a gown."

"Aye, but ye didna tell me how fetching ye'd look."

She drew a hand over her mouth as if stifling a grin. "I could use a bath, a comb and something with which to clean my teeth. Only then will I be somewhat presentable."

"Bah." William sat in Robbie's place. "I've been thinking."

"Oh?" Those damnable red eyebrows arched.

He'd started, so he might as well blurt out what he'd come over to say. "Ye should remain at Ellerslie until I can find a place for ye. Ye'll have Uncle Reginald's protection—and ye'll not starve."

She looked at him with a pointed stare. "Are you staying?"

"Nay, lass. Not while my father's murderer runs free."

"But I'm here to write your story." She crossed her defiant arms—far too self-assured for a woman. "I'm certain of it. How can I observe if I am tucked away on a croft?"

Oh no, he wasn't about to let a wench gain the upper hand. "As I said afore, no woman should be riding with a mob of rebels."

She had the gall to raise her chin and look him in the eye. "What about a lad?"

"Och, ye dunna make a convincing lad, especially with the way ye squeal." He leaned in to her and lowered his voice. "If the times were different, I'd court ye myself."

Eva's gaze softened and drifted down his body, the tip of her tongue moistening the corner of her mouth. "If only we weren't worlds apart."

Chapter Seven

Eva awoke with a start. Chilled to the bone, her hip had pushed a hole through the straw and ground into the packed earth beneath the pallet Robbie had fashioned. Positive she had a bruise, she rubbed the sore spot and sat up. Shrouded in midnight hues, she could barely see the stall gate. Of all the conveniences in the modern world, she missed electricity the most—then running water, a mattress, her car, men without knives and swords strapped to their bodies…the list went on.

The blanket dropped to her waist and she added central heating to the litany.

She pulled a bit of straw from her hair and stifled a sneeze. Lord, she thought she'd had it rough living in a caravan at the dig site? What she wouldn't give for a night on that foam mattress without barn smells tickling her nose.

She startled when a lamenting noise came from near the stall's gate. Initially, it didn't sound human. But gradually the deep wail grew louder. Eva leaned toward it. *Someone's trying not to cry.*

Crawling to the gate, she unfastened the hook. The blasted thing swung back. Before she could skitter aside, a man fell into her, so large Eva crashed to her back, sprawling on the dirt floor.

"Jeez."

An eerie ray of light shone into the stall.

"William?"

He quickly sat up and swiped his hand across his eyes. "Forgive me. I did not intend to wake ye." Ever the guardian, he'd been watching her door.

"No, I was awake." Eva kneeled beside him. "I have nightmares and wake up in a sweat nearly every night." Rocking forward, she peered down the corridor. Good, no one had seen them.

He squared his shoulders. "Ye as well?"

"Aye," she said, settling more into her native brogue, which was still a far cry from Auld Scots. "I'm haunted by knives and swords."

He dragged his fingers through his hair. "And I am haunted by all the faces of the weak and dying."

She shuddered. "I don't know which is worse."

He took in a breath and scrubbed his hands over face. "I'm so driven to fight. 'Tis as if Longshanks himself is calling me out. And now the bastard has struck my own kin."

Her heart twisting into a knot, Eva slid an arm around his shoulder. "I'm so sorry your father fell victim to this mess."

"Too many Scotsmen and women have lost their lives for naught." He leaned away from her and glanced over his shoulder. "Ye should go back to your pallet."

"I will," she whispered, resting her head against him and smoothing her hand over his back. The loneliness night brought was palpable. No one knew that better than Eva—and all too often there was nowhere to turn for comfort. "But not yet."

William didn't respond—only bowed his head and coughed.

She swirled her fingers into the muscular bands in his shoulder. "I know what you're going through. It's as if there's a chasm spreading so wide in your chest, you feel like it's about to burst. The pain hurts so badly, you want to score your palms to ease the burden on your heart."

William shook his head. "'Tis my burden to bear. I should have been with him."

At the campfire, Eva had learned from Robbie that Wallace and his men were on the borders defending villagers' homes from an English raid. They couldn't have known about his father's meeting with knights loyal to the Earl of Carrick at Lochmaben. "You cannot blame yourself. You would have been with him had you received word sooner."

His head dropped a bit further. "Every time Scottish blood is spilled, I feel responsible, as if God put me on this earth to defend those who are too weak to fight for themselves."

Eva sidled behind William and sunk her fingers into muscles made tense by too much anguish. If nothing else, she could help relieve his burden with a massage. A man who wore a heavy hauberk, the sinews supporting his neck felt rock solid. Mercy, it would take a month at a spa in the Bahamas to relieve such tension.

He stretched his head from side to side. "I ken in my soul I must carry the sword and face our oppressors, but how do I ken if I'm doing the right things?"

A man like William Wallace had doubts? In awe, Eva plied his flesh with deep kneading fingers. "You are following your heart and you cannot walk away."

"I wouldna be able to live with myself if I turned my back on my people." His muscles stiffened. "Edward Plantagenet humiliated King John and forced the nobles of this great kingdom to pledge fealty to him as suzerain." He spat. "The Bastard. I refuse to sit idle and stomach the crimes he has committed against my countrymen."

"I know." Eva rubbed in a circular pattern and his tension eased ever so slightly.

"The nobles are afraid. One misstep and they can lose their lands and their titles, but I have no lands and no title to lose. I am a vassal of the people."

"You are and you must continue to be." Eva moved to his outer shoulders, using the heels of her hands to loosen the taut sinews. "God gave you the mind of a great general—a man who can strategize and lead an army."

"I dunna ken about that." William harrumphed. "If only I had the numbers."

"You will."

He drew his head up. "How can ye possibly ken what the future brings?"

"I just do." She used her thumbs to coax the muscles in his lower back to relax. "You are charismatic. Men are drawn to you. *I* am drawn to you. And by your size, let alone your skill with weapons, they will be in awe of you."

He chuckled. "Ye are whimsical. I only desire to see my country as she once was—to have the rightful king returned to the throne."

Eva's nerves grated. If only she could tell William how wrong he was about John Balliol, but Walter Tennant's voice rang in her head—she must do nothing that might change the past. And at this point in history, Balliol was still the King of Scotland.

She mightn't be able to argue the future with William, but she could offer a man mourning the loss of his father a few words to bolster his spirits. "Scotland's people need someone to follow. A man of the masses. You have the heart."

She placed her lips beside his ear. "Be. That. Man."

William sucked in a sharp breath.

Eva slid her fingers to his neck and up through his hair. The medallion warmed against her chest, as if providing another reminder not to reveal too much. But she didn't need to tell William how he would rise to become a great man. On his own, he'd proved the strength of his character to the world and became a legend. In this moment, he merely needed a soothing touch in a time of sadness.

"I will," he whispered and leaned into her hands with a rumbling moan.

Eva massaged until her fingers ached and William's chin dropped to his chest. She finished with soft outward strokes, then studied his face. His eyes closed, she gently coaxed him down to the bed of straw. Though doing so was inordinately presumptuous, in the dead of night, shrouded by darkness in a barn, she'd never felt so connected with another living soul. No words were necessary to share their pain, and the comfort of an unconditional touch was something she'd longed for on many a lonely night.

Eva slid down beside him and spooned her body into his.

***

Awakened by the crow of a rooster, Eva opened her eyes. Someone had covered her with a blanket, but William was no longer beside her.

She rubbed a hand over her caffeine-starved head. *What the hell happened last night? Nothing. I did nothing but give a grieving man comfort. Yeah right, and you'd better not let things go any further than that.*

Shaking her head, she focused on her mission—to get her story and find a way home. Before setting out, she jotted a few notes, and then left to find Wallace.

Plopped on a stack of hay near the barn's entrance, Robbie Boyd sat alone. He hopped up with his bonnet in hand. "Good morrow, Miss Eva."

"Good morrow," she replied, figuring it would be easier to communicate if she adopted some of their archaic words. Turning full circle, there wasn't another soul in sight. "Where are William and the men?"

The lad kicked at a bit of straw. "Left me behind to watch ye. Bloody hell, they always leave me behind to clean up their messes."

"I'm sorry." Eva bit her bottom lip. "I didn't mean to be a burden."

"Och, 'tis not ye that angers me." He shook his fist. "'Tis just that I'm a man. I should be fighting alongside Willy and the rest of them, not staying here playing nursemaid to a lost lassie."

"Don't feel like you have to stay here for my sake." She craned her neck, looking for spare horses. "Where did they go?"

Robbie's lips thinned. "They've ridden after the man who killed Willy's da."

"Heselrig?"

He studied his boots, his shoulders shrugging so high they nearly touching his ears. "Aye."

Eva's heart lurched. "Then they're heading to Lanark."

"Nay." Robbie shook his mop of sandy hair. "They're setting an ambush."

"Ambush? Where?"

The lad scooted backward. "I shouldna tell ye."

But she could guess. The corner of her eye twitched. "Loudoun Hill."

"Boar's ballocks." Robbie threw up his hands. "Are ye a soothsayer?"

I knew it. Eva could have jumped out of her skin. "No, I'm just smarter than I look." She tugged his arm. "Come. I need to watch the battle."

"Oh no." Robbie's head shook like he had palsy. "I never should have opened my mouth. If we show our faces at the hill, Willy will whip my hide for certain."

"I'm not suggesting we ride close enough to join in the fight. But I cannot possibly write William Wallace's story without witnessing the man in action." She gripped the lad's elbow. "Just take me close enough to watch."

Robbie yanked his arm away and rubbed it. "Ye can write?"

“Aye, I can do a great many things that would surprise you.” She pulled a bridle from a nail on the wall. “Now help me saddle a couple of horses.”

“Och, no, Miss Eva. I’ll face a month of mucking out the pig sties, I will.”

“Robbie Boyd.” She fisted her hips and shot him a challenging stare. “If you’re not man enough to help me, I’ll go alone.”

Chapter Eight

William's shoulders weren't quite as tense as they usually were when lying in wait for the enemy. He'd been so distraught last eve, he hadn't realized how well Eva's deft fingers had eased his stiffness.

Though waiting was his least favorite part of battle, he'd never forget it was the most important. Impatient men ended up dead.

At least waiting gave him time to think as the water from the burn rushed past, unaffected by the ravages surrounding them.

He'd never encountered a woman like Eva. They'd only met, but she seemed to understand him better than many people who had known him for years. Her encouraging words wiped away all suspicion of her being a spy. As most had, she'd lost a great deal in this war with England—yet another victim of Edward's brutality.

Regardless, he'd most likely not see her again before she found employment. He almost regretted leaving her in the stall, but it was for the best. He couldn't court a woman—could give his heart to no one but Lady Scotland. Aye, he'd like to. And mayhap one day he'd settle down, grow crops and raise a family.

Take up the cloth? Fight with the Templars in the Holy Land as was his boyhood dream? Now he knew bonny Eva lived in Christendom, family life bore a bit more allure. The corner of his mouth turned up, picturing her hips swaying gently as she stirred a kettle of pottage over home's fire.

Holding her in his arms last eve had set his blood to thrumming for certain.

And there is nothing like a battle to reset my priorities.

There would be bloodshed for certain this day and he had no business thinking of anything but the task at hand. *A man whose mind wanders is a man who ends up with his throat cut.*

Regardless if there was nothing he hated more than waiting, Brother MacRae had drilled three critical elements of war to ensure success: *Wait for your quarry to come to you. There is nothing greater than the element of surprise. And stage your battles using the most advantageous ground.*

Aye, he'd live by this code and put a stop to his errant thoughts of a redheaded lassie.

William opened his psalter and pulled upon his inner calm by reading. When he finished the psalm, he looked to the top of Loudoun Hill. His archers stood ready with their bows and boulders lined up to push down onto the unsuspecting horsemen as they rode through the pass.

He and his best swordsmen crouched in their saddles, lying low in the gully of Winny Wizzen. Completely out of sight, they had not only the ground advantage, but the element of surprise on their side. If only the bastards would come.

"How many horse and how many foot do ye reckon there'll be?" asked Blair in a low voice.

"Two dozen mounted and forty or so pikemen," Eddy whispered, though he'd reported the same earlier that morn.

Two to one. They'd fought worse odds, and this day William's men had the ground advantage and, if nothing tipped them off, they had the element of surprise as well.

"We'll wait until they're trapped in the pass with nowhere to run, then I'll toot one blast from the ram's horn." William pointed toward the archers. "That'll be their cue to start firing."

Blair crossed himself. "May God have mercy on their souls."

William followed suit. "Och, John, put in a good word for us while ye're at it."

"I do that every waking hour."

"Wheesht," Malcolm scolded from behind. But Willy's elder brother was right.

Without another word they waited.

The silence before a battle always sent chills along William's spine. When not a bird called, the faint sound of hoofbeats carried on the breeze.

William squeezed his fingers around the hilt of his sword and made eye contact with Blair, then Little. Each man's face determined, Willy would be confident riding into battle with these men any day of his life. He raised his head high enough to peer through the brush at the pass. The English hadn't yet rounded the bend.

The archers atop the hill loaded their bows.

Movement at the forest's edge caught William's eye. *What the devil?* His heart stopped in his chest. *I'll murder that wayward ox-brained lad.*

Blair nudged William's arm and pointed.

All Willy could do was shake his head and roll his eyes. Now he'd have to worry about a woman and a lad of two and ten who thought he was a man. When this was over, Robbie Boyd would need to be taught a lesson in obedience—if he managed to survive this day.

The first rider came into view, carrying the king's pennant—and the next touted Sir Heselrig's colors emblazoned on his surcoat. William raised his ram's horn no higher than his shoulder—the men on the hill could see his signal, but in the gully, he and his rebels remained hidden from view of the English.

"Now," John Blair whispered.

William shook his head. *Let them come a bit farther.*

He waited until the iron pike tips reflected the sun over the heads of the riders. Slowly he drew the horn to his lips, holding his hand steady. With a single blast, he dug in his spurs and drove his mount toward the unsuspecting cavalry. Arrows hissed and enormous stones bounded down the hill. Horses whinnied and men howled with unimaginable pain.

Bellowing the rebel's war cry, "Scotland until Judgement," William led the charge straight toward the first horseman. With a gasp of horror, the man cast his pennant aside and reached for his sword. Before he drew, William dealt a killing blow across his neck.

The English cavalry surged forward, surrounding William and his men. One by one he fought the onslaught of riders. "I will avenge my father for his murder at Lochmaben!" He spun his horse in place, swinging his longsword from side to side.

His mount squealed with a high-pitched whinny and reared. Thrown from his seat, William crashed to the ground, his sword clattering beside him. Intently focused on the battle, no pain could sway him during a fight. Clamping his fingers around his swords hilt, he sprang to his feet. A horseman barreled in, bellowing like a madman, battleaxe held high. Planting his feet, William prepared to meet the bastard's blow. As if time slowed, he watched the weapon as it came down on a path to lop off his head. But the English soldier made a mortal mistake by wielding it with only one arm.

William ducked aside. With and upward strike, his great sword met the soldier's axe with a clanging scrape. The jarring impact shuddered through his arms, but Wallace held fast. The bastard's weapon flew from his hand, while William caught the attacker with his downward stroke. Cut in two, the man's corpse dropped to the earth.

William spun in place, searching for his next opponent. A shrill scream resounded from the forest edge. Robbie toppled forward as he took a bash with the hilt of a sword. Heselrig threw Eva over his horse's neck and galloped into the forest with a half-dozen riders behind him.

"No!" William yelled, racing for his horse. Before he took two steps, something crashed into his helm with teeth-rattling force. He dropped to his knees, the world spinning.

***

When William opened his eyes, Robbie's worried mug grimaced inches from his face. "Thank the good Lord, ye're alive."

William's hand shot up, his fingers clamping around the lad's throat. "Why did ye not stay at Ellerslie, ye fool-born milksop?"

Robbie clenched his hands around William's wrist. His face turned red as he croaked out a gurgling sound.

"If ye want him to answer, ye'd best loosen your grip," Blair said beside them.

William pushed the lad away and sat up. A miserable pounding punished his head. "Tell me, Robert Boyd. Why did ye bring Miss Eva here—a battle site, no less? She could have been run through or worse."

"She said she would ride alone if I didna go with her." The boy rubbed his throat. "I told her ye would throttle me."

"Ballocks!" William stood and glared at his men. "What are ye all standing idle for? Heselrig is the one man we wanted and now he's ridden off with Miss Eva."

Blair crossed his arms. "Good riddance if ye ask me."

The ache in William's head nearly burst through his skull. He balled his fist and smacked the priest across the jaw.

Stumbling to his arse, Blair rubbed his chin. "Why in God's name did ye have to go off and hit me? Ye're taken with the lass and she's marred your judgment."

"Ye think ye're so wise? What about Heselrig? As long as he's in Scotland, he'll not only rape our women, he'll burn and pillage our villages—regardless." William ground his teeth, forcing his mind away from what that monster could do to Eva.

"He's using the wench to lure ye into his lair." The priest lumbered to his feet.

"Aye?" William paced. "Well that's an invitation I'll gladly accept."

Blair swatted his palm through the air. "Bloody woman."

Wallace held up his fist and glared. "She changes nothing." Then he pointed east. "Heselrig will pay for his crimes against Scotland *and* Da."

"But we now have a bonny lassie to rescue from the Lanark gaol—if she's still alive," Robbie said.

"Aye." William glared at the lad and growled. "And shut your gob. That spineless boar will not murder Miss Eva. 'Cause I aim to find him first."

Chapter Nine

Stars flashed through Eva's eyes after riding face-down, draped over a horse for God knew how long. She smelled the burning peat a good quarter-mile before the road grew wider and the horse slopped through mud made soupy from heavy use. Out of the corner of her eye, stone buildings passed. *This must be Lanark.*

When Heselrig pulled her down, Eva's knees gave out. She strained to regain feeling in her legs while the ruthless toad dragged her through ankle-deep mire toward a stone building.

She twisted against his crushing grip to no avail. Though shorter, the man was a beast. The stench of raw sewage burned as he pulled her up the stairs. Her gaze shot across the scene—muddy street, stone buildings charred with smoke residue from endless burning fires—people gathered around and stared at her like spectators anxious for a public display. This brief glimpse was the first she'd seen of a medieval village and was every bit as ghastly as she'd imagined and worse.

With soldiers flanking her on all sides, she had zero chance for escape.

Shuffling her numb feet, Eva managed to keep pace with the scoundrel. "You have no right to bully me. I am an innocent bystander."

"That is yet to be seen." Even Heselrig's voice cackled unpleasantly.

He led her into a narrow stairwell and pulled her down the winding steps. Shoved into a dimly lit chamber, Eva crashed to the dirt floor.

Bracing herself with the heels of her hands, she blinked and forced her eyes to adjust. Then she wished she'd remained blind. Some of the torture devices she recognized from museums, like the rack, the iron branks and stocks. Lining the wall were whips, thumbscrews, even a heinous breast ripper. Beside them hung an assortment of deadly knives, saws and sharp axes—a torture chamber to rival any museum exhibit she'd ever seen.

But this was real.

The display of weapons made a cold shudder pulse through Eva's veins. *God help me.*

Heselrig sauntered up to her, a sadistic sneer stretching his thin lips. Eva scooted away until she hit the wall. She flinched when he swung his foot back, but wasn't fast enough to dodge the toe of his boot as he kicked her in the stomach.

"Gah!" Eva cried.

"I want his name."

Sharp pain shot through her abdomen like shards of glass. Eva curled into a ball, sucking in gasps. "I-I don't know what you're talking about."

Lurching forward, he grabbed her shoulders and pulled her to her feet. "Ye talk like a guttersnipe. Exactly what I'd expect from a backstabber's whore."

Clutching her arms around her gut, she glared at him through narrowed eyes. The man was shorter by at least three inches.

Eva twisted and struggled to wrench from his grasp. *Fight.* With another glance at the knives on the walls, she clenched her fists, threw back her shoulders and jerked her arms wide. As his grip released, she dashed for the stairs.

Guards crossed their poleaxes, blocking her escape.

She flung her arms over her head and prepared for impact.

Heselrig grabbed her from behind. Crushing her neck in his grip, Eva's arms clamped harder as he drove her body against the wall.

The iron taste of blood slid across her tongue. Everything hurt. The sheriff pinned her in place with his disgusting, smelly body, oozing with male sweat covered by a sickly concoction of musk oil.

Cold steel pricked the side of her temple.

Eva drew in consecutive stuttered breaths. That damned knife was too sharp. One twitch and his dagger could cut out her eye. God, she hated knives.

He pressed his lips to her ear, the foul stench of decayed teeth nearly made her heave. "I'll ask ye one more time afore I cut off your gown and take the lash to your bare flesh." He chuckled and thrust his hips into her buttocks. "And then I'll bend ye over and give ye a taste of King Edward's elite."

"You goddamn fucker." Eva bucked, only to have her chin slammed into the wall. Gasping, she stretched her jaw to the side while shirking away from the dagger.

"Ye are a spirited bitch. I like that," he cackled, rubbing his sickly erection across her buttocks. Sheathing his dirk, he whipped a rope around her wrists. "The giant phantom who descends from the darkness and murders my men. If ye want to live, ye'll tell me his name."

Eva regarded the brutish man over her shoulder and wrenched her arms against the grating rope. *He'll be dead soon and everyone will know William's name no matter what I do*. Then she pictured Walter Tennant's big tent at the caravan park. Blinking, the image quickly faded. The medallion warmed.

Heselrig stepped away and studied the assortment of torture devices on the table. He picked up a headman's axe and examined the blade.

"Stop this madness." Eva faced the man's back, emboldened by her knowledge of the past. "The man you fear will attack and cut you down in a matter of minutes. You want his name? Well, it's William W…"

Before she blinked, everything went black, her body spinning as if being sucked into the depths of a whirlpool. A deafening rush filled her ears, so painful, she wanted to clap her hands over them to muffle the roar, but she couldn't move even if she'd been untied.

As fast as it started, blackness turned to blinding light. The noise ebbed.

Eva drew in a sharp breath, recognition tickling the back of her mind. Tent walls flapped. Birds sang.

"Back so soon?"

Walter.

"Holy shit!" Standing in the center of the tent, she struggled against her bindings and stared at him wide-eyed. "W-what happened? One moment I was in Heselrig's torture chamber and then everything went black."

"Were you about to do or say something that could change the past?" He pulled out a pocketknife and opened the blade.

With a cry catching in her throat, Eva skittered away. Lord, she'd met with enough sharp objects for a lifetime.

He held up the knife. "To cut your bindings, unless you like being tied."

"Right." She forced herself to be rational, turned and presented her wrists. "Thank you."

"Honestly, I thought you would have returned days ago."

She eyed him over her shoulder. "I knew you and your medallion were behind this."

"I merely acted on a hunch." He ran his blade back and forth over the rope. "So, what's happened?"

"God." Her entire body shook. "Heselrig captured me and demanded I tell him the identity of the enormous phantom warrior who kept attacking his soldiers. I was about to reveal William Wallace's name and, poof, everything went black."

Her bindings released and Walter folded his pocketknife. "That must have been what did it."

"But why would it matter?" Eva rubbed her wrists. "We know Wallace killed Heselrig in May of twelve ninety-seven—*exactly* the time I was there. Would it have made any difference if I told him?"

The professor shrugged, his rolling eyes ginormous behind his thick lenses. "I've no idea, but evidently it would have."

"Why?"

"Perhaps it would have given him a chance to dispatch an army before Wallace attacked."

Eva pressed her palms to her face. "This can't end. Not now. I was just beginning to earn Wallace's trust—providing I escape Heselrig's sadistic torture." She gave Walter a pointed look. "How do I get back?"

Walter spread his palms, a bewildered frown stretching his jowls. "I've no idea." He offered her a folded handkerchief.

"What?" She wiped her bloody nose. Jeez it hurt. "You're the mastermind who gave me the medallion."

"Aye." He scratched his head. "But I wasn't sure it would work."

Eva paced. He couldn't be serious—playing with her life on a whim? "How long have I been gone?"

"A few days."

"That means time passed here while I was there."

Walter nodded.

"Where's my car?"

"I moved it here—where you always park it."

"Are the others worried?" She wrung her hands.

"Nah." He waved his hand and batted the air as if she'd never been in an iota of danger. "I told the team you had a big story you were chasing."

"Good…I think." Eva's mind raced. Wallace had looked directly at her before she was taken at Loudoun Hill. Never had she seen such a determined expression. Though in the midst of battle, she knew he'd ride after her. "I must return. William will come for me—I need to be there when he does or else he'll think I'm a turncoat."

The professor crossed his arms. "So it's *William* is it now?"

"Oh, please." She had to make Walter understand. "I've learned so much in such a short amount of time…" Eva quickly rattled off the details about Wallace's father's death, meeting Robert Boyd, Edward Little and John Blair. "Did you know Robbie was only twelve years old in twelve ninety-seven?"

Walter sat in a camp chair and gestured for her to do the same. "That stands to reason. As I recall he was still a young man when he rode for Bruce."

Eva remained standing. "But the history books make out like Robbie was William's right-hand man."

"You are as aware as I the history books are often mistaken. Besides, *Sir Robert Boyd* would have been a strong ally of Wallace in later years—perhaps even after William returned from mainland Europe."

"Right." Eva swiped a hand across her forehead. "Regardless of all this, I must return."

Walter guffawed. "And end up dead?"

"Wouldn't I hurtle through time before I got killed?" She blinked rapidly, trying to make sense of all that had happened in the past five minutes. "Come on—tell me I'm immortal when traveling to the thirteenth century."

Tennant threw up his hands. "How should I know?"

Holy shit. That made her gut clamp as she pictured Heselrig's torture chamber. The madman wouldn't think twice before he ran a blade across her throat. "What?" she shrieked. "You mean to say you picked me, knowing I could end up dead?"

Walter's gaze trailed sideways. "Well not exactly—not when you put it like that."

"Then why? Tell me, why did you give me the medallion?"

"Because you are a writer and a Wallace fanatic. I thought you'd have the best chance of staying alive and bringing back the truth—and then have the skills to tell the world about it. Besides, I honestly didn't believe you'd spend more than two minutes there, just like..."

Pacing in a circle, a bazillion thoughts warred in Eva's head. *I can't leave things with William thinking the worst. I must see him again.* "I have to figure out how to get back."

Walter removed his glasses and wiped them with the hem of his shirt. "I don't know if you can."

She gulped. "What are you saying?"

His exasperated mien grew more exaggerated when he repositioned his thick lenses. "You might have guessed that *I've* already tried."

"Shit." She plopped into the camp chair. "I figured you might have. What happened?"

"An old man gave me the medallion years ago at the Fail Monastery ruins. The only thing he said was the rule, the same one I told you."

She shoved her hands against her temples and rocked back. "Where did he come from?"

"I've no idea. I was sitting on the wall, writing in my journal, and all of a sudden he was standing in front of me. I looked down at the medallion and read the inscription. When I looked back up he was gone—almost thought he was a ghost."

"That's creepy." Eva shuddered. "Did you travel right then and there?"

Tennant nodded. "I landed in the midst of a battle, and fought for my life, shrieked when I was sure my head was about to be lopped off." He stretched his legs out and crossed his ankles. "I was only there for a few minutes before I was catapulted back. It's never happened for me again."

Dropping her hands, she grasped the camp chair's armrests. "So you traveled before you were killed?"

"Aye, I did."

She scooted to the edge of her seat. "Do you know if the traveler has any control over time and place?"

He shook his head. "You ken as much as I do, lass. And I'm not certain if Fail Monastery has anything to do with it or not."

"Then why did I end up in your tent and not at the ruins?"

Shrugging, Walter had no answer.

With a drum of her fingers, Eva recalled that she'd pictured the tent—her mind must have some sort of control. *But how?*

Filled with growing confidence, she jumped to her feet. "I need a shower and to collect a few things. Then I'm heading back to Fail."

Walter leaned forward in his chair. "Don't you have enough material for a story? I'll say it again, traveling back could be dangerous."

And now he was worried about her safety? But for the first time in her life, she wasn't. "Jeez. Did you think about that when you put the medallion around my neck?" She stopped at the tent flap and grinned. "Besides, I've got William Wallace watching my back."

***

Eva stood under the shower, reveling beneath the luxurious hot water. To think, just a few days ago, she thought it a paltry stream. If only she could linger, but not now. Anxious to be on her way, she turned off the faucet and grabbed her towel. Earlier, she'd rinsed out her musty smelling clothes and thrown them in the caravan park dryer. Who knew when she'd have the chance to clean up again?

After toweling off, she donned a pair of black leggings, convinced they would be more comfortable under her gown and blend in better to medieval Scotland than her jeans. Then she put on wool socks, her boots and a bra. Dashing to the dryer, she removed the shift and tugged it over her head, followed by the blue gown, the apron and the veil—well, she tossed the veil over her arm and ran to the caravan.

Thank God her roommates Linsey and Chrissy weren't there. Eva opened her laptop and quickly shot off an e-mail to her parents, telling them she'd found the story of a lifetime, and not to expect to hear from her for a while. Mom would have a gazillion questions, but Eva wouldn't be online to answer.

She grabbed a worn leather satchel because it was the only bag she owned that would pass for medieval. The first thing she packed was a handful of panties. She might have to wear the same clothes for days, but she'd go crazy if she couldn't change her underpants. Then she added her toiletries bag and her solar mobile phone charger. Without service, the phone could still be used as a camera and a recording device—as long as she could keep it hidden.

Money?

She plopped the satchel on the bench and turned in a circle. Opening the cupboard, she found a canister of salt and tossed it in, then opened her jewelry travel case and pulled out the gold band from her wedding set. She stared at the diamond engagement ring and matching earrings Steven had given her and opted to leave them behind. She could end up in more trouble than not with a couple of karats in diamonds…but she did pick out two silver rings and a silver pin in the shape of a thistle she'd had since high school.

If only I had a halfpenny or a few farthings dated 1297 or earlier.

She sighed, stood in front of the mirror and affixed the veil in place with the cord Wynda had given her.

The door swung open.

Eva whipped around and faced Linsey and Chrissy with her hands gripped behind her back as if she'd been caught stealing. "Hey! What have you two been up to?" She sounded like a cheerleader.

They exchanged exasperated looks. Chrissy with her brown hair and freckles stepped in and leaned against the counter. "The question is: where have *you* been?"

Eva shrugged into her down vest—Lord knew she needed it the most. "I wish I could say, but I'm following the story of my life, and its hush, hush."

Linsey raked her gaze up then down. "Bloody Christmas, you look like you're ready for a reenactment of the Battle of Bannockburn or something. I went to one last year and the women were dressed just like you are."

"Oh this?" Eva held out her skirts. "It's just part of my disguise."

"Sounds like a weird story you're writing," Linsey said.

"I know, right?" After picking up her satchel, Eva slung it over her shoulder. "Hey, well, I guess I'll see you later, then?"

"Yeah." Still leaning against the counter, Chrissy crossed her arms and her ankles. "I hope you can tell us what's going on when you get back."

"I sure will, just as soon as I know it's all right." Before Eva walked out the door, she opened the cupboard and grabbed a box of granola bars she'd brought with her. "See ya."

The girls hardly had a chance to say goodbye when she dashed out the door, running for her car. Hopefully Walter would bring it back again. Honestly, she had no idea if she could fling herself to the past from anywhere, or if she had to be at Fail Monastery. But this wasn't the time to find out. She must return to Lanark before William arrived, else the trust she'd began to build would be ruined forever.

The Fiat engine revved, and though Fail was only a few miles away, she couldn't drive fast enough. Skidding to a stop in the gravel, she ran to the old ruin and faced the rose window. Breathing heavily, she looked up and grasped the medallion. "I swear I will never do anything to alter the past. Please, whatever force is out there, take me back."

Eva stood staring at the window while the breeze picked up her veil. Thunder rumbled in the distance.

Please. Before it starts to rain.

She stood in place for a good fifteen minutes. Gusts of wind swirled around the ruined walls, then a splash of water smacked her cheek. Lightning streaked overhead. Eva crossed her arms and hugged them tight to her chest. "I'm not leaving!"

The skies opened with a deluge. Eva glanced at the Fiat—if she made a run for it, she could wait out the storm. But something deep inside told her to stay.

When she blinked, an image of Heselrig's back flashed through her mind's eye. She shook her head.

"I will not fail," she yelled at the gaping window. "I will do everything to bring back the truth." She shook her fist. "You know what I've been through. You know how much I need this story. And most of all, you picked me because I will obey your code of honor. I swear this on my life!"

A bolt of lightning turned the sky above pure white. Eva threw up her hands as the brilliant light transformed into utter darkness. This time her heart soared at the piercingly agonizing noise and the sensation of falling through a bottomless abyss.

With a sudden rush that nearly burst her eardrums, Eva found herself against the torture chamber wall, looking at

Sheriff Heselrig's back—the same image she'd seen when she blinked.

Holy shit!

He regarded the battleax just as he had before everything went black…but Eva's hands were no longer bound.

Chapter Ten

Dripping wet, she tugged on the satchel strap to conceal the bag in the small of her back. Eva hadn't thought through exactly what might happen when she returned. She'd kind of assumed she might arrive in a dungeon cell. The last time she'd hurtled through time, she'd landed in the midst of life-threatening danger. Why on earth would she have anticipated differently now?

When Heselrig set down the unbelievably sharp battleaxe, Eva exhaled. She could only think of one thing he might do with that weapon and she was pretty sure head severing was involved. Regardless of her fear of sharp objects, now that she'd returned, she refused to allow terror to control her mind—the hard knot in her gut insisted this was not her time to die. She inched toward a dagger hanging in a line of weapons on the wall.

"Let me see," he said. "I think I'd like to take my time with this one—young women always provide such interesting sport—and ye will be all the more entertaining when I hold court in the town square on the morrow."

She took in an inhale—good, he didn't plan to kill her immediately. Eva slid the knife from its peg and hid it behind her back.

The sheriff spun around. "What was that?"

Jeez, I barely made a noise. She knitted her eyebrows. "Pardon me, sir?"

He chuckled and sauntered toward her, his neck craning so he could look her in the eye. "Ye might be certain of yourself now wench, but I assure ye, I'll have ye singing the bastard's name from the bell tower by the time I'm done."

Eva tightened her grip around the knife's hilt.

He held up a pair of shears and grinned like *Batman's* Jester. "We'll start with these."

He yanked her veil from her head, then jerked away. Sucking in a gasp, he gaped at her in horror. "Miserable bleating wretch! I should have known someone might have already taken the shears to ye."

Then Heselrig narrowed his eyes, his initial shock replaced by a sneer. He fingered a lock of her hair—the veil had kept it dry. "What did ye do to earn this shearing? I'll wager ye're keeping company with more than one scoundrel dog."

Eva jerked her head aside, making her hair slip from his fingers. Her gut lost a bit of verve and clamped with terror. She needed to keep the sheriff talking—anything to prevent him from doing something unconscionable. "I-if I tell you his name, will you let me go?"

Lunging, his hands shot out and trapped her against the wall, his foul breath wafted up to her nose. "Ye've broken the law, for that ye must be punished."

She looked down at his beady eyes—black and without a hint of compassion. "But I thought a man like you might be a better negotiator," she baited him. "Telling me I'll pay penance regardless does nothing to loosen my tongue."

"Ye are a wicked bitch." With a sickly chuckle, he ground his crotch against her thigh. "Clearly ye're not daft." He inclined his head toward the table of torture devices behind. "If ye hold your tongue, the pain ye'll endure will be far worse."

Eva swallowed, perspiration prickling her brow. Though the man was shorter, he outweighed her by a good sixty pounds. She needed time. How the hell could she overpower

Heselrig and then take on the goons with the battleaxes by the stairwell? "What will you do if you catch him?"

"*When* I catch him." He licked her neck, an unwelcome column of hardness growing against Eva's thigh. "There will be a public display on such a grand scale, the king will grant me title, lands and riches."

"So you're pillaging Scottish villages—murdering innocents for a title?"

His hand snapped to her face, his fingers clamping around her chin. "I'm clearing vermin from the face of the earth."

The back of Eva's head ground into the stone wall behind, but she clenched her teeth against the pain. *I must keep stalling.* "What about the gentry—nobles like Bruce and Comyn? They own lands on either side of the border."

The vile man spat at the wall beside her head. "They're little better—aside from having the king's ear—and his bleeding protection."

"True," she hissed through her teeth with her face squashed in his grip. "Those who signed the roll pledging fealty to King Edward are all protected—but then some didn't sign."

Still pinning her with his body, Heselrig released his grasp on her chin. "And it is my duty to convict those errant bastards for treason."

Her brow pinched. "How can they commit treason when they are not English subjects?"

"Ye're one of them are ye not?"

"A Scot? Aye." Oh, how Eva would have liked to tell Heselrig how wrong he was, and describe exactly how psychotic the English king would become, but that would only serve to make her captor lash out—might even buy her a one-way ticket back to 2015.

The muffled sound of horses came from above. Eva prayed Wallace and his men had arrived. She doubted she'd be able to delay the sheriff's sadistic torture much longer.

Heselrig grabbed the back of her hair and yanked.

Eva braced herself against the wall and tightened her grip on the dagger. "What if the man you're after rides with Bruce?"

"Ye're boring me, wench. Ye know as well as I, Bruce sides with Edward."

"Does he?"

He yanked her hair to the side and held up the shears. Grunts and clanging echoed from above stairs.

Hesitating, Heselrig nodded at the guards. "Go take care of the skirmish."

With his attention diverted, Eva clenched every muscle in her body and stamped her boot on the sheriff's instep.

Hopping, he reeled back. "Christ! I'll murder ye for that."

He drew back his fist. Clamping onto the dagger with both hands, Eva swung. She gritted her teeth as the blade sliced across his arm.

"You cock-sucking whore," Heselrig shrieked, bending over his wound.

Eva sprinted for the stairs. "Help!"

Something clattered behind her. Heart racing, she ran faster.

Her foot stretched for the first step. She grasped the rope rail.

A blunt object thudded against the back of her head.

***

"Spare the innocent!" William held a torch high as he led the charge into the town of Lanark. "Burn out the vermin!"

The only way to break through Heselrig's defenses was to storm the city at night. It had taken every ounce of William's self-control, but he'd waited until the sun sank in the western sky.

The Sheriff of Lanark had murdered hundreds of his countrymen—had murdered his father, and now he'd taken Eva. The woman might be only a slip of a lass, but in the past hours she'd become a symbol embodying all of the suffering inflicted against Scotland by the trespassing English.

Ahead, the town gates had not yet been secured. Wallace waved his torch. "We shall have our vengeance."

An arrow hissed past his ear. His warhorse didn't flounder, pummeling the ground as together they barreled forward.

A high-pitched bellow shrieked from behind. William's gut roiled with his mounting ire. Aye, he would lose a man or two this night, but his losses would be nothing compared to the devastation his men would deliver.

English pikemen scampered in front of the gateway, awaiting their death.

Digging in his spurs, William demanded more speed as he galloped toward the doomed men. Holding his course, he drove with focused abandon. Two steps before impact, he leaned forward and cued his warhorse to jump over the unsuspecting guardsmen.

With a thud, the horse's front hoof caught a soldier's helm. The man grunted as he dropped to the ground.

William braced himself to land, casting a glance over his shoulder. As planned, Blair followed suit, along with Little. The miserable guards had no defense.

The warhorse hit hard, then raced ahead. William threw his torch at a thatched roof and reined his steed toward the gaol. By the time he dismounted, the burgh's roofs were ablaze. Women screamed as frenzied people raced through the streets.

"Spare the innocent," he bellowed again, hopping down with his sword firmly gripped in his hand.

William led the way up the steps straight toward a line of guards.

"Halt," yelled an emboldened fool, defending the door with a battleax.

The impertinent command only served to raise the hackles on the back of William's neck. Not stopping to parley, he raised his blade and dispatched the man with a sidelong swing. Metal clanged as William and his men deftly launched into battle, cutting through the line of guards.

Not a man in the burgh of Lanark could stand against William and his patriots. When not fighting the enemy, they trained from dawn till dusk for battles such as this. If Sir Heselrig thought he'd continue to demonstrate the ruthlessness of Edward Plantagenet, he'd soon discover the error of his ways.

Charging inside, William addressed a young soldier. The lad's sword shook as his neck craned to take in Wallace's extraordinary height. William glowered and advanced. "Where's the sheriff?"

The lad's eyes flashed toward the stairwell.

"Help!" Eva's voice shrieked.

William started toward the sound. The lad howled and attacked from the flank. With a twist, the great sword hissed through the air, colliding with the young man's blade. William attacked.

The boy quickly retreated behind a table.

In two strides, William skirted around it, slamming his pommel into the lad's helm. His eyes rolled back as he dropped to the floorboards.

William dashed to the stairwell, crouching low to descend the narrow passage without hitting his head.

Rounding the last bend, Wallace found the repugnant blackguard kneeling over Eva's body. Blood pooled beneath her face.

Heselrig sprang up with a sneer.

William roared and leapt from the last step.

Moving like an asp, the sheriff blocked William's strike and spun to behind the security of a table. The man's deranged cackle filled the dungeon. "Luring ye into my snare proved far easier than I'd guessed."

Together the men circled the table, laden with blackened iron tools of torture.

Heselrig lunged to the side with a tricky flick of his sword. William hopped away from the blade's pass and dashed around the board.

The Englishman made chase like a milk-livered swine. William stopped daring the bastard to make a move.

The scoundrel trained his blade between them. "'Tis a shame ye spoiled my fun. Any later and I would have impregnated her with English seed."

William's ears rushed with his inhale.

Each thundering beat of his heart rumbled as if the world stilled.

The shift of his eyes brought in a myriad of information.

As his lids lowered, William upended the table and hurtled it into Heselrig's body. Weapons clanked and clattered to the ground. The sheriff flew against the stone wall, his eyes stunned. Heaving the board aside, Wallace advanced. "Ye will not live to rape another woman or pillage another Scottish burgh."

Heselrig jerked, pulling his weapon up. "I'll murder—"

William's great sword hacked off his arm at the shoulder, opening a giant gash in the bastard's upper quarter.

The English sword clattered to the floor.

Dropping to his knees, blood spouted from the sheriff's wound before he fell to his face.

As time again sped, William dashed to Eva's body, praying she was alive.

Turning her over, he gathered her into his arms. Blood caked beneath her nose. "Eva, wake. Please." He clutched her body against his and rocked, the agony of the past few days hitting him with the force of an iron hammer. "God in heaven," his voice cracked. "Why are my people to suffer at the hands of a madman's rule—a man not of this kingdom?"

Beneath his arms, Eva's ribs expanded. Gasping, William regarded her face. "Eva?"

Her eyes remained closed.

Chapter Eleven

William sat beside Eva and read his psalter, something he often did to make sense of the world around him. The memory of his own brutality troubled him—deeply troubled. Amidst the fever of battle, he could be as ruthless as Edward Plantagenet himself. *But who else will take a stand against these tyrants?*

At least Eva could rest peacefully there in his private alcove of the cave. He'd never allowed anyone inside this space, but he'd brought her there because of her gender, not because…

William shook his head and read Psalm Eighty-eight—a favorite—one about his soul being in the depths of a pit. When he rescued Eva from Lanark, his soul had soared with the stars. But now doubt clutched his heart with iron gauntlets. How could he have allowed the woman to grow close? She'd shown him kindness in the wee hours one night and he'd assumed they had made a bond. And now it would be yet another black mark on his soul if she didn't wake.

When he finished reading, his gaze slid to the rectangular object that had fallen out of her pocket when he removed her doublet. Devil's spawn, the thing lit up without a fire when he grasped it. He tensed. Even Eva's doublet was not from this world. It possessed a metal tab that ran up and down a track, fastening and unfastening as if by magic. How he hadn't noticed the abnormality before, he couldn't fathom.

A sorceress.

William had never had dealings with a witch, but Eva appeared to defy all the rumors spewed about them. She certainly wasn't capable of saving herself from Heselrig, nor would she have escaped Fail Monastery alive if he hadn't arrived when he did.

His gaze slid to the worn leather satchel she had slung over her shoulder when he found her at Lanark. She definitely didn't have that before she'd been abducted by Heselrig—and in no way could Wallace imagine the sheriff giving it to her.

Did she come in contact with someone else?

William desperately wanted to believe she had been given the bag by a passerby, but it seemed so unlikely. *Could she have met another of her kind? A sorcerer?* He shuddered. *A Devil worshiper?*

He had noticed her boots before. Carefully, he unlaced them and removed each one. Thick soles with grooves that would provide good traction for certain, but once again, they were not of this world. The soles weren't made of leather or wood. He ran his thumb over the back of the heel. The material had pliability to it, and inside, the sole was spongy. He turned the boot over in his hand and sniffed. *She'd said these were waterproof, yet they've not been immersed in fat.*

The satchel stared at him like a calculating serpent. Had she witches potions within? William couldn't remember ever being afraid of anything in his life. He was a warrior. He ran into battle when others fled, and by the grace of God, he would fear nothing from this witch.

With a growl, he snatched the satchel and unfastened the buckles. Taking a deep breath, he quickly threw back the flap, ready to face any apparition that sprang out. When nothing untoward happened, he inclined the opening toward the candle and peered inside.

He reached in and pulled out another bag, pink in color, hewn of a foreign, iridescent material. This, too, had the fastener with the metal tab. Dreading what he might find inside, he opened it. Oddly, he recognized a few items—a hairbrush and another that might be used to clean one's teeth. He picked up the hairbrush and examined it. Indeed, the materials were a quandary. He placed his finger on a rounded point, surprised when it didn't prick him. The center of the brush was pillow soft, entwined with Eva's red tresses.

To his dismay, small vials of potions were tossed haphazardly inside, as if they wouldn't break. William held one up. Though the writing was bold and blocked—nothing like the script he'd seen used throughout Christendom—he thought he recognized the letters. "Sh-am-poo." *Whatever does it mean?*

He tugged on the stopper, to no avail, but it twisted beneath his thumb. Curious, he turned it again and again until the stopper pulled all the way off. *Amazing, yet so entirely alien.* Holding the vial to his nose, he sniffed. A pleasing fragrance of honey mixed with flowers—not a repugnant-smelling potion he'd expect from a witch. Still, the scent was so heavenly, it couldn't be of this world.

William didn't know what to make of any of it. That Eva was a witch was certain. He fingered the hilt of his dirk. Practicing sorcery was strictly forbidden by the church, punishable by burning. What havoc could she run with his men? *I should kill her now while she's still sleeping. That would be the most compassionate way to dispatch the lass.*

But William didn't draw his knife. He glanced at her face and then to the items scattered about him. He needed no more evidence of her guilt. The satchel and its contents must be burned, and when, or if Eva awoke, he'd send her away. He'd been a fool to take her in and clothe her.

"Where am I?"

William jolted. Things might have been easier if she'd passed away in slumber. "We're back at the cave," he grumbled. In no way would he mention Leglen Wood.

Her eyes peered open with a flash of green. "My head feels like it's been bludgeoned."

His gut clamped. She wouldn't be charming him ever again. "I'm surprised a witch can feel pain."

She pressed her palms to her temples. "What are you talking about?"

William held up the most incriminating evidence of all. "This, this *thing* lit up without fire when it fell from your doublet."

"Jesus Christ."

"Blasphemy!" He drew back. "So it is true, ye do worship the devil and practice sorcery?"

She sat up and swayed, holding her hand to her head. "No. I am a Christian. I'm sorry, my head is pounding so hard I can't think straight."

"Mayhap because I have uncorked your beguiling floral potion. I can still smell its wiles in my nostrils."

Her gaze trailed to the satchel. "You looked in my bag? That's my personal stuff."

"Aye? It became my duty to look inside when that *object* lit up like a streak of lightning."

She reached for the vial he'd opened and twisted the stopper. "This is not a potion. It is shampoo, used for washing hair—*ye ken*, scrubbing my tresses. The scent lingers and smells nice."

"A hair tonic it may verra well be, but nothing about ye is of this world. Your doublet fastens with magic, the soles of your shoes are not of leather or wood, or any material I've ever seen. Even that vial of sh-am-poo must be hewn by a sorceress' hand."

"Ugh." Eva rubbed her head. "You weren't supposed to look in my satchel."

He straightened. "So ye admit to being a witch?"

"No." She groaned and looked up, dragging her fingers through her hair. "I am not a witch. I promised you that before."

"Then explain all this." He gestured to the contents spread before them. "And ye'd best do it quickly, else I'll have no choice but to burn these things and ye along with them."

Gasping, she scooted aside. "No, please. I-I-I just don't know how to tell you. If I do, I might…" Her gaze trailed away.

"Ye might?" William didn't know if he wanted to hear more.

She took a deep breath and cringed. "Look, that thing that lit up? It's a telephone. People in my time use it to communicate when at long distances." Eva, glanced left and right with fear in her eyes, as if she expected someone to spring from the walls and seize her.

William had heard enough. Standing in a crouch so not to hit his head, he yanked his dirk from its scabbard. "*Your* time? Ye speak with a devil's tongue."

Eva held her palms in front of her mouth. "Just wait a minute. Before you haul off and cut out my tongue, sit your ass down and allow me to explain."

How dare she speak to him with such insolence? He hesitated. No woman had ever spoken to him thus. He should not allow it.

She swatted the fur beside her. "Sit."

Growling, he shoved his dirk back in its sheath. "I'll listen, but if ye lift a finger against me, I'll slit your throat afore ye can draw your next breath."

"I'll keep that in mind." Eva smoothed her fingers over her throat and waited for him to sit. "You are right. My things are not from your era, but they *are* from this world."

He gave her a leery stare. And to think earlier he'd grown to believe her tale of woe.

She placed her palm atop his hand. "Please hear me out. But first promise you will not strike out rashly at what I am about to say."

He didn't like it, but she had a right to make her peace. Though he couldn't make any promises about how he'd respond once she'd finished. He snatched his hand away and rubbed off the beguiling sensation of her soft touch. "Go on."

***

Staring at her with the most intense blue eyes she'd ever seen, Eva had no doubt William would take her life if she couldn't make him believe her story. But for some reason she didn't panic. She almost felt calm. After pulling the medallion from beneath her shift, she translated the inscription in her head: *Truth is like a beacon…but few choose to follow.*

No matter what his medieval mind chose to believe, she could no longer lie to William Wallace.

She took the medallion off and handed it to him, searching for words he would clearly understand. "A professor—an expert in thirteenth and fourteenth century antiquity gave me that after we had a discussion about reporting the truth. You see, I am a historical journalist—a *chronicler* from the twenty-first century. I was born six-hundred and ninety-nine years in the future, in the year of our Lord nineteen eighty-eight."

"That canna—"

She held up her hand to stop him. "I know what you're going to say, but you can't possibly imagine the inventions and progress that have occurred in seven hundred years." She reached for her phone. "Honestly, I have no idea how I ended up here, but it has something to do with that medallion and the fact that I have researched your life and deeply desire to know more about you."

"My life?"

She sighed. "You do become a great man, one who…ah…" Walter's warning echoed in her head. "I can say no more about that."

He nodded.

"I have pledged an oath not to change the past." She bit the inside of her cheek. "I think that's why I was allowed to return."

"To return?"

"Yes." She had so much to say and yet needed to be careful with every word. "In the torture chamber, Heselrig wanted to know your name. I figured it wouldn't hurt to tell, because I knew you were going to kill him—regardless if I was there or not." She couldn't help but delve into the stories. "But honestly, no one knew the real reason for your attack on the Sheriff of Lanark. A man named Blind Harry, who lived in the fifteenth century, wrote that you were married to a woman named Marion Braidfute, and that Heselrig murdered her—not your father."

"Me? Married? I've never met a woman named Marion Braidfute." He knitted his eyebrows. "From Lanark?"

Eva nodded. "There is no proof of her birth, though she would have been from a noble family with holdings in Lanark. She was said to be the heiress of Lamington."

"'Tis preposterous," he snorted. "How on earth could a lowborn man marry an heiress?"

"Many historians questioned exactly that…and then there was the quandary of your paternity. Because Harry quoted your birthplace as Ellerslie—"

"Which it was."

"True, but history got it wrong and assumed the poet meant Elderslie in Renfrewshire."

"Bah. What did they have right?" he grumbled sarcastically.

"You did brutally kill the Sheriff of Lanark—and other events of which I cannot disclose." Eva took a deep breath, relieved that he appeared to be willing to listen before he killed her. And thinking of that, she snatched the medallion and put it back around her neck just to be safe. "Anyway, I've veered too far away from what happened in the jail. When I tried to tell Heselrig your name, blackness engulfed me and I was flung back to my time. I thought it wouldn't hurt to disclose your identity to him, but I was obviously mistaken—though I still cannot understand why."

He scratched his head. "Is that where ye obtained the satchel? I ken ye didna have it afore ye were captured."

"Yes. I collected a few comforts from my time and then headed back to the Fail Monastery ruins."

"Ruins?" he groaned and rolled his eyes to the alcove's ceiling. "This is all preposterous."

She held up her phone. Showing him was a huge risk, but the pictures would provide undeniable proof. When she pushed the on button, William jerked away. She gave him a pointed look. "I bring no sorcery, no evil. This simply holds a glimpse into the future."

He pulled back as if he were about to be burned. "I dunna believe ye. 'Tis witchcraft hailing the future."

"No. It is pure unadulterated fact." After finding the picture of the sunrise over the ruins, she held it up. "My phone has a camera with which I can take pictures—it's like an artist drawing an image of a scene at a certain point in time. It never changes once the picture is taken or drawn."

He eyed her dubiously, then shifted his wide-eyed gaze to the phone as if afraid it might scorch his eyeballs. "Why, that's just a pile of rubble. It looks nothing like the monastery." He leaned closer. "And there's no forest surrounding."

"Most of Scotland's forests were cleared in later centuries." She pointed to the rose window. "Though not much remains, do you recognize the window? It is the same."

He crossed his arms. "I am not convinced. Most abbeys and monasteries have round windows."

She brushed her finger over the screen and displayed another picture she'd taken the first day of the dig. "This is Loudoun Hill."

He sucked in a sharp inhale. "'Tis sorcery."

"No, the deforestation, and the erosion happens over time, but the rock still looks the same." She swiped over to the picture she'd taken of the Wallace monument. "This was erected in your honor."

He looked closer. "Is there an inscription?"

She pulled the phone away. "Yes, but it is not meant for your eyes." She shook her aching head. "Remember, I cannot do or say anything to affect your future."

He growled. "It seems ye're willing to tempt me, but when I dig deeper, ye canna say. 'Tis the forked tongue of a soothsayer."

"Do you honestly think so? You are enterprising enough to realize that's not it at all." Eva held out the phone and inclined her head toward him. "Smile."

She snapped a picture before he had a chance to say a word.

William clapped his hands over his eyes. "Are ye trying to blind me now?"

"It's just the flash. Blink a few times and your vision will clear." She held up the still, praying he wouldn't freak out. "See? I've just taken of photo of us—in my time it's called a selfie."

He said not a word, but his eyebrows formed straight lines while he looked closer.

"You're a handsome man." But Eva cringed as her gaze slid to her mangled face. "Oh my God, I have a black eye. Why didn't you tell me?"

William gaped as if he hadn't heard her. "'Tis witchcraft for certain." He seemed none too concerned about the condition of her face.

She groaned. "You're not understanding me."

He grabbed the phone and held it two inches from his nose. "What other images have ye on this thing?"

She snatched it back. "Can I see your stamp—the one you use to seal documents?"

He eyed her. "Why?"

"Because I need to see it first."

"I suppose there's no harm in it. But ye best have sound reasoning behind your request." With a distrustful scowl, he untied a worn leather pouch from his belt and slipped his hand inside.

When he held it up, Eva's heart skipped about five beats. Clear as her nose, it was a brand new version, exactly the same with a backward inscription of *Filius Alani Walais.* She selected the picture Walter had taken of her with the seal. "I unearthed this at Winny Wizzen four days ago."

William sprang to his feet hovering in a crouch with his back inches from the low ceiling. "That is preposterous!" he bellowed, his eyes so wide they nearly burst from his skull.

Unwilling to lose the battle now she braced her hands beside her. "You are a smart man—a man with vision and purpose. Above all people in this century, I would expect you to be able to understand all I have shown you."

He thrust out his palm and held it in front of her face. "Ye will stop this immediately. Ye're an apparition of my imagination." He shook his finger at her phone. "And that sorcery must be destroyed afore it consumes the minds of good men. God willing, I have not been soiled by your display of witchcraft."

Shit! She'd pushed him too far—shown him too much. *I am so stupid.*

"William," someone called from behind the furs hanging in the alcove entrance.

Still crouching, Wallace lumbered over and pulled them aside. "What is it?"

John Blair held up a folded piece of parchment. "A missive from the High Steward of Scotland. He's requested a meeting at his keep in Renfrew."

He glanced back at Eva, then to Blair. "How do ye ken 'tis not a trap?"

"His messenger said to travel at night. Said all of Scotland is talking about Lanark, and the English are plundering every standing hovel looking for an outlaw the size of Goliath—say he's seven feet tall and wields an enormous sword the length of a poleax."

"The gossipers are always blowing tales out of proportion," Wallace groused. "At six-foot-eight, I'll disappoint them for certain."

"Bloody hell, most people canna see that high, let alone worry about a hand."

William took the missive. "Go ready the horses. I'll be with ye shortly."

After glancing at the writing, he turned to Eva and crossed his arms. "Tell me what James the Steward wants with the likes of me. Is it a trap?"

"No." A flicker of hope made her grin. "Bishop Wishart might be there with him. They will pledge their support and offer you troops. They could mention Sir Andrew Murray to the north and Sir Douglas to the south." She clapped a hand over her mouth, terrified she could reveal too much. "That's all I can say."

"Bishop Wishart is the man who approved my entry into Dunipace in Dundee. I studied under him as a lad." He reached for his sword from where it rested against the wall and gave her a pointed stare. "If ye're wrong, I'll expect ye to be gone afore I return. Else I'll have no recourse but to burn ye."

Chapter Twelve

Setting out with a small band of his closest men, William took Blair's advice and traveled at night. Moving through darkness slowed the pace, but any man his size would be suspicious to English patrols, especially now with news of the slaying of Heselrig spreading like wildfire. Regardless, William knew this country better than any scout in the shire. He'd be able to pick his way to Renfrewshire blindfolded if forced.

And this eve in particular, he welcomed the quiet ride. Listening to Eva's story had riled him more than he cared to admit. And regardless of what she'd said, the woman was a vixen. Even with the bruise expanding beneath her eye, her beauty intoxicated him. Nothing about the lass was natural. And the Almighty knew he could not entertain courting any woman, let alone a hellcat who possessed inexplicable things she claimed to be from the future. How could he ever believe her?

Seven hundred bloody years? He guffawed.

Worse, things grew more precarious by the day. Last eve when he and his men had struck the English garrisons at Lanark, he'd crossed the line. Aye, he'd battled with the English and killed in the name of King Balliol before, but Heselrig was the first member of nobility who'd fallen under William's blade. Willy may have been a wanted man for leading a score of resistance warriors, but now that Heselrig was dead, Wallace would be an outlaw with a price on his head. Showing his face in public would bear greater risks than ever before.

As he rode his mind kept drifting back to Eva. The further they rode from Leglen Wood, the more William recounted all the disturbing things the lass had shown him. *Is she truly from the twenty-first century? I cannot imagine someone wanting to travel back in time to be my chronicler. Of all the great men Eva could have sought, why would she choose me? I've no title, no lands to my name.*

Nothing about the woman made sense. Yet the pictures she'd shown him were so visceral. It was as if he could reach into her small rectangular telephone and touch the miniature scene. And how unnerving to see his seal without the wooden handle, rusted and decayed like it actually had been in the ground for seven hundred years.

Though she'd blinded him taking a *picture* of them together, he couldn't believe she'd captured their faces. Couldn't bring himself to comprehend all she had shown him. Aye, her clothing and trinkets were not of this world—that she was a sorceress was the only logical explanation for certain.

Even her name was synonymous with the first woman—the very enchantress who'd tempted Adam in the Garden of Eden.

William shifted in his saddle unable to pinpoint exactly what made him so damned uncomfortable.

On one hand, nothing Eva had shown him was meant for evil. *Shampoo?* What harm was there in wanting one's tresses to be clean and to smell nice? The *telephone*, however was a different matter. She'd said she used it to communicate with others from a distance. *Surely that defies God's holy order? Are the people in the twenty-first century playing God?*

Pushing a button and capturing their faces at a moment in time? He never would have imagined it possible if he hadn't seen it with his own eyes.

But how does that compare to capturing a picture on a canvas or tapestry?

He didn't care to examine her side. He'd built his life, his honor, his code of chivalry around the firmly set rules of Christendom. He'd be a man of the cloth at this very moment if Scotland hadn't come under attack by the oppressor to the south. William believed in the word of God, freedom, and the right of every man to live at liberty without the yoke of tyranny.

He could not abide sorcery of any kind. *Never.*

Riding into the open lea, Wallace drove his mount harder. He had no time for a damned woman, no matter where she hailed from, and no matter how much he wanted her. No sorceress could sink her wiles into his heart. He'd sworn his duty to Scotland and to rid the kingdom of English rule. He'd pledged his life to the cause and would die with a sword in his hand.

If Eva was still at the cave when he returned, he would send her away. Nothing would change his mind this time.

***

They camped in the wood beside the High Steward's keep in Renfrew, and after a few hours' sleep, William roused the men at dawn. Before breaking their fast, he pounded on James Stewart's thick wooden gates.

A guard opened the viewing panel and his eyes popped wide. "I didna expect to see ye so soon."

William looked toward Blair and shrugged. Fancy knocking on the gate of one of the most powerful men in Scotland and being recognized afore he opened his mouth. Something was afoot.

The gate opened. "I'll notify Lord Stewart of your arrival immediately." The guard gestured toward the keep. "Ye can wait in the great hall."

"My thanks." William glanced over his shoulder at Eddy Little. "Do ye think ye might find a bowl of porridge for my men? We rode all night and haven't had a morsel."

"I'll tell Cook straight away. Not to worry, there's food aplenty, especially for ye and your men."

William led his band into the great hall with a swagger.

"It appears our raid in Lanark tipped the scales in your favor," Blair whispered.

"I pray the lord of the castle greets us with the same sentiments. Meanwhile, fill your bellies while there's food aplenty."

Stepping inside, William couldn't remember seeing such opulence outside of an abbey or cathedral. He'd not much occasion to visit a castle that hadn't been plundered by the English. Rich tapestries lined the walls, woven with silk so brilliant, the scene could have been outdoors—not unlike Eva's pictures. Sturdy tables lined the hall, spotted with groups of guardsmen breaking their fasts. At the far end, a raised dais displayed a table with ornately carved legs and velvet padded chairs to match.

The Steward has the means to assist us.

After they'd found a table and helped themselves to the abundant fare, William spooned his last bite of porridge when the same guard who'd met him at the gate approached. "Lord Stewart will see ye now."

Blair and Little stood with William.

The guard held up his hand. "My lord asked to see only Wallace."

Blair wrapped his fingers around his hilt—a greater warrior of God did not exist in William's mind. But he patted the priest's arm. "We are among friends."

"Ye're too bloody trusting."

"And I'd expect a man of the cloth to be more so." William nodded to the guard. "Lead on."

As usual, Wallace had to stoop to climb the tower stairs. He never cared to be in a stairwell. They were too narrow and didn't leave enough options for escape. If he ever had the opportunity to build a keep, he would ask the mason to make the stairwells as wide as the structure would allow, and most definitely wider than his shoulders so he didn't have to ascend sideways.

They exited on the first landing, ventured down a passageway until the guard stopped and opened a sturdy door, fashionably rounded at the top. "My Lord Stewart and Bishop Wishart, allow me to present William Wallace."

The back of William's neck tingled. *Eva said Wishart might be here.*

He ducked under the lintel and entered. God's bones, if he'd considered the great hall to be opulent, this chamber was befitting of royalty. The hearth alone was crafted of white marble. Rich greens adorned the tapestries displaying hunting scenes. The oaken table had been polished to such sheen, it could have been used as a mirror.

An older man stood, dressed in a red doublet with a blue mantle closed at his throat by a large brooch fashioned with the Stewart coat of arms. "Thank you for coming, Mr. Wallace."

William bowed deeply. "The honor is mine, m'lord." Still bent, he looked to the bishop. "Your Worship."

"'Tis good to see ye again, William." The bishop remained seated. "It warms my heart to hear ye've taken up the mantle for Scotland."

"Please sit." Lord Stewart gestured toward a chair, so ornate it appeared far too fragile for sitting.

William tested the velvet seat for soundness before he sat. Already uncomfortable amid such wealth, he preferred not to further embarrass himself by breaking the chair with his immense size and end up sprawled across the floorboards.

Lord Stewart slid into his chair at the head of the table. "I see by your girth, ye are as great a man as the rumors tell it."

A servant appeared from a side room and placed silver goblets of wine in front of each.

"Pardon, m'lord?" William leaned over his goblet and inhaled the fruity bouquet, examining the craftsmanship of the stems, fashioned in the shape of lion's claws.

"Do ye not ken?" The High Steward slapped his palm on the table. "Since ye and your men rained havoc on Lanark but two days past, all of Scotland is agog with your action against that barbarous sheriff."

Wallace pulled his gaze away from the goblet. "Truly?"

"Aye, reports claim ye leapt your horse over a line of guardsmen, and plunged into the gaol, dispatching anyone who stood in your path."

"Nothing to put fear in the hearts of a line of pikemen like jumping a warhorse over their ranks." William grinned. "Besides, I had a bit of help. I've a score and ten men who ride with me."

Lord Stewart waved a dismissive hand. "Merely a score and ten? That might suffice for a quick raid, but ye need an army behind all that brawn."

William leaned forward. "What are ye saying?"

Bishop Wishart held up his goblet. "I was just apprising Lord Stewart of your tutelage in Dundee." He sipped and looked to the High Steward. "I've never seen a prospect more naturally skilled with a great sword. Though 'tis a shame his exemplary skills are not being put to use with the Templars in Jerusalem. William would have been my choice to put the fear of God in the hearts of the infidel."

"But we need him in Scotland." Lord Stewart assessed Wallace like he was a prize bull on the auction block.

"The bishop kens I left the order to drive the invader from our lands." William drank and savored the smooth taste sliding over his tongue.

"And have ye a title of any sort?" Lord Stewart asked. "A knighthood, perchance?"

"I am a man of the land." William unclasped his belt and held up his great sword and scabbard. "This is the only title I need. Not a man can best me."

His Worship gestured his palm toward Wallace. "His uncle on his mother's side is the Sheriff of Ayr. His grandfather was a knight as well. Wallace may not be nobly born, but he was raised a gentleman."

William didn't care to have the bishop speak in his stead. "If ye are looking for a nobleman, ye'd best set your sights elsewhere."

"Hmm." Lord Stewart circled his pointer finger around his gold brooch. "And your men, are ye their leader, or…"

"The men follow me because they choose to do so. We have but one goal, and that is to rid Scotland of Longshanks to restore the true king to the throne."

"I see." Lord Stewart cleared his throat.

Wishart rolled his hand through the air. "Go on James. This is what we agreed."

"Very well. As ye are aware, I am the High Steward of Scotland, and as such, my position is…" Lord Stewart brushed his velvet mantle as if cleaning it of lint. "*Political.* There are a great many eyes upon me and a great many nobles who have sided with King Edward."

Never before had the opportunity to question a high ranking noble presented itself so fortuitously to William. Though he knew the answer, he wanted to hear it explained for himself. "I heard ye also signed the roll pledging fealty to Longshanks."

Wishart removed his miter, as if to again speak in his lordship's stead. "True. Many men applied their seals to the roll, but under duress." The bishop placed the hat on the table. "How else were the nobles to retain their lands and keep their families safe from the wrath of the English army?"

The High Steward simply nodded in agreement.

William picked up his goblet and sipped. Then he looked from one man to the other. "I'm not faulting ye for protecting your lands and riches, but I have no tolerance for any man who sits idle while King John remains imprisoned in the Tower of London and his gaoler moves English tyrants in place to seize our castles, to plunder our towns and churches. Men like Heselrig have gone too far. Worse, we've stood idle and watched Cressingham flay our countrymen. My own father was murdered at Lochmaben. Have ye witnessed the tyranny for yourself? Women are raped, their throats cut, left dead with their skirts up around their hips. Children are hanged alongside their fathers." William again looked from Wishart to Stewart and swallowed back the churning bile in his stomach. "The nobles must unite their armies and make a stand."

"Your concerns have been duly noted," Lord Stewart said. "But as I mentioned, this is a war that must be fought by the heart and soul of our nation. To be blunt, Edward Plantagenet has the Scottish nobility by the cods." He pointed at William. "Ye own no lands, have pledged fealty to no one as far as I can tell."

William nodded. "The true king of Scotland is the only man to whom I will pledge my sword."

Wishart grinned. "I kent we could count on your verve, my son. We, too, have a vision for a united Scotland. We need a leader the common man will adore—someone who is not protecting title and lands."

"Ye're exactly the man for whom we've been searching," Lord Stewart added. "And your actions at Lanark have already made ye a legend."

"Bah." William picked up the damned goblet and guzzled his remaining wine. "I need an army to undertake a true rebellion. Aye, we've made some headway with our raids on

English garrisons, but the bastards continue to cross the border and pillage our towns."

"That is where we can help, lad," Bishop Wishart said, putting the miter back on his head.

The High Steward placed his palms on the table. "I'm prepared to give ye a cavalry of fifty horse and two hundred foot."

William's heart leapt with the prospect of having trained soldiers to his avail. "'Tis a start." But he'd need so much more to accomplish his dreams.

The bishop ran his hands across his velvet chasuble. "And Sir William Douglas is ready to ride with ye as well."

"Douglas?" William scratched his beard. "Did he not surrender his lands and castle in Berwick only one year past?"

"Aye," Wishart said. "And he wants them back with vengeance."

"Ye are not alone, Wallace." Lord Stewart held up a finger. "Word has it Andrew Murray in the north has made good headway in recapturing lands taken by the English. There are skirmishes all over the country."

Eva had mentioned both Douglas and Murray. The back of William's neck tingled yet again. "But we will not be successful until we join together."

"Sir Douglas is planning an uprising in Ayr—but I doubt he'll be successful if he goes it alone." The lord pointed. "I'll send ye word and provide my men when the date is settled."

William drummed his fingers on the table for a moment. He needed men, but Sir Douglas had an unsavory reputation—then again, this was war. Edward's policy was to show no quarter and Sir Douglas could very well be the type of man Wallace needed. *Can he be trusted?* "I accept on one condition." He panned his gaze from one face to the other. "If I ride into this skirmish, I lead the battle."

"That is what we desire as well." Wishart bobbed his head. "And in the interim, we'll ensure all of Scotland is aware a new leader has risen from the people."

Lord Stewart held up his goblet. "To the people's man-at-arms."

Wishart followed suit. "Here, here."

Holding up his empty goblet, William acknowledged the toast. *The people's man-at-arms*. Such a *nom de guerre* suited him.

Chapter Thirteen

Eva never should have brought a satchel filled with modern stuff. As soon as William left, she hid the thing in a crevice in the cave wall and rolled a boulder across it. If Wallace thought her a witch, the other men would completely freak out if they saw her phone and toiletries. She'd just have to do without—after she popped a couple ibuprofens for her pounding headache.

Her body might be getting used to going without caffeine, but it would take her a few days to recover from being knocked out by Heselrig.

Voices grew louder beyond the fur curtain that hung at the alcove entrance, blocking her from the rest of the men. She secured her veil in place and poked out her head.

Robbie turned—obviously keeping guard while she was inside. "What the bleeding hell happened to your face, Miss Eva?"

"That's not proper language to use in the presence of a lady, Robert Dominus Boyd." She grimaced and touched her tender nose. "But I know I look awful."

"Och, 'tis just a black eye. It will fade in a sennight or two."

"Wonderful, and I may have broken my nose to boot."

He peered a bit closer. "I think not. At least 'tisn't crooked."

"Thank heavens." Honestly, she would have died if her nose had been mangled. "I guess there's something to be said for having a box-shape to it."

"I think ye have a bonny nose."

"Thank you." She glanced toward the cave entrance.

Brother Bartholomew marched inside shaking his head, leading a pair of men at his flank. "I've no idea how we'll feed them all, let alone where they will sleep."

Eva glanced at Robbie. "What's going on?"

"Men are arriving in droves—say they heard about Willy killing the Sheriff of Lanark. They're all pledging fealty."

She clapped her hands. "That's wonderful."

"Aye, except they're hungry and carrying pitchforks for weapons. I doubt there's a trained foot soldier among them."

"I wouldn't worry about their training. The first thing is to see they don't starve." Eva drummed her fingers against her lips. "Can any of them hunt?"

Robbie shrugged.

She pulled his arm. "Come."

Outside, the bedlam was worse. Everywhere Eva looked there were groups of men shouting, each one louder than the next—at least a hundred men. She picked up on bits and pieces—a lack of a smithy, broken arrows, shelter, food. The only certainty? Tempers were flaring and fast.

She pulled Robbie to an enormous boulder, about five feet high. "Give me a leg up."

"There?"

"Aye, someone's got to take charge before a brawl breaks out."

Once atop, she shoved her fingers in her mouth and blew an ear-splitting whistle.

The noise immediately ebbed to a hum.

Eva planted her fists on her hips. "Wallace has gone to meet with the High Steward. Until he returns, we need food, shelter, and people to make arrows and sharpen weapons."

"Who are ye to tell us what we need? A woman, no less," someone yelled.

"What happened to your eye?" another voice chimed. "Beat for opening your flapping gob?"

"Heselrig walloped the lass—right before Wallace ran him through." Robbie jumped up beside her—the showoff. "She's Wallace's woman. Anyone touches her and Willy will lop of their—uh—ballocks right afore he lops off their heads."

Heat rushed to Eva's face. *Wallace's woman?* It would take her forever to convince William she hadn't contrived that lie. But she could show no sign of weakness, not in front of a hundred Scotsmen out for blood. She spread her arms wide. "Who can hunt?"

No one uttered a word.

"Very well. The first man who brings in a deer will be the first to meet with Wallace when he returns." God, she hoped William would humor her.

A man with a bow slung over his shoulder raised his hand. "We'll need more than one deer."

"Aye we will," Eva agreed, eyeing the stunned faces. "Do you want William to return to a mob of lazy milksops, or do you want to face him with a grin and say you felled a deer or snared a pheasant or a rabbit, and the men are feasting because of you?"

Another man stepped forward. "I'll hunt."

"So will I," said a man with a formal bow of his head.

"Me as well."

"Thank you." Eva gazed at the expectant faces. "Who among you can set up a smithy's shop?"

"What will we use for iron?" a big fellow asked.

Eva shot a panicked look at Robbie. The lad did nothing to help. Jeez, she had to give an answer or else she'd lose the tiny bit of authority she'd gained. "Ah…anything you can find—or swipe. What did we bring back from Lanark?"

"Plenty of pikes and poleaxes," a disembodied voice shouted from the crowd.

"Then they need to be sharpened—and arrows made." Eva pointed to a group of boys who looked about Robbie's age. "You lads, set to it."

Eva watched them leave and then glared at the crowd. "You all want to sleep in the rain? Who will build shelters?" She pointed at every man who hinted at raising his hand.

"The rest of you will help Brother Bartholomew prepare food, fetch water, and maintain a constant supply of firewood. I do not want to see a single idle soul…and if I do, so help me, William Wallace will hear about it."

A stout man with a thick, black beard stepped forward. "I'm a brewer, we'll need ale."

"Then set to work." She gave him a nod of thanks, then returned her gaze to the crowd. "Hard labor will make you strong, and when it comes time to fight, you'll be ready."

She stood, watching the men dispatch. Keeping her fists tight against her hips prevented her from wilting into a trembling heap. Heaven knew she had just set a mob of medieval men to task without really having any idea if she'd done right or not. Her heart beat a fierce rhythm, but aside from the deep breaths drawing in through her nose, she showed no outward sign of fear. *I won't back down, no matter how inept I might actually be.*

***

The following night, Wallace and his men left Renfrew just past the witching hour. At dawn, they reached the edge of Leglen Wood and proceeded to pick their way through the rugged scrub. Signs of passersby were everywhere—moss wiped from a tree, footprints in mud and freshly broken limbs.

"Ye think they've found our camp?" Blair asked.

"Mayhap," William said, looking at the deep impression of a boot. "Nonetheless, we'll ride around to the outcropping first."

Eddy turned his horse south. "Good plan."

After three sleepless nights, Wallace couldn't remember being this tired, but the detour would only add a half-hour to their journey.

As they made their way along the southwest game trail, there were signs of recent human traffic there as well. The back of William's neck bristled. He drew his sword. "Ready yourselves for battle, men."

But a fight didn't come. Instead, after the men tied their horses and climbed the big hill overlooking the camp, they all stood dumbfounded. It was as if a mob of carpenters had come into the forest and decided to build a hamlet right in the middle of the densest part of Leglen Wood.

In the center of it all crackled a roaring fire beside a man hammering on an iron anvil. Lads sat outside the cave, sharpening the weapons they'd brought back from Lanark.

"Someone's set them to task," Blair said.

"Och, aye." William slapped him on the back. "And we'll be making him a lieutenant forthwith." He held his ram's horn to his lips and gave a hearty blow.

Robbie Boyd hopped up from amidst the group of lads and broke into a run. Before William and the others reached the bottom of the hill, Robbie skidded to a stop. "Ye should have seen her, Willy. She took charge like a queen."

William didn't need to ask who. There could be only one she. Hopefully Eva hadn't used witchcraft to erect the lean-tos that had gone up in the clearing. "Did she now?"

"Aye. Brother Bartholomew was about to throttle the lot of them, but Eva climbed up on that rock and whistled like she was the Queen of Sheba—and someone asked who the hell she thought she was—and I jumped up and set them straight—said she was your woman."

"Pardon?" William grasped the lad's shoulders. "Ye said what?"

"I didna ken ye'd been swiving the wench," John Blair blurted with exasperation.

Wallace slapped the monk with a quick backhand. "I have not and ye will not be speaking ill of the lass even if ye are a priest."

"Bloody hell." Blair could swear with the worst of them. "Ye're a bit oversensitive."

"Aye? Well, I havena slept in three days."

Robbie tugged William's arm. "Ye should have seen her. She wouldna take a word of backtalk from anyone."

That was all Wallace needed. He was about to cast Eva out of the camp and now she'd singlehandedly organized an army of men. "Where do they all hail from?"

Waddling on his stout legs, Brother Bartholomew caught up to them, huffing with exertion. "There're coming in droves—tenant farmers and young fellas out to make a name for themselves, mostly."

"Anyone skilled with a sword or bow?" Blair asked.

The little monk drew in a deep breath. "Ye'll have to determine that. I've enough work for ten men just trying to keep this lot fed."

Once they reached the bottom of the hill, they were met by dozens of expectant faces. A man with a grizzly beard and a smithy's apron stepped forward. "We heard ye took a stand in Lanark. Scotland needs a man who is not afeared to face Longshanks."

"Aye," said another. "My village was burned, my family murdered. I will not rest until I have vengeance."

A pair of men marched through the clearing carrying a deer suspended from a pole. Robbie pointed. "Ye see. Miss Eva set them to hunting and set the lads to sharpening the weapons and making arrows."

"And I'm melting every bit of iron I can find to make swords and arrow tips," said the man in the smithy's apron.

William pushed his fingers under his helm and scratched his head. "I must thank her." Now she'd be even more difficult to send away. The lads even appeared to *like* her.

He addressed the assembled men. "We've a battle to fight one month hence and I'll not have any men march against trained English soldiers without being prepared. Edward Little I appoint over the archers. John Blair will train all foot soldiers in pole arms and I will teach each and every one of ye how to wield a sword."

A cheer rose above the forest and, at the moment, William hoped the English could hear. A new, more organized rebellion would soon be breathing down their necks.

He leaned toward Blair. "If this many men can find us, we need to post a watch in a perimeter around the camp. See to it groups of men are assigned a turn—no one shirks guard duty."

"I'll see it done, sir."

Wallace stopped to correct the cleric, but from Blair's stern countenance, he clamped his mouth shut. He heeded what Wishart and Stewart said—the commoners were in dire need of someone they could follow. If they deemed him a knight of the people, then so be it.

***

After eating his fill of venison, William still hadn't seen Eva. Too tired to face her anyway, he'd rather put off the unsavory duty of turning the lass out until the morrow. He could fight for hours and never grow weary, but days in the saddle followed by lack of sleep sapped him like the ague.

Still daylight, he picked up his kit with drying towel and soap and headed for the River Ayr.

In truth, it was a relief to have Eva set the men to task. William did need to thank her for that before…

Ballocks!

Damnation, he could hold on to no regrets. The woman posed too much of a distraction. She must go and that was the end of it.

On the morrow, after he'd had some rest, he would take up the reins and turn his group of men into warriors. They had all come to make a stand against the oppressor. Men like that had heart, and with that kind of vitality, he would find a way to mold them into a formidable force. He could be so much more effective with two hundred fifty trained soldiers from Lord Stewart, another hundred from Douglas, and mayhap he'd raise another hundred before they left Leglen Wood.

The English in Ayr won't know what hit them. This is what we needed to start an all-out rebellion.

Reaching the place where the water pooled, William disrobed and set his things on a rock just like he always did. It wasn't often the weather was nice enough to strip down to his braies and take a dip in the icy river. One of the things he missed most about Ellerslie was Ma's wooden barrel filled with warm water, though he'd never admit it to a soul.

He dove in, the bitter cold enlivening his tired limbs. He kicked his legs and pumped his arms, warming to the water as he swam against the current. Then he rolled to his back and floated down river, watching the tree limbs pass above. Nothing like cool water and the tranquility of nature to help him clear his mind.

A lily white flicker caught the corner of his eye.

William let his legs drift downward as he planted his feet in the sandy riverbed.

In a heartbeat, he scarcely could take a breath.

Wearing not a stitch of clothing, Eva stood in thigh-deep water with her back to him.

Before he blinked, his gaze slid from coppery tresses brushing feminine shoulders to a tiny waist which fanned into glorious heart-shaped buttocks. Heaven's stars, her flawless skin had to be as pure white as fresh cream.

God on the cross, save me.

Christ, he was only a flesh and blood man. Who on earth could resist such a temptation? He clenched his teeth and growled. Frigid water or nay, he lengthened like a stallion catching scent of a filly in heat. God's teeth, even his ballocks turned to balls of tight molten steel. Palms sweaty, chest heavy and heaving, his mind honed in on one thing. Lord, he had to bring himself under control…and why the devil was she naked, bathing in the wood with so many men about? Hell, if anyone saw her…

He clenched his fists.

She turned. The devil only knew why she did that, but her mouth formed an "O" with her gasp and she crossed an arm over her breasts and slid a hand in front of the triangle of red curls he'd already seen. He'd caught a glimpse of her breasts, too. He stood dumbstruck, his feet sinking into the riverbed. By the saints, he couldn't turn away from such perfection—full and ripe as melons, tipped with pink rosebuds. He licked his lips, forcing himself to clench his muscles against the blast of desire surging through his groin.

She blinked in rapid succession. "You-you're back?" Heaven help him, she was lovely even with the bruise surrounding her eye.

"Aye." The word came out with a husky growl. "Robbie told me what ye did with the men. I owe ye my thanks." As the vivid green of her eyes became more intense, he suddenly realized he'd started walking toward her.

Eva's gaze dipped down the length of his body. Her lips parted and a dainty pink tongue slipped out and moistened them.

William looked down. The water all but covered his braies and the thick column that refused to ease. But she was so close he could practically reach out and touch her. If only he could pull her naked body into his embrace and kiss those bow-shaped lips—enjoy those soft, pliable breasts pressing into his chest.

She dropped her arms and took one step toward him—an inordinately bold move for a lass. It made the fire in his groin burn all the more. When her brilliant green eyes met his gaze, her chin ticked up and she smiled.

Wantonly.

"Someone needed to set the men to task until you arrived." Her voice turned sultrier than a midsummer's day.

"Eva, I—" Blessed be the saints, he didn't know what to say—could scarcely inhale—especially with those unbelievably desirable breasts now pointing straight at him. Jesus, he wanted to taste them, his fingers ached to sink into her softness and run across those deliciously hard tips.

With one more step, she placed her palm on his chest. "Yes?" she asked breathlessly.

God's bones.

It took every bit of self-control he could muster not to drag her into his arms—devour those enticing lips—grind his hips against that red triangle that screamed for him. Lord, if she was half as delectable as she looked, he'd come undone in two blinks of an eye.

But no. He could not act on his base desires. With a surge of restraint, he grasped her wrist. "Ye must return from whence ye came."

Her lips thinned, but she took her free hand and brushed the hair from his face. Bloody hell, why did she have to touch him like that? "I know I pushed you too far—showed you too much." She glanced back to the shore. "Look, I borrowed a cake of soap from Brother Bartholomew."

William's mouth grew dry.

She stepped so close, the heat from her naked body warmed him. "Please don't send me away. I am convinced I'm meant to be here." The green of her eyes grew darker.

God, she was too close for him to form a rational thought. "With you."

William shook his head and turned his back before she could further distract him with her wicked body. "Scotland is at war. I'm living in a cave. 'Tis no place for a woman, no matter in which century she was born."

"I can take care of myself."

Och aye, now she sounds self-assured. "Nay, ye cannot. Ye proved that at the gaol in Lanark when I found ye unconscious—look at your blessed eye. 'Tis still black and blue. Besides, even if ye were to stay, how could I trust ye?"

She coughed out a high-pitched gasp. "I've been completely truthful with you."

"Aye?" He rubbed his eyes, trying to forget the image of her succulent breasts prone to him—pink tips—silken skin. God's teeth, he needed to dunk his head in the icy river and hold it there. "'Tis easier to believe ye lost your home in Dunbar than ye came from the future."

"I fabricated my story at first, because I knew you wouldn't believe me then. Once you found my things—well, I had no choice but to be honest." By the stars, she spoke with a forked tongue.

He folded his arms to steel his resolve. "Ye see? Ye'll lie to me if ye think I'll believe it."

"I will not." The water sloshed. "I hate lying. I have pledged my life to telling the truth. If I weren't afraid you'd slit my throat with that gargantuan sword of yours, I would have told you the truth from the outset."

William regarded her over his shoulder. She'd climbed onto the shore and wrapped a drying cloth around her body, thankfully hiding those distracting breasts…alluring hips—but those slender legs still attracted him like a cock to a hen.

She jutted her foot to the side and tapped the damnable thing. "Tell me. If you awoke unarmed in some strange place with a crazy man—clearly not from your time—swinging a sword at you, and were dragged from the scene by an enormous brute and put on a very large horse, the likes you'd never ridden before—would you be forthcoming about your identity?"

He waded to the shore, moving his hands to his hips. "Of course I would."

She groaned. "Let me put it another way. You've heard of the Egyptians, right?"

"Aye."

"So if you awoke in an Egyptian temple, before the time of Moses, and they identified you as an Israelite, wouldn't you try to do what you could to stay out of chains…until you figured out how to get home?"

Damnation, she could take an argument and turn it into a muddle. "So are ye an English spy?"

"No, you aren't understanding me at all." Her face flushed red as she shook her finger. "I'm just trying to say that I had no choice but to make up a story until I was sure you wouldn't kill me."

"Ye think I willna?"

She glanced back to her clothes, spread out to dry in the sun. "I suppose it is a possibility, but you are William Wallace, not a bloodthirsty murderer. I now know I was meant to find you."

Now she had *him* tapping his foot. "How can ye be so sure?"

"Because I swore I could uncover your story without changing the past—I swore I would bring the truth to the world." She was being nonsensical.

"I am but a crofter's son—a younger one at that, meant to become a monk. I lead a small band of rebels." Heaven help him, his gaze slipped to the points of her breasts straining against the linen cloth. With a growl, he forced his eyes to look at her face. "Aye, we've gained some recognition from our raid on Lanark, but I'll soon fall into obscurity. History remembers kings, bishops and popes. Even if 'tis as ye said and I become a commander. When John Balliol is returned to the throne, Scotland will once again be at peace, and I can return to Dundee and take my vows."

Raising her chin, her gaze met his, then drifted aside as she sighed. William couldn't shake the sense that she disapproved of something he'd said—knew there must be something she wasn't letting on to. He wanted to ask her how she'd known so much about what would happen during his meeting with Lord Stewart, but discussing it with the woman would only encourage further soothsaying.

"My mind's run amuck." He gestured toward her clothes. "Put on your gown. Ye shouldna be out here alone with all the men mulling about. 'Tisn't safe."

"But Robbie told them I was…that you would, um, have words with anyone who touched me."

William knew well enough what the lad would have said and it had nothing to do with a conversation. "Aye? With a body as sinful as yours, mayhap no God-fearing man in Scotland is safe." He turned his back. "Now put on the damned dress afore I do something we'll both regret."

Chapter Fourteen

Eva hadn't been able to look William in the eye after they'd returned to the camp. And he obviously wanted to distance himself from her—hadn't said a word. He'd taken the evening meal sitting with Eddy Little and John Blair, pretty much like he always did.

But Eva couldn't ignore the tension in his silence. Lord, he said he'd burn her if she was still there when he returned from Renfrew. The reason she didn't flee to Fail and beg to go home was because she hadn't lied—prayed he figured that out during his meeting with the High Steward. He had to learn to trust her—believe her story, and fleeing would only serve to solidify his misgivings and errant assumptions.

Why is he so tight-lipped? He must be pleased about all the men flocking to him to pledge their fealty.

Now that their numbers had tripled, men filled their trenchers and sat wherever they could find a place, mostly outside. As usual, Eva sat with Robbie. At least he seemed to like her, and though he was just a lad, she felt safe beside him. He didn't look at her with leering eyes and she had no doubt the boy would stand up to any man in her defense.

Though the boy yammered about his day and all the new recruits, Eva hadn't listened. She pushed her food around her trencher, too wound up about acting so embarrassingly bold when alone and naked with William. At first she'd been mortified that he'd caught her bathing, but when he moved in her direction with that look on his face—lips slightly parted, his hungry eyes drinking in every inch of her bare flesh—she'd misread his intention.

God, she was a lamebrain. Why on earth did a man seven hundred years her senior happen to be the only guy who'd stirred any sort of desire since Steven's death? Oh yeah, William Wallace wasn't just the greatest hero Scotland had ever known, he was hot, sexy and as rugged as the Highlands. The gruff alpha male wasn't usually Eva's type, but heaven help her, the man had the most chiseled set of ripped abs she'd ever seen.

Michelangelo would have killed to sculpt him…but jeez, even the brilliant artist won't be born for almost two hundred years.

She chewed her thumbnail. An affair with William wouldn't have been so bad—if he'd shown any interest at all. She could have allowed herself a fleeting tryst. *Why not? I'm a widow.* They could have both enjoyed a zippy romance with no strings attached.

Not that she'd ever in her life considered doing anything so daring.

A lead ball sank to the pit of her stomach. For the first time since she'd arrived in the thirteenth century, she thought about William's gruesome end. She could have heaved all over her trencher.

Forget lust, it was probably best they remain at odds after all. She needed to stop acting like a total idiot. The first love of her life was murdered—nothing like setting herself up to fall head over heels for someone she knew would…

A man climbed onto a rock and began to play a wooden flute and the noise in the cave ebbed to a low hum. Spritely music echoed off the cavern walls and whirled around them. Goodness, the acoustics were ideal for a performance.

Robbie tapped his foot. "I like a good tune."

"Me, too." Eva clapped her hands together, but when she met William's gaze across the fire, her smile waned.

He looked at her with such intensity she could have sworn she was still naked. *I'll never live down that slip of judgement.* She smoothed her hands over her skirts to ensure everything was in place. But she couldn't drag her eyes away from William's stare. It made her breath come in short gasps. Had he decided to rid himself of her once and for all?

I should have run.

But I couldn't.

God, why does he have to be so…so…male?

Damn, I always want that which I can never have.

Robbie elbowed her in the ribs. "Do ye sing?"

"Aye." She licked her lips and forced herself to tear her gaze away from William and regard the lad. "I used to…" *When I was at uni.*

He rolled his hand through the air. "Go on then. Give us a tune."

"Oh no." She shook her head. "I doubt I know any songs that would be familiar to you."

Robbie stood, stretching his arms wide. "Who wants to hear Willy's woman sing us a tune?"

Eva's panicked gaze shot to William. His jaw tensed like he could kill the lad—she could too, damn the little pipsqueak.

But the others hollered and clapped, egging her on.

William shook his head, then shrugged. A lot of help he'd be. Eva bumbled to her feet and stood while her mind recounted all the tunes she'd ever sung from *Itsy Bitsy Spider* to *Ave Maria* to the top ten she'd hummed with on the radio last week. Not a one would do. Even *Ring Around the Rosy* hadn't been composed yet. Lord, the Black Death wouldn't hit for about another fifty years. She shuddered and closed her eyes.

Making a snap decision, she drew in a deep breath and launched into a song she loved, *You Raise Me Up*. Her choir at NYU had sung the modern Irish folksong. She'd even been given the solo, which had been one of the highlights of her year.

She started softly. "*When I am down and, oh my soul's so weary…*" Even without a microphone, the acoustics in the cave were surprisingly resonant. Chills spread down the backs of her arms as she looked at the stunned faces of her audience.

Even Robbie and the lads beside him sat perfectly still, their mouths agog.

She sang the second verse mezzo forte, but when Eva hit the refrain, she crescendoed to fortissimo, the sound almost palpable. What a time to realize how much she missed singing.

Filled with the uplifting spirit of the moment, she swayed and lifted her hands, holding them above her head for the ending. "…*I am strong when I am on your shoulders*…" Eva took in a deep inhale and lowered her arms, emphasizing the retard and decrescendo. "*You raise me up to more than I can be.*" As the last note echoed, swirling around the cavernous walls and gradually faded, the men sat in complete silence.

Someone sniffed—another rubbed his eyes.

Eva chanced a glance at William. Sitting erect, his dark stare made her stomach totally flip with butterflies. It wasn't a look of anger, oh no, Eva knew the look well enough. Predator came to mind—a deadly hunter honing in on his prey.

She liked it—craved what she'd seen at the river and more.

But even Eva knew better than to humiliate herself twice in one day. Oh no, besides, this time an audience would watch her every movement.

Before another thought popped into her head, deafening applause filled the chamber. Robbie hopped up and raced beside her. "Bloody oath, ye can sing. Why didna ye tell me ye were good enough to be a king's minstrel?"

"Och aye," hollered John Blair from across the fire. "If ye're intent on having the woman remain in our army, we might be able to make use of her talent to create a diversion. What say ye, William?"

The priest actually had sort of a kind word to say? A lump stuck in Eva's throat. The dark stare gone, Wallace glanced at her, then to Blair, but his reply was swallowed up by the noise of the crowd.

Her singing probably made him want to be rid of her even more now. She'd drawn too much attention to herself.

Jeez, why do I always have to ruin things?

After bidding goodnight to Robbie, Eva headed for the alcove to hide. Maybe sleep would help her recover from a thoroughly embarrassing day.

***

William watched Eva pick her way to his makeshift bedchamber. He didn't know if the lass realized she'd taken over the space he'd carved out for himself when he and his band of upstarts had discovered the cave—they'd only been five strong at the time.

Growling under his breath, he looked to young Boyd curling up on his pallet of pelts. So Robbie had told everyone Eva was William's woman? If only Wallace *could* have a woman as bonny and spirited as that redheaded lass for his own. And who knew she could sing like an angel? She possessed a voice clear as a flute and still swore she wasn't a witch? Bloody hell, Eva MacKay meant trouble. Doubtless, by the time she'd finished her tune, she had every man in the cave wanting to bed her—including Wallace. Ballocks, it had taken an iron will not to ravish her by the river earlier in the day as well.

He nursed his tankard of ale and stared at the furs covering the entrance to his place of solace. Had she removed her apron and kirtle? Was she brushing her hair wearing nothing but a thin linen shift? Though only shoulder length, her tresses reminded him of copper shimmering in sunlight.

The hum of the crowd started to ebb as it usually did at this hour. Beside William, Blair held a flask of whisky between his palms, his eyes closed, snoring louder than a builder's saw.

William sat quietly for a time, pulling on his ale, staring at the furs shrouding the recess. He should be thinking about all the new men and how he'd start training them on the morrow.

She's probably asleep by now.

Curiosity consumed his mind. His tankard empty, William set it aside and crossed the cavern to her—his alcove. He stood for a moment well aware entering would only serve to make things worse, but now he was there, the men would think him weak if he didn't slip inside, especially since Robbie told them she was his woman.

Blast Robbie Boyd. This is all his doing.

William ducked under the low ingress and stepped inside. A lone candle had nearly burned to a nub.

Eva sat up, clutching the blanket beneath her chin. "William?"

"Aye." The word came out thick and raspy.

She sighed. "Thank goodness it's you."

Unable to stand upright, he pulled himself alongside her and reclined on his elbow. Thankfully there was ample room for them both, as touching her would drive him over the edge. "Who else did ye expect?"

"Not sure. The men have been respectful—you know—they haven't tried *anything.*" By the stars, her scent was more alluring than a field of heather. Bartholomew's soap had never had him smelling so bonny.

He toyed with a lock of her hair and twirled it around his finger. "Would ye like me to leave?"

"No, not at all." She placed her palm on his chest. She'd done that by the river, too.

God's bones, William's heart thrummed so fast, he gasped.

"I want you—ah—to stay." Her exhale shuddered. "We—um—don't have to…" Her gaze trailed down the length of his body as she bit her bottom lip. "…you know."

God save him, he bloody well knew. His entire lower half ignited into an unquenchable raging fire, he knew so well. And lord knew what it did to his insides to have her eyes upon him—look at him with such unfettered desire. He'd been living like a monk for far too long not to be painfully aware his cods were about to burst with want for her. But doubt crept up his spine. Had she changed her mind since they'd been at the river? He unwound her hair. "Ye dunna want to—ah—with me?"

He'd intended to train his gaze all the way down her body, but he only got as far as her lips. Red, petal-soft lips, slightly parted just as they'd been earlier. He adored the femininity of them—bow shaped, begging to be kissed. Before a rational thought crossed his mind, William's hand slid behind her neck. Ever so slowly, he lowered his lips to hers. Eva's sweet, minty breath caressed him, sending a fireball of heat through his chest. When finally their mouths joined, his heart thundered as the floodgates of desire spread through his groin.

Holy Moses, the moist heat of her lips stripped away every ounce of resolve he had left. They were so damned soft—why had he waited? Why didn't he pull her into his arms at the river and take her? Och aye, by the way her tongue danced with his, the wee whimpers of her voice, she wanted him as much as he craved to have her in his arms.

William's blood thrummed faster. The woman's fervent response, her passionate wildness did unholy things to his cock. Lord, he wanted to be inside her—feel the warm wetness milk him—holy hell, he wanted her so badly, he mightn't be able to wait.

She moaned, her fingers sliding from his chest to his shoulder, showing him her mind hadn't changed in the slightest.

Thank God.

A fresh spike of heat hit William low in the gut. His body craved friction and he arched his hips toward her. When he finally pressed his cock against her, his entire body shuddered. How long had it been since he'd been this aroused?

Never.

Kissing him as if she'd been starved for days, Eva slipped her leg over his hip. She nestled her crux against his solid erection and rubbed. Holy hell it felt good—too good. All he could do was hold on and try not to come undone. God bless her, this woman proved to be a vixen in every way.

She sighed as their kiss eased. "I didn't think you wanted me."

"Ye're wrong there." He'd wanted her since he'd discovered she was a woman. How could he have ever thought her a lad? "I'd be a daft fool if I didna want ye, Eva."

Sitting up with sultry, half-cast eyes, her fingers fumbled to unbuckle his quilted doublet. William started to help, but she brushed his hands away. "I'll do it." God's teeth, even her voice seduced him.

His desire heightened with her every movement. When the last buckle released, she shoved the doublet from his shoulders. Tugging his shirt up from under his belt, William helped her pull it over his head. His chest heaved while she stared at him—lips parted—taking in quick stuttered breaths.

Her trembling fingers traced a line down the center of his chest. When she passed his navel, gooseflesh sprang across his skin. Willy's breath caught when she stopped at the belt holding up his chausses—Lord it was only an inch above the tip of his erection. He groaned and pinched his bum cheeks already feeling her hands upon him—Christ, not touching it nearly made him loose his seed.

She pulled the buckle.

In a moment of sanity, he placed his hand atop hers. "Now ye, lass."

She stopped, her green eyes turning dark as midnight. Rolling to her knees, she allowed him to tug her shift over her head. Bare to him, her breasts formed the most perfect feminine flesh he'd ever seen. Och aye, he'd ached to touch them at the river—had been able to think of nothing else since he'd seen her naked, those delectable rosebuds demanding he taste them. Unable to resist, he cupped them with his hands. God Almighty, her skin was softer than silk—softer than anything his rough fingers had ever caressed. He plied her flesh, aching to taste the tips that had teased him so unashamedly. Slowly he bent his head and captured heaven. Lord, he didn't think he could grow harder, but the tip of his manhood strained and pushed out the top of his braies.

Eva arched toward him with the moan of a hellcat. As if she could read his mind, she straddled his lap and let him explore her perfection. Her hips rocked against his aching member while he suckled her. God on the cross, it took an iron will to contain his raging desire.

Gradually, her fingers slipped down and released first the belt holding his chausses, bless her—she was not a vixen, but an angel. Then she loosed the rope holding his braies. Unrolling the linen, she exposed all of him. Heaven help him, her fingers touched him—tempting him beyond all imagination. She rose up on her knees and William glanced down.

She wore something pink—something like braies. He slid his fingers down and tugged them out from her body, revealing the perfectly shaped triangle of red curls. Licking his lips, he swallowed his urge to pull them down. "What is this?" The material snapped back in place.

"Panties."

"Pan—t—ies?" He said, emphasizing the T.

"Um hmm, I wear them for comfort. But right now I want you to tear them off me."

Oh Lord of lords, his ballocks squeezed with the stretching of his erection. How could she make him spill simply with words? All that separated them was the thin strip of cloth she called panties. William blinked. "I could get ye with child."

"No." She leaned forward, growling in his ear, rubbing up and down the length of him.

"Are ye barren?"

"No." She captured his mouth and kissed. "I have an IUD—a device that prevents pregnancy." Deepening her kiss, she swirled her hips faster as if she feared her words would give him pause.

But blessed be the saints, "no" was the only thing William needed to hear—at least for now. William tugged the thin strip of cloth. Eva lifted her hips and let him pull the panties free.

She wrapped her hands around him and kneaded, massaging her fingers like nothing he'd ever experienced. "God's bones." His voice quavered.

"I want you."

William couldn't talk. The seductress had spoken. He could think of nothing but his own deep-seated desire to claim her. Now. He grasped her shoulders to roll her onto her back, but Eva did something completely unexpected. Rising up, she slid over him—took him inside her right there straddling him.

Her molten, soft core milked him. William buried his face in her neck and moaned. She worked her hips up, down, side to side. Eva's every movement took him soaring to new heights of pleasure. Her breathing sped. Her arms clung tighter around his shoulders. With no choice but to let her dictate the pace, William gave himself over to her wiles.

Och aye, no ordinary woman could fill him with such mind-consuming desire.

A gasp caught in Eva's throat. She arched back, her breasts heaving. William could withstand no more. He clenched his teeth to keep from bellowing as together they rode the wave of passion.

Chapter Fifteen

Awaking in the dim light, Eva moved ever so slightly, spooning her body tightly into William's chest.

Did last night really happen?

Her skin sizzled where he pressed against her. Deep inside, her breasts swelled again, just as they had when he'd finally placed his hands on her. If only there could be a future for them. But she couldn't allow herself to think beyond the present.

She blinked and listened. *What time is it?*

Sleeping inside the cave, Eva had difficulty discerning the time. Since she'd hidden her phone with her satchel, her internal clock totally twisted around. Normally, she preferred to sleep late. She didn't know why she'd suddenly started waking early. Her candle had burned out, but a faint glow shone in through a crack in the fur curtain. The lack of voices beyond the shroud indicated that dawn hadn't yet arrived. William's inordinately warm body beside her was another clue. In the short time she'd known him, he'd been an early riser—and yet he slept.

Eva's cheeks grew hot as she rose up on her elbow and studied him. She didn't have to be a mind reader to know he hadn't accepted her story. Regardless, she'd stand by the truth from here on out. She mightn't be able to answer his every question, but she'd be honest about that, too.

Ever so peaceful rolling to his back, William's lips were closed, though they pursed slightly with every exhale. Eva loved his profile. With an angular forehead, his nose slightly bent at the bridge, forming a straight line all the way down to the tip. His nostrils flared as he inhaled. Like most of the statuary and paintings of men she'd seen in this century, he wore his red beard cropped close, not long and bushy like some. He kept it neatly groomed around his mouth, and his masculine lips pursed slightly—as if always waiting for her to kiss him.

In my dreams. This can only be a fleeting liaison.

Eva tried to picture what he'd look like shaved clean. That he had a strong chin beneath those wiry curls was certain and she imagined a dimpled cleft as well.

Mm. No thirteenth century man should be so sexy.

The plaid covered his lower extremities, but his chest remained bare. In slumber, his muscles still looked sculpted like a Greek statue. The curls on his chest, thickest in the middle, were also red. During their frenzied moment of passion the night before, that he'd been red *down there* hadn't gone unnoticed. Though the hair atop William's head was chestnut brown, she loved the fact the rest of him was a ginger just like her.

Did I honestly sleep with him?

From the tingling throughout her entire body, Eva didn't need to ask. It had been too long since she'd made love with a man. And the rugged Scotsman sleeping beside her could rock her world in ways she'd never dreamed.

She refused to allow her mind to make comparisons, however. Her heart welcomed this new experience as if starting life afresh. No one here knew her. She could be anyone she desired. She could lust after a seven hundred-year-old man if she chose—a least for a little while.

Compelled to make an entry in her journal, she continued to be religious about daily notes. Her leather-bound journal looked adequately dated. Eva opened it and recorded most of the previous day's events, omitting the details of her blossoming affair. That was private—something she'd never include in an article for any major magazine.

Sucking in a deep, hissing breath, William opened his eyes.

Eva set the pen and journal aside and slid down onto her elbow. "Good morning."

He swiped a hand over his face. "Good morrow," he said in an authoritative tone.

"Oops. I beg your pardon." She giggled. "Good morrow." She'd been trying to use more medieval words and phrases. Every time she ended up separated from William, she could be in danger if she spoke like a twenty-first century Scot. She swirled her fingers through the hair on his chest. "Did you sleep well?"

"Better than I have in a long time." He sat up and scrubbed his knuckles over his thick, shoulder-length hair. "I've a great deal to do this day."

Eva gestured toward her journal. "And I need to get serious about writing your story."

He knit his brows. "What in the blazes is that?"

She picked it up and turned to her most recent notes. "My *chronicler*—I use it to jot down notes." She reached for her pen and underlined the date. "See, I've just started today's entry."

Frowning, he snatched it from her fingers and thumbed through the pages. "This is not how we keep records." He held the book closer to his face. "How did ye make the ink so even? I see no light or dark, no splotches. Is this another example of your witchcraft?"

Eva's face grew hot. "For crying out loud, no."

He pointed to her notes. "I cannot read these scratchings."

She rolled her eyes. The man could be like Jekyll and Hyde. "I thought—"

"What? Because ye beguiled me last eve, I would turn a blind eye to your sorcery?"

Her blood pressure skyrocketed so high, Eva's ears thundered. Snatching the journal from his grasp, she glared at him. "I did no such thing, you heartless brute. You're the one who came in here after I'd gone to bed." She tossed the damned thing aside by her pen and grabbed her bra, clasping it and shoving her arms through.

"Ye harness your udders?" The man was insufferable.

"For your information, it's a bra—short for brassiere, something that wasn't invented until the twentieth century." Eva groaned with sarcasm and yanked her shift over her head. "But then you're so pigheaded, you wouldn't believe that, either."

William's lips pursed though he didn't say a word. He reached over, grabbed her pen, snapped it in two and threw the pieces against the wall. Then he opened a small wooden box and made an exaggerated gesture toward it. "If ye're planning to scribe anything whilst ye remain in my company, ye'll find vellum, ink and a quill right there. I meant it when I said I dunna want to see any of your newfangled bits of sorcery." He lowered his voice. "Even if they are not of the devil, every other soldier in my army will see your trinkets as an omen for evil." He snatched her wrist and squeezed. "Can ye not understand me, lass?"

Nodding, Eva yanked her arm away and rubbed her wrist. "I hid everything but my journal. I do not want to be responsible for jeopardizing your chances of success." Though she figured she would have been hurtled back to the twenty-first century by now if she had. *And*, he'd not said anything about sending her away—even talked about remaining for a bit. *Yippee*. She tried not to grin.

"'Tis good to hear." William pulled on his shirt. "Now tell me, how did ye ken Bishop Wishart would be with Lord Stewart, and that they'd offer their support?"

Eva's mind raced. What should she say? She'd vowed not to lie to him again. On the other hand, he didn't believe anything she uttered. If she told him she'd read countless articles and books about his life, he'd freak. Taking a deep breath, she met his soul-piercing gaze. "I know *some* things, major events, but not all." There. She'd told the truth without mentioning anything from the future.

"Now I think I can believe that." He grinned. Wow. He had the most captivating, broad grin with healthy white teeth. "Ye're a seer."

A cough caught in her throat as she threw up her palms. "What's the bloody difference?"

His grin twisted into a smirk. "Ye dunna ken?"

She snorted. "Not in this century."

"First of all, seers are valued by commoners as well as the gentry." He shook his finger, nearly hitting her nose. "But most importantly, they are good-hearted. They do not worship the devil or cast hateful spells."

Shifting her gaze to her shattered pen, she nodded. "Ah—if that's what you want to call it, I suppose *seer* would make more sense, especially since I cannot incant a spell to save my life."

"Why didna ye say so in the first place?"

Because I can see about as far as you can.

If William accepted her presence as a seer and wouldn't cast her out of the camp, she'd resolve to play along. "Honestly, the thought hadn't crossed my mind." Still, his assumption didn't sit well. Why couldn't he trust in the truth? That would make things so much easier.

With a sigh, she reached in his box, pulled out a sheet of vellum, and the quill. She removed the cork from the small bottle of ink and dipped it in. At least *seer* was a step toward gaining his acceptance. "My first entry today will include this conversation. I do not wish for either of us to forget it."

Using a script that she hoped would appear something like Auld Scots, she wrote: *William Wallace has decided I am a seer, though I am not convinced of it. However, we both agree I am not a witch.*

She read it to him, panning her finger under the words to help him follow her modern penmanship.

His eyes met hers and held her gaze, connecting lightning to earth. His drew in a sharp inhale—one that made hot blood thrum beneath her skin. For a brief moment, the passion from last night returned full force. But William cleared his throat. "Agreed."

"Let us make it official, then." Eva dribbled a bit of ink onto the parchment. "Affix your seal."

"In the ink, not wax?"

"Aye, it'll make a mark. But hurry before the ink dries."

***

Great sword in hand, William walked down the line of bedraggled men. A few showed up with swords, most rusty and looking like they hadn't seen a smithy's rasp in a score of years. "The first lesson is to care for your weapons." He held up his well-oiled sword. "Does anyone see a speck of rust?"

"Nay," all agreed.

"Too right. A man's sword should be his most prized possession." William swung a cross cut through a blade of grass. "Your sword and your dirk should be deadly sharp at all times. Any knife ye carry on your body has the potential to be used to kill an attacker." He stopped and scanned each face in the line of men. "Who here would prefer the best odds for survival to be in his favor?"

The men held forth with exuberant ayes.

"On the morrow, every one of ye will have a well sharpened and oiled blade, else I'll send ye back to your mas. And every day henceforth ye'll allow nary a speck of rust to soil your weapons." William pointed at a soldier. "Agreed?"

"Aye, m'lord."

William stepped past the man, then batted the fool's chin with a flick of his elbow. "I am no man's lord. I am a murdered crofter's son—studied for the priesthood, and drawn into this war upon the invasion of our land and wrongful imprisonment of King John."

"Here, here!" the men bellowed, some pumping their swords in the air.

"In battle, your blades and your wits are the only things that will save your lives. Your sword and your pike will become an extension of your arm. Your feet will dance and your legs will be as solid as oaks. This day I will teach ye the foundation of a fighting man. Before any solider can wield a sword, he must first make his body strong." He glared at the staring faces. "Cast aside your weapons."

A bull of a man stepped forward, rusty blade held in challenge. "I can fight with the best of them." He flexed an arm. "I dunna need a lesson in gaining strength."

"Nay?" Wallace faced the braggart and beckoned him. "Ye're bigger than most, I'll give ye that, but still a good two hands shorter than me."

The man shrugged. "But I've a greater girth."

"Aye?" William assessed the man's form. "Mayhap around the middle."

"Ye're a smug bastard. I'd like to see ye prove ye're as good as they say."

God knew William needed every able-bodied soul he could recruit—even a vainglorious codfish such as this measle. "Verra well. Come, let's give it a go." He crouched, readying himself for attack.

Bellowing, the man raised his weapon above his head and barreled in with a downward hack. Exerting little effort, William lifted his great sword and deflected the blow. With a grunt, he used the man's momentum, slid aside, and continued to circle his hands downward in concert with the man's blade. Then snapping up his arms, the beef-witted goat flipped head first and landed on his back.

His eyes stunned, the puffed-shirt clutched at his chest, gasping for air.

William faced the men, their mouths agape. "Let this be a lesson to ye all. Put it in your heads this verra day—there is always someone who can best ye. The only way to overpower a man with more size or skill is to outlast and outmaneuver him." He slapped his hand to his chest. "That kind of doggedness takes stamina—air in your lungs and quickness of feet."

The man on the ground sat up, his head dropped between his knees with a fit of coughing.

William offered his hand. "What are ye called, soldier?"

"Graham of Peebles."

"Well then, Mr. Graham, I suggest ye step back into line and pay heed to the lesson."

William started at the beginning, just as he and Blair had been trained by Brother MacRae, the old Templar monk in Dundee. The timeworn knight had driven William hard and now Wallace knew why. He'd been born to be a leader in a rebellion against a tyrant. He would drive these men harder and longer than he himself had been driven in Dundee and nary a soul would have cause to complain because William would work alongside them every step of the way.

Making a competition of it, he showed them how to build strength by tossing the caber—a very long tree trunk as heavy as a man. He made them stand in a crouch, holding enormous boulders until their thighs could take no more. He ran them, forcing the men to leap over logs and dance between the trees as if each protruding branch were an attacking English spearman.

William stopped only once to take a swig of water. Over the top of his cup, he watched Eva carry a sloshing bucket toward the cave with both hands. She glanced at him and smiled with a subtle nod. His heart leapt. Och aye, that wee gesture could give him enough verve to last the entire day. Bless it, she made him want to beat his chest and bellow—and right out in the open she could beguile him so subtly, none were the wiser.

Indeed, few women would ken to mind their own affairs when the men were hard at work, and William appreciated her taking the initiative to help Brother Bartholomew. Perhaps he had chosen right to allow her to stay—for the now.

He chuckled and took another drink. If Eva had been a man, he would have made her a lieutenant. They needed someone who could organize the men and take charge, but aside from her gender, Wallace had seen her blanch at the sight of a blade more than once. She'd even told him of her nightmares. No, the woman was best kept beside the cooking fires or in the cave with her quill. Besides, now he'd realized she was no witch, but had the gift of sight, William kent she'd be of use. And thanks to Robbie Boyd, the men had already accepted her.

But why had he? She still posed a quandary—so many secrets—so many unanswered questions. Did it matter? Mayhap not when they were alone.

The lass disappeared into the cave. Aye, he liked having her near—not that he'd boast about that actuality to anyone.

Chapter Sixteen

William had been back from Renfrew for a couple of weeks when Eva hastened back to the clearing with a camphor-smelling clump of yellow tansy in her hand. It had been drizzling all day, but now the sun had moved to the western horizon, the clouds parted to reveal a violet sky.

Across the clearing, William caught her eye.

The men had stopped sparring for the day, and he stood frozen, as if seeing her for the first time.

Pushing an errant lock of hair under her veil, she glanced sideways. No one else mulling about seemed to notice William's intently focused attention. She gave him a questioning look—it was unusual for him to pay her much attention away from the alcove. Usually he was deep in conversation with his inner circle or training the new recruits. Only behind the deerskin shroud of the alcove did she command his full attention, and in their quiet space very little was said, yet very much was expressed.

In the fortnight since the first time they'd made love, she'd grown to prefer things being passionate but not too open, especially given *her* past and *his* future.

Striding directly toward her, William's intense expression didn't change. He clasped his fingers around her wrist. "Come."

Eva held up the tansy. "Brother Bartholomew wanted this to keep the mosquitoes out of the cave."

His dark stare slipped from her eyes to her breasts. William snatched the bouquet from her grasp and dropped it near a tree. "Ye can take the flowers to him later."

The rumble of his deep growl made shooting heat sear between Eva's legs—so intense her reaction, her knees nearly gave out—right there in the clearing with others about. How this man could make her melt with a stare and a few gruff words, she'd never understand. Wallace embodied raw male—passionate, intense and powerful.

Eva had never been one to fall for the alpha type. But, Lord, this attraction defied all sensibility.

He moved his hand and laced his fingers through hers. Long, powerful fingers roughened by hours and hours of training pulled Eva down the path to the river, not forcibly, but with conviction, demanding she follow.

She hastened her step to keep pace with him. "Is everything all right?"

"Aye."

Not much for words tonight, I see. "Where are we going?"

He glanced back with that same dark glint in his eye. "Where I can gaze on your bonny face without a mob of rebels surrounding us."

Her heart fluttered. "But it's nearly dark."

"Not to worry. We'll be there afore the light's gone."

He pulled her a distance down the shore and together they climbed a craggy outcropping. At the top, the ground was flat, covered by a cushion of moss. Above, more green moss draped from the canopy of trees with sunlight streaming through and flickering as if the fairies had prepared a haven solely for them.

He stopped and smoothed his hands over her shoulders. "Here."

She gazed up at his handsome face. Intent, starved, determined—with a look he could express so much. The hardened warrior she saw during daylight hours stared at her like a wolf, but not as he regarded his opponents. He looked at her with penetrating intensity, his mouth slightly parted, his chest rising and falling with every breath.

Barely able to breathe, Eva's tongue slipped across her lips.

He moved a bit closer. "Every time ye walk past, I want ye. Your scent sends my insides into a maelstrom of need."

She closed her eyes and drew out the moment, wishing he'd say that again. Oh, how delectable to listen to a medieval Scotsman declare his desire. A wry grin turned up the corners of her mouth, and she circled her finger around the center of his chest—ah yes, he'd taken off his hauberk and arming doublet. Only a thin slip of linen lay between her fingers and his muscular flesh—did he have any idea what his exquisitely toned body did to a woman?

Eva's tongue slipped to the corner of her mouth as she untiled the bow and loosened his shirt laces. William's breathing grew more labored.

With a throaty chuckle, she lifted the hem of his shirt, but William finished the motion, whipping it over his head and casting it aside. His bold fervor heightened the stirring in Eva's panties. "You notice me when you're working with the men?" Her fingers trembled as she traced the defined muscles rippling over his abdomen, her need moving from simmering to a rolling boil.

He yanked her into his arms with unmitigated strength—forceful, but not quite savage. She liked it—a hint of danger with a surge of passion. "I ken when ye are within a mile, lass."

Rocking her hips forward, his erection drove into her mons. With a soft moan, she swirled against him, desperate for more intimacy.

Powerless to resist his advances, Eva's knees buckled as he crushed his mouth over hers. This wasn't a deep, exploring, sultry kiss like the many they'd shared in the cave.

This was a claiming, fervent expression of passion that demanded a response in kind. All she could do was hold on and mirror every swirl of his tongue, every little suck, every deep, guttural moan.

Ignited by the bone-melting fire that spread between her hips and up through the tips of her breasts, she cupped his face with her hands while he eased her down to the bed of moss.

Kneeling, her fingers fumbled with his chausses while he untied the front of her kirtle and shift. Slipping his hand inside, he pushed beneath her bra and cupped her breast, teasing his finger over her sensitive, hard nipple. Heaven help her, how on earth could this man be so virile?

With one last tug, she released the ties, shoved down his woolen chausses and his braies with them. Beautiful, long and hard as an oak branch, William growled and covered her mouth with another mind-claiming kiss. Every sinew in her body shuddered as he ground his exposed flesh against her.

Eva's thighs trembled with need as she arched her hips against him. "I want you."

"I need ye as much as I need the air I breathe," he growled with a breathless burr.

William tugged up her skirts and he tore down her panties. In a fluid motion he lifted her with one arm and laid her on the exquisitely soft bed of nature. Naked, potent, he held himself above her.

Their gazes locked.

She could take no more.

Reaching down, Eva smoothed her fingers along his shaft and guided him into her. His breath trembled as he slowed the pace, allowing her time to adjust to his size. Needing him deeper, she sank her fingers into his solid buttocks and demanded he speed his thrusts as if their very lives depended on their joining.

The desire in his eyes connected them as if their very souls passed through their bodies. Wetting his lips he devoured her mouth as he made love to her with languid strokes—controlling the pace—controlling her.

Mind-consuming passion flowed through Eva's every nerve ending. Fierce and hot, William could make her soar to the stars and hover there until sweet release finally allowed her to drift to a place of blissful inner peace.

***

As the weeks passed, Eva continued to settle into a routine. With so many mouths to feed, and more arriving by the day, there was never a lack of something to do. She journaled in the mornings, then spent the majority of her days helping Brother Bartholomew with what she called administrative tasks. He wasn't only the cook. No taller than five-foot-two, the little monk played the role of chief healer as well. Though she'd never done anything aside from applying antibiotic ointment and a Band-Aid, by necessity she applied herself to learning medieval healing arts—some of which were surprisingly effective—and others—well, Eva figured there was always the power of the placebo effect.

Stealing a moment's rest, she climbed the hill overlooking the clearing. A few days ago, she'd done the same while the men still practiced. At that time, she'd made the decision to do a little training herself. One thing she knew for certain—their time in Leglen Wood was nearing an end. She posed as Wallace's woman there, but outside their small community, who knew what dangers she'd face? And truth be told, Eva preferred being outside the dank cave whenever possible.

William's routine had become predictable as well. Daily he trained with the men until the sun set. He took the evening meal with his inner circle—the men who always stood beside him, rode with him—the most trusted and most talented warriors. Though his gaze would meet hers across the fire and linger, Wallace still rarely ever spoke to Eva unless behind the furs in the alcove.

She chuckled. The great legend changed from hardened warrior to ravenous lover behind the privacy shrouds. Eva almost liked it that way. She couldn't fall in love with him—lust, yes. But the everlasting-get-married-have-your-babies kind of love? She couldn't begin to allow herself to consider it.

Never.

Even though she was living and breathing in thirteenth century Scotland, one day she must return home. She might stay a year and that would be it. The end. The grand sayonara and, *poof*, she'd be gone.

Heated stares across the campfire Eva could handle.

Unbridled passion with an incredibly hot seven hundred-year-old Highlander in the middle of the night? *Mm Yeah. Bring it on.*

Mad declarations of love from a Don Juan? *No. Possible. Way.*

With William, she could remain anonymous, her past life hidden beneath the rock in the alcove alongside her satchel.

Eva reached the hill's summit and gazed over the throng of activity. William and the swordsmen sparred with their deadly sharp weapons flashing in the sunlight. John Blair's group was busy fashioning longer pikes. Eva shuddered. She didn't want to guess at what they'd be used for. Edward Little and the archers had quite a setup of targets—some of the men who were wealthy enough to own a horse practiced firing from horseback. Then there were the workers who hunted, set snares, chopped wood and fetched water among other chores.

William blew his ram's horn four times per day. With each sounding, the groups would change—that way no one ended up saddled with the same tasks day-in and day-out. A certain harmony beat like a heart among the men. If only they could remain like this and let the War of Independence pass them by.

With a sigh, Eva stepped away from the summit and picked up a good sized boulder. Holding it in front of her chest, she performed leg crunches, just like William did with the men. She also added some additional exercises to her routine, similar to those she'd learned in the weight room when training with the team at NYU.

Funny. People in her time went to gyms to stay in shape—at least city folk did. They never had to worry about waking up to the enemy pillaging their homes and attacking their families. New Yorkers and Edinburghers alike didn't till fields with hand tools, or hunt for their evening meal—butcher their own meat—brew their own ale.

Eva picked up a stick and lunged, thrusting it forward. Last time up on the hill she'd practiced with an imaginary sword, but now wanted something sturdy to hold in her hand. Sharp weapons still gave her the willies, even though she'd been surrounded by them for weeks. Though she hadn't yet convinced herself to carry a knife, she might need to defend herself here in medieval Scotland more than anyplace she'd ever been.

Having watched enough of William's lessons, Eva worked through the exercises, imagining a sparring partner opposite.

"Thinking to ask Willy to let ye join the resistance?"

Eva nearly jumped out of her skin at the sound of the rumbling voice behind her. She whirled around. "Father Blair? You startled me."

He drew his palms together and tapped his fingers to his lips, his grey eyes calculating. "I saw ye venture up this way. Thought mayhap it would be an opportunity to talk."

"Oh?" She'd been bothered by his cautious stares and on numerous occasions. It didn't take a nickname of seer to know he didn't trust her—even if he did enjoy her singing.

Squeezing her stick at her side, she returned his pointed stare. "Is something weighing on your mind?"

"Aye, there is." He wasn't an attractive man. Aside from shaving the top of his head like a monk, he had a narrow face and a long angular nose to match.

She looked at him expectantly. The priest certainly didn't remind her of any holy man she'd ever met. But then monks in the Middle Ages weren't only clerics. Some were warriors—like the Hospitallers and the Templars. She stepped toward him. "You and William studied together, correct?"

"Aye."

"But he did not take his vows and you did. Why is that?"

"I didna come up here to give ye a lesson on Willy's past."

His gruff response brought no surprise. After waiting a few uncomfortable seconds, Eva turned and continued with her exercises. Lunging, she jabbed the stick forward.

Blair snatched her wrist and the stick dropped to the ground. "I want to ken why ye are here."

Eva tried to wrench away, but he held fast. "You're hurting me," she hissed.

"Ye havena answered."

If she told Blair she was from the future, he'd have her tied to the stake and burned before sunset. And if William didn't buy her story, this guy had no chance. She stopped struggling. "Aside from having no other place to go, I've remained to help the patriots in any way I can. I wish no harm upon William or anyone else." She glared at the fingers wrapped around her wrist. "You, however, I'm not entirely certain about."

"Me?" He released his grip.

She rubbed her arm, a purple bruise spreading across her skin. "You are a man of the cloth, yet you did not approach me kindly first. You glare at me during the evening meals. What am I to think of you? Are you planning to betray

William's confidence?" There. Possibly using a touch of reverse psychology might encourage him to back off.

He snapped a hand to his chest. "How dare ye doubt my fealty? William Wallace and I have been friends since we were lads. We are of one mind in this rebellion—but *ye*. Ye came from nowhere. Ye have no kin. Ye speak like a heathen sent from the depths of hell."

Gaining her confidence she stepped closer. "You've met such a heathen?"

"I ken loose women such as ye." He shifted backward. "They all have one thing on their minds and 'tis not the goodwill of their lovers."

Cheeks burning, Eva's mouth dropped open. Her? Loose? "You, sir, do *not* understand anything."

He held up a finger and shook it. "I ken what I see, lassie."

Eva flinched. "You are wrong. I have done nothing to incite your ire." Even if she had been a tad improper with William, the passion they shared behind the shrouds was no one else's business.

He splayed his fingers and dropped his hand. "See to it things remain that way, else I'll be the first to run a blade across that bonny neck of yours." He started off.

"Wait." Though she could have picked up her stick and clobbered him over the head, she didn't want this disagreement to end badly. Things were uncomfortable enough.

"Aye?" he asked without turning

"How can I earn your trust?"

Blair regarded her over his shoulder. "Ye'll ken if it ever happens. Until then, ye'd best watch your back."

Eva watched him walk away, then kicked the damned stick. Thank God they would be leaving soon. She wouldn't consider giving up her time with William Wallace for anything or anyone—especially an uptight warrior priest. Aside from the story of a lifetime, she'd found exactly what she needed—an intelligent and desirable man with no strings—a man she could place on a pedestal yet continue to keep her heart locked away, not to be twisted and torn apart by medieval brutality.

***

Eva collected the strips of cloth she'd washed from the drying line. Brother Bartholomew watched her, gripping his hands on his hips. "With so much to do, ye waste your time washing thcsc linens."

Inside she cringed. "Cleanliness is next to godliness."

He harrumphed. "Where on earth did ye hear that drivel?"

"I thought everyone said it."

"Aye, in what country? Egypt? The Bible tells of the Great River Nile, do people there bathe as much as ye?"

"Yes. Bathing is of great importance to a person's wellbeing." She rolled a bandage. "And using clean bandages will help the men's wounds heal faster."

The monk snorted. "And so ye're thinking ye're a physician now?"

"Not at all. I just know a thing or two about personal hygiene." Something medieval physicians knew nothing about. But jeez, the first time she'd seen the monk wrap a dirty cloth around a bloody cut, she'd gathered up all the rags she could find and washed them in boiled water. Eva shook her finger. "Please, if you pay heed to nothing else I say, do not apply a dirty bandage to any wound, especially one that has already been used. Someone could die…" She stopped before saying "from blood poisoning."

"I think ye're being overly cautious."

She placed her roll in the medicine basket and pulled the next bandage off the line. "Just humor me on this one thing. Please?"

"Verra well." The little monk held up his palms and shrugged. "If ye are willing to wash the bandages, I shall use those first."

"Thank you."

"Miss Eva." Robbie approached, leading a scrawny, dirty-faced lad by the elbow. "Lachlan got sideswiped with a lance."

Eva shot a pointed look at Bartholomew. "We're running low on avens water, too."

"Because ye use it on every wee cut. 'Tis a wonder they're all coming to ye now for their healing. Ye spoil the lot of them." He turned on his heel and headed into the cave.

"We'll need to gather more avens root on the morrow," she called after him. Fortunately, the medicine basket sat beside her and Eva could tend the lad right there. "Come, sit on this rock."

Lachlan did as asked and held out his arm. "'Tis not bad. It'll come good in a day or so."

Eva crossed her arms. "And how am I supposed to examine the cut through your sleeve?"

Just like most everyone else, the lad's shirt was dingy with eons of ground-in dirt. Soaked with blood, the sleeve had a gaping hole that would need repair too.

"Do you have a needle and thread?" she asked.

The boy clamped his lips taut and shook his head of brown hair.

"He's an orphan," Robbie said with a matter-of-fact shrug. "Just like me."

"I see." Most of the lads Robbie's age who'd made their way to William's camp were orphans. No twelve-year-old's mother would allow her son to join a rebellion. Not even in medieval Scotland. *Would she?* "Well then, take off your shirt and give it to me. I'll see it's returned to you by the evening meal."

"Thank ye, Miss Eva. 'Tis the only shirt I own." He pulled the filthy garment over his head.

"You and everyone else, it seems." She grasped it between her pincer fingers and dropped it far away from her clean bandages. "Now let's have a look at that cut."

Lachlan held out his arm and grimaced.

Eva did too. Then she hissed. "It appears the lance clipped you pretty good."

"Aye."

"What on earth is Father Blair thinking allowing you lads to play with spears and poleaxes?"

Robbie tapped a stone with the toe of his boot. "We're not playing. We're training."

"Well, lads your age should be playing."

Both boys glowered.

"I thought wooden sparring weapons were available to prevent the *men* from being hurt." She added emphasis to men to bolster the boy's esteem.

"Och." Robbie crossed his arms. "Willy says sparring with toys makes a man soft. In the heat of a battle, he needs to ken what 'tis like to swing blade hewn of iron. Says we need to be ten times fitter than our opponents—'tis the only way we'll win."

She had to agree with them there. This bedraggled lot needed stamina to stand up to English soldiers and this wasn't the first time she'd heard it said. "In that case, I suggest you swing your lances at something inanimate, like a tree."

Lachlan gave her a quizzical stare. "Ye sure do talk peculiar."

Eva doused a clean bandage with avens water. "'Tis so I can entertain the likes of you." She held it near his arm. "Now this might sting a bit."

The lad proved to be a tough little bugger, and when Eva had the congealed blood cleared away, she peered closer at the wound. "Looks like this needs to be stitched as well." Her stomach squelched—she hadn't needed to sew up a wound yet. Two days ago, she'd assisted while Brother Bartholomew stitched a cut to a man's flank. The well-meaning monk jabbed the bone needle through the skin like he was picking nutmeat from a walnut as blood streamed all over his fingers.

Panic filled the boy's eyes. "Can ye not tie a bandage around my arm and call it good?"

She pulled a needle and thread from the basket. "I'm afraid not this time. Would you prefer I ask Brother Bartholomew to do it?" She grimaced.

Lachlan snatched his scrawny arm into his chest. "Nay. He'll skewer me for certain."

"All right then. I'll be as gentle as I can." After threading the needle, she pinched the flesh together, willing her stomach to stop its queasiness.

Robbie leaned in and peered a bit too close. "Are ye not going to give him a tot of whisky first?"

To a twelve-year-old? Eva looked at the wound—it needed the whisky more than Lachlan, though avens could be used as a mild antiseptic, which is why she'd used it so profusely. She regarded the cut—the stitches were going to hurt. How much damage would a wee swig do? She waved her hand. "Quickly—run in and ask Brother Bartholomew for a flask."

After Robbie dashed away, Eva sat on the big rock beside Lachlan. "Where do you come from?"

"Berwick."

A lump formed in her throat. She didn't need to ask what had become of his parents. Grasping the hand of his uninjured arm, she held it between her palms. "If you should ever need to talk to a grown up, I hope you'll feel comfortable coming to me."

"Why would I want to talk to ye?" Lachlan's mouth twisted with his quizzical look. "Ye're a lass."

She grinned. "Perhaps one day something will come up. Who knows?"

Robbie raced back with a flagon and pulled the cork. "Drink this down."

"Just a sip," Eva cautioned.

But Lachlan gulped the spirit as if he were drinking a cordial. Belching, he wiped his mouth and handed the flagon to his friend.

"Give me that." Eva reached out, just missing.

Robbie took a swig before handing it to her. "Ye mean ye drink whisky? But ye're a woman."

She poured a bit over the needle. "I can drink it if I want to."

"But now ye're just wasting it." Robbie snatched the flagon and clutched it against his chest.

"Wheesht." Eva held up the needle with a steady hand and regarded Lachlan. "Are you ready?"

"Aye."

"I'll be careful." *After all, I've sewn seat cushions in Girl Scouts.* Every muscle in the boy's body tensed as she pushed in the bone needle for the first stitch. Perhaps she should have gone into nursing rather than journalism. *If only I'd known I'd be spending time in the thirteenth century.* Eva chuckled under her breath as she pulled it through.

Lachlan blanched.

"That wasn't so bad," Eva squeaked. "Are you ready for another?"

"More whisky," he croaked.

She nodded to Robbie. Given the choice between causing pain and an inebriated minor—she'd choose the later.

When Eva tied off the last suture, a horse and rider trotted into the clearing. He spun his mount in a circle before he stopped and pulled a folded piece of vellum from beneath his surcoat. "I've a missive for William Wallace."

Chapter Seventeen

William ran his finger under the red wax seal of James, the High Steward, and unfolded the missive. Written in Latin, he read the scrolling penmanship.

"Who is it from?" Blair asked while the men crowded around them.

Wallace handed the missive to the priest. "Lord Stewart." William looked to Eddy Little and Malcolm, who'd arrived from Ayr earlier that day. "Come, we need to talk."

"What does it say?" someone hollered from the crowd.

William regarded the expectant faces. "All of ye, prepare to march at dawn."

"To face the English?" another asked.

"Aye." William nodded. "I would have preferred to train ye a bit longer, but there's a garrison moving northward carrying out 'peacekeeping' demonstrations. I'm sure ye all ken what that means."

Robbie pushed his way in front of Wallace. "Why do we not set out straight away?"

He mussed the lad's hair. "Because we must follow the plan."

"But I want to skewer the bastards who killed my da."

"Ye'll get your chance, lad." He raised his voice so all could hear. "Pay heed to my words. If we stand unified, we'll not be beaten. But every one of ye must follow me. If anyone has a mind to haul off and become a hero, ye have leave to do so…but ye'll be going it alone."

Then William turned and led his band of lieutenants up the hill—the only place they'd be away from prying ears. Eva stepped aside and allowed him to pass, their gazes connecting for a moment. Must her green eyes be so intense—so inquisitive? Why did a wicked storm brew in his loins every time he met the lass's stare? Grinding his teeth, he walked past her. She kent this day would come, damn it all.

Once they reached the summit, William gathered his men in a circle.

Malcolm spread his palms. "What's afoot?"

"Lord Stewart is sending fifty horse and two hundred foot from Renfrew—and Sir Douglas is marching a hundred more cavalry from Galloway."

"Douglas?" Malcolm asked, a hint of distrust inflected in his tone.

"He's bringing a hundred men." William sliced his hand through the air. "We need his numbers. Besides, if anyone has a bone to pick, it is he. The knight lost near everything when Edward sacked Berwick."

Eddy elbowed his way further into the circle. "Did that missive mention anything about a plan?"

"We're to rendezvous at Fail Monastery on the morrow. But tell no one. Even if we havena spy in our ranks, ye never ken when someone will turn tail and join our enemies."

"Aye," Blair said. "And I still dunna trust that lassie ye brought into our camp."

Wallace stepped up to Blair so their faces were but a hand's breadth apart. "That's right. Ye havena had a good word to say about Eva since she arrived."

Blair squinted. "She's a harlot."

Clenching his fists, William leaned even closer. "Ye took an oath of celibacy and now your cods are aching. Is that it?"

Blair took the first swing—a fisted jab, aimed at the temple.

William blocked and thrust an undercut into John's gut. Best friend or nay, Wallace wouldn't stand for Blair or anyone spewing foul words against Eva. Locking arms, they wrestled to the ground.

William shoved the heel of his hand in the priest's face. Straining through his teeth, he growled, "She's done nothing but work her fingers to the bone since she's been here."

Blair's palm squished Willy's nose to the side. "And keep your miserable bed warm at night ye swiving bastard!"

William swung back with his fist.

"God's teeth, Willy." Malcolm grabbed William's right elbow from behind with John latching on to his left. "What the bloody hell have ye been doing whilst I've been away?"

Arching his back, Wallace struggled to break free. "I've been training an army to fight the rebellion, ye beef-witted swine."

From his back, Blair grunted and took a dirty swing, connecting with William's jaw. "Aye, but 'tis time to leave the wench be and let her find another bed that's not so important to our cause. God bless it, William. Ye fight with the power of six mace bearers. We canna afford to have your mind anywhere but on your duty to Scotland."

The blow could have been harder, but regardless, William didn't care to be hogtied by his brothers while his best friend tried to knock some sense into him. "Eva is no one's business but my own." It was one thing for *him* to question her presence, but that's as far as it went. She'd earned her keep as far as William was concerned.

Blair squirmed out from under Wallace and stood. "She doesna belong here."

William wrenched his arms away and glanced at Eddy. "Ye're being quiet all the sudden. What say ye, Little?"

He shrugged. "Not certain. She's been a help, but if ye canna fight because of the likes of her, I'd sooner run the lassie through."

Blair clasped his hands together like as if he were ready to say a few prayers now he'd had the last swing. "We're going to Fail—'tis where ye found her, no?"

William rubbed his aching jaw. "Aye."

"Well then, why not leave her there?" Eddy reasoned. "One of the Trinitarians ought to recognize her, otherwise how else would she have ended up inside when ye found her?"

Malcolm tapped a finger to his lips. "Unless the marauding English brought her in."

"Nay." Rubbing his jaw, William opened and closed his mouth to ensure it hadn't been knocked out of place. "One of the bastards was trying to kill her when we arrived."

Blair chuckled. "Now that's a quandary. I pegged her as a spy and the English want to kill her?"

William blinked then looked each man square in the eye.

Eva's prediction about his meeting with Lord James Stewart weighed on his mind. He hadn't told anyone—more for her protection than anything. But it was time these men knew. "Ye breathe a word of this outside this circle and I'll slit your throat myself. Eva's a seer. She kens things—says she sought me out."

Eddy shook his head and pinched the bridge of his nose. "So then what was she doing at the monastery?"

"Trying not to get herself killed." William slapped him on the back. "Never mind that. I'll be the one to decide what is to be done with her."

Everyone seemed satisfied with William's answer except Blair. "Ye ken she's been up here swinging a stick around as if she thinks she's going to march into battle with us?"

"Aye?" William puzzled. "That makes no sense. She's afraid of sharp weapons."

"Another good reason to leave her in the hands of the monks at Fail," Malcolm said.

"Enough about the woman." William sliced his hand through the air. "I said I'd determine what to do with her. And in the meantime, I'll appreciate it if ye leave her be. Now, we've a battle to plan."

He pointed to his brother. "Malcolm, I want ye to steer our uncle clear of the English garrison."

"Consider it done."

Wallace crouched down and drew a map in the dirt. "Stewart's missive said the English are hunting for the giant who killed Heselrig. I reckon we should make sure they meet their end with no doubt of exactly who I am."

***

After a downpour started, too many smelly bodies crammed into the cave. Eva sat in her usual place beside Robbie and now Lachlan. The lad hadn't left her side since she'd stitched his arm.

Robbie reclined on his fur, holding a tankard of freshly brewed ale, his eyelids drooping. "I hope the rain stops afore the morrow."

Now that he'd swilled the flagon of whisky and joined with his partner in crime, Lachlan grinned with a glassy look to his eyes. "It has to. I'm ready to face the English."

"I'm afraid you're on injured reserve." Eva would do anything to keep the lads from picking up weapons and facing grown men—trained soldiers, no less.

"Wha-d-ye mean?" Lachlan flexed a scrawny arm. "I'm ready."

Eva gave him a mothering stare. "Aw, come on lad, even a grown man knows it is madness to run into battle with a wound as grave as yours."

"But I feel fine."

She pointed at the flagon. "Aye—because you've had a wee bit too much to drink, I'll say."

Lachlan hiccupped. "I'm fair to middling."

Robbie sat up and thumped his chest. "Too right, we've both been practicing for days. We're ready. Lachlan isna about to let a wee scratch keep him from skewering the English."

Eva clamped her lips together and glanced at William, holding court across the fire. The man hadn't so much as glanced her way after he'd come down from his secret meeting up on the hill. Nor had any of them said where they'd be off to come dawn. She rifled through her memory, but couldn't tie anything to June, 1297. If she knew where they were headed, she might be able to figure out what they'd be facing.

Eva pinched the bridge of her nose. *After Lanark, William's next battle of record is in Scone—and I figure that should occur within the next three to six weeks. What happens leading up to that is a quandary—unless it was detailed in the cryptic writings of Blind Harry.*

She forced her mind to clear, but nothing came.

"Ye look like ye're in pain, Miss Eva," Lachlan said.

"What?" She regarded the boy and ran her hand over his tangled hair. "You should try to get some sleep. Doubtless, with all the marching, tomorrow will be a tiring day."

"Aw, I can go for days without sleep."

"Really?" Eva didn't believe it for a second. The boy looked like he wouldn't last another hour. "Let us hope you're not sore in the head as well as your wing on the morrow."

"Ye worry more than my nursemaid used to," Robbie said.

"Well, someone should be worried about you lads. You're not really old enough to be out on your own."

"Says who?" Lachlan asked.

"Me." Eva stood. "The pair of you might be ready to swill ale all night, but I'm heading to my pallet."

Once sitting cross-legged in the alcove, Eva struck a flint to light the tallow candle, pleased with herself for the progress she'd made surviving in the wood with all the mosquitoes and midges and men wilder than Alaskan lumberjacks.

She reached for a piece of vellum and recorded the day's events, including her trouble recalling what was on the horizon in the next few days:

…News of Wallace's actions in Lanark has most certainly spread like wildfire, evidenced by the new troops arriving at the campsite every day, and by the growing interest from the nobility. Things will become unsettled and tumultuous in the coming weeks and months. I wouldn't miss it for the world.

She blew on the ink as she read, then rolled it with her other pages and secured them in place with a leather thong.

The furs parted. William stooped and crawled up beside her. "Do ye ken what will happen on the morrow?"

"This isn't one of your bigger battles. Where are we heading?"

His eyes shifted sideways, then he picked at the fur beneath. "We'll be meeting up with more men at Fail Monastery."

A shiver tickled up her spine. *Four thousand strong that night did lodge in Ayr, and in the bloody barns without the town*[1]. The verse from Blind Harry's poem came to mind with the force of a lightning flash. She blinked in succession. "Are the English taking their 'peacekeeping' demonstration to Ayr?"

When he looked up with that acute intensity reflected in his eyes, Eva knew he'd never be able to lie to her. "Aye."

"You'll come upon them after dark—holed up in the barns on the outskirts of town." The medallion against her chest burned, but Eva wasn't ready to hold her tongue. Not yet. "Who are you meeting at Fail?"

"Lord Stewart is sending an army." Those eyes shifted again.

"Who else?" she pushed.

---

[1] William Hamilton of Gilbertfield translation version, *Blind Harry's Wallace*, The Luath Press, 2003 Edition, p. 86

"Douglas—Le Hardi."

"And so it begins." Eva smoothed her fingers along William's forearm. "Watch out for that man. He's as vain and barbarous as they come."

"That I ken. His reputation was bad afore he lost Berwick. What more can ye tell me?"

She shifted the medallion to the side, but it burned like a branding iron against her skin. "All I can say is there will be fire and death."

I hope it is the English who will bc dying and not my men.

Eva couldn't look him in the eye. "Oh, yes." If Blind Harry's account was accurate.

William adjusted his seat and then did it again. "I want ye to remain at the monastery."

A gasp caught in the back of her throat. "Will you return for me?"

"I plan to." This time *he* didn't meet *her* gaze.

She leaned toward him. "Where will Brother Bartholomew and the lads be?"

"They'll come along to tend the injured—but I'll ensure they remain at a safe distance."

A fire ignited beneath Eva's skin—this was so unfair. "So it is all right for clerics and children to follow you into battle, but not me?"

William inclined his head against the wall and looked at the low ceiling as he let out a deep sigh. "I canna in good conscious allow ye to stay with us. I've thought about our arrangement and it is selfish of me to keep ye as my *leman* even if ye are a seer. The monks at Fail will help ye find a husband."

Eva groaned loudly. Wallace didn't understand anything about her. "How many times do I have to tell you that I'm here only because of you?" She scooted away from him. "I refuse stay behind at the monastery—and there is no way you will be able to force me."

"Aye? I could hogtie ye and tell the monks not to release ye for a sennight."

"Oh, right." She crossed her arms. "That would be a humane thing to do."

"Humane?"

"Nice, thoughtful, genuine, caring." She took a deep breath. "Chivalrous."

"Ye will never cease to befuddle my mind." He stretched out his long arm and stroked her shoulder. "By leaving ye at the monastery, I am being all those things, especially chivalrous."

She swatted his hand away. "No. You are being callous and demeaning and…and thoughtless."

"But ye'll be safer there."

"Oh? Was I safe when you found me?"

He swiped his hand through the air. "That was different."

She rolled her eyes in disgust. "Men are all the same no matter the century. They argue points only to the extent that they benefit their case—all other sides are superfluous even if they are relevant to an informed decision."

"Och, your babble is making my head swim." His eyebrows slanted over his angry glare. "I've a great deal on my mind and I dunna need a harpy addling my thoughts."

"Is that so?" Eva pointed to the fur curtain. "Well, why don't you go out there with your mates and sleep with them for the night?"

"All right then." He scooted toward the exit. "I'd thought we could have spent one last night together, but if ye'd prefer to end it now…"

"Go." She waved him off. Bloody hell, his heart could be as callous as his hate for the English. "Find a ewe to keep your bed warm if that's what you want."

He paused and stared at her almost as if he were fuming enough to take a swing. But with a groan, he just shook his head and turned.

Eva pushed her back against the far wall and watched William's enormous form retreat. She clutched her arms tightly against her body. How in God's name could she make that man understand? Talk about a generation gap. Holy hell.

Do I mean nothing to him?

Her shoulders slumped. *Just leave me behind at a monastery because I'm a woman? Who the hell has worked her tail off to fit in to this miserable mob of rebels?*

Damn him!

He cannot leave me. I won't stand for it.

The back of her eyes stung and she buried her face in her palms. *Dammit. I am not in love with him. I cannot be. Even if I was, just a little, it wouldn't matter. I still have to go home eventually…but not now. Not when he is only beginning to rise to greatness.*

Chapter Eighteen

The men roused early as the clatter of weapons began before dawn. Regretting the stupid argument from the night before, Eva wasn't sure if she'd actually slept. Her head throbbed. *Oh to have a heavenly cup of coffee today.*

Before leaving the sanctity of her alcove, Eva pushed away the boulder hiding her stuff. She slid her roll of notes into her satchel, brushed her hair and smoothed wonderfully minty toothpaste over her teeth. William could be damned if he expected her to leave her things behind, and knowing a little about what lay ahead, she couldn't be sure if she'd ever return.

After securing the satchel over her shoulder, she took one last look at the alcove and chuckled. "Never in a hundred years will I forget the passion shared in this tiny haven."

She blew out the candle and placed it in her bag along with the flint.

The cave hummed with a flurry of activity. Men rolled up the furs and tied them with leather thongs. Brother Bartholomew lumbered across the uneven ground with his arms laden with pots and baskets. Eva hurried over to him. "How can I help?"

He inclined his head toward the back of the cave. "There're parcels of oatcakes and bully beef. Fetch them and meet me by the pack mule. Miserable heathens didna give me enough time to prepare. I fear we'll all starve."

Wallace's resourcefulness was one thing she didn't doubt. "If I know William, he'll find a way to feed everyone."

"Dunna be so certain. He has more mouths to feed than ever before, lassie. Sooner or later, there'll be too many."

Eva chuckled and headed to retrieve the food. *Brother Bartholomew has no idea exactly how large this army will grow.*

After collecting all she could carry, she headed outside. A horse sped toward her at a brisk canter. Eva dodged aside nearly dropping her armload of food. "Watch where you're going." Straightening her bundles, she looked both ways before taking another step. Though mud squished beneath her boots, only wispy clouds sailed above.

The entire clearing aflutter, shoulder-to-shoulder the men worked, helping each other tie their weapons and possessions to their backs or waists. She spotted the monk with the pack mule already laden with parcels. Brother Bartholomew beckoned her. "Come, lass. We've no time to dawdle."

Eva huffed. In no way had she been wasting time. "Where is William?"

Bartholomew took the parcels from her arms. "How should I ken? He's probably preparing to set out like all the others."

She scanned the tops of the heads for Wallace's exceptional height. "Will most of the men be marching, then?"

"They're not fixing to crawl." With a hearty shove, the monk stuffed the parcels of food into a cooking pot, somehow defying gravity as it hung precariously strapped to the side of the mule's harness. "At least God has seen fit to hold the rain at bay for today's march."

"Thank goodness for that."

"Hello, Miss Eva," Robbie called from his horse. Lachlan rode double behind him and waved.

"Lachlan, how are your stitches?"

He pointed to the patch she'd sewn on his shirt. "They're itching a bit, but not so bad it'll keep me from fighting the English."

She vigorously shook her finger. "You mustn't do anything to tear the sutures or else it will take forever to heal."

"Not to worry, Miss Eva." He patted Robbie's shoulder. "That's why I'm riding today. It'll help my skin grow back together."

"Ha." She sounded more like her mother every day. "The only thing that will set you to rights is time."

"Och, dunna worry about him." Robbie grinned. "He's tougher than a badger."

Eva strode toward them, noticing the quality of the youngster's gelding for the first time. "You have a nice horse, Robbie. Where did you find him?"

He patted the bay's neck. "This Galloway was me da's."

"You're lucky to have a mount."

The lad nodded. "I'll be leading the cavalry soon."

Eva gave him a wink. "Perhaps once your voice changes."

"Och, I'm the chieftain of my clan now. Ye mustn't continue to treat me as a child."

Lachlan planted his fists on his hips. "Right. We're old enough to carry a sword. We're old enough to fight."

Eva bit her bottom lip. Arguing with them would only encourage their misplaced ambitions and possibly make them do something stupid. So far, William had been good about keeping them away from the real danger. She had to trust that he'd continue to do so—especially since she knew Robbie would grow up to be the First Lord of Kilmarnock. *He must survive this.*

Eva smoothed her hand over the horse's shoulder. "Was your father a knight, Robbie?" Though she knew the answer to her question, she had a point to make.

"Bloody oath he was. The most fearless knight in all of Ayrshire."

"Well then, you must make him proud—live to see his legacy endures through your progeny."

The lad regarded her with a serious, thin-lipped nod, then dug in his heels and rode away.

Brother Bartholomew stepped behind Eva. "Not to worry. Willy will look after the lad. 'Tis why he's taken him under his wing."

Eva sighed. "I thought no less."

The ram's horn sounded from atop the hill. William stood towering atop the crag like a champion, his hair blowing sideways, triumphant as a flag. An imposing sight he made, dressed in a hauberk with a surcoat sporting the St. Andrew's Cross on his chest. The warrior cradled his helm under his arm, the hilt of his sword peeking over his right shoulder. Eva's gaze swept down to his quilted arming doublet hanging below the mail, with his muscular legs planted firmly.

The hum of the crowd fell silent while the cool breeze swept through the clearing, giving her a welcomed chill.

Eva placed a hand over her heart. She'd never seen a more magnificent sight.

William moved a fist to his hip. "This will be a long day of marching, I willna argue that. But as ye travel, know that ye are on the path to meet our enemies. Together, we will drive Longshanks out of Scotland and demand our rightful king is restored to his throne."

Cheering, the men thrust their weapons in the air.

"John Blair will lead us to Fail where we will meet up with the armies of the Douglas and the Stewart. Mark me, afore this year is ended, we will see a united Scotland!"

A deafening roar spread through the clearing.

Eva wished she could have taken out her smartphone and snapped a picture. It was far too risky—especially after meeting with John Blair's threat.

Her heart thrummed with the roar of the crowd. The men's excitement made her giddy—ready for adventure, and she didn't want to miss a single moment of it. Not now—not for the next several months. If only she could run atop the hill and tell them exactly how much things were about to change.

But the men seemed to know. With John Blair's whistle, the retinue began to move, the faces of the rebels determined, excited. Even Eva's heart raced while she watched them pass.

Straightening her satchel on her hip, she strode to the rear of the entourage. William intended to say goodbye at Fail? The thought only made her more determined to find a way to stay with the rebels.

"Are ye planning to walk with the foot soldiers?" William's deep voice resonated behind her.

Glancing over her shoulder, she regarded Wallace in his glory, mounted atop his great horse. The helm low over his brow gave him the menacing look of a hardened warrior. "I've nothing but my feet to carry me."

He tapped his heels and walked his steed alongside her. "So ye want nothing to do with me now?"

She shook her head. "I don't recall having said that." If only they hadn't argued—she hadn't pushed him, they would have had at least one more heavenly night in each other's arms.

"Come on then." He reached his hand down. "I'll pull ye up."

But he'd insulted her—was casting her aside because of her gender.

Oh no, she wouldn't give in that easily. Eva tucked her fingers under her armpits to keep them from his reach. "I'm perfectly capable of walking."

He bent down and peered at her. "I ken, but I want a word."

Eva's insides squeezed. How this man could constantly look her in the eye and make butterflies swarm throughout her entire body, she couldn't fathom. Jeez, she was twenty-seven. Regardless, she caved to his devilish look, reached up and he clamped his fingers around her wrist so she had no choice but to grasp his.

"I'll swing ye up now. Are ye ready?"

"You'll what?"

Before she could say another word, William hefted her onto the horse, smack dab between his thighs.

He wrapped his big arms around her and pressed his lips to her ear. "Ye all right?" His low growl softened her resolve a bit more.

"I think so." She gestured to her legs, sideways across the horse's withers. "Do I need to straddle him?"

"Nay, just hold on."

The warhorse broke into a canter. Eva leaned into William and looped her arms around his neck, squeezing her eyes shut. "Where are we going?"

"I'm riding ahead a bit."

Jostling in the saddle against an iron shirt of mail wasn't half as romantic as the books made it out to be. But still, his warmth drew her in, and as she grew accustomed to the horse's gait, she relaxed and opened her eyes.

Mm. At least William's thighs certainly made for a comfortable seat.

The trees passed by in a blur, the horse splashing through mud puddles until William reined the horse to a walk.

Eva let out a long breath and leaned into him. She definitely preferred the horse's stride when ambling. "Are we far enough ahead?"

"Should be."

She craned her neck and met his blue-eyed gaze. So many emotions brewed behind his stare, but when he reached up and tucked an errant strand of hair beneath her veil, he smiled. A genuine, make-your-heart-melt type of grin. But it didn't last. William scraped his teeth over his bottom lip. "Ye ken ye are fine to me."

Oh dear, she'd heard breakup words before. Swallowing, Eva nodded.

"I have nothing to offer ye. No lands, no title, no wealth aside from a few groats in my purse."

"I—"

He held up a palm to silence her. "Ye said now's my time. Ye said I would lead an army of men and in my heart, I ken ye're right."

"Yes."

"And I ken I cannot have a woman holding me back from what I must do. The only way to beat the English is to stay ahead of them—to attack when they least expect it—to outsmart and outmaneuver their armies."

She hated that he thought her a burden. Dammit, she could work harder to prove her worth. "Yes, but—"

"I'll not argue this with ye. My own feelings cannot take precedence over the needs of Scotland."

"I know."

"I cannot…" He regarded her. "Ye do?" The inflection in his voice rose as if she'd knocked him off guard.

She nodded. "I definitely do not want a husband. All I ask is to follow and be your chronicler. Brother Bartholomew needs help with the food and healing. And the greater your numbers grow, the more assistance he will need."

Furrowing his brow, William blinked. "Ye are a quandary. What woman does not want to marry and bear children?"

"It's complicated." But right now, she wanted to hold on. This couldn't be the end.

"What isna with ye? Ye're nothing like any woman I've ever met." He pulled the horse to a stop and kissed her forehead. "My mind's made up, Eva. Ye will remain at the monastery. I couldna live with myself if anything happened to ye. I care for…" He shook his head and dug heels into the horse's barrel, his lips disappearing into a line.

He does care. He doesn't want to leave me. Eva's gut clenched into a knot. "If I stay at Fail, will you return for me?" she asked carefully.

"I can make no promises." He kept his eyes on the path.

She swallowed against the thickening in her throat. "I know that, too."

"Then why did ye ask?"

"Because I don't want to lose you." *Not yet.*

William wrapped an arm around her shoulders. He inclined his head and studied her face, his eyebrows slanting outward as if he were in pain. "Mayhap one day when this is over."

But it will never be over—not for William.

The horse slowed his gait.

Reaching up, Eva drew his face down and plied his lips with a kiss. Closing her eyes, she willed her emotion to pass through to him. Their physical connection spoke volumes about honor and respect and tenderness. She didn't want to hear him say a word about the future. Blocking events to come from her mind, in this moment she wanted to savor him, fill her mind with William to ensure she would never forget. As his lips softened to her, she deepened the unhurried and languid strokes with her tongue, showing him the depth of her desire. William Wallace's kisses were like a drug, his mouth greedy—in complete contradiction to his words.

Completely breathless, Eva eased away. If only she could beg and plead for more.

William nuzzled into her neck, his breath hot against her cool skin.

Eva closed her eyes and inhaled his feral scent. "You may leave me at Fail, but I refuse to bid you goodbye."

***

Eventually John Blair and the retinue caught up to them about at the same time Eva spotted the stone walls of the monastery. It looked so new and enormous compared to the ruin. What had Walter said? The monastery was commissioned less than fifty years prior. Surrounded by a wooden fence, the sanctuary with its rose window loomed majestically above a long dormitory building—she'd seen no trace of it in the ruins.

As they approached, a pair of riders galloped toward them. To the west of the monastery, an army of men gathered. Just as Lord Stewart had promised in his missive, the soldiers had arrived. Though Blind Harry gave William credit for Ayr, Eva wondered. *Will things play out as the poet described?*

"What? Did ye find a wood nymph along the way?" A man with broad shoulders, dressed in mail from head to toe, eyed Eva with a lecherous glint. An ornate brooch at his throat clasped a red mantle closed.

"She'll be staying with the Trinitarians." William reined the horse to a stop. "Sir Douglas, I take it?"

"In the flesh." Douglas stared at Eva. "Though with such a tasty morsel, 'tis a wonder ye made it this far, Wallace."

"The maid is none of your concern." William helped Eva slide down before he dismounted. "I've business inside, then I'll tend ye directly."

A rueful laugh rolled from Sir Douglas' lips. "Ye best make it quick, else ye'll have all my lads wanting their turn."

Eva had enough. "Pardon me, but you are a pig. How dare you insult—"

William's firm fingers gripped her shoulder. "I'll be but a moment," he growled, pulling her toward the gate.

Once out of earshot, she wrenched her shoulder from William's grasp. "Did you see how he looked at me?"

"Aye, and I'm surprised I didna have to fight half the camp to keep my men away from ye as well."

She'd known that was why Robbie had told the rebels she was Willy's woman in the first place, but she didn't expect such an indecent appraisal from a member of the gentry. "Where is his sense of respect?"

"For himself or for a woman dressed in a crofter's gown?"

"I am not a slave."

"No, but as far as Sir Douglas is concerned, if ye are not married, ye are fruit for the plucking."

"That is preposterous. He's *married* to Eleanor of Lovain."

"Aye and his first wife was James Stewart's sister. He's a noble with connections with lofty lords. We dunna want to cross him."

Eva bit her bottom lip. "Because he's bred of nobility, he has the right to act like an ass?" Her own father was knighted—Sir David MacKay, the UK Ambassador to the US. If anything, the nobles of her time went out of their way to be more congenial.

William opened the door leading into the courtyard and shrugged. "Ye ken as well as I, ye must be respectful when it comes to your betters."

"Betters?" Eva dug in her heels. "But you are no one's man. I would expect you to stand up to the likes of Douglas."

He grasped her elbow and started forward. "Had he placed a hand on ye, I wouldna have stood for it."

"Right, but it is just fine for him to insult me."

"Enough." William clamped his lips together and led her across the courtyard to a monk working in the garden. "Is the abbot in?"

The man pointed. "In his chamber I believe, though we'll be heading for the devotions of sext soon."

"I willna be long," William said, still leading her by the arm. He gave her a sideways glance. "Ye should be familiar with the abbot."

Her heart squeezed. Must he continue to fixate on the exchange from their first meeting? "You know I am not."

"I ken ye've lied to me." He glowered as if convincing himself he needed to be rid of her.

Eva yanked her arm away "Which I did when I thought you were an outlaw about to murder me. And must I keep reminding you I will *never* stretch the truth again?"

Without another word, William knocked and stepped inside the abbot's rooms. Tallow candles burned with black smoke in the center of an oblong table. The threadbare rug curled at the corners. Walter had been right when he mentioned this was not a wealthy order.

The withered man looked up from his seat at the table and stood. "Willy, 'tis good to see ye, lad."

William greeted the man with an embrace. "Father Semple, I've come to ask ye a favor."

The abbot looked at Eva for the first time and knit his eyebrows. "What is it?"

Pulling Eva forward, Wallace gestured with one hand. "I need ye to take this lassie in and help her find a husband."

"I don't want to get married." Eva yanked her arm away and clutched it tight to her body.

"Willy, what is this?" The abbot gave her a once over. "We dunna take in subjects who are not in need of our assistance."

"Och, Miss Eva needs help for certain." William spread his palms to his sides. "She just doesna ken how much."

Eva rolled her eyes to the exposed beams in the ceiling.

"Please." Wallace placed his hand on Father Semple's shoulder. "I'd like to see her cared for, and a rebel's band is no place for a woman."

The abbot frowned. "I suppose she can stay in Brother Murdach's cell. He passed away a fortnight ago."

William crossed himself. "I'm sorry for your loss."

"Not to worry, lad. He is walking with the Lord now." Father Semple drummed his fingers on his chin. "Are ye another victim of this mindless war with the English, lass?"

Shifting her gaze to William, she nodded. "Aye."

His eyebrows shot up. "Can ye take her in—at least until the fighting has ended?"

She could only shake her head. *Lord, you have no idea.*

"I suppose I'd be no abbot if I refused." Father Semple moved toward the door, beckoning with his fingers. "I must away to sext. Come with me, Miss Eva. We live simple lives, and whilst ye're here, I'll expect ye to be respectful of our order."

She glared at William and pursed her lips. "Of course."

By the holy man's glum frown, he didn't seem any happier about taking her in as she did about staying. It didn't matter one way or the other. She had no intention of remaining behind. Besides, how difficult would it be to track an army?

William gave her a squeeze and kissed the top of her head. "I'll never forget ye." He blinked in succession, then with long strides he hurried out the door.

Eva just stared. Nights of passion reduced to a hasty goodbye? Her entire body went numb while tightness gripped her heart all the way up through her throat. *How could he just turn his back and abandon me?*

He'd said by leaving her, he was doing the right thing.

How could he be so wrong?

She followed the abbot through the cloisters while her heart ached.

Left.

Rejected.

Why did every good thing in Eva's life crumble to nothingness? God, she wanted to scream.

The abbot stopped at a narrow door and pushed it open. The cell was no more than a closet with barely enough room to stand beside a narrow cot. "We live modest lives with few luxuries." He gestured for her to step inside. "If ye'll excuse me, I've a mass to chant."

Lips dry, Eva couldn't manage to make a sound, so she nodded instead. Tears rimmed her eyes as she shuffled inside.

When he closed the door behind him, Eva's heart skipped a beat. A brown habit and hood hung on a nail.

Chapter Nineteen

The vise clamping around William's heart was exactly what he needed to focus on the battle ahead. At least that's what he told himself. Heaven help him, he'd been daft to become involved with Eva. And she always twisted every argument to her favor. How could a woman continually sound so bloody right? Well, he needed to end it now, and the battle to come would only serve to release his pent up agony. He never should have let things go so far.

And why did the lass have to look so forlorn when I left?

Blast it, she said she didna want to marry me.

And by God, I canna allow myself to think about marrying her.

Sir Douglas rode beside him. "My spies report a thousand troops marched into Ayr this morn."

William blinked, snapping from his thoughts. "What is their purpose?"

"Public hangings or irons for all who haven't sworn fealty to King Edward. Same as always."

"Ye have proof of this?"

"Who needs proof?" Sir Douglas spurred his mount faster. "They all follow Longshanks and I'll wager half of them pillaged Lochmaben—same place your da was murdered."

William's gut churned. He'd not forgotten the massacre of that day, nor would he ever.

John Blair and the Douglas man-at-arms who had ridden reconnaissance from Fail, galloped through the open lea straight toward them. By the determination on Blair's face, they'd struck gold.

"What did ye find?" William asked as the riders neared and slowed their mounts.

"'Tis true. There's an entire army." Blair looked at Douglas. "But I estimate only a thousand troops, all bedding down in the sheep barns of Ayr." The priest took in a deep breath. "This could be a grand win for us."

William caught Sir Douglas' eye and grinned. "Timing is everything."

"I say as soon as the last lamp is snuffed, we burn them out."

William looked back from whence they came. The Douglas cavalry weren't far behind, but the foot had not yet come into sight. The pikemen provided their greatest muscle. "I say we'll wait for the infantry to catch up and then we'll make camp a mile out. It has been a long day. The men will be hungry. They'll fight better on a full stomach and a good night's kip."

"Are ye daft, man?" Sir Douglas spat. "I say we ride now and burn them out."

"Now?" William looked down the length of his nose. "In daylight? Afore the foot have a chance to move into place *and* after a full day's march? Ye expect a hundred cavalry men to be victorious against a thousand trained English soldiers?"

Douglas guffawed. "Ye're soft."

"And ye're reckless." Wallace hailed the cavalry men. "Only the patient man succeeds against a stronger foe. We make camp here and rise afore dawn."

"Then we set fire to the barns and burn them."

Wallace nodded his agreement. "We'll strike with vengeance as they flee."

Sir Douglas looked stunned. “Ye’re planning to let them out?”

“I woudna kill a man without allowing him a wee chance for a fair fight.”

“Och, ye’ve a lot to learn about war. I all but lost my head in Berwick—would have if I didna sign Longshanks’ Ragman Roll.”

Gut roiling, William regarded the knight. “Ye bore false witness to save your head?”

“Bloody oath I did.” Douglas clamped his hand around his mail-clad throat. “Saved my neck so I could return and murder every last one of them.”

William dismounted. “Ye’ll have your chance—come the darkest hour.”

Grumbling something imperceptible, Sir Douglas led his men a good fifty paces away and gathered them together.

Blair strode up beside William. “I dunna trust a one of them. The man-at-arms wanted to ride clear into the English camp and make a ruckus. That would not have been right—alert the bloody bastards to our presence.”

Wallace peered toward the Douglas camp. “Inform the watch to keep an eye on them. If we lose the element of surprise, we might as well all run for home.”

***

Dressed in the monk’s habit, Eva waited until the chanting from the sanctuary resounded across the monastery grounds, before she slipped out the front gate, somewhat surprised there was no guard posted to stop her, especially since the monastery had been under attack not long ago.

She closed the gate behind her and stood back from the curtain wall. When the monastery had been in ruins, there was no sign of the wall’s existence at all. Had the stones been used to build fences for the paddocks that crisscrossed the modern landscape?

She dug in her satchel for her mobile phone and pushed the "*on*" button.

The battery warning immediately flashed. Clicking "*ok*", she stood back and snapped a picture. *Good.* She'd caught the angle of the building from the same place where the modern street would one day be paved—now only a narrow dirt trail.

After connecting her solar charger, she placed the phone in her satchel with the solar panel hanging out the side. Alone, she wouldn't need to worry about prying eyes, and she just might snap a few more pictures that would totally blow away Walter, even if she couldn't use them in a story.

Hmm. I wonder if the medallion would work in the reverse and send me back to the thirteenth century if I tried to publish pictures from this era. She laughed out loud. *I doubt anyone would believe me. They'd all think my pictures were Photoshopped.*

All set with the hood pulled low over her brow, Eva followed the boggy tracks west. On occasion, she'd catch sight of the tail-end of the entourage as it crested a hill, but she dared not move too near. She couldn't risk having William discover her and do something that might change the course of the battle.

If her intuition was right, this would be a fight she'd prefer to miss—one she'd like to caution William against.

The medallion burned hot against her flesh. Stopping, Eva clamped her hand over it. *Right. I can change nothing. My job is to observe only.* The burning cooled.

Eva's feet ached by the time she crested the hill and found the men making camp. The sun glowed orange, low on the horizon. A burn trickled eastward along her path while Eva crept as close as she dared. Two groups set up about a football field apart. The one to the south had fewer men and more horses—that had to be the Douglas contingent.

She snapped another picture.

William's army included the Stewart pikemen, but she was too far away to make out any individuals.

Next problem. She'd been walking for hours with nothing to eat or drink. Digging in her satchel, she found the granola bars she'd dumped inside a month ago. Her hands shook as she tore the wrapper. As soon as she caught the sweet scent, her salivary glands watered. She shoved half the bar in her mouth and chewed.

Mm.

Eating mostly meat with the odd bland oatcake, the honey and chocolate sent her taste buds into overdrive. She crammed the rest of the bar in her mouth and reached in her satchel for another. The sugar hit her blood like relief filling her veins and she strode to the burn, dropping to her knees.

The water ran clear and swift. Scooping greedy mouthfuls, she drank her fill. No, she mightn't be able to survive for long on granola bars and water, but her meager meal would see her through till morning. And the woolen monk's habit she wore over her clothes would help stave off the cold night air.

Straightening, Eva shook the water from her palms.

A metallic hiss sounded behind her. "Luck is not with ye today, Friar."

Chapter Twenty

Shit. Why couldn't one of William's men have found Eva rather than the brute who dragged her into the Douglas camp with her hands tied behind her back? Gripping her elbow, the man thrust her forward.

"I reckoned I'd found a friar until the wench opened her mouth." The bastard chuckled. "Thought we might have a bit of sport."

"Ye dunna say?" Though it was dark, she recognized Sir Douglas' voice. He sauntered toward her.

Eva lowered her gaze while her heart thundered in her ears. Damn it, everything in her life always backfired. Couldn't God allow her a break?

Sir Douglas yanked off her hood. "What have we here? The wench Wallace discarded at the monastery come to spy?"

"Nay." She dared not let him hear her accent.

He fingered a lock of her hair and held it to his nose. "Why were ye with the likes of that rebel?"

She jerked her head away.

"Ah." He chuckled. "I like a spirited wench." He leaned closer and sniffed. "Ye're too bonny to be roaming these parts alone, even if ye are his whore."

"How dare ye?" she spat out.

"Then what are ye to him and why did Wallace dump ye with the Trinitarians?"

Eva squared her shoulders. "I'm his chronicler."

He threw back his head with a deep belly laugh. "Now that's the tallest tale I've ever heard come from a woman."

She stared at him without allowing a modicum of emotion to show on her face. *He doesn't get out much, does he?*

"Now tell me true, lass, what are ye doing dressed in a monk's habit?"

She cleared her throat and affected her best Auld Scots. "I canna verra well record historical events locked behind the gates of a monastery." She twisted her wrists to test her bindings—the thug who'd caught her had tied them a bit hastily. "Now if ye'll allow me to head over to Wallace's camp, I need to have a word with him."

"I think not." Douglas rubbed his palms together. "We'll be keeping ye with us until I find out just what Wallace had in mind leaving ye behind at the monastery."

"I can look after the wench," grunted the vile beast who'd captured her.

Sir Douglas backhanded the dolt. "Ye'll nay be touching her. Not yet. We've barns to burn first."

With a gasp, Eva looked west, the barns were out of sight, but she had no doubt they were there. *Another of Blind Harry's legends with a thread of truth.* "Will ye lock the English inside?"

His gaze snapped to hers. "What say ye? How the bloody hell did ye ken my mind?"

She shook her head with her shoulders shrugging to her ears. "Fortuitous guess?"

"Mayhap Wallace discarded ye at the monastery cause ye're not to be trusted." He narrowed his gaze and scowled. "Ye talk like ye're spewing lies."

"If ye'd allow me to seek him out, I'm certain William would vouch for my character." Eva took a deep breath, satisfied with her delivery of that stream of prose.

"Ye'll remain here." He pointed to the guard. "Bind her feet and silence her beguiling mouth."

"But—" As she began to speak, someone gagged her with a dirty cloth.

Sir Douglas sliced his hand through the air. "I'll not have a woman's squealing alert the English to our plan."

After they'd bound her, Eva sat on the damp grass and watched the Douglas men fan out and creep over the crest of the hill. Odd, the cavalrymen left their horses hobbled. Over her shoulder, the Wallace camp remained quiet. *Why wouldn't they attack together?* She sniffed. *Unless Sir Douglas plans to undermine William's authority.*

Tugging her wrist against her bindings, the rope gave a bit. She tucked in her thumb and made her hand as narrow as possible. Slowly twisting back-and-forth against the coarse rope, her skin burned. Teeth clenched she tugged, but her hand stuck. Jeez, only a fraction more and her palm would slip free. Stars crossed Eva's vision as she pulled harder, biting into her gag as the grating rope tore her flesh.

When unable to force her hand further, Eva stopped and sucked a reviving breath through her nostrils.

Wrenched behind her back, her arms ached. But she had to warn William. Gathering her strength, she bore down and heaved. With a sudden jolt, her hand tore free—along with a layer of skin. Hissing at the pain, she quickly untied her gag and then released her ankles.

Now all she needed to do was to find William and not end up in the clutches of an overzealous guard in the process.

***

A light sleeper, especially before a battle, William's eyes flashed open at the faint rustle of brushing grass. Lying on his side, the sound came from behind. He tightened his grip on the dirk cradled in the upper crux of his arm. Then a footfall lightly crunched the grass, closer this time.

"William," a voice whispered.

His muscles tensed. Was this friend or foe? With the price on his head, he couldn't be sure. Remaining still, he shifted his eyes. The intruder was so close, Wallace could sense him now.

"William," the whisper came again.

Taking a deep breath, he forced himself to wait.

The hair on the back of his neck stood on end.

Now.

With an abrupt turn of his head William seized the brigand's wrist. Twisting his hand, he flipped the cur onto his back and he leveled the point of his dirk against the scoundrel's neck.

"No!" Eva squeaked in a high-pitched whisper.

With a sharp twist to his gut, he focused on the whites of her eyes. "What the bloody hell are ye doing here?"

Shirking away from his blade, she gasped, taking in short inhales. "I-I-I…" She waved her finger up over her head. "They-they—Sir Douglas and his men—"

"God's teeth." William released his grasp. Eva didn't need say another word. The western sky glowed with flickering amber. A sickly chill spread across his skin. Only one thing lit up the sky like that. He sprang to his feet. "Everyone up! Sir Douglas has moved without us."

Eva clambered up beside him. "What can I do to help?"

He flashed a narrow-eyed glare. "'Tis looking as if ye willna listen to me no matter what I say."

"That's not true. I refuse to remain left behind, but otherwise, I'm quite good at following orders."

"That's yet to be seen." He pointed. "Stay close to Brother Bartholomew and keep out of trouble. I canna be dragged away from every fight to save your arse."

She nodded, muttering something that started with "ungrateful".

He sauntered close, jutting his face down to hers to make his point. "How many times do I have to tell ye a battle is no place for a woman?"

Craning her neck, her sharp stare challenged him. "But—"

"Hide." Damnation, he shook her shoulders. "Ye're a blessed *female*. Do ye ken what the English will do if they find ye?"

She bit her bottom lip, the corners of her lips cringing as if reality finally set in.

But William was about to leave it there. Oh no, she needed a good tongue lashing—and mayhap a whipping when this day was over. "I've seen their hospitality to Scotland's women and none of them have lived to tell about it." He grabbed her arm and squeezed. "I reckon that's God's blessing, because if a woman lived through that sort of plunder and defilement, she'd be a lunatic for the rest of her days."

By Eva's shudder, William may have actually made his point this time.

Blair stepped beside them. "Ye ready?"

William held his finger under Eva's nose. "Stay hidden."

"I will. I promise."

He nodded to Blair. "Let's away."

"Where did she come from?" asked the warrior priest.

"Fail—where else?"

Blair threw up his hands. "God on the cross, she'll be a thorn in your side until she ends up on the wrong end of an English pike."

Wallace hastened the pace. "Shut your gob and tell me why the watch didn't see Sir Douglas slip away without us."

Cresting the hill, William's gut churned before Blair had a chance to answer. Screams of men being burned alive howled from within the barn's walls.

The roof was ablaze. Hammering and pounding came from the men inside, attacking the timbers with weapons. Sir Douglas had sealed the doors before he lit the fires—just like he said he would.

"Lord have mercy on their souls," Blair growled, keeping pace beside him.

"Amen." William would opt for a fair fight any day—so would Blair. But now the fires had been lit, saving the bastards made not a lick of sense. His men would only be forced to cut them down as they gasped for air.

In the forefront of the fire, Sir Douglas was an easy mark, laughing and hollering taunts as if the shrieks of the men and horses inside were more entertaining than a minstrel's display. Aye, William relished a good fight, and had killed many an English enemy, but locking them in a barn and burning them alive went against every grain in his body.

"Douglas," he bellowed.

The knight faced him, sword in hand—a deadly mistake. "'Tis about time ye showed up for the fete." The man made an exaggerated bow. "Watch them burn!"

William planted his feet wide, his hackles standing on end. "Made it easy on yourself, did ye now?"

"Why should I not?"

"Because we are not murderers. We are warriors."

The man raised his sword—a reckless risk. "I've killed men for less insolence." Surging forward, Douglas lunged with a stab of sword.

Spinning away, Wallace snatched his dirk and faced the cur.

Every sinew in his body clamped taut as the two men circled.

"Ye're soft. Just like ye were with that redheaded vixen. Ye told her to stay put, but she followed ye—and now she'll be my whore." Douglas swiped his blade.

William hollowed his stomach, scooting back from the hissing iron. "What are ye on about?"

"My guard found her spying—followed us all the way from Fail." Douglas darted in.

William hopped aside and the knight stumbled forward with the momentum of his thrust. "Ye're bloody daft." William slapped Sir Douglas in the backside with the flat edge of his blade. "And I'll not stand for it."

The spineless maggot brandished his weapon over his head. "Who do ye think ye are?"

"I am your commander, by order of the High Steward of Scotland—and now I ken why."

When Sir Douglas swung, William caught his sword arm and spun the blackguard into his body, leveling his dirk against the man's neck. "Ye'll not be usurping me again. If ye try, I'll not act so kindly next time." He pressed his lips against the varlet's ear. "And ye'd best curb your tongue when ye're speaking about *my* woman. I, too, have killed for less. Ye ken?"

William pushed the bastard to the ground and backed away. "I call an end to our quarrel. All of Scotland must stand together to drive the English back to their own soil. I canna stomach drawing a sword against one of my own."

Sir Douglas sat up and shook his head. But it wasn't until William walked away that the coward cleared his throat. "I still think ye're soft."

Sheathing his dirk, Wallace kept going. *If he crosses me again, he'll not survive the length of time it takes him to draw his sword.*

After joining Blair, he crossed his arms and regarded the burning barns. Heat from the blaze scorched his eyes. And now the only sound was the rush and crackle of the fire. The men within had all perished, their cries whisked away with the breeze blowing the black smoke eastward.

Together, William and his men walked back over the hill toward the violet and orange hues of dawn. The events of the morning weighing heavily on his shoulders, William looked forward to seeing only one face. Perhaps he could find a role for Eva. She'd made herself useful in Leglen Wood—could be as handy as Brother Bartholomew if William allowed it—if they could keep the woman safe from the enemy.

And then he spotted her standing at the crest of the hill, wringing her hands.

He had no doubt she'd seen all that had happened. That's what she continued to say she wanted. Though now she might have a change of mind—especially if she'd heard the horrific cries resounding from the barns.

Wallace marched up to Eva and grasped her by the elbow. "Come."

Her face dazed, she stumbled a bit, but she uttered not a word.

Robbie raced toward them with Lachlan right behind. "Ye didna even have to fight."

"Dunna speak ill of the dead. We may have killed the English, but this was no victory." William inclined his head toward the horses. "Go saddle my mount and tell Father Blair to march the men to Ellerslie. I'll meet ye there on the morrow."

"Will there be another fight?" Lachlan asked.

Wallace regarded the dirty-faced lad. "As sure as ye're breathing, there will be battles to come, and we'll nay stop until we drive Longshanks from Scotland for good."

After the boys sped away, Eva's footing became surer. "I'm not going back to Fail."

"I'm not taking ye there."

Chapter Twenty-One

For the second time, William didn't ask Eva ride to behind him. He cradled her across his powerful thighs, his arms encircling her waist as he held the reins. She closed her eyes against the trembling. She'd asked for this—asked to witness it all. Not once did she think it would be like going to the state fair or the movies. But seeing footage of war-torn countries on the big screen was a far cry from watching it in person.

How could she remain impartial? How could she have stood on the hill listening to the pleading shrieks of the dying? Even the livestock inside brayed with unconscionable fear and pain. The horse hooves kicking the walls were unmistakable. Eva even had wished more for the animals to break free than the men.

When William had walked toward her, it crossed her mind to run, but she couldn't force her feet to move. All she could think of was the strength of his arms when they surrounded her. The inexplicable bond they'd made—her driving, ever present need to be a part of this—to share his life.

God damn it, she needed his touch more now than ever. The warmth of the arms formed a protective barrier shielding her from the ugliness of the world.

"Why didn't you open the doors?" she asked in a whisper.

"Open them just to cut the men down as they ran?" A tic twitched in his jaw.

She nodded. She'd seen it all. By the time William and his men reached the barns, the flames leapt from the thatched roofs and through the gaps in the wooden walls. Even standing on the hill, the blaze burned so hot, it warmed her face.

He pressed gentle lips to her temple. "We'll not speak of it again."

She only nodded. Closing her eyes, she tried to force the horror to the back of her mind—tried to compartmentalize it so she wouldn't break down. This was a time of cold brutality. Only the strongest could survive it and she had no intension of wilting like a sniveling weakling. She'd risen above her share of hard knocks. Now was no time to sink back down into the doldrums.

With her resolution, she pushed up her sleeves and examined the raw skin, irritated by the habit's coarse wool.

"Ssss," William hissed. "What happened there?"

"Rope burn, compliments of Sir Douglas." She blew on the sting.

That jaw tic twitched more prominently this time. "I could kill him for that."

She brushed her fingers across his beard. "I know you can, but you're a better man than he is."

"Mayhap ye give me too much credit." He let out a wry chuckle and kissed her again. "Ye're a wise woman. Perhaps that's why I canna stop thinking about ye."

Sighing, Eva relaxed against him. Heaven help her, she'd never be able to stay mad at him. Wallace was running just like her. Confused and angry, maybe even more than Eva. She'd been running from her tragedy in New York and William blocked the gruesome memories of his every battle. No wonder neither one of them could sleep.

Together they rode for miles, not saying a word. William relaxed the reins and let the horse amble until they wove through deep wood and stopped on the bank of a river. The rush filled her ears with the sound of water babbling over boulders and skimming the bottom limbs of trees.

"Where are we?" Eva asked.

"The River Irvine."

The musical flow of the water helped to calm her inner turmoil. "Near Loudoun Hill?"

"Aye, though nearer Kilmarnock." He helped her slide down, then dismounted. "Are ye hungry?"

She should be. Now away from the warmth of his chest, she shivered and shook her head. Stepping in, she smoothed her hands around his waist. "I don't want to let go of you."

He raised her chin with the crook of his finger. Lips parted, his gaze met hers with an electric pull. "I've tried to walk away from ye, but every time ye've fought me."

Eva swallowed back a lump forming in her throat. "I know."

"And now ye've seen me at my worst, yet ye havena fled."

"But it was Sir Douglas who…" They'd agreed not to talk about it. Eva's breath became shallow as she kneaded her fingertips into the back of his exposed neck. "I want to be with you so badly, I cannot bear the thought of walking away. Not now."

"And I can no longer turn ye out." He cupped her face between his palms. "Ye are in my blood. My every heartbeat thrums for ye."

Eva's mouth went dry and she focused on the rugged lines of his face, refusing to allow her mind to wander.

He brushed his fingers along her jaw. "Why do ye want to stay with me when ye ken we cannot marry?"

"Does it matter?" Her face reflected in his fathomless, crystal-blue eyes while she dug deep for her answer. "Our souls are one. I want to be with you."

Intense, his gaze dipped to her mouth. "And I with ye."

"Then why worry about what the future holds? Love me for today. Love me like you may never have the chance again." Eva refused to consider the future and thinking about the past brought too much pain. "The only time we have is the now."

His eyes dipped to her mouth and he moistened his lips. "The now," he whispered. Sliding his hands to her neck, he crushed his mouth over hers possessively, as if the pressure of the day's events surged through him with a burst of passion.

"I need to feel the warmth of your flesh against my skin." He tugged up his hauberk. "Help me take this off."

He kneeled and Eva hefted the heavy mail over his head and placed it on the grass. The electric current that always connected their souls shot between their heated stares. Taking his hands, she pulled him into her arms.

Moving her fingers up his spine, Eva clung to William as if she needed his touch to breathe. His mouth fused to hers, exploring with the same fervent hunger that thrummed under her skin. Never in her life had she been so spellbound by a man. Her body on fire, she drew her fingers to his waistband, groped for the ties and spread open his chausses.

He fumbled with the rope tie on her habit, but when it released, he pushed the garment from her shoulders and cast it aside. Eva couldn't get to him fast enough. So many layers—the arming doublet, the linen shirt, the braies. With every piece of his clothing, he removed one of hers.

Urgency demanded they move quickly, but still Eva's fingers fumbled with her mounting desire. When finally the breeze caressed her bare skin, she rubbed her body against his hard. Bliss sent tingles skittering along the goosebumps on her skin. She ran her fingers through the fine hair in the center of his chest. "Beautiful."

"Ah, lassie. Ye are bonnier than any woman in all of Ayrshire. Just looking at ye stirs a maelstrom of passion in my blood."

With a wink, he turned and untied a blanket from behind his saddle, showing her the most powerful masculine back she'd ever had the pleasure of gazing upon. A back that would fight for freedom—a back that could carry the weight of a nation.

Eva's heart sped. His perfectly chiseled derriere rounded down to long powerful thighs, peppered with auburn curls. Heat seared deep inside with a longing so intense, her thighs shuddered. Stepping to him, she smoothed her hands over his rock-hard buttocks and circled her fingers inside his cleft, lightly brushing his scrotum.

"Mm," he growled, leaning into her. "If ye keep doing that I'll follow ye anywhere."

Chucking, she pushed her hand further and cupped him. "I like that."

"Come with me." Turning, he took her hand and led her to a patch of moss. "There's no better bed in the wild—if ye dunna mind a wee bit of damp."

"I remember," she chuckled.

After he'd spread the blanket, he drew her into his embrace. "I ken I shouldna allow myself to feel so strongly about anyone, but merely breathing in your scent has me transfixed. How can ye possess me so?"

"I have no idea." She closed her eyes and focused on the now. Being near him filled her with life. "I've said it before and believe me when I swear there is no one I'd rather be with than you."

Leaning in for a languid kiss, he lifted Eva and reclined on the blanket. "Are ye cold, lass?"

She shivered. "Not when my body is pressed to yours."

"Mm. I've enough heat for the both of us."

A seductive chuckle rumbled from her throat. "You can keep talking to me with that deep Scottish burr all day." Pushing him down to the blanket, she straddled his robust hips and rubbed her slick core up and down along the length of his erection.

His big hands plied her thighs, until his thumb snuck up and slid over her. "I want ye too much."

She wouldn't last long either. Not this time. Maybe not ever with this man. The hunger sizzling deep inside her core burned so hot, she might come with one more brush of his thumb. Raising her hips, she caught the tip of his cock and took him inside, just far enough.

His breath caught. So did hers. She held very still while her body gradually adjusted to his size. Then staring into his glassy eyes, she slid down his length. Supporting herself with her hands, she watched his face as the spike of arousal escalated to an urgent frenzy.

A current stronger than the pull of electricity connected their souls as their bodies moved in perfect tandem.

A cry caught in her throat. She closed her eyes.

"Look at me," William growled, drawing her back into the power of their bond. He sank his fingers into her bottom, demanding more.

The pressure mounted, driving Eva toward glorious release. Thrusting faster, a bead of sweat rolled down from her temple as, all at once, she cried out as her inner core burst into euphoric splendor.

Still holding on to her hips, William drove harder until his entire body shuddered with his muffled growl of pleasure. Eva collapsed atop his chest, sighing with every deep breath.

She lay atop him while their breathing gradually returned to normal. In this moment, William Wallace, leader of the resistance, the greatest legend Scotland had ever known, was hers alone. There were no rebels lingering outside an alcove, no nosy priests accusing her of being a loose woman, no Sir Douglas making lewd remarks. Right now, Eva held her William in her arms, bound as man and woman, savoring every blessed second.

"Thank you for not forcing me away," she whispered.

"I didna want to let ye go."

She rolled to her side. "Then why did you?"

"I've said it afore—a man hell-bent on rebellion has no business loving a woman." William pulled the blanket over her back.

She swirled her fingers over his chest. "Even if she's willing to live with the consequences?"

"Even then—but dunna take me wrong. It tore my heart to shreds when I left ye at the monastery. I told myself I'd never see ye again. 'Twas the blackest day of my miserable life."

She nestled her head under his chin. "Never abandon me again."

"I'll not on one condition."

"Aye?"

"Ye listen to me when I tell ye to stay put."

"I can do that, as long as I know you're coming back."

He smoothed his hand over her hair. "Aye, lass. I give ye my word."

Eva closed her eyes and relaxed into his comforting arms. Exactly where she wanted to be, she blocked her mind from thinking about anything but William. In the past year she'd become adept at compartmentalizing her thoughts, and if it was therapy she needed, she'd found it right there in the arms of William Wallace.

"Eva?" he asked.

"Yes?"

"Will ye promise me something?"

She inhaled his scent—delicious spice and danger. "Anything."

"When I ask ye for the truth, ye will give it willingly."

She'd only ever wanted to be forthright. "I've shown this to you before." Reaching down, she grasped the medallion and held it up. "If ever I had a motto, this is it."

He read the inscription on both sides. "Ye said a wise man gave this to ye?"

"A man who believed I would find you and discover the truth."

"Have ye been disappointed?" William ran his thumb over the smooth bronze.

"No, on the contrary. I've experienced more…more stirring of my blood than at any time in my life. I must say, I'm not ready to go back."

He pressed his lips to her forehead. "'Tis good, 'cause I am not ready to have ye leave."

Chapter Twenty-Two

The sun rose all too soon, even for William. Though anxious to rejoin his men, he couldn't deny how much he needed this time away. And the woman cradled between his thighs, sharing his horse, had an uncanny way of soothing the horrors he'd witnessed—if only for a little while.

Over and over he would relive every murder he'd seen, and every man he'd fought, until the day he died. William envied those who tilled the soil and raised bairns. Their lives must be rich and unfettered as God had meant for men to live, knowing their seed would continue through generations. But the Lord had made Wallace a warrior. Unimaginable, gruesome death lurked in the recesses of his mind, soothed ever so lovingly by Miss Eva's gentle touch.

Sure, John Blair would have something cheeky to say about William's absence, but Willy hadn't taken a vow of chastity. And now he knew he'd never be able to walk away from Eva. She'd taken a great risk to wake him in Ayr. He wouldn't abandon her again.

He couldn't deny that leaving her at the monastery had torn what remained of his heart to shreds. How in God's name had he become so attached to the lass in such a short period of time? *But these are fast and furious days. Life is short, brutal, fleeting.* That she possessed gifts not of this world was certain, but William had seen enough to decide for himself that she, indeed, had a good heart. The final thread of proof came in Ayr. If she was a vassal of King Edward, she would have alerted the English in the barns rather than seek him out.

Eva rested her head against his chest. "Thank you for taking me to your hideaway. I wish we could have stayed there for a sennight."

"Me as well." William released a rumbling sigh. "If only I weren't embroiled in this revolution."

"But you are."

"Aye." Bloody oath, when the news of Ayr came to light, the price on his head would increase tenfold.

"Where was your father raised? On the croft in Ellerslie?"

"Nay." William ran his reins through his fingers. "Da was the youngest son of Sir Adam Wallace of Riccarton."

"Isn't that near Kilmarnock?"

"Aye. And we slept on Riccarton lands last eve."

She inclined her face up toward him and met his gaze. "So then we're near Ellerslie?"

William's heart swelled—he could gaze on that lovely face all day. "A mile or so." He pointed with his thumb. "Ellerslie is part of the family estate."

"Wow, I wouldn't have guessed." She tapped her delectable lips with her pointer finger. "Am I correct in assuming though your father was a tenant farmer, he was prosperous?"

"Wallaces always prosper." He nuzzled into her fragrant tresses. "My da was renowned for raising the tastiest beef in all Ayrshire. Not to mention the finest Galloway ponies."

"That is impressive." Eva swirled her fingers on the outside of his thigh. Somehow she always knew exactly where to touch him. "Is everyone in your family tall?"

"Da was close, but no others. I dunna ken why I'm so much taller than everyone else. Ma always said 'tis on account of the marrow."

"Marrow?"

"I always sucked the marrow from the bones when I was a lad. 'Twas my favorite part."

Eva's mouth twisted. "Sounds awful."

"Mayhap to ye." He glanced down at her fingers still swirling. "But if ye keep touching me like that, we'll never make it to Kilmarnock."

"Sorry." She drew her hand away.

William chuckled. "I'm not sorry in the slightest."

With a playful whack, she giggled.

They rode for a time when her dancing fingers next tickled the back of his hand. "How did you learn to read and write?"

Though the soft strokes on his hand were nice, he preferred to have her stroking his thigh. "Ma made certain of that. Said regardless if we were the sons of a crofter, we would fare better in life if we could read and write in Scots, French and Latin."

"What's your favorite?"

He thought for a moment. "Aside from my native tongue, I rather like Latin. 'Tis the foundation for so many languages. After I left home, I went to study with my uncle in Dundee."

"Why so far away? Why not Paisley Abbey or Fail Monastery?"

"Och, ye are full of questions this day." William chuckled. "One of my uncles is a priest. He introduced me to Bishop Wishart, who encouraged me to study at Dunipace to be a Templar knight. A monk named MacRae who'd fought in the Holy Land with the Order of the Knights Templar taught me everything about war. But he trained knights of God to fight for Christendom. I once had dreams of traveling to the Holy Land and fighting for the church."

"And here you are fighting for your country."

"I reckon God wanted me to remain in Scotland."

"So you left the order and took up your sword?"

"Aye, I suppose ye could put it like that." William again ran the reins' soft leather through his fingers. But he'd had enough talk about his life. So much of Eva's was still a mystery. "Is anything ye told me about your past true?"

She craned her neck so her green eyes shimmered with the sunlight—pure artistry. "My father is a knight and he is an ambassador abroad."

"Is?" He puzzled. "Ye mean to say he's still alive?"

Her gaze drifted down as if William's simple question troubled her. "Not exactly alive."

"Ye dunna make a lick of sense." He dug in his heels, requesting a trot. Why must she be so baffling when talking about her past? "I'll hear no fabrications. Ye promised to always tell the truth."

"And I have—it's just that you won't listen." She crossed her arms tight against her body. "All right, then. I'll make it easier for you to understand. I can honestly say I have no family—not a single relation living at this point in time."

William let out a labored sigh. If there was one thing he'd change about Eva it would be her cryptic past—or her reluctance to talk about it. But he did believe she had no living kin, else she wouldn't be riding with the likes of him.

Moreover, he cared for her deeply, as she did him. She'd asked William to live in the now, and with so much death and war around them, he agreed with her perspective. Their souls craved each other like the flowers of spring needed rain.

He bowed his head and nuzzled into her slender neck. "Ye needn't worry about your care whilst ye're with me. On that ye have my promise."

***

As they rode onto Ellerslie lands, Eva pressed her hands to her abdomen. She'd enjoyed their time alone so much, ending it made her stomach clench. Who knew when she'd have William to herself again and if they'd ever be able to speak so candidly?

Men sprawled everywhere around the barn and house.

"It looks like Father Blair beat us here," she said.

"'Tis a good thing. We'll take our nooning and then be off."

"How can your mother feed all these people?"

"With luck Blair has already set meat to turning on a spit."

"He's a good man." *Though he doesn't trust me.*

William purred against her ear. "None better."

Robbie and Lachlan raced toward them, shoving each other as if there were a prize at the finish line. But Robert Boyd arrived a step ahead of the other orphan. "Where have ye been? Ye had a good head start and we were forced to ride at a snail's pace to allow for the footmen."

A hundred excuses warred in Eva's head, but William pulled his mount to a stop and tossed Robbie the reins. "Feed and water my horse, then go saddle an old gelding for Miss Eva. Tell the troops not to make themselves comfortable, we'll be setting out right after we've et."

Robbie threw back his shoulders, hanging on William's every word. "Yes, sir."

After they dismounted, the lad led the horse away with Lachlan on his heels.

Eva nudged William with her elbow. "You didn't answer his question."

"'Twas none of his affair. Had he asked again I would have given him a firm rap to the side of his head."

"You're serious? Jeez, if you did that where I come from, you'd be arrested for child abuse."

He stopped. "Edinburgh grows odder and odder to hear ye tell tale of it."

She raised her chin and eyed him. Things would be a lot easier if he'd have believed her story in the first place. How much more convincing could she have been? Even the picture of his seal hadn't swayed his stubbornness. But

William's stern stare told her it wasn't wise to argue. She huffed. "Never mind."

He chuckled. "Come, I'll wager my mother will pour us a tankard of warm cider."

Before they reached the door, Wynda opened it wide with a gaping grin. "Master Willy, ye've arrived, and with Miss Eva." She opened her arms and gave him a warm hug, then turned to Eva. "I'm surprised to see ye, lass."

Her mouth twisted. "I'm a bit surprised to still be here."

Wynda led them into the cottage. Wearing black from head to toe, William's mother stood. But her mourning clothes did not prevent her from smiling. "'Tis good to see ye, son."

He pulled her into his embrace. "How are ye, Ma?"

"Well enough." She held him at arm's length. "News has come telling of your rebellion. Is this true?"

"Aye, mother. Ye ken it is." He kissed the top of her head.

"But why do ye have to be in the center of it?" She clutched her hand over her heart. "I've just lost a husband and I'm not ready to lose a son."

"We've been over this afore. I'll not stop until we drive Longshanks out of Scotland. If I tucked my tail now, I would dishonor Da's memory." He gestured toward Eva. "Do ye remember Miss Eva MacKay?"

"Aye, though we were not properly introduced the last time she was here." Mrs. Wallace stepped forward and grasped Eva's hand. "'Tis lovely to make your acquaintance."

"Miss Eva is the daughter of a knight," said Wynda.

"Truly?" Mrs. Wallace regarded her with intelligence reflected in her careworn eyes.

Eva smiled. "Yes ma'am."

"And where do ye hail from?"

"Edinburgh, and abroad," William answered, moving toward the table. "Do ye have a cup of cider for us? The trail gives a man a thirst."

Mrs. Wallace motioned to Wynda, then took a seat on the bench across from them. "And I reckon ye're not intending to stay?"

William helped Eva to sit on the end, then climbed over and sat beside her. "Aye. We'll take our nooning and then head to Renfrew."

Eva eyed a pewter plate of oatcakes sitting in the middle of the table.

Mrs. Wallace picked up the cakes and offered them to her. "Pray tell me, why is the daughter of a knight riding with my son?"

"Um…" Eva accepted the treat and clipped a bit with her teeth. "I'm his chronicler."

William snatched two oatcakes from the plate. "Bah. She's a seer and learning to be a healer under Brother Bartholomew's tutelage."

Eva shoved some more of the bland biscuit in her mouth. Of course she should have thought before she said anything. As a woman, a seer and healer made far more sense than a chronicler.

Mrs. Wallace arched an eyebrow and appraised Eva's gown. "Have ye nothing nicer to wear? Something more in line with your station?"

Wynda set three steaming tankards on the table. "Och, Willy, ye should have taken Miss Eva to a tailor."

William passed a tankard to Eva, then took one for himself. "There hasna been time."

Selecting an oatcake for herself, Mrs. Wallace pursed her lips. "If ye're heading to Renfrew, ye'll not want to be presented to his lordship in a servant's gown."

Eva glanced down at the gown she'd been wearing for nearly a month now. Though back home she dressed well, she hadn't thought much about the style of her gown, and no one at the cave had commented one way or the other. As far as she knew, she blended in well enough—way better than when she'd arrived in her jeans.

William grumbled under his breath. "I'll see to it Miss Eva sees a tailor once we reach Renfrew afore she meets the High Steward." He turned his lips to her ear. "That ought to keep ye out of trouble whilst I meet with his lordship."

Eva coughed into her cup, peeking up to see if Mrs. Wallace had caught William's whisper. The woman frowned as Wynda placed trenchers of cold meat and bread in front of them. "What business have ye with Lord Stewart?"

"We need troops." William broke the bread in half. "I've a plan to drive the English garrisons out of Scotland's villages one by one and John Stewart has the ear of the nobles. With him behind me, I'll be able to grow an army—and feed them as well."

Ma drew her palms to her cheeks. "Ye mean to say ye're taking your feud beyond Ayrshire?"

"I did that when I struck in Lanark."

Eva pointed to William's eating knife. "Can I borrow that?"

"Again?" He grinned at her, then cut a slice of meat and dropped it on her plate.

Mrs. Wallace frowned, then reached across and placed her palm over Eva's hand. "Ye see to it my son doesna forget his ma."

Eva gulped down a bite of cold mutton. No matter how hard she tried, she couldn't smile. The worst of her warring thoughts? She knew far too much about William's future to be able to make any promises to his mother. She turned her hand over and wrapped her fingers around the woman's palm. "Och aye, Mrs. Wallace. One thing is for certain. A man never forgets his mother, especially one who loves her son as much as you."

Chapter Twenty-Three

Thank goodness Robbie had selected an old sorrel gelding for Eva to ride. The horse even had grey peppering his muzzle. Yes, riding double with William had been fun, but they couldn't do it for long. Though Wallace was a hearty warrior, Eva was five-foot-eleven with hips like a female to match. She imagined his thighs grew awfully sore by the end of the day.

Though her nag ambled along at a snail's pace, the last thing Eva could handle was a spirited mount. Horses were so darned enormous and nowhere near as predictable as a car.

When the tower of a church came into view, a commotion rose with the clang of the bells and a blast from a ram's horn. Eva turned to Robbie and Lachlan, still riding double. "Where are we?"

"Kilmarnock." Robbie thumped his chest. "My family lands are here."

She had to bite her tongue. It seemed like eons ago when she'd done some touring before joining the dig team. One of her stops was in Kilmarnock to visit Dean Castle, built on lands Robbie would be granted for his service to Robert the Bruce. In the near future, the lad's holdings would grow exponentially, but she dared not speak of it.

Before they crossed the bridge over the River Irvine, townsfolk came running, flinging fern branches and petals onto the pathway. A chant of "Wallace, Wallace, Wallace!"

rose over the throng. Eva's heart soared. *How unbelievably fantastic to be a part of his rise to fame.*

A man ran in and grasped William's bridle. "Ye're a hero to us all." His grin split his face wide. "We kent ye'd be riding this way. I've been watching out for ye all day."

William glanced at Eva.

She waggled her brows. "They're lining the streets to see you."

He grinned—God, she always had a fit of butterflies when he smiled. "Then let us not disappoint."

Waving and greeting everyone as they continued on, William led the retinue through the city gates and into the town square. He dismounted and handed a boy his reins. "Will ye mind my warhorse, lad?"

The young fellow beamed. "Aye. I'll hold him throughout the eve if ye want me to."

Head and shoulders above the crowd, William marched up the stairs of the stone platform while people reached out to touch him. At the top he turned, raising his hands to request silence. "'Tis good to see my countrymen filled with vitality and hope."

A deafening roar rose. Still mounted, Eva looked at the faces with her mouth agape. The mob was as frenzied as a mosh pit at a rock concert and they all shouted "Wallace" at the top of their lungs. Goosebumps tickled her outer arms.

It took William ages to get them to quiet down enough for him to speak, but he showed no sign of upset. He grinned beneath his auburn beard, nodding at his adoring fans, holding his hands out as if welcoming every one of them. "We have only begun," he finally shouted. "This will be a long road, but we will drive out the oppressor and fight for our freedom!"

As William thrust his fist into the air, the crowd again launched into a boisterous chant, but this time, Wallace quieted them easily by pushing his palms down to request silence. "The English have committed unconscionable crimes against our families—good men, women, and innocent children have perished for no sound reason. And I *refuse*—" He stopped and panned his gaze across the crowd of hopeful faces. "I *refuse* to stand aside and watch England strip away Scotland's liberty."

Another roar filled the square. Eva laughed. William commanded a natural presence with a crowd and they adored him.

He planted his fists on his hips, looking like a born leader. "We will be victorious. Scotland needs every man who can wield a sword, brandish a pike, or shoot arrows." He eyed their faces as if he were intimately speaking to each soul. "And for those of ye who are not able to fight, we need food. Spread the word throughout the kingdom: Feed Scotland's sons and starve the English. As a nation we must join together and stand against Longshanks and his tyranny. Without food they will be weak. Without food they will be unable to fight!"

The uplifting shouts grew deafening. Even Eva's old nag stutter stepped, sending her heart flying to her throat. Relaxing her seat as she'd been taught, she smoothed her hand down the horse's neck. "Easy boy."

William pointed directly into the crowd. "Who among ye is Kilmarnock's crier?"

A man stepped forward with his bonnet in hand. "I am, sir."

"Go forth and spread the word. Scotland's sons and daughters will no longer tolerate the yoke of tyranny. Not for another day!"

The frenzied crowd parted as Wallace descended the stairs.

Tears welled in Eva's eyes. *Wow. They love him.* Undoubtedly, William could win the hearts of a gathering of multitudes.

"Long live the king!" William shouted and boldly strode to his horse. He gave the lad who'd been holding the reins a coin and hopped aboard in one fluid motion.

Eva watched in awe. *Lone Ranger, eat your heart out.*

The retinue marched north in a whirlwind of excitement, picking up countless recruits. Onward they headed to Paisley, where outside the abbey, William and his men were met with the same fervent support. By the time they reached Renfrew, their numbers had tripled.

Riding at a pace to match the foot soldiers, Eva stayed beside William with Robbie and Lachlan right behind. She glanced over her shoulder and chuckled at the sea of men. "I hope Lord Stewart will be able to feed them all."

William gave her a pointed look from beneath his helm. "As do I."

***

The ride to Renfrew sped past quickly, and once inside the city gates, William left Eva with the tailor and made his way to the keep where he requested an audience with Lord Stewart. The valet told him to wait in the hall, but William hadn't a mind to pull up a bench and drum his fingers.

The valet regarded him over his shoulder. "I bid ye to sit and await his lordship's summons."

"Aye?" William asked. "A man could wither away whilst he waits. I'll see him forthwith."

"Oh no." The valet shook his head, though he continued up the stairwell. "'Tis improper to barge into his lordship's apartments demanding to see him."

"I'll take my chances."

At the landing, the valet held up his palm and frowned. "Wait here."

William stopped for a moment just to appease the beetle-eyed weasel. Then he watched the man open the same solar door William had entered sennights ago.

"M'lord, William Wallace has requested an audience."

William strode forward and planted his palm against the door. "We've near enough to a thousand mouths to feed, though it could be closer to fifteen hundred. Men are flocking to the rebellion by hill and glen."

"Sir!" the valet admonished.

Lord Stewart dropped his parchment on the table and stood. "That many?"

William pushed into the solar, grinning like a lad. "Och, aye."

The valet wrung his hands. "I shall summon the guard at once for this impertinence."

"Nay," Lord Stewart dismissed the little man with a flick of his wrist. "Go to the kitchens and tell them to start cooking."

William pulled out a chair and sat. "Ayr was a massacre."

Lord Stewart also took his seat, a sharp arch of his brow the only indication that William's brash behavior annoyed him. "From the report I received, Ayr was exactly what we needed on the heels of Lanark."

"I agree, but Sir Douglas is raving mad. His tactics are as reprehensible as Longshanks'."

"I don't disagree there."

"I dunna trust him. He undermined me and turned backstabber. He's out for his own glory, that one."

"What man isna?"

"Ye're serious? I, for one, put the needs of Scotland above my own. I expect everyone under me to do the same." William pounded his fist on the table. "Douglas is a cold-blooded killer. After watching him pillage in Ayr, I reckon the man is excited more by the opportunity to murder—and not only the English. He'd kill his own kin if he didna need their muscle behind him."

Lord Stewart reached for a flagon and poured two tots of whisky. "As ye said, he has good men supporting him—cavalry."

"Aye, but if the Douglas willna adhere to the plan, his men are worthless to me." William picked up the cup and drank. "The people of Scotland are ready for battle. I saw it on their faces as we traveled from Kilmarnock to Renfrew today. I canna risk losing momentum because of a backstabber."

"I've heard report of the same." Lord Stewart narrowed his gaze. "If I agree to have a word with Sir Douglas, where will ye next strike? With Murray growing stronger in the north ye must take the south."

William thumped his chest. "Then we should march on Stirling."

"Not yet. With so many new recruits, ye couldn't possibly be ready to take on Edward's forces in Stirling—'tis the heartbeat of the English garrison. No, no. We can ill afford a misstep." Lord Stewart stroked his fingers down his long, pointed beard. "I've received word of excessive brutality inflicted by Sir Ormsby at Moot Castle in Scone. His atrocities mirror those of Heselrig. Ridding Scotland of yet another of Edward's high-ranking executioners will further promote the cause of the Patriotic Party."

Narrowing his eyes, William leaned back in his chair. "Patriotic Party?"

Lord Stewart waved a dismissive had through the air. "A term Bishop Wishart and I agreed to with a few other like-minded nobles."

"Well, I suppose 'tis good to hear. If ye could unite the nobles, ye'd make my job all the more painless." Though William saw this as good news, his hackles stood on end. He swiped his hand across the back of his neck, brushing away the warning.

"Right ye are." Lord Stewart raised his cup. "To Scone?"

"Agreed." William drained the rest of his tot and set the cup on the table. "We'll remain here for a fortnight. That'll give Blair a chance to train the new men."

"Here?" Lord Stewart's eyes bugged out—not a becoming expression for the man.

Pushing back the chair, William rose. "Aye, and as ye're lord and master, I'll expect ye to feed us."

His lordship's noble chin ticked up. "Ye are quite sure of yourself for a commoner."

"Possibly. But unlike others, I'll not rest until His Grace, John Balliol, is returned to the throne. Only then will I settle and farm the land as my father did. Then I'll be more than content to sit back whilst the Scottish aristocracy quibbles about their borders. Until that day, I'll continue to lead this rebellion, unless a man who can best me with a sword earns the right to take my place."

***

When William left Eva with the tailor with orders to create a wardrobe fitting for a knight's daughter, she'd hoped she would end up with another complete change of clothes. She'd even offered to pay with her gold and silver rings, but William would hear none of it.

Mr. Tailor eyed her from head to toe. "Your gown is the most hideous woolen garment I've ever seen in the twenty years of my trade."

Eva could only laugh. The man's gaunt face was entirely serious, but he reminded her of a weathered accountant who wore a visor and crouched over a desk all day. The only thing missing was a monocle or a pair of glasses. She brushed her hands over her dingy skirts. "This *gown* was loaned to me by a Good Samaritan, and I assure you, you don't want to see what I was wearing before that."

"I couldn't agree more." The man frowned and shoved a handful of pins in his mouth.

For the next several hours, Mr. Tailor measured, pinned, cut and stitched all the while grumbling about Eva's ill-fitting and completely unstylish gown.

When he finally allowed her to sit, to her astonishment, the speed at which the man's fingers worked the burgundy damask was practically as fast as her grandmother's Singer sewing machine. Eva leaned forward and studied his impeccable craftsmanship.

"Must ye crowd me?" he asked.

She straightened. "Sorry, but your stitches are so perfect, they look like they could have been sewn by a machine."

"Och. That will be the day." He shook his head. "Young people come up with the most harebrained ideas."

Eva covered her mouth with her palm. If only he knew what a treasured skill he had.

He flicked his wrist her way. "Remove that godawful veil. I've a snood made of gold thread to match this fabric. It'll suit your coloring nicely."

Before she thought, she pulled off the cord and veil and scrubbed her knuckles through her hair. Jeez, it always felt good to take off her veil.

The old man's fingers stopped. "God on the cross, what happened to your hair?"

Eva cringed. *Might as well use the same old story*. "Lost it during the battle of Dunbar."

He clapped a hand to his chest. "Glory be, ye dunna mean to say ye survived that massacre."

Her gaze dropped to her hands as her eyes rimmed with tears. She may not have been in Dunbar, but she'd been through enough strife to warrant his sympathy. With a deep inhale, she looked up. "Will I be able to wear that tonight? I cannot be seen by his lordship wearing this old rag."

"Not to worry, lass. I'll set ye to rights." Somehow, people always grew nicer after they learned about her past—either factual or fabricated. If only she could just tell everyone the truth.

He glanced down and sucked in a gasp. "What is that ye have on your feet?"

Eva tapped her toes together. "They're hiking boots."

"While I'm finishing this, ye'd best go next door to the cobbler and put in an order for a pair of proper shoes like those on my shelf." He pointed over his shoulder to a pair of dainty slippers that looked more like they belonged in a production of Swan Lake.

Eva tucked her feet beneath her wooden chair. "These boots serve me well, thank you."

Mr. Tailor grumbled under his breath and continued to furiously whip stitches.

Training her gaze upward, she spotted a man's leather hip purse hanging above the slippers. "Would you be able to make something for William?"

"Of course, as long as ye dunna need it today."

"I've a canister of salt. Would that pay for a leather purse?"

He looked up. "How much salt?"

Eva squinted. "A pound."

"That is quite a lot."

"Aye."

He whipped a half-dozen more stitches. "Well then, I'll throw in a linen shift for ye as well."

She clapped her hands. "Oh my, that would be wonderful. Thank you."

When Eva left the man's shop, she wore a new burgundy damask gown complete with matching veil and snood. He'd even had a polished copper mirror for her to assess his handiwork. Indeed, she looked quite the medieval lady. She'd also requested he craft at least one kirtle for riding that didn't drag on the ground when she walked. How women in this century kept their dresses from caking with mud or horse manure, Eva couldn't surmise.

As she bid the tailor good day, she felt sort of like she'd spent the day in an upmarket dress shop, being primed and measured for her every whim. And it thrilled her to no end to be able to have a change of clothes. *How such small things seem huge when forced to go without.*

Across the courtyard, William faced her. Eva startled. After spending the entire day with a tailor a good head shorter, William Wallace took her breath away. Not only was his hair combed away from his face, he wore a shiny, black leather jerkin over a pair of black chausses that made him look as devilish as a pirate.

"My, you are a handsome man, William Wallace." She strode up to him and waggled her shoulders in tandem with her eyebrows. "Were you able to speak with Lord Stewart?"

"Aye, half a day ago. What have ye been up to in there, weaving the cloth?"

She chuckled. "Indeed. I never thought that sadist tailor would unpin me."

He stepped back and raked his gaze from her head to toe. "Well, if this is the result of his efforts, I heartily approve."

She held out the skirt. "You mean this old thing?"

His mouth twisted.

Rapping him on the arm she simpered, "He insisted I have a fine damask gown in line with my station. When I told him I needed something practical for riding a horse, I thought he might whip me with his tape measure."

"I dunna see why. My mother wears day gowns and her father was a knight."

"Honestly? You didn't tell me that." Eva blinked. "Anyway, he found a length of blue wool for the kirtle. He's also planning to make a mantle and I'll be ever so grateful for a new shift."

William grasped her elbow and led her toward the keep. "Sounds as if he'll have ye clothed right proper."

"Yes, and thank you." She strolled beside him. "At least stays aren't in fashion yet. I'd die if I had to wear one of those contraptions every day."

"Stays?"

"Oh yes, at first they had wooden slats, and later whale bones and women cinched them around their ribs and waist to make them look smaller." Eva shuddered. "They're torture devices that make it hard to breathe."

William looked to the skies. "That seems complete gibberish to me. I canna see any woman putting up with torture simply to look bonny."

Eva stopped gave him an incredulous stare. "You didn't have any sisters did you?"

"Thank the good Lord for such mercies."

She held up a finger. "Never underestimate how much a woman will be willing to suffer to be beautiful."

He blessed her with a knee-melting grin. "Well, ye're the bonniest lassie I've ever seen, and it doesna look as if ye're suffering overmuch."

"Thank you, and you should smile more. It makes butterflies flit around in my stomach."

He gave her a squeeze. "'Tis good to hear I'm not the only one around these parts with those fluffy-feathered vermin ticking my insides."

Giggling, Eva slipped her fingers over her mouth. William hadn't complimented her often. Their attraction had been powerful—carnal, but he kept his opinions to himself. She liked that she had a visceral effect on him and he thought her beautiful, but it made her nervous at the same time.

He is an attractive man, so why should I be uptight? She bit her nail and regarded him. Yes indeed, he could charm every maiden's heart in the county. *Okay, I'm not bothered at all.*

Eva gestured toward the keep. "I hope you are taking me to a place where there's food, because I'm starving."

"Ye're in luck. Lord Stewart has invited us to dine at the high table this eve."

"Us?"

"I told him ye were under my protection."

Eva's stomach flipped. "You mean a feast in a great hall with the High Steward of Scotland?" *If only I had a video camera. Linsey and Chrissy would totally die from envy.*

"I thought ye'd be pleased."

Her mind snapped to her bag. "Do I have time to freshen up?"

"Ye spent the entire day with the tailor, how much more primping do ye need?"

"I could use a bit of makeup on my face—perhaps some rouge?"

"What the hell is that?" He pinched her cheeks. "Ye look fine."

"Right." He could repeat that a hundred times and she wouldn't believe him. "Red eyelashes and all."

William's tongue tapped his top lip and his eyelids dipped. "The red adds to your character."

"'Tis a very good thing you continually make those butterflies squirm or else I'd not believe you one bit." She gestured toward the keep. "Lead on, Mr. Wallace. After all, it's not often a girl has the opportunity to meet the High Steward of Scotland and dine at the high table in the year of our Lord twelve ninety-seven." The way her insides bubbled, she felt as if she'd imbibed in a glass of wine—though she was stone cold sober.

Chapter Twenty-Four

Eva had toured the great hall at Edinburgh Castle when she visited with her family before they moved to America. Even at the age of fifteen, the enormity of the hall had impressed her. Though it had appeared more like a museum with swords and poleaxes on display, as well as coats of armor adorning either side of the marble hearth. She chuckled. The very great hall she'd seen at Edinburgh Castle hadn't even been built yet—not for another two hundred years or so, if her memory served her correctly.

This evening when she stepped into the hall of James Stewart, High Steward of Scotland, she reached down and pinched her thigh through her skirts just to ensure she was lucid. Tables and benches filled the room, packed full of people. Overpowering smells of humanity mixed with welcomed aromas of baking bread and roasting meat. The men outnumbered the women about five to one, which made sense, given Lord Stewart's large army.

Eva leaned into William. "Where are your men eating?"

"They've fashioned a spit and encampment just beyond the Renfrew walls."

"So it's just us receiving the royal treatment this eve?"

"Aye."

"No wonder you look so dashing."

William grinned and led her toward the dais.

Covered with rich tapestries, the walls absorbed some of the sound echoing off the stone floor. Above, candelabras supported countless candles, all flickering in harmony. As they approached the dais, the sound of minstrels playing a flute and lute up on the gallery became clearer.

Now this is more in line with what I imagined living in the thirteenth century would be like.

Ahead on the dais, the lord and lady were unmistakable. They sat in the center of the table as they presided over the throng, sipping from golden goblets and dressed in rich velvets in line with their station.

Eva looked to the side. The people sitting in the main part of the hall drank from pewter tankards. And the further away from the dais they sat, the more bedraggled their appearance. Truly, the scene established the social pecking order of the Middle Ages. But the disparity between classes did nothing to quell the exuberance in the hall as these medieval folk made merry, laughing and talking above each other. Eva couldn't make out a word.

Her palms began to perspire as William led her up the three steps to the dais. When he bowed, she dipped into a curtsey, hoping she didn't appear too awkward.

"Lord and Lady Stewart, may I introduce Miss Eva MacKay. She has fallen victim to King Edward's severity as have so many in these trying times," William said, obviously curbing his passionate dislike for England's king.

Lord Stewart spread his palms before him. "Welcome, Miss Eva. It is our pleasure to have ye share our table this eve."

"Thank you." She again curtseyed, though not as deeply this time.

"James tells me you are the daughter of a knight," said Lady Stewart. "Pray what was he called?"

Eva gulped and glanced up at William who arched his eyebrow, giving her no encouragement whatsoever. "Sir David MacKay," she said with conviction.

Lord Stewart stroked his pointed beard. "I do not recall a knight named thus."

She hated being called to the carpet. *Dammit.* "Do you know every knight dispatched to the Holy Land, m'lord?"

He used his pinky finger to dab the whiskers at the corner of his mouth. "Most, I'd say."

Shrugging her shoulders, Eva feigned a dismayed grimace. "Then I have no answer for your lack of recall." *Perhaps I should have told William my father was a Norwegian knight. Had I only the forethought. But then again, that would have been a lie and I hate lies.*

Lady Stewart reached for her goblet, jostling the silk wimple that covered every last strand of her hair. "I recall a knight named MacKay. Hmm. Ever so long ago."

"Then if ye recall him, it must be thus." Lord Stewart patted his wife's hand. "Regardless, Miss Eva, if ye are an ally to Mr. Wallace, then I welcome ye to my table."

Eva bowed her head. "Most gracious of your lordship."

William led her to a pair of seats toward the far end of the table. As soon as they sat, a servant placed goblets of wine in front of them. Everything was so new, but archaic. Eva ran her finger around her empty pewter plate, thinking how excited the dig team would be to unearth one of them.

Lord Stewart clapped his hands. "Let the feast begin."

At once, servants laden with trays of food paraded through great double doors and up to the dais. The smells made Eva's mouth water. She leaned aside while a servant placed a trencher of roasted meat in front of her—three whole chickens, two legs of lamb and another fowl. She looked up at the man. "Is that duck?"

"Nay, 'tis swan."

Eva looked at William and cringed. "How can anyone eat a swan?" she whispered under her breath.

He reached out with his eating knife and sliced off a piece. "Eat it. 'Tis tasty."

She should have kept her mouth shut, but she clipped off a piece with her teeth and swirled it in her mouth. After all, as the daughter of an ambassador, her parents served all manner of food depending on the guests. Eva thought she was rather diverse because she'd eaten emu—a bird no one from Scotland had even seen yet. When hit with a combination of mutton and fish, she swallowed the swan meat and washed it down with her wine.

"Did ye like it?" William asked.

Eva pointed to the tray. "I think I'd prefer a bit of chicken, thank you."

Chuckling, William held up an eating knife with a bone handle, sheathed in an ornately hammered leather scabbard. "This is for ye. I'm tired of lending ye mine."

"For me?"

He smiled as if very pleased. "Aye."

Accepting the gift, she turned it over in her palm. "Oh my, this is exquisite." Without a moment's hesitation, she pulled out the blade and examined it. Oddly, the sharpened steel gave her no tremors at all, and the handle molded to her fingers like an expensive steak knife. *Perhaps being surrounded by knives is the therapy I needed after all.* "Thank—" Her voice caught and she drew in a breath. "Thank you. I shall cherish it."

William beamed. "I thought ye'd like it." The candlelight flickered in his eyes and he stared at her as if there were no other people surrounding them.

She liked it when he looked at her like that. Probably liked it too much. Glancing down, Eva rolled the blade between her fingertips. "This is almost too nice to use for eating."

William reached for a loaf of bread and broke it. "What else would ye do with a wee blade such as that?"

"Good point. I guess I have no china cabinet in which to display it." She plucked a portion of bread from his grasp with the knife. "You were very thoughtful to think of me. I don't know how to thank you for all you've done—new clothes and now this."

"'Tis nothing." He gave her a wink. "Besides, I couldna let my woman traipse across the country dressed like a serving maid."

Eva's heart caught in her throat. Yes, he just called her his woman, and oh, did she relish the idea. Since arriving in the thirteenth century, she'd mostly been living in a cave. Worries about her attire had been miniscule compared to everything else. But now she would be out in the public, riding with William Wallace and his growing band of rebels. *Please, Lord, do not let me do anything that will send me back. Not now.* She glanced at William. *Not for a very long time.*

Presented with more food than at a presidential banquet, Eva ate until she couldn't swallow another bite. Even the apple tart was delicious.

A servant stopped by her shoulder, holding a ewer. "More wine, miss?"

"No. I've had quite enough, thank you."

William held up his goblet. "I'll have more and her share as well."

"Aren't you gorged to your teeth?" she asked.

"Me?" He took a healthy sip of wine. "Never, and when prosperity presents itself, a man learns to take advantage and store up as much food as possible."

She chuckled. "I wish it worked that way, but I know I'll be hungry come morn."

He poked her waist. "Aye, but if ye had a wee bit of fat on your bones, ye might not fall to hunger sickness so quickly."

Eva folded her hands and nodded. How different the medieval mind when it came to food—and health. Though without a grocery store nearby, she might do well to gorge herself at every opportunity.

On the gallery, a drummer and a piper joined the minstrels.

William clapped his hands. "Do ye fancy a dance, Miss Eva?"

"No, no." She shook her palms. "I wouldn't know what to do." *Nothing like the Cupid Shuffle, I'm sure.*

Lord Stewart leaned forward and regarded her. "I would assume a daughter of a knight would be well versed in all manner of dancing."

A Norwegian peasant would have been a preferable occupation for my father. Eva feigned a smile. "It has been ever so long."

Sitting erect, Lady Stewart clapped her hands together. "If not dancing, are you skilled in any of the other finer arts?"

Eva started to shake her head, but William placed his big palm on her shoulder. "Miss Eva sings like a meadowlark."

She kicked him under the table.

He knit his brows and gave her a dark frown.

"Honestly?" Lady Stewart looked like she'd just slipped a Godiva Chocolate in her mouth. "You must sing for us."

Leaning toward William's ear, Eva considered kicking him a lot harder. "The minstrels won't know my song."

"Please do entertain my guests," Lord Stewart said, gesturing toward the center of the dais.

William squeezed her arm. "Ye cannot refuse," he whispered.

Eva stood, giving a timid wave to the minstrels. "I'll be but a moment."

They bowed.

She gagged like her mouth had suddenly filled with cotton. There was no use trying to give medieval musicians a key. She'd just sing *You Raise Me Up* and slink back to her chair. Hopefully the song would buy her the pardon she needed to avoid dances with intricate steps she'd never seen before.

***

William sat back and closed his eyes. He could listen to Eva sing all night. Once she opened her mouth, the entire hall fell silent, and now her voice rang out even clearer than it had in the cave.

If only he'd met her at a different time—a time when he could make a firm commitment and pledge his love. True, the lass continued to be a quandary, insisting on traveling with him. He should ask Lady Stewart if she needed a lady's maid, though Eva had repeated she had no interest in staying behind.

She was so different, so independent, yet needy in some ways. She was intelligent, yet lacked sensibility when it came to the most elemental of practicalities.

By her education and manners, she obviously grew up in a knight's home. But she cannot ride a horse, and claims that she does not dance—that is truly puzzling. She writes endlessly, though her penmanship is quadratic and full of words I can only surmise as Pagan. For all that is holy, I dare not let Blair lay eyes on any of her writings. His distrust of the lass would be compounded tenfold.

William opened his eyes and watched her while his heart swelled. A woman any man would be proud to have on his arm, he'd put her oddities out of his mind and simply accept her. She'd said more than once she wanted nothing from him that he couldn't give. For a rebel, Eva MacKay made an ideal companion.

But why do I feel guilty?

He had no answers for his internal strife, but deigned to hold on to two things. Eva was welcome to remain beside him as long as she wanted and he would put no harness upon her. William could not pledge marriage and she did not desire such a pledge. Regardless of her mysterious past, he trusted the lass almost as much as he trusted Blair—the only thing that kept him from trusting her fully were those damned trinkets in her satchel and the sorcery she'd shown him. The only option to forget about what he'd seen was to block it from his mind.

But how long will she stay?

William pushed his doubts aside as Eva finished her song to a rousing applause. Bloody oath, the woman amazed him.

Lord Stewart clapped louder than anyone in the hall. "My word, William, ye were not jesting when ye said she could sing."

He bowed his head in gratitude as Eva returned to her seat. "Well done." He grasped her hand. "Your singing brings me joy."

Smiling, she squeezed his fingers. "Thank you."

The drum rasped from the gallery and William pulled Eva to a stand. "But now we must dance."

Shaking her head she gasped. "I don't know how," she groused in a strained whisper.

Lord Stewart clapped his hands. "What's this ye say? A knight's daughter truly does not know how to dance? Preposterous."

William pulled her behind him. "Miss Eva—"

"Apologies my lord." She twisted her wrist from his grasp and faced his lordship. "I am able to dance, 'tis just I'm afraid I have not been taught the local dances. My father took me away from Scotland at a very young age."

"Most intriguing." Lord Stewart twirled his finger around the point of his beard and looked to his wife. "A talented vocalist who can also show us new dances from the Holy Land."

William closed his eyes and shook his head. He shouldn't have pushed her.

"Perhaps you should join a traveling band of minstrels, Miss Eva," said Lady Stewart, fanning herself. "What do you call your form of dancing?"

"Um." Eva's cheeks turned as red as the color of her gown. "A waltz."

"Waltz? Truly?" questioned her ladyship. "That sounds so inexplicably foreign. By all means, do give us a demonstration. I should like to see how people dance in other parts of Christendom."

"Yes, my lady." Eva curtseyed and grasped William's hand. "But I'll need a partner."

"Och, this time I dunna ken the steps." He tugged his hand away.

Lord Stewart chuckled. "Wallace, a warrior such as ye should not be afraid of anything."

William's brows pinched. "I didna say a word about being afraid."

"Then it is settled." Eva looked up to the minstrels on the gallery. "Can you play a tune in three-three time?"

The flutist looked at her like she was daft. "Pardon?"

"One, two, three." She swayed and rose up on her toes. "One, two three. One, two three. Preferably with a strong downbeat on one."

The musicians leaned their heads together and mumbled. Finally the flutist rolled his hand through the air. "Verra well."

Eva grinned. "Come, William, you wanted to dance."

He ground his back molars and allowed her to pull him to the floor. "What the bloody hell are ye on about?"

"Just count and you'll be fine." She was all too chipper when she placed one hand on his waist and held his left out to the side.

"Touching?" he grumbled. "This feels most awkward."

"Oh?" She smiled as if she were enjoying his discomfort. "A bit like I felt when you were planning to pull me into a medieval line dance."

"A country dance, mind ye. Something with which everyone in Christendom is familiar."

"I'll have to keep that in mind."

The minstrels started, and Eva pulled him side to side. "One, two, three. One two, three. Down, up, up. Down, up, up." She smiled like she'd just had a taste of plum tart. "Good. See, it is easy."

William tried not to trip. "Mayhap for ye."

"Now let's waltz in a circle."

"What?" Before he could stop her, she led him down, up, up-ing in two complete circles.

"And now we go around the room." She headed off as if she were the Queen of Sheba.

"Och, aye?" he growled, stumbling over his feet. "When ye least expect it, I'll pay ye back for this."

She chuckled. "Sounds like a promise."

"'Tis a bloody oath."

But by the time the music ended, William's feet had managed to come up to tempo. Though this was the most confounding dance he'd ever attempted.

Eva dipped into a deep curtsey. "Thank you, Mr. Wallace."

He offered a stiff bow. "Remind me not to dance with ye again."

The crowd's applause was slow to come. On the dais, their lordships were staring with open mouths.

Eva leaned into William's shoulder. "It appears waltzing will not become popular in Scotland for some time."

Chapter Twenty-Five

With Lord Stewart providing the food, William was able to spend more time training his new recruits—at least those who'd shown up with a weapon and armor. Blair was in charge of sending the outcasts home—those who had only arrived in hopes to be fed. God bless it, the day prior, William had watched Blair turn away a blind man and another with a peg leg. Next thing the lepers would be coming to fight. William didn't even want to think about how to quarantine the infirmed—though mayhap a mob of lepers would instill enough fear among the English ranks that they'd all turn tail and go home.

William assessed a new recruit who brandished a two-handed sword like it was a dagger. "If ye're planning to hold your blade like a lassie, I may as well slit your throat now and be done with it."

The young pup lowered his weapon and snorted. "I ken how to fight as well as the next man."

"Och aye?" William strode toward the braggart, watching him out of the corner of his eye. When near enough, he clamped his fingers around the man's wrist. With a sharp twist, he disarmed him.

"Bloody hell." The recruit looked at his hand with disbelief.

"Your weapon's too heavy to wield with only one hand." William jutted his face down to the man's to ensure he had his attention. "If ye're hell bent on joining the rebellion, ye'll do as I say, else I'll have Father Blair give ye a blessing and send ye on your way."

The lad hung his head. "Apologies, sir."

That was better. William motioned to the fella's sparring partner. "Go again."

As the pair faced off, Bishop Wishart lumbered around the corner of the bailey. "William," he called. "Would ye walk with me?"

Wallace bowed. "Indeed, your Worship."

The bishop pointed his staff toward the trees. "Let us take a turn along the burn, away from prying ears."

"Is something bothering ye, m'lord?"

"I am a vassal of God." He chuckled. "There is always trouble causing me grave concern."

William knew better than to press the holy man before they reached the soft babbling of the burn, so he opted for pleasantries first. "How are the lads?"

"You mean my *nephews*?"

William cringed. He deeply respected Robert Wishart, but his indiscretions with his leman were no secret. The lads were his sons, regardless. "Aye." William continued along the stony path. "'Tis why I said the lads."

"Ah. They are well enough—hidden at my manor in Ancrum." The bishop smiled. "Paden is now four and ten."

"Almost a man," William said. "What are his aspirations?"

"The boy likes music." Wishart sighed. "I'm afraid he won't make much of a warrior."

"Och, with a bit of training with Brother MacRae in Dundee, he ought to come good."

The bishop shook his head. "Ye ken as well as I God makes warriors. A man must be born with the heart of a lion—like ye, Willy. Another man of the same size wouldna be half as effective if he didna have your heart."

"I suppose I've seen it in my ranks as well. There are men I choose to be on my flank because I ken they'll stand and fight until they draw their last breath." Nearing the burn, William turned the discussion to more pressing matters. "'Tis good to see ye have the ear of The High Steward."

"The time for action is nigh." Wishart stretched his arms out from the long sleeves of his vestments and clasped his hands. "There are a great many nobles who have come to me and voiced their disapproval of Edward's tactics."

"Disapproval? I'd say ye used too soft a word. Outrage is the first that comes to mind."

"Aye, Willy." The bishop patted William's shoulder. "'Tis the lion's heart from which you speak, but the nobles must tread verra, verra carefully."

"I ken, though I'd prefer to see a united Scotland."

"Perhaps we will soon."

"Who are those who have come to ye?" William needed to know.

The bishop peered left then right. "'Tis best if I didna say."

Wallace's gut twisted. "Och aye? Ye asked me to lead the rebellion, but canna tell me who is for and against?"

Wishart licked his lips. "Ye ken as well as I, with lands on either side of the border, 'tis a verra dangerous path we walk."

"I grow weary of hearing about men who put their holdings before king and country. Who?" William demanded. "I ken Douglas. Bruce? Comyn? Eglington?"

"Those are all names with which I am familiar." Bishop Wishart swiped his hand across his wet lips, his movements stilted, nervous.

"Aye, and ye're talking out both sides of your mouth, with all due respect." William would be made a fool by no man. "I'll assume that's a yea to all parties I named." He kicked a stone into the burn. "United, we'd be strong enough to invade England, march all the way to London and free our king."

Wishart expressed his dissention with a tsk of his tongue. "I've been to the tower. 'Tis the most impenetrable fortress in all of Christendom."

Squeezing his fist so tight, his knuckles cracked, William made a quick decision. "Then we must first drive the English out of Scotland—weaken their forces here."

"Agreed." The bishop stopped and placed his hand on William's shoulder. "And your rise in popularity has been most impressive. Seize this opportunity. Let nothing stand in your way."

"Ye ken, I will." William swallowed. "But above all, I need your support."

"Ye have it. I brought ye out here to affirm that the church is behind your rebellion wholeheartedly. I want ye to drive out the enemy and show no mercy."

"I'm ready to make a stand. But I cannot stress enough that all of Scotland needs to be united behind me in this uprising."

Bishop Wishart firmly patted Wallace's shoulder. "Leave that to me, my son."

"Verra well." William let out a long breath. "I will expect ye to act swiftly. The nobles will pay heed to ye and the High Steward. With God's help we will rid our home of the oppressors afore autumn's end."

"Well said, lad." The bishop turned and started back. "Now let us go see how your new recruits are faring."

***

Oh yes, living the life of an aristocrat in the Middle Ages definitely had its advantages. Eva could sleep as late as she desired in her four poster bed made blissful by a feather mattress, which was exactly what she did this morning. The room served as a perfect example of a medieval bedchamber, with a red canopy above the bed, a window embrasure with furs that could be pulled across the glassless window. And since it was summer, Eva could sit on the bench in the embrasure and write, enjoying both fresh air and natural light.

The most glorious thing of all was privacy. Living in a cave with a mob of rebels for a month sure did reestablish a girl's priorities.

At the moment, she stood beside the hearth and watched the serving boys carry pails of water to fill the enormous oblong tub they'd brought up for her bath. Sarah, Eva's chambermaid oversaw the parade, standing by the door with her hands on her hips. "Mind ye don't splash water on his lordship's floorboards."

Eva liked Sarah and they were close in age. Better yet, she didn't ask many questions and treated Eva like she was royalty. With her own bedchamber equipped with a garderobe and a personal servant, all the food she could eat in the hall, or room service if she asked, it was akin to staying in a five-star hotel in any major city.

Sarah even provided turndown service.

Watching a lad pour in an iron pot of steaming water, Eva couldn't help but question, "What do you do with the water after the bath?"

"Take it out the same way it got in—scoop it out with the buckets, except we toss the water out the window so the lads dunna have to haul it all the way back down the stairwell again." Sarah moved her hands to her hips. "I'm surprised ye need ask, Miss Eva."

"Of course, it was the same in my father's keep." Eva pretended to brush some lint from her shoulder and took a seat in one of the two padded chairs near the hearth. She folded her hands atop the round table. "Is there a bathhouse on the premises?"

"Aye, for the servants, though. His lordship and the family all bathe in that basin right there."

The last lad finished pouring his portion of water and walked out the door.

"Off with ye, now." Sara gestured to the tub. "Can I help ye wash your hair, Miss Eva?"

"Oh no. I can handle it from here."

"Truly?" Sarah wrung her hands. "His lordship and lady make a grand occasion of their baths. We set up a privacy tent around the basin and a board across for food. The minstrels play whilst they have a grand feast and all manner of servants attend them."

Eva chuckled. "I assure you, no such display is necessary for me. I'd simply like to have a good soak and I need no one attending me for that."

The chambermaid curtseyed. "Verra well. I suppose I'll leave ye be, then."

"Thank you, Sarah."

After the chambermaid took her leave, Eva disrobed and stepped into the warm water. Though cooler than if she'd run a bath with a tap, it still caressed her feet with heavenly luxury. She lowered herself in, releasing a long sigh. Ah yes, she could languish there all day.

Allowing the water to buoy her arms, she closed her eyes and gave in to the sensation of weightlessness. If given the choice, Eva could handle being a member of the gentry in the thirteenth century, no question. Her spacious bath was almost as relaxing as a massage. Perhaps this was where she was meant to be. Aside from her parents, she had no real ties to the twenty-first century.

Then her eyes flew open. *I have to go back. In no way do I want to be here in 1305.*

Though it had nothing to do with the temperature of the water, a cold chill coursed over her skin. She sat up and rubbed her outer arms.

Stop it. I'll allow a year and then I'm going back. End of story.

Taking in several consecutive breaths, she closed her eyes again and sought to blank her mind. She focused on her breathing and on the image of the sun radiating from her core to the tips of her limbs, then slid deeper into the welcoming water.

One day at a time, remember? Live for the now.

After washing her hair with real shampoo and languishing in a state of bliss, the door opened and closed. Pulling herself up enough to peer over the basin's edge, Eva chuckled. "How did you know I would be naked and wet?"

William stepped into the chamber, turning up one corner of his mouth. "Mayhap I'm a seer as well."

"I believe you are." She sat up, giving him a peek at her breasts. "Why don't you join me? There's plenty of room."

He reached for his sword belt. "'Tis exactly why I slipped inside."

Nothing could stir Eva's passion like a tall, muscular Scotsman disrobing. Lordy, she could watch him stand before her in the nude for hours. His every movement heightened the flame burning deep inside as if her mind snapped a picture at each angle and pose. After he kicked off his hose, he grasped the edge of the basin, but Eva held up her palm. "Wait."

"Aye?" He looked up with the dark look in his eye she'd grown to crave.

"There's a present for you on the table." She inclined her head.

His gaze shifted. "What? Ye needn't give me anything."

"I know, but I wanted to." She flicked her wrist and watched the defined muscles in his legs flex as he strode across the floor.

"Och," he whispered and reached for the leather purse. He held it closer to the candlelight. "'Tis sturdy."

"I asked the tailor to make it for you." She gestured to the ties. "It goes on your belt."

"Aye lass." He grinned. "'Tis where a man carries his purse."

Eva's heart skipped a beat. She adored his smile. "So you like it? I had a St. Andrew's Cross stamped into it."

He traced his finger over the cross that would one day become the flag of Scotland. "'Tis the most thoughtful gift I've ever received."

She leaned against the edge of the tub and regarded the firm edge of his jaw. *What would William think of a modern Christmas with dozens of presents under the tree?*

"Are ye all right?"

She shook her head. "Never better…Are you coming in now?"

"Aye, lass." Leaning forward, he cupped her chin in his palm and lowered his mouth to hers. His kiss spilled through her soul as if their bond could never be broken.

When William lowered himself into the water, it nearly sloshed over the sides. "Ah," he sighed. "My ma used to fill a wooden tub at the croft." He looked side to side. "It wasn't as large as this, though."

Eva slid forward and straddled him. "The chambermaid says his lordship's whole family can have a merry time in this tub."

He responded with a deep moan and brushed his lips across her mouth. "I rather like it with two."

She held up a bar of rosemary soap that Sarah had given her. "Let me bathe you." Though William had chosen to bed down with his men outside the gates of Renfrew, he'd probably spent more of the wee hours in her chamber than not.

As the lather foamed, Eva swirled her hands over his chest and he leaned back with a satisfied moan. "Lower."

A spike of need shot through her body as she moved her hands down and wrapped her fingers around his manhood. "We must pay special attention to cleansing this."

"Ye do understand me, lass."

She pleasured him with languid strokes, watching his face grow dark and impassioned.

He opened his eyes to half-cast. With a low rumble he lifted her onto his hips. "Take me to heaven, lassie. For no one but ye can cool the fire thrumming in my blood."

Chapter Twenty-Six

With war imminent, the luxury of Renfrew Castle could never last, and deflecting Lady Stewart's questions about Eva's parentage had grown thin. With leather saddlebags filled with her new clothing and two rolls of parchment, she mounted her old gelding and rode out the gates of Renfrew where she crossed the River Clyde with William and his growing ranks of foot soldiers. At least she'd stolen an opportunity to sneak through the keep and snap photos. She patted her satchel with her phone hidden in a secret pocket she'd made. Her pictures would be priceless one day.

Robbie and Lachlan rode in beside her. "I thought ye may have left us," Robbie said.

Lachlan planted a fist on his hip. "Och aye, ye didna come to the camp once."

"I'm sorry." Eva bit her bottom lip. "I should have been more thoughtful."

"Mr. Little fashioned me a longbow." Lachlan held up his new weapon with a broad grin stretching his freckled face. "I wanted to show ye how good I shoot."

"How well I shoot," Eva corrected.

"Huh?" The lad scrunched his nose. "They're putting me with the archers."

"Aye, and me with cavalry." Robbie patted his gelding's neck. "This fella is fearless."

Eva made a mental note to again speak to William to ensure the boys stayed far from harm. "I am impressed." She tried to mask her horror. "Do you know how long we expect the march to Scone to be?"

"Three days," Robbie said.

"Good, then you shall have plenty of time to tell me about all that happened at Renfrew." She gave Lachlan a wink. "As well as show me how to shoot arrows." *And I'll have time to talk to William.*

Traveling with an army was slow. Scouts rode ahead to look for ambushes and sentries were sent ahead to ensure there would be enough food. All the while, stragglers joined along the way. And Eva didn't balk when William told her he and his lieutenants had decided they'd only accept men who possessed arms because it did little good to have beggars in their ranks who consumed precious food.

On the second day, they gave Stirling Castle a wide birth, skirting to the north and west. Riding through the edge of a forest, William looked to Eva and pointed upward. "'Tis Abbey Craig. Blair and I hunted there when we were studying at Dunipace."

Eva's gaze trained up the forested cliff. Up there, the Wallace Monument would be built in the nineteenth century. She'd climbed its narrow tower stairs with her classmates in grade six. But it all looked so different in the twenty-first century, Eva didn't recognize a thing.

Her limbs quivered in concert with a horrible tightening in her chest. The reality of 1305 wrapped itself around her throat like a hangman's noose. Her nightmares may have ebbed, but the trepidation creeping up her skin increased her anxiety tenfold.

Eva closed her eyes and willed herself to breathe. *Go on sickly dread. Back to your corner.*

"Are ye unwell?" William asked.

She glanced at his concerned expression and forced a smile. "I'm fine—just had an unpleasant thought haunt me from my past."

"Och, your elusive past, aye?"

She nodded and ran her fingers through her gelding's mane—anything not to look William in the eye. True, this adventure had pulled her away from thinking about Steve and his murder. But now she must keep thoughts of the year 1305 from her mind too. Besides, she doubted the forces behind the medallion would ever allow her to remain in medieval Scotland for eight years.

No, no, no. *One year.*

She must continue to live life one day at a time. Neither the past nor the future existed for Eva.

She clenched her fist around her reins, drilling in the words she must never forget: *there can only be the now.*

***

In the wee hours before dawn, outside the tent the trees of Scone Wood rustled and moaned with the wind. After spending an hour on his knees with psalter in hand, William watched Eva in slumber. Gazing upon her stilled his heart. What on earth had he been thinking leaving her in Fail? Living without the lass was like living without air to breathe.

He placed his palm on Eva's shoulder. "Would ye help me with my hauberk?"

Stirring, she rubbed her eyes. "What time is it?"

He shrugged into his quilted arming doublet and fastened the ties. "Time to ask Sir Ormsby to vacate Scone Castle and head back across the border."

She mumbled something about coffee while she stood and hefted up William's mail armor.

Knee-length with half sleeves, the blasted thing weighed near three stone, and even for Willy it was near impossible to shrug into without help.

Once situated, Eva held up his surcoat with the St. Andrew's Cross emblazoned on the chest. "Remember you promised to keep the lads away from harm."

"Aye. Given the wooden battlements around the city, we aim to attack first with cavalry." Now dressed for battle, he stretched his shoulders back to allow the chain links of his mail to better mold to the quilted arming doublet beneath. "Keep them with ye and set up a makeshift hospital with Brother Bartholomew."

She frowned. "I hope the injuries will be minimal."

"As do I." He grasped her shoulders. "I mean it when I said stay clear of the fighting. If ye want all the gory details, I will relay my account after 'tis safe."

She smoothed her hand down his surcoat as if clearing it of wrinkles. "You needn't worry about me."

"Aye? Well, this would be the first time."

She thwacked him on the shoulder. "I beg your pardon?"

"Think on it, lass." He picked up his helm from the base of their pallet. "Since I rescued your fair arse in Fail, ye've managed to wind up in a world of trouble at every skirmish."

She cringed. "Well, I didn't mean to."

"No one ever means to, but ye sure do have a knack for finding it." He grasped her wrist and pulled her into him. "Come here and kiss me."

He loved how her green eyes grew darker when she pressed her body against his. Eva's tongue moistened her bottom lip as she rose up on her toes. Clasping her face between his palms, William closed his eyes and savored the taste of pure woman. Aye, when he walked out of the tent, he would assume his role of hardened warrior. But having Eva MacKay in his arms helped to remind him that he was also a man with a compassionate heart—a heart he once thought hewn of stone.

With one last kiss, he headed for his horse. The others had begun to rise and prepare their mounts. God willing, this would be a victorious day.

Robbie had William's Galloway saddled and waiting. "Are ye sure ye dunna need me to ride beside ye? My horse is as fast as yours."

William mussed the lad's hair. "I need ye to look after Miss Eva and tend to the fallen."

The lad dropped his arms to his sides. "Again?"

After mounting, William regarded thc lad. "Robert Boyd, I ken ye're the leader of your clan, but that does not allay the fact that ye're still a lad. Once your beard has come in, I'll be more than honored to have ye fight beside me. But until then, 'tis my duty to ensure ye live to lead your people."

"But—"

William sliced his hand through the air. "That's the last I'll hear of it. If I see your bony arse on a horse anywhere near the skirmish, I'll lock ye in the stocks for a week. Ye ken?"

"Och."

William gathered his reins and leaned down to the boy. "Ye ken?"

The lad kicked a rock. "Aye."

"Now off with ye. Go see what ye can do to help Miss Eva and Brother Bartholomew—and take Lachlan with ye." William tapped his heels and trotted to the cavalry men.

"He's with the archers," Robbie yelled.

William looked to the group of men with their bows. They probably would see no action this day and at least an archer wouldn't be in the midst of the fighting. Lachlan stood on the outside of the mob with his bow in hand. William steered his horse toward him until Sir Douglas blocked his path.

"Are ye ready to skewer some English vermin?" Douglas asked from his black steed, caparisoned with the white-and-blue Douglas shield embroidered over the beast's hips.

William reined his mount beside the knight. “Ready to take back Scotland’s lands for Scotland’s people?”

Douglas smirked. “And send Sir Ormsby to an early grave.”

“Aye.”

William turned his attention to the ranks and rode down the line of mounted men. “This day we shall stand against an uninvited trespasser. A man who mistakenly believes himself superior. A man who has committed heinous crimes against our kin.” At the end of the retinue, William drew his sword and turned. Digging in his heels, he demanded a gallop. “We will not stand for another day of tyranny!”

With an uproarious cry, the men followed him. Thundering through the wood and out into the open lea, William and his cavalry raced for the sleeping village of Scone with the Douglas renegades alongside.

From the ramparts, the ram’s horn sounded. Ahead the gates opened and out poured a line of cavalry men all clad in English surcoats depicting the red-and-yellow Ormsby coat of arms.

The wind at his face, William tightened his fist around his hilt and bellowed a battle cry. He raced toward the enemy at breakneck speed. His senses honing, every sound, every blink of the eye, every breath became acute. Even his mount’s hoofbeats thundered like the pounding of a drum. The rumble of the horse’s snorts intensified as the beast took in deep breaths through his enormous nostrils.

From beneath his helm, William stared at the onslaught of mounted English soldiers. He focused on the whites of one opponent’s eyes. The man bared his teeth with a challenging bellow, galloping toward him with his sword held high. At two paces to impact, William chose the point of his target. The man’s exposed neck would be the first place Wallace would strike. Without hesitation, he swung his blade, hacking through the neck sinews of the attacking guard.

The man toppled backward off his horse, but William couldn't stop to watch. Surging forward, he swung his sword, fighting his way to the town gates. The thundering roar of the battle infused him with strength. On and on he fought the onslaught of mounted Ormsby men.

As he neared the gates, out of the corner of William's eye, Sir Douglas and his rebels had also broken through the line of English horse.

"Battering ram!" Wallace shouted.

Thrusting his blade, William dispatched his next opponent, then spun his steed. Eddy Little's archers moved into place while infantry men marched forward. They carried the iron-tipped ram and protected their bodies with targes held over their heads.

A volley of arrows hissed, raining above as the soldiers on the battlements made a feeble attempt to stage their defense.

The battering ram boomed against the gates.

Eddy's archers shot flaming arrows into the wooden fortress. Within two blinks of the eye, fires across the battlements crackled and grew.

Boom. The ram smashed again, this time with a splintering crack. Again and again the ram hit its mark until the heavy gates gave way.

William led the charge through billowing black smoke, straight into the town square. The remaining enemy stood with their weapons above their heads whilst an English cleric pleaded for leniency.

"Blair!" William shouted. "Send them back to England and bid them never return." William dismounted along with his men. He would not attack soldiers who were willing to lay down their weapons. "Only but one will pay for the crimes committed against Scotland. Where is your leader, Sir Ormsby?"

"F-fled," said a brave soldier. "Deserted us in the night."

Dropping to his knees, the friar continued his chant, begging for God to have mercy on their souls.

Sir Douglas spurred his horse forward with an ugly bellow.

William broke into a run. "No!"

With one swipe of his sword, the bloodthirsty knight lopped off the defenseless cleric's head.

Stunned gasps rang out across the courtyard. William's gut roiled. The last thing he wanted was to have the Scots become reputed as murderers of innocents, something of which Sir Douglas couldn't give a rat's arse about.

"Ye bloody bastard." In three strides, William latched onto Sir Douglas's bridle. "There'll be no more killing for the sport of it under my command."

"And who named ye commander of this army?" The knight tried to rein his horse away, but William held fast.

"My charter comes from High Steward of Scotland, James Stewart, and ye'd best not forget it, else your head will be rolling on the cobblestones alongside the friar's."

Douglas scowled. "Ye talk like a milk-livered fool."

"Ye're wrong. Let no man say I raised a hand against the innocent. Send these Englishmen back from whence they came. Furthermore, we will have Scottish born holy men presiding over Scotland's abbey's and churches," William spoke loud enough for everyone to hear, though his gut roiled. To have this victory sullied by Sir Douglas's vulgar brutality left a sour pall hanging over the town.

"My men and I will lead the survivors to the border," Douglas said.

It would be good riddance to have him do so, but Wallace refused to let him go without a warning. "Only if ye can manage it without massacring the lot of them first."

"Ye're a bleeding miserable bellyacher." Douglas pointed to his man-at-arms. "Bind their wrists. We leave at once."

A high-pitched cry came from outside the city gates. By the shudder crawling up William's back, he knew who had uttered it. *Why does that woman find trouble at every turn?* With haste, he ran, finding Eva on her knees, cradling Lachlan. It only took a glimpse to spot Robbie speeding toward them on his horse.

William's stomach dropped to his toes. Eva had asked him to look after two souls and one lay in the grass with an arrow protruding from his chest.

The woman rocked back and forth, her bottom lip trembling with her wails. Looking at her swollen eyes and tears streaming from Eva's eyes, his heart could have stopped beating.

But the boy's face was snow white and his eyes held a vacant stare at the sky.

William looked to Eddy Little. "How many dead?"

"Only three."

"Three with one child's life cut short." William's jaw twitched. "I told ye to watch after the lad."

Eddy's face fell. "I ken."

"Then what happened?"

"Christ, William. If ye didna want anything to go awry, why did ye allow him to carry a bow?"

William pursed his lips to keep them from trembling. Och aye, only one man could be blamed and Wallace clenched his fists against the guilt. The worst part of war was the aftermath. "Three dead? Now tell me how many injured," he groused.

"Lachlan!" Robbie cried, hopping down from his mount.

"He's…" Eva looked at the lad with a tear streaked face. "We've lost him," she whispered.

Robbie stood motionless for a moment, tears dribbling down his cheeks. He wiped his face with both hands, then glared at Wallace. "You made me stay with Brother Bartholomew and Miss Eva, but you let him join the archers.

Now look what happened! I hate you. I'm the one who should have been shot through the heart with an arrow. Not Lachlan. He never did anything to hurt anyone." Robbie dropped to his knees beside Eva. "Why does everyone I love have to die? My ma, Da…and now—" The lad couldn't finish. Curling into a ball over his friend's body, he broke down and wept while the lass pulled him into her arms and cradled the child to her breast.

William's self-loathing sank to new lows. He pointed to a group of men standing by. "Dig the graves. I'll see to it Blair kens he has a funeral mass to chant."

Clenching every muscle in his body, he strode away to the woeful laments of two people he had grown to love. In a heartbeat, William would give his life for either Robbie or Eva. They both had such generous souls. If only he could give his life to bring back that young lad lying in the grass.

Chapter Twenty-Seven

Completely numb, eyes swollen with tears, Eva stood beside William and listened to John Blair's bass voice chant the Latin funeral mass.

I'm a fool.

She'd run away from the tragedy of death only to find it tenfold. No wonder Lachlan wasn't mentioned in the history books. The child hadn't even lived to see adulthood.

Eva held out her trembling palms and stared at her fingers. Only hours ago, Lachlan was alive. And what would have happened if she'd been able to save him? Would she have been sent back to her time, never to return? It didn't matter. If she'd been with the archers, Eva would have tried to save him no matter what.

She clenched her fists and squeezed her eyes shut as tears dribbled down each cheek. *What am I doing here?*

When William placed his hand in the small of her back, Eva tensed. She stepped forward enough to relieve the pressure of his fingers. She didn't want his comfort right now.

Too many conflicting emotions warred inside her. If she continued to stay with William, she would see death—much more unconscionable death. If she chose to leave, she would walk away from the most fascinating experience of her life. But how could she bear to lose people—*children* she cared for? Life was not supposed to be about misery and struggles and death. Life was supposed to be about love, achievement and reward for hard work.

To her left, Robbie sniffed. The lad was hurting even more than Eva. And he had no opportunity to leave this century and travel to a gentler period in time.

She stepped beside him and pulled the boy into her embrace. The lad's body trembled as he drew in a stuttering inhale.

"You're a brave young man, Robbie Boyd. Don't ever let anyone tell you differently," she whispered against his temple. "When you weep for a friend, it shows you have a heart, and as you become a man, you will need compassion—something that is very lacking in these times."

Wallace caught her eye and frowned, his eyes rimmed red as well. Yes, he'd shown compassion and heart, but he could ill afford to mourn his losses—not with the victory won this day. And Eva resented him for it.

After the mass ended, William tugged her hand, but she pulled away and shook her head. "Leave me alone."

He hesitated and stepped toward her, but when Eva crossed her arms and shook her head, he backed away.

She stood by the grave until the crowd of mourners dwindled. Her eyes blurred with tears, she knelt, running her hand over the moist earth. "You have no kin to say goodbye. No one to write your epitaph. But I give you my promise that one day the world will hear about the brave young archer who gave his life at Scone. You will be remembered, Lachlan. I swear it."

Eva scooped a handful of dirt and watched it stream through her fingers. "I couldn't tell you, but I'm not from this time. I live in a world where all children in Scotland go to school and find engaging work, and raise families with no worries about invasion from England or elsewhere."

She wiped her face in the crux of her arm and cleared her throat. "I must admit my world is not entirely safe. My husband was murdered in a subway in New York City." She sucked in a long, shuddering breath. Looking up to the tops of the trees, tears again streamed from her eyes. It took her a minute to find her voice again. "In this century neither New York nor America has been discovered. That won't happen for about another two hundred years."

Eva sighed as a weight lifted from her shoulders. It was as if telling Lachlan's spirit about her secrets lessened the heavy sorrow of losing him. She scooped another handful of dirt and watched it stream through her fingers while she gently sang a verse of *Oh Danny Boy*. As the words, *Oh Danny boy, Oh Danny boy I loved you so* faded with the breeze, a footstep moved behind her.

With a quick inhale, she glanced over her shoulder.

"Ye were married?" William's deep voice was but a whisper.

When Eva blinked, a tear dribbled down her cheek. Oh God, she thought he'd gone with the others. "Yes."

"Why did ye not tell me?"

Still looking down, she shook her head. "I never talk about it." And since she'd arrived, she hadn't thought as much about it either.

He moved closer. "What is this *America* ye spoke of?"

She dabbed her eyes with her sleeve. "Were you listening to me the whole time?"

"Aye, for the most part, I'd reckon." William's weapons jostled as he knelt beside her. How had he kept them quiet while sneaking up behind her?

Eva smoothed her hand over the dirt she'd mussed.

He covered her fingers with his enormous palm. "I want to hear your story, no matter how farfetched."

"But you won't believe me." She met his intense blue-eyed stare. "And I cannot risk losing you."

Lifting Eva's hand, he laced his fingers through hers. "Ye dunna ken how much your words bring joy to my heart, for I cannot fathom losing ye. But tell me true. I promise I'll not judge ye. Not this day."

She took in a deep breath. *He needs to know, even if he turns away*. "My father *is* a knight—knighted by Queen Elizabeth for outstanding service to his country. But he bears no arms—civilians have no need of them in my time." Eva's voice strained and she again wiped her face in the crux of her arm. "Dad's full name is Sir David Archibald MacKay, and as of the year of our Lord two thousand and fifteen, he has been the U.K. Ambassador to the United States of America for twelve years."

"U.K.?" William asked.

The warmth of the medallion against her chest warned her to tread carefully. And right now she couldn't handle being ripped away from William and landing in Walter Tennant's tent. "Let's just say he's Scotland's Ambassador to the US."

A line formed between William's brows. "But what does U.K. stand for?"

She should have known he'd be persistent. "Ah…It's an alliance of nations, sort of like Scotland, Ireland and the Orkneys." Lord help her, she couldn't tell him that eventually England and Scotland would live in harmony. From the increasing heat of the medallion, Eva would be gone before the words formed on her lips.

He nodded his understanding with an arch to his brow.

A relieved breath whistled through Eva's lips. *Thank heavens he didn't ask me to explain more.* "My accent is strange to you, because aside from the seven hundred years between us, I attended school in the United States, or America as my countrymen call it. There I studied at university and became a historical journalist, or chronicler as you would say."

"'Tis an unusual profession for a woman, but not surprising to me, given all the writing ye do." He glanced down and drew crosses in the dirt. "Tell me about your husband."

I've been wrung out like a dishrag today. May as well get it all out. "I…I met Steve while I was studying. He was an attorney—a lawman with a promising career. We dated—"

William gave her a questioning look.

She patted her chest and changed her tack. "He *courted* me until I graduated from university, and then we were married at my parents' church in a city the size of London, called Washington D.C."

His fingers snuck over and smoothed around Eva's knee. "It sounds so strange."

Reassured by his touch, she continued, "What's even stranger is that in my time, the United States is the most powerful country in the world—and in your time it doesn't even exist yet—at least not as a country."

"Ye say in the world, but I say in Christendom. 'Tis another difference between us."

"True." She closed her eyes and willed herself to hold it together. How could she explain a subway? "We have many different methods of transportation—and there's no longer a need for horses."

He snapped his hand away. "No horses?"

"Horses are only used for pleasure and sport. You could have no idea of the technological advances that will occur in the next seven hundred years." He opened his mouth, but Eva held up her hand. "Let me try to explain…In big cities there are trains that transport people for miles very quickly. You can live in Glasgow, for example, and work in Edinburgh and if a person takes the train, he or she can arrive at work less than an hour."

"Fascinating."

"It is, and in New York the underground train is called the subway." She swallowed—she'd already told William what a phone was used for. "Steve called me on the telephone right before he left his office—uh, his place of work—and told me he was taking the subway home. I asked him to take a taxi, which would be safer, but he chuckled and said the train would be faster at that time of night." Eva shook her head and buried her face in her palms.

"God dammit. I should have insisted he take the taxi." With a groan she swiped her hands down her face. "I wish I would have known it was the last time I would ever hear his voice."

William moved closer so their arms touched. "Ye dunna have to tell me what happened if it hurts too much."

"No. You need to hear the rest." *And I need to say it.* Eva tried to think of words William would understand. "He was attacked by outlaws and stabbed in the kidney. By the time the paramedics—sorry—the healers arrived, my husband had bled to death." She pressed her hands against her cheeks and cringed, trying not to cry. "He would have lived if they'd been faster."

William slid his arm around her shoulders and squeezed. "I'm sorry."

"Me too," she squeaked, wiping her nose on the back of her sleeve. "After that, I was completely numb for *months*—lost in my own home. I stayed in my luxury apartment for a year until I couldn't take it anymore. You know? Everywhere I looked something reminded me of him."

"I think I ken what that's like." His hand rubbed her shoulder, offering a world of comfort. "Ye must have loved him verra much."

"Yes. But I had to say goodbye." Eva drew in a stuttered breath. "So, I returned to Scotland and joined an archaeological dig for the summer."

"An archol-olol what?" His quirked expression was priceless.

She let out a laugh—at least it was better than crying. "That must be another recent word. It's where a group of historians get together and dig up ancient artifacts."

William formed an "O" with his lips, as if putting the pieces together. "Where ye dug up my seal—at least the lump of rust ye showed me in your shiny black box…uh…telephone."

"Yes. You remember? I thought you'd blocked the pictures from your mind."

"I tried, but I canna forget." He brushed a lock of hair away from her face. "Ye see me as an ancient?"

"No." She cupped his face with her palm. "I see you as the most amazing man I've ever met."

With a stuttered inhale, he held her gaze for a moment, then rested his forehead against hers. "Ye dunna hate me after what happened this day?"

"I wanted to, but I can't." She blinked back tears. "You have great goodness in your heart, and a vision from which you cannot turn away, no matter what."

"And ye are a mystery to me."

"Do you believe my story?"

William looked to the grave while his Adam's apple bobbed. "I dunna think 'tis a case of belief. 'Tis just difficult to accept or understand." He met her gaze. "There are those who would condemn ye to burn if they kent your secrets."

The idea of burning made sweat spring across Eva's skin with an unwelcome shiver. "That may be what I fear most."

His lashes lowered as he leaned forward and nuzzled against her cheek. "Ye have my sword, m'lady. On that there shall nay be any question."

Eva's heart swelled as he brushed his lips across hers. She slipped her hand to the back of his neck and slowly joined with his mouth. Ever so warm and inviting after a day of victory and devastating sorrow, Eva closed her eyes and allowed him to melt her pain away. Two souls joined together against impossible odds. God, this was the most heartrending experience of her entire existence.

Holding on for dear life, they shared a moment of intimate peacefulness.

"Do you ever wonder why you were chosen to be Scotland's rebel?" Eva asked.

"Nay. Besides the job didna choose me so much as I chose it." William splayed his fingers and looked at his palms. "God made me strong for a reason. 'Tis written that 'tis a sin to ignore your gifts. I would be no kind of man if I didna stand and fight."

Eva reached in and threaded her fingers through his. "Aye, but you run into adversity where most others choose to flee."

"I make a stand where it needs to be made." His shoulders slumped. "Only…"

Releasing her grasp, she ran massaging fingers over his back. "Is something troubling you?"

"I look at this young lad's grave and it makes me doubt everything I've done."

Moving behind him, she kneaded the solid knots between his shoulders. "This was both a great and terrible day. But while we honor the dead, you must also build upon your success."

William shook his head. "It seems when I take a step forward, I'm always met with a step back in this miserable rebellion. I think I'm doing the right things and then something happens to quell my progress."

"But you've come so far, even since I arrived." She kneaded harder. "News of the uprising has spread and people are flocking to you."

"Aye, but if I had the gentry behind me, we would be all the more strong. I ken in my heart we would send Edward back to England never to return. If only all of Scotland could stand together."

"But the nobles are all watching out for themselves. And there are those who *want* English rule. This is why you alone have been chosen."

"Unfortunately ye are right." He stretched his spine. "With great clans like Bruce and Comyn—even the Stewart with lands on the English side of the border, alliances are oft misplaced, and their armies follow their leaders which leaves my rebels lacking in talent."

"Have you thought to seek help from the north?" Though she knew the answer, the decision had to comc from William. "What about Sir Andrew Murray?"

"I must write to him."

"He's proved he's committed to ridding Scotland of Edward's tyranny. And his father is a member of the gentry. Joining with him will only bring credence to your cause."

"And more skilled men." William sat taller.

"That, too."

Eva pulled out the medallion and looked at it in her palm. The metal cooled in her hand, as if pleased. She doubted she'd see Walter Tennant's tent any time soon.

Chapter Twenty-Eight

In London, King Edward Plantagenet sat at the head of the board with his advisors. "I fully intend to attack France before the leaves of autumn begin to turn. Philip is at his weakest. If we wait a moment longer it will give him time to lick his wounds."

"With three ships in refit, I must advise you to wait," said the Earl of Norfolk.

Edward was not a patient man. He narrowed his gaze. "You have a month, and those vessels had best be ready to set sail, else your title and lands will be forfeit to the crown."

The Earl of Norfolk's countenance took on a shade of green. "We shall be ready, Your Grace."

John de Warenne, the Earl of Surrey, drew a noisy breath through his large nostrils. "I'd like to sail with more infantry as well. Since our last crusade, there are fewer in Ireland and Wales fit to draw upon."

"Is that not why I brought Scotland under my rule?" King Edward leaned forward on his elbow. "Aside from the acquisition of trade and lands, those miserable sheep are dispensable. Put them in the front line."

With a rap, the door opened and Edward's valet strode inside. "Sir Ormsby has arrived with news from Scone, Your Grace."

Edward gripped the armrest of his throne. "The question is what is Ormsby doing in London and not at his post in Scone?"

The valet bowed. "If I may show him in, I'm certain you'll find his story diverting."

Glancing at Norfolk, Edward rolled his hand through the air. "Mayhap you should alert the headsman."

The knight entered dressed for battle, carrying his helm cradled in the crux of his arm. His beard did nothing to hide the man's frown or the fear in his eyes.

Edward let him squirm for a moment while he scrutinized the man. Ormsby had been reasonably useful last spring when they sacked Berwick and Dunbar. "Well out with it, sir. Why in God's name are you not holding my castle at Scone?"

The man shivered to his boots. "Sacked, Your Grace."

Edward's fingers itched to issue the cur a well-deserved slap. "Sacked? Then why are you standing before me unscathed?"

"I-I was able to spirit away—with the aid of my men."

"How fortunate for you. But you managed to lose my stronghold in the interim?"

"There is an uprising underway, led by a vassal of the people. A great behemoth of a man."

Edward's shoulders tensed. God, he hated imbeciles. "One man? And who is this giant?"

"William Wallace. He killed my unarmed cleric in cold blood…a-and only a handful of my men managed to escape his capture."

"You witnessed this murder of your cleric?" Raising an eyebrow, the king picked beneath his fingernail.

"No, Your Grace, but it was reported to me in Roxburgh." Ormsby bowed. "En route to inform you, sire."

"You sniveling maggot." Edward threw up his hands. "You cannot manage to keep the miserable Scottish heathens in line? Those people are the outcasts of society. How could you have allowed them to gain the upper hand in Scone?"

"I—"

Lord Warenne cleared his throat. "Pardon me, Your Grace, but as I recall, William Wallace is also the same scoundrel who killed Sir Heselrig in Lanark."

"You mean to tell me, we've allowed a murderer to run loose up there? Of all the lawlessness. Why has he not yet been arrested and made an example of?"

"He's enormous s-sire," Ormsby stuttered. "Seven feet tall and twenty-six stone."

"And my greatest lords to the north are afraid of Goliath?" Edward slammed his fist onto the board. "King David killed that Philistine with a pebble."

Sir Ormsby bowed his dull-witted head. "Forgive me, Your Grace."

"Perhaps 'tis time we crush this Wallace once and for all." Edward looked toward John de Warenne, the most trusted man in his court. "Surrey, I shall assign the Earl of Cornwall with mustering new recruits for Flanders. You shall depart for Scotland at once and put an end to this petty uprising."

Lord Warenne stood and bowed. "We shall ride at dawn."

Another rap came at the door and the valet stepped inside. "Your Grace, a missive has arrived from Mr. Cressingham on the northern border."

Edward beckoned the valet with his fingers whilst eyeing Warenne. "You may as well wait for the news, John. At least my treasurer has the sense to send a missive rather than travel all the way to London to bring word himself."

After reading, Edward folded the vellum and placed it on the board. "It appears all the nobles of Scotland need to be reminded as to who is suzerain over their miserable country. I thought Robert Bruce, William Douglas and James Stewart were securely under my thumb, but Cressingham reports they've caused a skirmish in Irvine, which I might add was swiftly quelled by Lords Percy and Clifford."

"'Tis grave, indeed," said Lord Norfolk.

"Not too terribly concerning." Edward twisted the garnet ring on his finger. "Warenne, you'd best collect Lord Percy and Lord Clifford on your journey north. Clearly they have demonstrated the ability to stop the uprising with their *victory* at Irvine."

"Yes, Your Grace." Warenne bowed.

"Appeal to those Scottish nobles who have pledged their fealty and remind them their lands will be forfeit on both sides of the border if they so much as hint at refusing my call to arms." Edward panned his gaze across the faces of his councilmen. "Meanwhile I shall continue to focus on more important battles to secure my holdings in France."

***

By the time the news arrived of the Scottish noble's failure in Irvine in early July, William and his men had Perth under Scottish control. But his army's success did nothing to quell his ire. The only color William could see was red. He balled the missive in his fist and ground his teeth. "Bloody backstabbers sought terms from the English rather than stand and fight."

"Is it about Irvine?" Eva asked from her seat at the table in the hall at Scone.

He slapped the missive down. "God's bones, woman. How did ye ken?"

She heaved a huge sigh. "By now you ought to know I am not a seer."

For the love of everything holy, he needed to hit something. Hard. "If ye kent, then why couldna ye have told me about this? 'Tis the lowest blow to a man's character."

Her face turned bright red. "What would you have done if I'd told you?"

"I would have ridden like hellfire to fight beside them."

"Right, and I would have been taken from your life for good *before* I had a chance to utter the words. Regardless, the outcome would have been no different. You know as well as I that I can do nothing to change the unraveling of history. I can only share things that will not affect your true story."

He kicked a chair leg. "Then what good are ye to me?"

Eva turned her face away with an exasperated cough.

"Och." His heart clamped tight as a rock. "Forgive me. It didn't come out the way I'd meant it."

"I know." She stood and pulled her medallion out from under her shift. "This is my gauge. It heats up against my skin when I'm beginning to let a little too much out of the bag. When I was about to tell Heselrig your name, I was flung back to my time—remember? If I say *anything* that will change the past—I mean your future, I will be taken away, and I have no idea if I'll be able to come back."

He spread his palms to his sides. "But ye came back once before."

"Only because I prostrated myself in the Fail ruins in the midst of a storm and begged."

William grasped the medallion and rubbed it between his fingers. "It feels like a lump of bronze to me."

"Same as it does to me most of the time."

"Dunna distract me with trinkets." He let it drop back to Eva's chest. The last thing he needed was to have his mind run amuck. "I cannot believe both Wishart and Stewart backstabbed me thus. 'Tis contemptible. Blast them. How in God's name am I to stage a rebellion if the nobles undermine my every move?"

She tucked her medallion back inside her bodice. "They have their sights set on fattening their coffers as well as their holdings of land."

"That they do." William jammed his fists into his hips. "Their avarice exceeds all reason."

"But you've said yourself that is why you were chosen to lead the rebels. Because you are a second son with no title, no lands, nothing but your sword and your psalter. You have nothing to lose."

"I have everything to lose." His heartbeat thrummed beneath his skin. "The freedom of my people is more precious than all the gold in Christendom. That is what I am fighting for."

She crossed her arms. "So you will go burn Wishart's home?"

"Och aye, now ye can tell me what I will do, yet you canna say what will be done against me? Ye are a vixen." William stood and strapped on his sword. "I will ride this verra night and rain down vengeance on those who choose to supplant me. It would be one thing if they had succeeded, but now they sit in the company of Percy and Clifford negotiating for lands? The shite-eating dogs would sell their own mothers to increase their wealth."

Eva watched him from under her thick red eyelashes. God's teeth, she could be maddening with her secrets.

"What else do ye know that ye're not telling me?" he groused.

"Wishart's 'nephews' are really his sons."

"I already kent he'd gone against his oath of celibacy. He's not only a backstabber, he's a blasphemer and a hypocrite."

"Possibly." Eva tapped her toe. "And when you return, there will be a reply from Andrew Murray. I hope you will have recovered from that sore head of yours, because not all news is bad."

"Ye'll not be cosseting me this night. The only news that would pull the dagger from my heart would be to see King John restored to his throne." William turned on his heel and headed for Little, Blair and the stables.

***

Wallace refused to allow thoughts of Eva to cloud his mind as he thundered south to Wishart's manor at Ancrum. Why in God's name didn't she warn him about the backstabbing nobles in Irvine? Only stopping to rest the horses, William and his men rode tirelessly.

The blood boiling beneath his skin propelled him forward. No man could grow tired when cast aside and used as thresh on the floor like Wishart and Stewart had done. To send a man to rain havoc across the country and then to undermine him? Worse, to fail at their pathetic attempt to make a stand and then to submit to the English?

Wishart deserves every moment he spends in Roxburgh gaol.

Though it was midday when they arrived, the sky was dark with heavy clouds, and rain pelted from the sky.

William turned to Little and Blair. "A nobleman would never fight in a squall such as this, but I say, nothing will stop men of the earth. We were born to work, to trudge through the mire and harvest the crops, and we will stand for what is right regardless of the tempest."

"I say we burn the rafters," Blair said.

William sliced his hand through the air. "I didna bring the whole army because I aim to make a point. My quarrel is with Wishart. We'll not burn him out this day. There are Scottish servants depending on the living he provides." William leaned in. "But I will take his silver and his children."

"Children?" Blair asked.

"The two lads he calls nephews."

"Bloody miserable hypocrite. He's a bishop for the love of God."

William chuckled. "Mayhap he'll answer for all his sins when he comes to collect the lads."

Ahead, two guards huddled under the archway of the portcullis, holding their hands out to a brazier stocked with burning peat.

Little slipped behind one and Blair the other, swiftly disarming them.

William stepped out from the side of the outer bailey wall. "We mean no harm to any Scottish subjects."

"Ye're Wallace are ye not?" asked one.

"I am."

The other nodded. "We'll not stand in your way."

It didn't surprise William to meet with no resistance. He gestured to his men. "Take all the silver ye can carry." Then he bounded up the stairwell, exiting at the third floor passageway. He opened and slammed doors until he found the lads. The eldest, Paden's hands shook as he pointed a dirk at Wallace, shielding the younger with his body.

Holding up his palms, William stepped inside. "Och, Paden. Lay down your arms. I've no intention of hurting ye or Adam."

The lad paid him no mind, shaking his damned dirk. "Aye? Then why have ye entered my *uncle's* home by force?"

William removed his helm and sat in a chair by the hearth—though not once did he shift his gaze away from the armed lad. He stretched out his legs and crossed them at the ankles. "Mayhap if I explain from my viewpoint. Your da asked me to lead a rebellion, and after a successful battle where I reclaimed the city of Scone for Scotland, your da rode off with a number of nobles and led an uprising in Irvine." William leaned forward. "Where he not only deserted me, he undermined the verra authority he granted my army from the outset."

Adam sniffed. "But he's been captured."

"Aye, and imprisoned in Roxburgh," William added. "Which means someone needs to foster ye lads until he's released."

Adam peeked out from behind his brother. "Will we ever see him again?"

"Wheesht," Paden admonished, his voice cracking.

Again William sat back. "Who kens how long the English will hold him. But in the interim, the pair of ye will learn to be men serving Scotland."

"Ye mean for us to fight?" Adam asked, his eyes round as coins.

William held up his two-handed sword. "Are ye skilled with a weapon such as this?"

The lad shook his head rapidly. "Naaaaay. B-but I can shoot arrows as good as Paden."

The elder brother elbowed the lad. "Now ye're telling tall tales."

Adam rubbed his arm. "Ow."

"I'll tell ye what. Ye'll go with me this day and join the greatest army Scotland has ever seen. Ye'll work with my commanders. I'll say it will not be easy labor either, but I will look after ye until your father is released."

Paden tipped up his aristocratic chin. "What if we refuse to go?"

"Then I'll hogtie ye and throw ye over the back of my horse like a sack of oats."

Adam gaped. "Ye wouldna do that?"

"Och aye, I would." William tightened his grip on his hilt. "Your da backstabbed me for certain, but I aim to make sure ye two lads ken the meaning of honor afore ye reach your majority. Ye can choose to come along peaceably or I'll force ye. But ye've no business hiding here with no one to teach ye how to be a man."

"What if I try to kill ye while ye're sleeping?" Paden asked.

"Well, then." William stood, grabbed the lad by the wrist and disarmed him. "That would be the last mistake ye'd ever make."

Chapter Twenty-Nine

Out of necessity, Eva had taken charge of the tower house in Scone until a Scottish sheriff was appointed. The locals showed their gratefulness by providing an abundance of food and allowing William's army to camp in their fields and barns.

But today her jaw dropped when William walked into the hall and introduced her to Paden and Adam—Wishart's *nephews* who were fourteen and eleven. Leaving the boys standing in the center of the hall, she pulled William into the alcove that led to the kitchens. "What the hell were you thinking, kidnapping a bishop's sons and forcing them to join your army?"

He looked at her as if she'd lost her mind. "They need to learn to become men."

"With swords in their hands? What if one of them is killed?"

"Och, ye ken I willna allow that to happen."

"Right." She thwacked his beefy shoulder. "Just like you did with Lachlan."

He threw his hands to his sides. "I canna believe ye are bringing that up. Lachlan's death was an accident."

"Aye? And these boys won't meet the same end?"

"Not if ye're looking after them." He leaned in.

"Me? So you expect me to be their babysitter—" Eva jutted her face toward his. "I mean nursemaid?"

"These lads no longer need a nursemaid, but with their father imprisoned in Roxburgh, they need someone to teach them about honor and obedience."

Eva pursed her lips. "Don't they have another relative to foster them?"

"Aye, but I dunna trust any kin of Robert Wishart—not after he deceived me in Irvine."

"And so you aim to take these younglings and mold them to your way of thinking?"

"What better way? There's an enormous void between the minds of the gentry and the minds of the commoner in this country. Mayhap when they return to their home, they will have a greater appreciation for the common good."

Christ, the man does have to make sense.

She glanced over at the two lads, standing in the center of the hall, bonnets in hand. They could have been orphans by the forlorn looks on their faces. Then she remembered the history books mentioned that William looted Wishart's home and took his children, though she couldn't recall anything ever being said about what he did with them. *Great.*

Holding up her palms, she eyed him. "I will not be saddled with these boys alone. I fully expect you to assign them with work, just as you've done with Robbie—and that work had better be something guaranteed to keep them from harm."

"Aye, Miss Eva." William bowed deeply. "And my thanks."

She pointed at his sternum. "You owe me."

"Och aye?" He waggled his spiteful eyebrows. "I'd be more than happy to deliver on that promise above stairs this eve."

She groaned, forcing herself not to giggle. "You are incorrigible."

He gave her a pat on the behind. "And ye are irresistible."

She thwacked him on the arm as she headed to the lads. Lord knew babysitting wasn't one of her strong points. "I hope you came ready to work, young men."

"Us?" Paden asked with an adolescent voice that had just started to change.

Eva picked up his hand and turned it over. Just as she'd thought, the boy had no calluses. "There will be no sitting on your laurels waiting for servants to wipe your…" She looked at Adam. "Noses."

Paden threw back his shoulders. "I can take care of myself."

"Good, because I have enough to worry about."

"Ye'll help Miss Eva and Brother Bartholomew," William said. "And if ye cause trouble, ye'll answer to me."

"Yes, sir," said Paden. Evidently, William had already instilled the fear of God into them.

"But when do we shoot arrows?" Adam asked.

Eva tensed. "You will not be touching a bow within five miles of the enemy."

"Miss Eva speaks true." William placed his hand on the youngest lad's shoulder. "Ye can train with the men if there's no threat. Meanwhile, Sir Edward Little and Father John Blair need squires. Robbie Boyd will take ye under his wing and show ye the ropes."

Eva breathed a sigh. At least she wouldn't be lumbered with the boys at all hours, and Robbie could use new friends—lads who were gently bred to train him how to be the nobleman he would become.

A messenger marched through the big double doors. "I've a missive for William Wallace."

All eyes turned to the runner.

William strode forward. "I'm Wallace." He took it and ran his finger under the seal.

Eva tiptoed up to him. "Who's it from?"

"Sir Andrew Murray."

Her stomach flipped.

He looked at her with a grin. "We march to Dundee on the morrow."

She plucked the missive from his fingers. "Well, what does it say?" Though she had studied Auld Scots documents, Eva still had difficulty discerning the script and lack of spelling convention.

But she caught the gist. She glanced at Wallace, raising her brows. "Murray and his army intend to be in Dundee by the beginning of September. You will beat them by a fortnight if you leave now."

"Aye. And with the siege engines we've captured in Scone, why not rid the city of English afore Murray arrives? That way we'll be able to focus on laying plans to drive the English out of Scotland. This is exactly what we needed."

Chapter Thirty

After Wallace led the army to Dundee it had only taken him a week to sack the castle with its motte-and-bailey stronghold. Mayhap the English had grown soft in their year of occupation. William sat with his commanders in the second-floor solar planning their next maneuvers. Wallace hadn't liked the latest report from his spies. He looked across the faces of his men—every one of them had grown more assured. But he held no illusions. "Our greatest enemy is overconfidence. And my oath, we've only just begun." He eyed Eddy Little, then John Blair. "Word came today that the Earl of Surrey is marching three hundred horse and ten thousand foot north from Berwick."

The warrior priest rapped his fist on the table. "I say we set out for the south forthwith and meet them head on."

William studied the map on the table in front of them. "Nay. If we march, we run the risk of losing the advantage. We must draw them to us."

"Here in Dundee?" Eddy asked.

"They'd recapture Scone if we allowed them to come this far." William pointed. "Mark me, Warenne would attack there first. To be successful we must not split our forces."

"Agreed there." Blair crossed his arms and leaned back in his chair. "But I dunna want another massacre like Dunbar."

Wallace thumped his fist on the table. "They'll not be striking castles they already hold."

Eddy leaned forward. "Ye have an idea, do ye not?"

William first pointed to the border on the map. "They occupy Berwick, Dunbar, Edinburgh and Stirling." He trained his finger northwest and pressed it firmly on the cluster of trees indicating Abbey Craig. "We'll lure them to Stirling. First, the River Forth flows too strong and too deep for the cavalry to cross except over Stirling Bridge. And they'll not be able to march more than two or three wide across the bridge."

Blair chuckled. "And our army will be out of sight up on the ridge. They'll have no notion of our numbers."

"Not to mention, we can see for miles up there," Eddy added.

With a rap at the door, Robbie stepped inside, looking officious. "Sir Andrew Murray has arrived." The lad grinned, all pomp fleeing his expression. "He's waiting in the passageway, Willy."

"Then show him in, young squire." William pushed back his chair and rose, taking long strides toward the door.

Clad in armor, Andrew stepped across the threshold and gave Wallace a good once-over. "By God, ye *are* as large as Goliath."

William held out his hand. "I reckon ye're no runt. What are ye, eighteen hands?"

"Aye, near enough." Andrew gave a firm shake.

William liked what he saw, a sturdy warrior with an intense glint to his brown eyes. He made the introductions and gestured to a seat at the head of the table, opposite William's. "Ye arrived just in time. We've word Edward has sent the Earl of Surrey against us. They marched from Berwick this morn."

Andrew rubbed his hands with an eager grin. "Then I've arrived in time."

"Robbie," William said. "I'm sure Sir Andrew has a thirst from his journey. Bring us some ale and a trencher of bully beef and bread."

"Yes, sir."

Returning his attention to Andrew and the others, William explained the plan.

"I like it," Andrew agreed. "We lost in Dunbar because we were not prepared—nor did we have the numbers to fend off the English. It pains me to admit it, but Edward's army is as fierce as Satan. Ye'll find no better trained fighting men in all of Christendom."

Robbie entered with a ewer of ale, followed by Adam who carried four tankards, and Paden with a trencher of food.

William grinned. "Good lads."

Andrew reached for a tankard and held it up for Robbie to pour. "Do ye have the numbers of the English attack?"

William reached for the bread and broke it. "My spies report they've mustered three hundred horse and ten thousand foot."

After taking a long pull on his ale, Andrew let out a deep breath swiped his hand across his mouth. "How many men are in your ranks?"

"A hundred fifty horse and near two thousand foot."

"And mind ye, some of those foot have just come from the crofts with nothing but a homemade pike in their hands," Blair said, taking a tankard from Adam.

"I've fifty horse and five hundred foot." Andrew looked around the table. "We mustn't delay—we need more men for certain."

"Aye, but they must come with their weapons," William agreed. "This is an army, not a mob of benefactors. No matter how much I'd like to, we're not feeding the poor."

"Well said." Andrew reached in and grabbed a piece of meat, making himself at home. "And the Scots failed in Dunbar because we summoned only landholding and propertied classes. We may have had an impressive show of horse, but we lacked in foot."

William took a tankard and motioned for the lads to leave. "Then we must make a call to Scottish service that applies to all males in the horseless classes past their majority. We'll inspect them for arms and armor. After all, how difficult is it for a man to fashion a pike of twenty-four hands?"

"I like ye more with your every word." Andrew grinned. "Agreed. The majority of our force must be pikemen. And for leadership, one in five will command their unit."

"We'll send out criers at once to spread the word. All fighting men are to march to Abbey Wood immediately."

Andrew held up a finger. "Why Abbey Wood? Why not assemble them here and then march together?"

With a chuckle, William sat back. "If we brought them all to Dundee, the English would ken what we are up to afore we had a chance to meet them. In the wood, no one will be able to count our numbers."

Andrew raised his tankard. "Then shall we set out for Abbey Wood on the morrow?"

William lifted his in salute to Andrew's and nodded to the other men. "Aye, and we'll stick to the byways."

All four men toasted to their plan and drank.

William knew this union of armies was right—the camaraderie at the table was profound. At last he'd found a leader as passionate as he. Och aye, Andrew Murray embodied a knight he could join with—and since the man's father was the Justicular of Scotland north of the Firth of Forth, the nobles would be all the more amenable to providing their support.

***

Eva rolled the dice onto the table and clapped her hands. "Sixes!"

"Holy Moses," Robbie said, his voice echoing off the rafters in Dundee Castle's great hall. "Ye are the luckiest person in all of Scotland."

She brushed the grains of barley from the center of the table into her heap. "At least we're not playing for coin."

"Too right," said Adam. "I'd have pledged ye all my earnings for the rest of my life."

Beside her, Paden strummed a lute. "That's exactly why I refrain from playing games of any sort. Gambling is Satan's vice."

"I don't know about that." Eva picked up the dice and plunked them into the cup. "Our game is all in fun. No one is losing his shirt."

"But many a man has gambled the clothes from his body and then crawls to the church asking for alms."

My, Paden is inordinately serious. "Do you plan to follow in your father's footsteps and take up the cloth?"

"Ye mean my *uncle*." Paden glared at her and strummed another chord. "I certainly wasna cut out to wield a sword."

Eva shrugged off the lie about his uncle, but jeez, he was every bit as much a hypocrite as many of the clergy in power during this era. "Do you prefer the arts?" Trying for more pleasant ground, Eva gestured to his instrument. "Why not play us a tune? Music surely is from heaven."

Paden snorted. "But minstrels are not."

"Then play us a religious tune." Eva looked to Robbie and the lad rolled his eyes. Evidently Paden's "holier than thou" attitude was wearing thin with everyone. But Paden began strumming. In a minor chord, the tune was eerily moving. Eva regarded him for a moment. The lad certainly showed talent as his deft fingers moved effortlessly, playing at a difficulty level that would match a professional.

"Willy's been in the solar forever," Robbie said, drawing her from the mesmerizing music.

"Aye." Eva had to agree. She'd been working in the kitchens when the boys came in and told her Andrew Murray had arrived, bringing with him another five hundred mouths to feed. In such a short time William's army had gone from thirty men living in a cave to a garrison of thousands.

Wow.

Footsteps echoed from the stairwell. Eva grinned. "It sounds like their meeting has finally ended."

Robbie and Adam jumped up and raced for the stairs. Eva followed at a more respectable pace.

"When are we going to boot the English out of Scotland?" Robbie asked as soon as William rounded the last few steps.

"Soon." He laughed and mussed the lad's hair. "What have ye been up to whilst I've been planning our attack?"

Adam pushed in beside William—the younger lad appeared to accept his predicament in stride, far better than his older brother. "Miss Eva has won all our barley playing dice. And Paden says it's the devil's game."

William looked at Eva. "Oh?"

"Just a bit of fun to pass the time." She smiled and pointed to the musician, still seated at the table. "Paden was playing his lute for us. He's quite good."

Followed by the men, William walked farther into the hall, giving a nod to the elder Wishart lad. Then he stopped and gestured behind him. "Allow me to introduce Sir Andrew Murray." William bowed. "Miss Eva MacKay, daughter of the late Sir David."

Something in her chest tightened. That was the first time William had referred to her father as "the late" and she didn't like it at all. But it would have been rude if Eva didn't smile at the knight and hold out her hand. "I'm pleased to meet you."

Andrew took her palm and met Eva's gaze. Full of life, the man was in his prime. With chiseled features, he could have passed for a fitness model in her time. He grinned, his sparkling brown eyes inquisitive and friendly.

As he tapped the back of her hand with a chivalrous kiss, cold chills fired across Eva's skin. Her stomach squelched.

Snatching her hand away from his grasp, she covered her mouth. The room spun. "I…I…" What could she say to explain her sudden panic? Her gaze darted to William. "Forgive me." Throwing him an apologetic grimace, she ran for the door.

She couldn't take it—she knew too much.

"Eva," he called after her, but she couldn't stop.

Tears blurred her vision as she pushed past groups of soldiers. She couldn't breathe. How in God's name was she supposed to remain impartial when doom pounded on the door of someone so young and vivacious? It had only taken a look, and in that instant every fiber of her being screamed of injustice.

A vile man she'd never seen before grabbed her by the elbows. "I'm in luck. Mayhap I'll have a tasty wench warm me bed tonight."

Eva tried to twist away from the filthy, gap-toothed wretch. "Get your hands off me."

"Och, a tall lassie with spirit. I like that even better." His fingers dug into her flesh. The brute smelled like the sewage outside Renfrew as he stuck out his tongue tried to pull her head down to his face.

Gasping, she strained to keep from meeting the man's vulgar kiss.

Footsteps slapped the mud behind. A deep, guttural roar thundered.

Before Eva could blink, William barreled in and slammed the thug up the side of the head with a fist. "I'll tolerate no pillagers of women in the ranks. Especially *my* woman."

The cur cowered, clutching his hands to his head.

Eva skittered backward. *William's woman?* How could she continue on with her charade? With a sharp gasp, she turned and fled for the open gate. Harder and harder she pushed her legs. Her side cramped as she cried uncontrollably, forcing her legs to run faster.

Suddenly, her feet were whisked out from under her. The rushing in her ears started. *The medallion*? She clenched her fists. No! She didn't want to return home.

Or did she?

As her head stopped spinning, strong arms cradled her against his powerful torso. Inhaling the scent of masculine spice, she realized she'd only been hysterical—not whisked away by the forces behind the medallion. Eva curled her head against William's shoulder. Only a man as potent as Wallace could carry her in powerful arms and sprint for the seclusion of the trees.

Once completely alone, William stopped in a clearing. Taking in a deep breath, he kissed her forehead and set her down upon the soft moss. "What happened to ye back there?"

The medallion burned so hot, Eva ripped up from under her gown and rubbed her chest. God, sometimes she hated knowing. "Is Andrew's wife here too?"

William shrugged. "He didna mention that she was. And a man with property wouldna risk taking his wife away from his keep and lands."

Eva covered her face and rocked forward. "Send for her."

"Are ye serious?"

The medallion burned through her clothing. She yanked it over her head and threw it on the ground. "Trust me, for God's sake. What harm will it do to send for her?"

William strode to the medallion and picked it up. He held it in front of his face, then wrapped his fingers around the metal. "'Tis hot."

Eva nodded.

He swung his arm back. "I ought to—"

"Stop." She marched to him and grabbed the leather thong, clutching it tightly in her fist. "This lump of bronze is my passport home."

His face fell. "Ye want to go home?"

Oh God. "No." *Not now.*

He thrust out his hand. "Then why dunna ye let me toss it into the brush? I hate that damned thing."

"I cannot, dammit." She pulled the thong over her head. "You agreed to live for the now. Remember?"

"Aye, but I didna ken how much I'd grow to…" He ran his palm across his mouth and looked away.

An errant tear dribbled from her eye and Eva stepped into him, smoothing her hand around his shoulders. "I care deeply for you, too. I'll be with you as long as you need me."

He grasped the middle of her bodice and tugged her against his body. "Ye'd best mean that."

Chapter Thirty-One

Ninth September, the year of our Lord 1297

Across from the fire pit, William reclined on a fur atop the Abbey Craig, his belly full of venison. Murray did much the same, but Eva kept an impartial distance when it came to Andrew. Her manner toward the knight was distant and tight-lipped. Wallace didn't want to know why. A few days ago, he'd capitulated to Eva's request and sent for Murray's wife, but something had told him to just let the lady's arrival be a surprise.

With luck, Lady Murray would arrive after the battle.

And, och aye, a battle was coming for certain. This day William's spies had delivered news that the Earl of Surrey had marched his great army thorough Edinburgh. In their company rode Edward's underhanded treasurer, Hugh Cressingham, the very man who made a public demonstration of flaying Scottish prisoners one year prior.

"I think we're ready," Murray said.

Wallace grinned. "I still canna believe we've amassed over six thousand men in a fortnight."

"And every one of them armed and trained by our best." Murray sipped from his tankard of ale. "Holy Moses, even your cavalry is impressive at a hundred and eighty."

William pursed his lips and nodded. "I wish it were more."

"We could always use more, but we'll not fail this time. I feel it in my bones." Andrew rubbed his palms together. "At Dunbar we not only didn't have the numbers, verra few of the men who died that day had a lick of training."

"No sense dying for a cause when ye've nary a chance." William reached for the ewer and poured for them both. "I'd rather fall back and build my strength, stand and fight when the odds are more in my favor."

"I couldna agree more." Andrew drew his tankard to his lips. "'Tis why I started my rebellion in the north. The English have concentrated their forces between Stirling and Berwick. Now that we've driven them out of the Highlands, we'll turn up the heat."

"Just as we did in Scone and Dundee. Drive them out one stronghold at a time."

John Blair stepped into the glow of the fire. "Riders await on the fringe of the forest carrying the flag of parley."

William turned to Andrew. The shake of the knight's head confirmed Wallace's sentiments. "Tell them unless they take their soldiers and march back across the border, we've nothing to discuss."

"Ye might want a word with these two characters."

William raised his eyebrows in question.

Blair just shook his head. "James the Steward and the Earl of Lennox. The bloody backstabbers are bringing word from the English camp."

That made his gut clamp into a lead ball. "Miserable traitors." Grasping his sword belt, William stood. "After the noble's bungle in Irvine, it must have taken an enormous set of cods to ride into my camp."

Andrew followed suit, testing his sword by sliding it out then back into his scabbard. "They most likely want to offer terms."

"Not to me." Taking a torch, William started down the path." If I wasna busy laying siege to Dundee, I would have sacked the Steward's keep in Renfrew along with Wishart's."

Andrew kept pace beside him. "Why one over the other?"

"With Wishart it was personal. The bishop was responsible for my training with the Templar priest. I thought he had more confidence in me."

"And then he undermined ye by leading a raid on Irvine?"

"Aye." William ground his teeth. "I still canna believe it."

"Ye need a knighthood. That'd garner ye a bit more respect with the nobles."

"Mayhap if we restore Balliol to the throne, the king will see fit to grant one." William stopped. Below, Stewart and Lennox were mounted, flanked by a score of men, their torches burning bright. Unless they'd somehow managed to post archers in the trees, they had indeed come to talk.

After handing the torch to Andrew, he cupped his hands around his mouth. "Meet us halfway. Alone. Any men-at-arms follow, ye'll both be dead men."

Mumbles rose from below, but the two leaders dismounted and started up the hill.

William snuffed the torch in the dirt. "'Tis a clear night. I can see all I need by the glow from the moon."

When James Stewart's face came into view, illuminated blue by the moon and shadowed by the foliage overhead, William smoothed his fingers around the pommel of his sword. How satisfying it would be to lop off his smug head.

"William." The cur had the audacity to smile. "'Tis good to see ye've found Sir Andrew Murray."

Wallace clenched his fists. "Ye'd best explain what ye're doing keeping company with the Earl of Surrey."

"Pardon?" Lord Stewart admonished. "'Tis not like ye to speak so discourteously to your betters."

"Presently I have the longer sword, and in *my* forest, that makes me *your* better." William crossed his arms against his urge to wring the noble's neck.

"Och, ye must ken, the nobles received a call to arms. I had to march, else be accused of treason and my lands forfeit."

"Thus ye acknowledged the slip of worthless parchment forced upon ye by a foreign king."

"William." Lord Stewart spread his palms deploringly. "These are troubled times. Every landowning baron must have a care, else he'll not only lose his holdings, his family will be imprisoned or worse."

A tic twitched over Wallace's eye. "Or flayed by Cressingham."

Andrew stepped forward. "In all seriousness, m'lord. Some of your cavalry is still in our ranks. Surely the pair of ye do not intent to ride against Scottish subjects."

"But that is why we're here," Lord Lennox found his words. "We can grant ye both lands west of Loch Lomond. Lay down your arms and leave this night. They have over six thousand foot and three hundred fifty horse. Ye cannot win."

William smirked. "We've the same. And we have ground advantage. It sickens me that ye think we are so weak."

"English annihilated us at Irvine," said Lennox.

Andrew chuckled. "And we were ill prepared at Dunbar, but ye've forgotten. Everything from Scone and to the north is now ours." His hands moved to his hips. "And in a fortnight Wallace has turned six thousand foot into a wall of muscle. Ye mustn't discount the odds. My wager is on Scotland."

"God save it be true," said Lord Stewart.

William crossed his arms. "Then what will ye do to help us? If ye must answer the call of the English, surely ye willna pit your men against Scotland."

Lennox and Stewart exchanged glances, but it was the High Steward who spoke, "Once the battle is underway, we'll give the order for our men to stand down. No Scottish blood will be spilled by our hand. On that we can give our word."

A taste as bitter as bile filled William's mouth. "I'll hold ye to it on one condition." He could end both their lives right here and now. And he'd do so if they didn't agree to his terms.

Lord Stewart shifted his feet. "Aye?"

"Ye never double cross me again. And when this is over, I'll have fealty from both your armies."

"Agreed." The High Steward held out his palm.

William looked to Andrew who nodded, then he gripped the nobleman's hand with crushing force to show exactly how serious he was. If either man ever backstabbed him—noble or not—William would show no mercy.

"We've one last matter to discuss," said Lord Stewart.

William had already given away more than he cared to. That blasted tic above his eye twitched again. "Aye?"

"I've had word ye abducted Wishart's nephews." Stewart huffed. "Is this true?"

"The lads are safe and working as squires for two of my commanders."

"And when Wishart is released from Roxburgh?"

"*If* he's released." Wallace sliced his hand through the air. "He'll need to own to his transgressions, just like any man."

Lord Stewart took a step back. "I'll send him word the lads are well. It should still his troubled mind."

"Verra well." William bowed. "I shall see ye gentlemen anon."

***

Early evening, Eva sat on the furs in the tent she shared with William and recorded an entry on her scroll of parchment:

11th September, 1297

Interesting that this date is significant throughout history, I personally will never forget the tragedy of the events on 11th September, 2001. I was only thirteen and my family hadn't yet moved to America. Still, the broadcast of the twin towers billowing smoke in New York forever burned an image on my mind.

This September 11th marks the date of the Battle of Stirling Bridge. William awoke before the sunrise and I haven't seen him since. Though I can hear footsteps beyond the flap of my tent, the men are silent. The forest is silent, as if the birds are aware of the terrible events that will unfold this day.

Honestly, I cannot believe I am still here…It's been four months. Six to go, God willing.

Her hand paused. Then she blinked and shook away the sudden sadness.

To me it is unconscionable that Lord Stewart and Lord Lennox are riding with the English and to complicate the insult, many of their men have sided with Wallace. This war of independence has put landowner against crofter and neighbor against neighbor. The lines of loyalty are not defined—jeez, they're not even grey. How William got this far with so many odds against him amazes me.

But the men love him. His words of encouragement always manage to touch that place in the heart where courage resides in every warrior in this camp.

I have never felt so alive or proud to belong to any cause.

This will be a terrible day indeed. I want to hide, yet I cannot bring myself to miss a thing.

Eva would have liked to have written more, but she put her quill aside and headed for the ridge.

In full battle armor, William stood beside Andrew. Lord, he looked magnificent—a living statue—a god. His broad shoulders tapered to a sturdy waist, with his white surcoat belted low. His great sword hung in repose at his hip, gauntlets protected his fingers, and an iron helm covered his dark tresses with curls peeking beneath. Before her stood a warrior. A man with such courage, he would never turn his back on his country, never flee from a fight. A man who knew of honor and respect and loyalty. A man who would die for right. Before her stood a man who could love with such ferocious passion, any woman who lay in his arms could never be satiated by another. She knew that to her very bones.

Together the two warriors gazed down upon the verdant Carse of Stirling, flatlands through which flowed the River Forth. Beyond and up the far hill loomed the grey stone walls Stirling Castle. From the distance, the grand fortress looked small, as if part of a landscape portrait of the horizon. Still early morning, the sun in the east was partially blocked by a hazy layer of clouds.

Eva kept her distance. In no way could she interfere with the events that were about to unravel. Without uttering a word, the lads surrounded her. Adam wrapped his fingers around her waist and leaned close. She hugged his shoulders and kissed the top of the boy's head. Though she wanted to send them away to tend the flock of sheep amassed to feed the garrison, she could not. In the Middle Ages, children were not hidden from the realities of war, and this would be a significant day for Paden, Robbie and Adam. One they would remember for the rest of their lives.

Chapter Thirty-Two

William watched the English start across the bridge, so narrow, only two horsemen could cross at a time, making their progress slow—but their retreat impossible. At dawn, he gave the command to the commanders of the Scottish schiltrons to stand ready for his order to form up in battle array below the Abbey Craig. One hundred men wide and six deep, when he gave the order they'd trap the English army on the lip of land jutting into the curve of the River Forth. 'Twas the most brilliant plan he'd ever dreamed.

In all of William's raids, he'd never had such a ground advantage. Once the English crossed the narrow bridge, they would have nowhere to run. Aye, they had more cavalry and crossbowmen in their ranks, but William prayed this time the Scottish plan was sound. He'd been patient and Lord knew they needed a win. With Sir Andrew Murray joining his army, a victory would most definitely swing many borderland nobles to side solely with Scotland.

William's heartbeat rushed in his ears as he watched.

"When shall we order the cavalry to mount?" Andrew asked.

"As soon as the crossing reaches a third, we'll ride down the crag at breakneck speed and lead the foot into battle. Racing horses with their commanders leading the charge will bolster our men with the courage they need."

"Look at that!" Robbie hollered, pointing. "The milk-livered hogs have turned tail."

William snapped his gaze to the bridge. Indeed, the English were heading back. He squinted for a better look. A rotund man mounted on a horse was flinging his arms and gesturing up the far hill toward the castle.

"Is that Cressingham?" Wallace leaned toward Andrew.

"Och aye." Murray pointed. "The verra swine who ordered the butchering of Scottish men, women and children in Dunbar. I dunna need to ride closer to recognize that murdering codfish."

William scratched his head. "What the blazes are they doing?"

***

John de Warenne, the Earl of Surrey opened his eyes when the latch to his chamber door clicked. Throat burning and raw, he felt like shite.

"My lord?" Lawrence, his valet called from the doorway.

Warenne rolled over. "Yes?"

"Tis well past Terce. The men have assembled."

The earl's heart thrummed with a jolt and he sat bolt upright. "Why did you allow me to sleep so late?"

"Apologies. 'Tis not like you to oversleep, my lord."

Warenne pushed aside the bedclothes and swung his legs over the edge of the mattress. "I've a miserable ache in the head and my throat. This Scottish air is disagreeable, indeed."

"Shall I send for a tonic?"

"Heaven's no. I must dress immediately." Warenne stood and stretched. "The men are assembled at the bridge, you say?"

"Yes, my lord. Sir Lundie started the infantry over the bridge, but Sir Cressingham insisted they return until you joined them." As always, Lawrence had Lord Warenne's armor neatly laid out on the table.

"Did he now?" Warenne stood with his arms wide while his groom dressed him.

"Yes."

"It seems the king's treasurer is quite a military tactician. Edward was very impressed with his victory in Irvine."

"Truly?" Lawrence carefully lifted the hauberk while the earl slipped into it. "I thought Lords Clifford and Percy quashed the rebellion there."

"Ah yes. A slip of the mind, I'm afraid, though Cressingham was the man who reported the incident. I was there when His Grace received the missive—'twas when I was dispatched to carry out this unsavory task."

"Would you like to break your fast, or should I have the groom ready your horse, my lord?"

"Since the men are assembled, I'll venture to my mount. Dispelling this rebellion shan't take long." Lord Warenne slipped his feet into his boots and watched the groom tie them.

"'Tis a shame this Wallace jester refused to surrender."

"Agreed." Warenne smirked. "We shall imprison him in chains and take him to London. I'm sure the king will enjoy using the beggar as an example to all of Scotland."

"'Twill be good to see, my lord." Lawrence held up a surcoat with the Surrey coat of arms. "I for one would like to have peace on our island. The war with France is enough."

After donning the garment, the earl smoothed his hands down the emblem on his chest. "Let us dispel this battle and then tonight we shall feast."

Once dressed and armed, Warenne made his way to Stirling Castle's courtyard and mounted his warhorse. Flanked by his personal guard, they rode down the hill to Stirling Bridge and the English army. Sir Cressingham met them at the rear of the company. "My lord, all is ready for the battle to commence. Do we have your approval for the bridge crossing?"

Warenne sat high in his saddle and ran his fingers down the point of his beard. "Before we begin, let us recognize the merits of our men. First I call forward the five garrison leaders who have acted for England on this foray. For they shall be knighted this day."

"Well said, my lord." Cressingham turned to the ranks. "Drake, Bastion, Snelling, Weaver, and Morton come forward and remove your helms."

Warenne dismounted and drew his sword. Holding it above his head, he stood perfectly still as the five men assembled and kneeled. "Our illustrious and revered King Edward, ruler of England, recognizes you for your service to our sovereign nation. I hereby bestow upon you the esteemed rank of knights of England's Royal Infantry. Long live the king."

"Long live the king!" The unison shout from three thousand men was quite uplifting. John dubbed each man on the shoulders, certain this act would inspire the troops. Then he led them parading across the ranks to bring inspiration to the soldiers. "Fight well, men, and we will drink Scottish whisky this night," he repeated again and again.

"Shall we now begin the march, my lord?" Cressingham asked after they rounded the last line of infantry.

"So be it." Warenne raised his arm and his voice. "Fight with might and be victorious. For England!"

"For England!" responded the resounding roar.

With the beat of foot soldiers on the wooden bridge, the crossing began.

"The bridge is quite narrow," Warenne observed.

Cressingham shook his finger at the procession. "But two horses can cross side by side and I cannot yet smell the Scots."

"Then ensure the infantry crosses first." Warenne chuckled at the treasurer's jest. "Scots don't know how to fight on horseback."

Nearly a quarter of the army had traversed the bridge when Stewart and Lennox returned from their sortie. Warenne breathed a sigh of relief. Mayhap there will be no bloodshed this day. "Cressingham, look there. And you thought the Scottish nobles had deserted us."

"Shall I recall the garrison?"

"Yes, do," Warenne agreed. "I'm certain their news will be favorable. They are not accompanied by the forty horsemen. 'Tis a sign the surrender has been favorably negotiated."

The treasurer scoffed. "Mayhap that is why the lowlife swine haven't shown their faces. Poor men cannot resist an opportunity to increase their personal wealth."

The battalion commander shouted the order to return, and by the time the Scottish Lords reached the bridge, most of the English soldiers had marched back across.

Warenne waited on his mount until the nobles rode all the way up to him. In no way would he present like an excited youth and meet them halfway. Besides, they were Scots—hardly of noble blood. "Tell me this William Wallace character has finally agreed to surrender. Did you offer him my terms?"

Lord Stewart frowned. "We did, my lord, though Wallace is as stubborn as a goat on a lead line."

The Earl of Surrey let out an exasperated cough. "What un-propertied man would refuse the promise of lands?"

Lord Lennox shifted in his saddle. "Wallace believes acceptance of a grant of lands would be a betrayal of his allegiance to Scotland."

"But he is a traitor—an outlaw with no scruples," Warenne puzzled.

"Mayhap from your point of view, my lord." The High Steward bowed his head, but his words bordered on the unpatriotic.

Warenne looked again from whence the nobles came. "If you could not negotiate terms, where are the forty horsemen you promised?"

Lord Stewart spread his palms. "Alas, we could not persuade the men from Lennoxtown to join us."

"Is this true, Lennox? I thought you were a powerful earl? Did you not take the horses and weapons from them?"

"No, my lord." Lennox bowed his beef-witted head. "We couldna because the men have already joined the rebellion."

"This is treasonous." Warenne could not believe his ears. "You met with Wallace, yet your men remained standing beside him?"

"Our men were out of sight." Lord Stewart's gaze shifted to Lennox. "It was dark and we were not invited into the outlaw's camp."

The Earl of Surrey jutted his finger forward. "I expect you to hang every one of the survivors when this is over. And the two of you clearly are incapable of negotiating a farthing from a blind beggar's alms basin." This was preposterous. Surely Wallace didn't want to be responsible for massacring his men.

Warenne snatched the missive containing the terms for the outlandish pirate and pointed to two Dominican friars. "Take this. Quickly cross the bridge and deliver my terms to Wallace and Murray. Tell them their refusal will result in the slaughter of their entire garrison of men."

As soon as the two friars set out, Sir Richard Lundie rode in. "Lord Warenne, with all due respect, if we wait until the entire army crosses the bridge, we are dead men."

"That is absurd," said Cressingham. "Are you another Scottish noble turned backstabber?"

"Please hear me out," Lundie deplored. "We can only cross the bridge two abreast, and the enemy is keeping their numbers hidden which makes me very wary indeed. Let me take a hundred and fifty cavalrymen and cross at the ford downstream."

Warenne stroked his beard. "We've not that many horse to spare."

Lundie pointed down river. "Then make it fifty. At least that will increase our odds."

"We cannot divide our forces, my lord." Cressingham rode his mount alongside the earl. "To do so would weaken us at our very heart. And it will pay us no service, my lord earl, to misuse the king's money with vain maneuvers."

Warenne peered across the grassy carse. "The heathens are hiding in the forest for Christ's sake." He frowned at Sir Lundie. "I'm afraid I agree with the king's treasurer on this. We need the strength of our cavalry here with the heart of our forces."

***

William watched in disbelief as two Dominican friars now crossed the bridge and made their way through the Carse of Stirling.

"What do ye make of that?" asked Andrew.

Unable to do anything but shake his head, Wallace smirked. "As farcical as this day has transpired? It could be the two monks are carrying a missive declaring us both to be saints."

"I could live with a sainthood." Andrew gave a wink and a grin.

William chuckled. "So could I, but only after we boot the bloody English off our lands."

Andrew inclined his head to the path. "Shall we ride down and meet them at the forest edge or make them climb the hill?"

William cued his horse to a walk. "If we dunna go down there, the sun will be setting by the time they reach us."

Riding down the hill had been the right decision, because the two holy men were breathing heavily by the time they stepped under the cover of the forest.

"The right honorable Earl of Surrey requests your surrender on threat of annihilation of your men. Please, for the love of all that is holy, stop this madness." A friar held up a missive. "Lord Warenne has offered you good terms—lands and riches—even a title. You and all your men could walk away and live."

William snatched the vellum from the friar's fingertips and handed it to Murray. "Do ye want to bargain with a backstabbing tyrant?"

Andrew shook his head. "No more than I want a rat to crawl up my arse."

"Then burn that bloody thing afore I use it to gag these two wayward monks. I will not accept a bribe to accede to defeat and play Judas to my countrymen." He held up his finger and eyed each one. "Tell your commander that we are not here to make peace, but to do battle to defend ourselves and liberate our kingdom. Let them come on, and we shall prove this in their verra beards."[2]

The second man shook his finger toward the Scottish ranks. "Then their deaths shall be on your head."

The other made the sign of the cross. "May God have mercy on their souls."

"And on yours for taking the side of oppression and injustice." William reined his horse toward the crag. Bless it, he'd have his battle this day.

---

[2] Andrew Fisher, *William Wallace*, (Birlinn Limited, 2007) pg. 102

Chapter Thirty-Three

After the friars returned to the English camp, for the third time that day Longshanks' army started across Stirling Bridge. When nearly half of the English vanguard had traversed, Father Blair approached, wearing mail atop his habit and carrying a psalter in his hands. "It looks as if we will have our fight after all."

William took in a deep, reviving breath of air. "Aye, friar, and a blessed day this is."

Father Blair bowed his head. "Let us pray."

Andrew and William kneeled, as did the other men in their company. Bowing his head, Wallace clutched his fist to his heart.

"In the name of the Father, Son and Holy Ghost, we beseech thee, oh Lord to grant these brave souls courage to face triumphant death and stand against the oppressor. We carry your cross over our hearts as we fight against tyranny. For rebellion to tyrants is obedience to God. Amen."

"Rebellion to tyrants is obedience to God," William repeated. "Amen," he chorused with the others, then stood. "I expected a prayer the length of Sunday mass."

Blair's shoulder ticked up. "Aye, well sometimes the Lord needs us to get on with it. Besides, I'll not tire our men by making them kneel for hours."

Andrew pointed. "I think it is time."

Indeed, the numbers of Englishmen who'd crossed the bridge had begun to march on. With a nod, William held his ram's horn to his lips and blew for God Almighty and the liberty of his people.

He and his cavalry sprinted for their horses, while William's heart thrummed a fierce rhythm. A year of building his forces and fighting Edward's rouges, he would finally wreak vengeance on a large scale.

At long last he had the army behind him to make a formidable stand. "Scotland until Judgement!" he roared, leading the charge down the crag and into the open lea.

The enemy sped their pace across the bridge, but still a good third of their numbers remained on the southern shore.

Swinging his great sword, Wallace led the cavalry around the English vanguard toward the north end of the bridge before the English troops realized they'd been trapped and surrounded.

Behind, Little and Blair ran on, bringing forth the Scottish infantry. The hiss of arrows overhead infused William's determination. The bloody English had nowhere to run and he would show no mercy.

Every beady eye of the English trespassers reflected Longshanks' tyranny. Every grimace mirrored the English king's disdain for Scotland.

The enemy attacked with pike and sword. Spinning his horse, William defended his country in the thick of battle, blocking the cowards from retreat. His arms grew stronger with every swing of his great sword. A heinous blackguard attacked screaming like a banshee, his hideous face splattered with blood. Clenching his gut, William eyed the doomed murderer while his sword swept down and beheaded the cur, silencing his shrieking screams.

"Send them to hell!" he bellowed as he hacked off the arm of another assailant.

Blood spewed across the ground while William pushed forward with his army of pure grit.

Wallace and his cavalrymen fought in the midst of mayhem, whilst Andrew skirted around and attacked those brave enough to face them on the bridge itself.

The bloodcurdling cries of battle rose to the beat of the English drums. The snare only served to incite William's rage as he fought one adversary after another. "Drive them into the river!" he shouted as brave Scotsmen gained ground, pushing the English back.

In the blink of an eye, the sounds of armored bodies hit the water with thundering splashes. Mud stirred from the riverbed, mingled with blood from the dying. English infantrymen weighed down by heavy hauberks tried to swim while the angry current pulled them do their deaths.

Behind him, a clamorous pounding reverberated above the deafening throng.

"They're destroying the bridge," Andrew shouted.

"Let them!" William spun his horse. The faster he swung his blade, the greater his bloodlust grew. The battlefield glistened red with the blood of the enemy and the river had turned as maroon as the mud in Lochmaben where William's da had been murdered. "Fight until none are left standing! We. Will. Be. Vic-tor-ious!"

***

Eva couldn't drag her gaze from the gruesome battle unfolding before her. The thunderous battle cries and the hideous shrieks from the dying held her stunned by the horrific bloodshed unfolding before her eyes. Her stomach churned while she clenched her fists tight to her body. All the movies she'd watched glorifying battles were child's play.

No wonder she hated sharp objects.

They hacked off limbs and stabbed through flesh, maiming and killing. In a matter of seconds, the exhilaration of watching courageous men charge across the battlefield was replaced by revulsion as metal scraped and the howls of dying men shrieked above the wind.

Tears stung her eyes as she trained her gaze to the front of the mayhem and focused on William. He fought with the strength of ten warriors and moved with the speed of a cobra. Though she knew the outcome of this battle, she feared for his safety most of all. From her vantage point, he could be hit by an arrow or cut open by a blade with her next inhale.

She couldn't blink.

Breathing became labored.

Every inch of Eva's flesh tremored.

Then the pounding started. On the far shore, Warenne's men used axes to hack away at Stirling Bridge.

"My God, they're condemning their own men to die."

Beaten soldiers fled into the river, only to be dragged under by the force of the current and their heavy armor. She watched in horror as enemy soldiers cried out as they were swept downstream.

"They're retreating—admitting defeat." Brother Bartholomew clapped his hands beside her. "Come Miss Eva, there will be many wounded to tend in short order."

But Eva couldn't move.

The Earl of Surrey, marked by his coat of arms and his horse covered with a caparison in the Surrey colors rode south, surrounded by a vanguard for protection. The entire English garrison remaining on the north shore fled.

From the trees, a mounted attack engaged the earl's forces. Eva pointed. "Lord Stewart and the Earl of Lennox."

"In the hour of victory they choose their side," said Bartholomew. "Let us pray they remain loyal to Scotland."

Then she saw it. Speeding through the air like a bullet, an arrow pierced through Andrew's shoulder. Grasping at the shaft, the knight fell from his horse. Eva's entire body shuddered at the jarring impact when he hit the turf, flat on his back. The brave warrior didn't move.

"My God," she whispered again, her heart seizing.

Then Murray sat up and lumbered to his feet, the arrow shaft protruding from his wound.

She stood frozen in place as she watched the brave knight stoop for his sword and whistle for his mount, his every move sluggish.

Only when the sound of agonized moaning approached, did Eva drag her gaze away from Murray as he stiffly mounted and crouched over his horse's withers. Her head swimming, she flicked her wrist at the dazed lads beside her. "Quickly. We'll need bandages and hot irons to cauterize wounds."

Robbie and Paden headed off, but Adam remained completely still, his eyes round as coins, frightened out of his wits, no doubt.

Eva kneeled and wrapped her arms around the lad. "This is why I insisted you remain up here. Never forget that war is a last resort. Always try to negotiate if there is a way."

Adam's bottom lip trembled. "But people tried to talk to William."

"True, though the Earl of Surrey tried to bribe him. That's different and would not free Scotland from the tyranny of Edward the Longshanks. William and Sir Andrew had no choice but to make a stand this day."

The lad dropped his chin. "Longshanks has my da locked away in the dungeon of Roxburgh."

"Aye." Eva smoothed her hand over the lad's cap of curls. "And one day he will walk free because William Wallace took a stand."

"Do ye think so?" Adam asked with a hopeful lilt.

"I know it, lad." She patted his shoulder. "Now come. We must do what we can to help those who have fallen, for they are the true heroes today."

"Ye sure do talk funny."

Eva chuckled. And here she'd thought her accent was becoming more archaic by the day. "Well, at least you can understand me."

***

Eva worked endlessly, tying bandages and repeating over and over how well the men had done. Even if she'd wanted to use avens water on every cut, she couldn't because supplies had run out. It was all she could do to staunch the bleeding and move on to the next wounded Scot.

When Andrew Murray rode his horse up the hill with the arrow protruding from his shoulder, Eva swallowed her urge to hurl. She dashed to Brother Bartholomew, looking down at his patient. "I'll take over here. You must go tend to Sir Andrew."

The monk peered over his shoulder. "Dear Lord. 'Tis a crossbow arrow with which he's been skewered."

"How do you know?" she asked.

"Thicker shaft." The monk shook his head. "And the arrowheads are near impossible to remove." The monk turned in a circle. "Father Blair, I'll need your muscle over here."

Eva hadn't seen William yet, but by the sound roaring from below, the battle still raged.

By God, she would help every man she possibly could, but couldn't bring herself to look the young Murray in the eye. Besides, Bartholomew knew more about pulling out crossbow arrows. Eva kneeled beside an injured man, his armor only a quilted doublet like many of the foot soldiers. "Looks like you had a nasty gash to your arm."

"Aye." The man gave her a wincing grin. "But not afore I skewered a half dozen English swine."

"You fought bravely." She held a balled up bandage against his wound and pressed.

He hissed. "'Tis a victorious day for Scotland."

"Indeed, and you must rise to tell about it." She used another bandage to wrap the wound tightly. "Keep this clean and at your first opportunity wash it with spirit." The medallion warmed against her skin. "Or avens water—anything that will keep it from festering."

"It'll be right." He grimaced. "I've a family in Bannockburn."

She patted his hand. "Then do as I say, and you'll live to watch your children grow."

Chapter Thirty-Four

It was dark when William trudged up Abbey Craig's steep hill to camp. His mail hung on his limbs threatening to drag him to his knees with every step. Aye, this was a day of great victory for Scotland, but he'd been going since dawn.

Every step punished him.

Never in his life had he fought so long and hard. He thought he was conditioned for battle? Lord, his every muscle, every sinew ached.

But when he saw her his heart fluttered with a wee surge of energy—enough to see him to the top of the hill.

Holding a torch, Eva waited on the path. "I was wondering if you'd make it back to camp or if you decided to sleep in the king's chamber at the castle."

He chuckled. "I'd never be so presumptuous as to enter the king's chamber, let alone rest my head on His Grace's pillow."

Moving forward, she took his hand. "I know. That's what makes me—ah—so attracted to you."

He winced when she looped her arm through his.

"Are you hurt?"

"Just sore."

She inclined the torch in the direction of their tent. "Come, I have some oil. I'll give you a massage."

"No sweeter words have ever been spoken, m'lady."

She chuckled and gave him another squeeze. "I'm proud of you."

"I'm proud of my men." But victory was bittersweet—battles were never waged without losses and that's what would always haunt him.

"But *you* are amazing."

William stretched his back. "I dunna feel too bloody amazing at the moment." His lip slit when he smiled—Lord, even that hurt. "I most likely canna even lift my sword I'm so bone-weary—but dunna tell anyone."

"I'll keep it to myself." With a sweet giggle, she held the flap to the tent.

But William wasn't so bone-weary he'd forgotten his manners. "After ye."

With a smile, she doused the torch and slipped inside.

It didn't take long for her to help him remove his armor.

She gestured to the pallet. "Lie down."

"Not yet." He pulled her into his arms and held her against his chest. This is what he was fighting for. Not just for himself, but for all men to hold their women in their arms—and to raise families free from tyranny. Lord, Eva felt so damned good, he never wanted to release her. "Home," he whispered.

"Pardon?"

William closed his eyes and inhaled her scent. "It doesna matter whether we're at Leglen Wood or Stirling, or Scone. Wherever ye are, I'm home."

She took in a sharp breath.

"Are ye well?" he asked, sensing his words had struck a chord.

Cupping his cheek with her palm, darkness shrouded her smile. He could have sworn he saw a hint of sadness in her green eyes. "I'm fine. It is you I'm worried about."

He stretched his neck from side to side. "Nothing a good night's sleep willna cure." He kissed her fingertips. "Or your deft fingers."

Her smile brightened. "I'll fetch the oil."

"Now that's music to an old warrior's ears." He stretched out on the pallet.

She chuckled. "You're not old."

"I feel it this night."

Sitting beside him, she ran a gentle hand along his spine. "Perhaps I can help with that."

He moaned. "Your touch can revive my verra soul, m'lady."

"And that is music to my ears, m'lord." Her lips brushed his ear. "Close your eyes while I massage some life back into your weary shoulders."

"Och, Eva. Ye're so fine to me." Her fingers started making their magic, swirling across his back, rubbing deep into his aching muscles. "What would I do without ye?"

He closed his eyes and let her take him to heaven.

***

By dawn the next morning, the air was still. William hated that Andrew had taken an arrow to the shoulder, but by the grace of God, none of his inner circle of men had been killed. The losses on the Scottish side were minimal compared to those on the English. He estimated a third of Edward's men had drowned, being sucked under the current of the River Forth by their heavy hauberks.

William ducked under the flap of Andrew's tent. The knight grimaced as he struggled to sit.

"How are ye feeling, my friend?" William asked, cringing at the blood soaked bandage wrapped around Andrew's shoulder.

"I'm coming good."

This was one time William hoped that Eva's cryptic prediction was wrong. But the man who had grown to be his closet comrade-in-arms in a few short sennights looked like shite. "Ye're a bit pale."

"Nothing a tot of whisky willna remedy." Andrew licked his cracked lips.

William found a flagon at the foot of the pallet. "Good thing ye've a bit of spirit right here."

Andrew reached for the whisky with a pained grin. "Ye're a man of great talents and a nose for fine spirit." He took a long swallow.

"I've sent for your wife. She should be here anon."

"Do ye think I'm that bad off?" Andrew swung his feet to the side of his pallet. "'Cause I'll beat ye to Stirling's gate."

"No need. We secured the castle for Scotland last eve. But ye do need to mount for the triumphant ride through her gates for certain."

Andrew chuckled. "We gave them a good run."

"Och aye." William sat beside his friend. "If only the bastards hadn't destroyed the bridge, we would have given chase to Warenne and the rest of his sorry lot."

"Not to worry." Andrew took another drink. "With our victory, Scotland's nobles will join us for certain."

"'Tis music to my ears. The High Steward has dispatched criers to take the news throughout the land." William shook his head. "Said this was the victory we needed to wash our hands of the English. Lord Stewart has even called a meeting of parliament."

Andrew passed him the flagon. "At last our dreams have come to fruition."

"Indeed." William took a swig. "Did ye ken we sent Cressingham to his grave?"

"Now that's the best news I've heard today. I only wish I would have been the man to run him through."

"Och, aye. But the men had a bit of sport." William shuddered and took one more tot. "They flayed him—just as he did to his victims in Dunbar."

Andrew straightened a bit and winced. "Ye dunna look too happy about it. Why not let the men have their vengeance? After all, Cressingham was the worst tyrant of them all—aside from Edward himself."

William let out a long sigh. "Ye're right." How could he stand in the way of a mob of three-thousand Scotsmen when they were hell-bent on repaying crimes committed against their kin? These were brutal times and why should he not settle up with the English in kind? "An eye for an eye, a tooth for a tooth." He passed the flagon to Andrew.

"Ta." Murray took a long drink this time. "We should mount his head above the castle gates."

"I'll see it done." William patted the wounded knight's elbow. "Are ye up to a triumphant march?"

"I wouldna miss it for all the gold in Christendom." Andrew grimaced and started to stand, but William held up his hand.

"Rest for a bit longer. When 'tis time I'll send in your squire, and when ye're ready, we shall parade through Stirling's gates and make merry."

***

Eva's toe nudged an arrow. She stooped to pick it up as Brother Bartholomew stepped beside her. "That's the nasty thing I pulled from Sir Andrew's shoulder yesterday."

It was ghastly—three-dimensional with four barbs. "Is it made of lead?"

"Aye, like so many."

Eva tested the jagged tip with her finger. "Did the point break off?"

Squinting his beady eyes, the Monk studied the arrow. "It looks as if it has. Regardless, Sir Andrew's fighting days are over. He'll never have full use of that arm again for certain."

Eva threw the vile arrow into the wood. It made her sick. If Andrew didn't die of infection, a chunk of lead in his shoulder would ensure a slow and painful death. "I hate violence."

Brother Bartholomew patted her arm. "There, there lass. People like us canna do much about keeping the men from fighting. But we can provide support through healing and prayers."

She nodded, staring down at the dirt.

"Miss Eva." Robbie came running with Adam on his heels. "Lady Murray has arrived and is already in the tent with Sir Andrew."

"Honestly?" asked the monk. "How did the lady arrive so quickly? She had to travel all the way from Inverness, no?"

Eva shrugged—no use telling anyone she'd insisted William send for her. "'Tis just good she's here. Her presence will give Sir Andrew strength." She looked to the lads. "Do you know where William is?"

"Last I saw, he was meeting with Lord Stewart down by the river." Robbie threw his thumb over his shoulder. "I canna believe people are arriving in droves. Are ye ready for the grand march through Stirling's gates?"

"Och, aye," said Adam, clearly recovered from his shock from watching the battle. "'Twill be a magnificent parade. Willy says we're making history."

"True." Eva patted his shoulder. The lad didn't know exactly how well the Battle of Stirling Bridge would be remembered. "You are at that. Is your horse saddled and festooned with brilliant colors?"

The lad shot a panicked look to Robbie. "We need caparisons for our horses."

The twelve-year-old threw up his hands. "Och, where will we find that much cloth?"

Eva looked to Brother Bartholomew and grinned. "Don't each of you have mantles? I think they would look splendid adorning your horses."

Robbie grabbed the younger boy by the arm. "Come. We must make haste."

"Ye do have a way with the lads," the little monk said.

"Thank you." Eva scanned the grounds and spotted John Blair. She excused herself and headed toward the priest. "Father Blair, may I ask a favor?"

He turned and assessed her from head to toe. "From me?"

It was time to test the waters with the priest again. "William is by the river and I can find no one else suitable to introduce me to Lady Murray."

He clasped prayerful hands together and bowed his head. "Of course. I'm sure the lady will be pleased to meet another woman amongst the rebels."

"Thank you." They strolled toward Andrew's tent. "Congratulations on your victory."

"God was with us."

"Will you be marching through Stirling's gates this afternoon?"

"Aye. I'll be right behind William."

"And I'll bring up the rear with Lady Murray if she is willing to ride beside me."

"Why would she not? Your father was a knight."

"True." Eva nodded. "May I ask you a question?"

"Verra well." He cleared his throat and looked skyward. "If ye must."

"Can we be friends?"

He frowned and met her gaze. "Priests dunna make friends with women."

"I see." She stopped outside Andrew's tent flap. "But surely you must know by now that I'll never do anything to compromise William's success."

"Dunna ye mean the success of the rebellion? Taking back our liberty is not about one man. It is about regaining freedom for Scotland."

"I know." She bit her bottom lip. The last time they'd talked, he thought her a traitor and warned her to watch her back. "But you and I are on the same side."

He bowed his head. "I'll give ye that, lass." Then he rapped on the tent. "Father Blair here. May we have a word with Lady Murray?"

"A moment." A woman's voice came from inside. In no time, the flap opened and Andrew's wife stepped through. She wore a light green kirtle with a darker green mantle draped over her shoulders and fastened at her neck with an enormous, round brooch. She looked at Eva and smiled. With alabaster skin, she had natural beauty, and though her hair was hidden by a wimple, she had mahogany colored eyebrows.

"My lady." Father Blair bowed. "Please allow me to introduce Miss Eva MacKay, the daughter of the late Sir David MacKay."

Eva's heart stopped for a moment. She'd never grow accustomed to anyone referring to her father as "the late", but "the future" would make no sense to anyone but her and William. She reached out her hands. "I am ever so pleased to make your acquaintance."

"And I yours." Lady Murray offered an aristocratic smile. "Andrew mentioned William's wife rode with the rebels."

Wife? Eva clapped her hands to her burning cheeks and looked to the priest.

Sucking in his gaunt cheeks with a pointed glare, he imparted no sympathy whatsoever. "If ye'll please excuse me, I've preparations to make." The priest hastened away before Eva could thank him.

She returned her attention to the lady. There was no use correcting her. "William and Andrew will be leading the procession through Stirling's gates and I was wondering if you'd care to join me at the rear?"

"I would be delighted." Lady Murray looped her arm through Eva's. "Would ye walk with me?"

"Of course." Eva hadn't expected the woman to be so amenable. "How was your journey?"

"Long." She absently rubbed her hand over her belly.

"When are you due?" Eva asked.

"How did ye know I was expecting?" She looked down at her stomach, which showed no signs of pregnancy. "Ye cannot possibly tell."

"William thinks I'm a seer," Eva chuckled. "But you did just rub your tummy."

"Tummy?" Lady Murray chuckled. "Andrew warned that your speech is odd."

"Apologies. I traveled a great deal with my father."

"How interesting," the lady said with a warm smile. "So if ye are a seer, can ye tell me if my child will be lad or lass?"

Eva stopped and held up her hands. "May I?"

The lady grinned and nodded.

Making a show of placing her hands on the woman's abdomen, Eva closed her eyes and hummed, noting no annoying heat from the medallion. "'Tis a lad for certain."

"Honestly?" Lady Murray clapped her hands, beaming excitedly. "Andrew will be delighted."

Eva forced a smile. "The bairn shall become a great man. I'm sure of it."

"Please forgive me, but I must inform my husband at once."

Eva curtseyed. "By all means. I shall see you anon."

Chapter Thirty-Five

As planned, Andrew's wife met Eva at the back of the parade. "Hello, Miss Eva."

"You look stunning, Lady Murray."

"Please call me Christina."

"Very well, and I am just Eva." She gestured ahead. "Are you ready? Even from here, people are lining the road to the castle. There must be thousands up at the top."

"And so there should be. 'Tis time all of Scotland united in our cause."

Eva looked away and rubbed a hand over her mouth while her gaze trailed sideways. Yes, Scotland would face many, many battles large and small before her people completely regained their liberty. But as with so many things, she couldn't allow herself to fixate on the future. For today was one reserved for great celebration. Tapping her heels against her horse's barrel, Eva followed the procession up the hill.

The crowd cheered wildly, throwing flowers onto the cobbled road, shouting Wallace at the top of their voices. Eva looked to Christina, but the lady showed no outward sign of concern that William's name was the one being hailed.

And Eva had been right. The closer they moved to the castle, the more crowded the route became. The wall-walk was lined with guards standing at attention with bows and quivers of arrows over their shoulders.

Before they crossed under the portcullis, Eva spotted yet another gruesome medieval custom. Cressingham's head hung above the Scottish coat of arms, flanked by the heads of other English victims.

She swallowed back her urge to be sick and looked to Christina. "Do those severed heads give you pause?"

"Oh no. That man received his due if ye ask me. 'Tis right to honor our men by displaying the spoils of their victory."

Eva had never thought of it like that. "You mean everyone *wants* to see grotesque heads on the castle walls?"

The lady looked as if Eva had lost her mind. "Aye, lassie, it gives the men courage for the next battle."

"Ah, of course." Eva swallowed hard and averted her eyes from the gruesome sight.

Once inside the crowded courtyard, grooms took the horses, and Eddy Little approached. "Willy and Sir Andrew will be at the high table with the nobles, but he's reserved a place for ye near the dais. Follow me."

Eva looped her arm through Christina's. "This is so exciting."

The lady stumbled into her. "Aye, if we make it to the great hall without being trampled."

"Just stay close to Eddy and we might live." Eva laughed.

Inside the enormous hall, the ceiling had to be fifty feet high, supported by thick beams. A gallery surrounded the entire chamber, and aisles of tables filled the room. Joyous music resounded between the walls. The smell of roasting meat and baking bread wafted up from the kitchens, making Eva's mouth water. "This should be a grand feast indeed."

Eddy stopped at a table beside the dais. "Here ye are ladies."

"Thank you." Eva sat on the bench beside Christina, facing the dais.

She spotted William right away. Lord, what a grand picture he made, head and shoulders above them all. "I recognize Lord Stewart and the Earl of Lennox. But aside from Andrew, I cannot place a one. Can you tell me who each man is?"

Christina leaned in. "It has been a time since I was last at court. Hm. On the left is Robert Bruce, Lord of Annandale, and his son, the Earl of Carrick." Christina giggled. "I see John Comyn, the Lord of Badenoch, is seated at the opposite end of the table. Ye ken their families hate each other?"

"Yes, I am aware." Eva could scarcely believe she was seeing these great men in the flesh. If only she could play seer and tell the Earl of Carrick he'd one day become king. But, given the enormous egos at the high table, such a declaration could start a riot.

"Let us see, Father Lamberton is the Chancellor of Glasgow Cathedral, acting Bishop for the duration of Wishart's absence."

"My, he's very young." Eva bit her tongue, well aware that Lamberton would become pivotally important to William in the near future.

"Aye, but his father's Lord of Kilmarus," Christina said with reverence, and then pointed. "Beside him is Lord Campbell, Lord Eglington. I'm surprised not to see Sir Douglas. He has been verra active in the rebellion."

Eva's gut squelched. "I'm happy he's not here. I had the misfortune of meeting that man and he is most disagreeable."

Christina made a sour face. "I've heard the same. Though he is a good soldier."

"And a good backstabber to boot."

"Well then, 'tis fortuitous he is indeed absent."

Eva stared at the Earl of Carrick. Broad shouldered with bold eyebrows, he was handsome with an aristocratic mien. He looked out over the throng with a hawk-like gaze. The man exuded intelligence and cunning. Though all the men seated at the high table wore fanciful airs, and fur-lined cloaks, the future Robert the Bruce had the most commanding presence. Even if she didn't know it was he, she would have picked him out of a lineup to be future king.

"Is something amiss?" asked Christina.

Eva blinked. "Hmm?"

"You're staring at the Earl of Carrick like his head is twisted backward."

With a laugh, she reached for a ewer of wine. "Forgive me. I was deep in thought."

"Did ye have a vision?" Christina held up her cup. "I understand seers have visions."

Eva poured for the lady, then for herself. "No. Just being silly, I suppose." Thinking or talking about the future would only land her in a world of trouble.

Servants processed up the dais carrying trenchers laden with food, while throughout the immense hall people made merry. Eva closed her eyes and listened to the delightful music and inhaled the delicious aromas swirling about the candlelit hall. Oh how lucky she was to be included in this momentous feast.

When she opened her eyes, William stared directly at her from behind his goblet. Robert the Bruce might be an imposing future king, but William's dark stare took her breath away. No other man at the table was as tall, as broad shouldered, or as completely magnificent as William Wallace.

Then the High Steward stood and raised his cup. The men pounded the hilts of their eating knives on the table, demanding silence.

"This eve, I dedicate this feast to Mr. William Wallace and Sir Andrew Murray for their heroic seizure of Stirling's palace. May they continue to lead our forces to drive out Longshanks and restore Scotland's freedom."

A triumphant cheer rose together with trumpeters atop the gallery. But it didn't slip past Eva's observation that Lord Stewart had omitted John Balliol from his toast, or any mention of the imprisoned Scottish king.

She looked again for William's reaction, but her attention was drawn away when John Comyn stood, a slight, rather pale man. "My vote is to nominate Scotland's two heroes as the new Guardians of Scotland."

Nearly every man at the table frowned.

William glanced at Andrew, who had a sheen of sweat across his sallow brow.

The High Steward shot a stern nod Comyn's way. "Your suggestion is a decision for parliament. We shan't consider it now, for tonight we feast."

***

When the meal was over, William bid good eve to Andrew and his wife. Turning to Eva, still seated at her table, he bowed and placed a tender kiss on the back of her hand. "Ye look like a queen."

A lovely blush enlivened her cheeks as she glanced down at the burgundy gown he'd purchased for her in Renfrew. "You've seen me wear this once before."

"Aye, and ye looked like a queen then as well." He tugged on her hand. "Come. Let us stroll along Stirling's wall-walk and watch the sunset."

"Don't you want to talk with the nobles? I've never seen such a gathering of dignitaries in all their finery." She lowered her voice. "And they've all come to see you."

"There will be plenty of talk on the morrow and for the next sennight to come. But presently, I want to enjoy a moment holding the bonniest woman in all of Scotland in my arms." He let out a rumbling chuckle. "During the entire feast, I wanted nothing more than to take ye away to a place of solace."

"Since you put it so eloquently, there's no way on earth I could refuse." Eva's smile radiated more brightly than the candelabra on the table. When she stood, she inclined her lips to his ear. "I'm proud of you, William." By the stars, the woman could make butter melt in a snow storm.

Wallace's chest swelled as he led his woman out to the courtyard and up the winding steps in the stairwell. Up they climbed as he crouched to avoid hitting his head. Glancing back, Eva had to crouch a bit too. Lord, she was tall for a woman. Once atop the walk, a brisk breeze tousled his hair and he took in a reviving breath. Built high upon a rocky cliff, the castle was as great a fortress as he'd ever seen. Verdant pastoral lands and forest stretched until it met with the mountainous Highlands.

He smoothed his hand up her back and rested his fingers on her shoulder. "'Tis as if we're standing above all of Christendom."

She fearlessly leaned through a crenel notch. "Almost like being at the top of the Empire State Building."

"What?" William pulled her back by the arm before she fell. Goodness, Eva could say the damnedest things.

"Sorry. You must think I'm an idiot." She shook her head. "I should have said we are at the top of the gateway to the Highlands. Anyone who controls Stirling controls Scotland."

"I agree there." Wallace had no doubt that she spoke true about the building of the Empire. He still couldn't imagine her world or the things she'd described, but he no longer feared them. He offered her his elbow. "Let us stroll to the western walk."

She smiled. It wasn't the innocent smile of a maid, but a knowing smile of woman who knew what she wanted. "Do lead on."

The western sky turned pink and orange as they ambled toward it, their feet lightly tapping the stone. After they'd passed over the main gatehouse, Eva released her grip and leaned against the wall. "The River Forth looks so different from this vantage point."

"Aye, as does Abbey Craig." Pride swelled in his chest as he gazed across the Carse of Stirling to the hill where he and his men had lain in wait.

With a sigh, she straightened and rested her head against his shoulder.

William closed his eyes and allowed himself to drink in her sweet fragrance. Together they stood as contented lovers until brilliant hues of sunset faded.

"May I remove your snood, m'lady?" He slid his hand atop her crown.

She glanced over each shoulder with a playful grin. "Won't someone balk about my short hair?"

"If they do, they'll answer to me. Besides, 'tis growing and I want to watch your tresses shimmer in the moonlight."

She bowed her head forward and allowed him to remove it. When she looked up, her hands flew to her temples. "Is my hair smooshed?"

He ran his fingers through the silken copper tresses. Such a simple gesture, but it calmed the ferocious beast in his soul. Aye, he would fight for his country, but after every battle, he yearned for peace—yearned for Eva to soothe him as her lithe fingers had done last eve. William smiled and gazed into her fathomless green eyes. "Your tresses are bonny. 'Tis a shame ye have to cover them."

"I like letting my hair loose in the wind." She stepped closer, sliding her hand around his waist. "But more so, I like what you're doing right now. Your touch makes me feel wanted."

He pressed his lips against her temple. "Never for a moment should ye think I dunna want ye, Eva."

"Honestly?" she whispered. "Even though I'm from a different time?"

"Even though. Besides, I dunna think there's so much time between us, ye and I. We are two drifting souls. In such a short time, we've come to share so many things—come to mean so much to each other."

She rose up on her toes and kissed his cheek. "I cannot tell you how happy it makes me to hear you say that. We *are* soul mates."

He chuckled. "I love your twists of phrase."

She rested her head on his chest. "I love your honor and honesty, and the deep burr that rolls across your tongue."

He took his left hand and held out her right, placing his other in the small of her back. "Shall we waltz?"

She looked up with wide eyes. "Up here?"

"Aye." A warm chuckle rumbled through his chest. "The walls are high enough, I doubt we'll fall to our deaths should I stumble over my feet."

Her feline eyes crinkled at the corners with a delightful giggle. "You are ever so reassuring, sir knight."

His shoulders tensed a bit. "I am no one's knight."

"You are mine," she whispered.

"Verra well. I'll give ye that. I *am* yours." He glanced down at their feet. "Now how does it go? One, two three?"

She picked up the steps. "Aye, down, up, up. One, two three."

Her lovely voice hummed an enchanting tune as they danced in place. William hadn't a mind to be anywhere else. In his arms he held the only woman he'd ever met who'd suited him in every way. And oh, could her voice lull the savage beast within his heart.

He pulled her close and filled his senses with the intoxicating bouquet of her wild tresses. "Ye are so fine to me, Eva MacKay."

"As you are to me, William Wallace."

Excerpt from Amy's Next Novel:

Follow along as William and Eva's saga continues with *Guardian of Scotland* volume two:

In the Kingdom's Name.

Here's a wee peek:

Chapter One

Selkirk, Scotland, late September, 1297

Holding her breath, Eva MacKay shot a glance over her left shoulder then her right. Alone at the rear of the nave, she stood behind a gathering of the most influential nobles in Scotland. Temptation made her fingers twitch. This might be her only chance. Gingerly, she slid her hand into the pouch hanging from her belt and palmed her smartphone. She'd be a total fool not to snap a photo of such a momentous occasion.

But if caught…

With a shudder, Eva looked again to ensure no one watched.

She pushed the "on" button and drew the phone out. With a quick swipe of her finger, familiar icons illuminated. After selecting the camera, she turned off the flash and held it up, snapping two quick pictures. Before Eva dared look at them, she slipped the shiny black rectangle back into her pocket—more like a purse, really, fashioned from the same material as her thirteenth-century gown.

The sound of a man clearing his throat came from Eva's left. Jolting, her stomach somersaulted with a queasy leap. John Comyn, Lord of Badenoch, stepped from behind an enormous stone pillar. He stood for a moment and squinted at her with suspicion etched across his hard, pinched features. Eva folded her arms, raised her chin and tiptoed to resume her place beside Lady Christina while watching the snake out of the corner of her eye. In the short time she'd come to know Scotland's nobles, she trusted Comyn the least, with the Earl of March a close second.

As the Lord of Badenoch brushed past her and joined his wife, Eva exhaled and turned her attention to the front of the Kirk of the Forest. Lord John Stewart, the High Steward of Scotland, presided over the ceremony, flanked by Canon Lamberton. "Kneel," he instructed William Wallace and Sir Andrew Murray.

They complied as commanded, wearing full battle armor of hauberks and mail coifs, adorned with surcoats emblazoned with the St. Andrew's Cross. Lord Stewart placed his palms upon their heads. "By the power invested in me granted by the Privy Council of this great nation, I hereby declare Mr. Wallace and Sir Murray joint Guardians of the Kingdom of Scotland. As witnessed by your gallant bravery and cunning defeat of the English at Stirling Bridge, ye shall not only preside over matters of state, ye shall be Commanders of the Army of Scotland and the community of the same Kingdom."

The High Steward paused for a moment and panned his gaze across the gathering of Scotland's highest ranking nobles. "Do ye swear to uphold all laws and decrees of the Kingdom of Scotland?"

"I so swear," each man said in unison.

"Do ye swear in the presence of all in attendance to defend this great nation against Scotland's enemies?"

"I so swear."

"Do ye promise to safeguard the rights of the crown until Scotland once again sees our monarch returned the throne?"

The two men regarded each other with a solemn nod. "I so promise."

Then Lord Stewart stood back and raised his palms. "Go forth and act to uphold the interests and decrees of Scotland. From this day henceforth, all subjects shall honor ye as the undisputed Guardians of this blessed Kingdom."

Eva pressed her palms together and touched her fingers to her lips while tears blurred her vision. Unwilling to miss a single moment, she blinked in rapid succession. Indeed, this day was the most uplifting in the five months since she'd been hurled into the thirteenth century.

Together William and Andrew stood, bowed, then turned and strode down the aisle. Though at six-foot, Sir Andrew Murray was inordinately tall for a man of this era, Wallace towered over him by more than a head. Of all the nobles in attendance, William was the only commoner, but by far, the most impressive warrior. Chestnut curls peeked from beneath his coif, framing a handsomely chiseled face made fierce by his cropped auburn beard. Even though he wore thick mail armor, anyone who saw him would be impressed with his well-toned, iron-muscled frame. Wrapped in tight chausses, William's powerful legs stretched against his thigh-length hauberk with every stride.

When he caught Eva's eye, a slight smile turned up one corner of his mouth, his crystal blue eyes sparkling with the flicker of the aisle candles nested in their tall, iron stands. In truth, William Wallace could make Eva melt merely with a look and today was no different. She clapped a hand over her heart to stifle its rapid pounding.

No one knew why the mystic powers behind the ancient medallion chose her, pulling Eva from the twenty-first century ruins of Fail Monastery through some sort of time warp where Wallace rescued her from nearly being murdered by the sharp blade of an English sword. Since arriving in the midst of a battle between the English and the Scots, three things had guided her decisions. First: as a historical journalist, she religiously chronicled all of the events she witnessed. The second: she could not change past events. If she did anything to materially change the past, her time in William's arms would come to an abrupt end. And finally, Eva refused to lie to William, which always seemed to land her in more sticky situations than she ever would have thought possible.

But none of that mattered right now. The only man in the thirteenth century, or the twenty-first for that matter, who could rock her world just strode past and gave her a sexy wink.

"Goodness, Andrew grows paler by the day," said Lady Murray from behind.

Eva's elation immediately ebbed when she turned and regarded her friend's worried mien. Sir Andrew had been injured during the Battle of Stirling Bridge and had suffered since. Worse, the bairn in his wife's pregnant belly had begun to show. If only Eva could do something to help him—help the pair of them. She patted Christina's arm. "Today is momentous for him."

"Aye, I am ever so proud."

"As you should be." Eva stepped into the aisle and grasped Christina's hand. "Come, let's join them."

At five-foot eleven, Eva could see over most heads, and she pulled the petite woman through the throng. Once they squeezed out the thick double doors of the church, she spotted William surrounded by men dressed in more velvet than it would take to stitch together a set of curtains for a theater. She led Christina off to the side, away from the stream of foot traffic. "Perhaps we should wait here."

The lady smoothed her hands over her silk wimple and nodded. "Verra well."

Lord Comyn stepped to Eva's right and folded his arms. "What's in your purse, lassie?"

"Pardon?" She feigned an exasperated expression. "I have no idea to what you are referring."

He smirked. "Och aye, ye do. And whatever it is, I've every suspicion 'tisna something meant for a house of God."

Eva's chin ticked up. "Are you threatening me, m'lord?"

Scoffing, he gave an exaggerated eye roll. "Heaven forbid someone threaten William Wallace's woman."

Narrowing her eyes, she glared at him for a moment. Even if he'd seen her take the pictures, he wouldn't have a clue what she was up to. And she'd turned the flash off. He had absolutely no grounds on which to make any accusations. With a dismissive nod she turned her attention back to Christina.

"But—" Comyn stepped closer, making the hackles on the back of Eva's neck stand on end. "One day that big fella will fall out of favor and then a pretty mistress such as yourself willna be so smug."

"I beg your pardon, Lord Comyn?" Lady Murray threw her shoulders back. "Ye overinflate your station. Regardless of your noble birth, Miss Eva is the daughter of a knight and I daresay she ought not to be spoken to like a mere commoner."

"Not to worry." Eva flashed a wry grin. "I am very comfortable being identified as among the loyal servants of Scotland. Unlike some high-ranking gentry present whose questionable actions have proved their very hypocrisy, *and* their willingness to change allegiances on a whim only to protect their personal wealth."

"Is all well here?" William's deep voice rumbled as he climbed the steps toward them.

"Ye'd best put a leash on your barb-tongued wench." Adjusting his collar, Lord Comyn stretched his neck and strode off.

With a gasp, Christina drew a hand to her chest. "How discourteous."

Wrapping his fingers around the hilt of his dirk, William's gaze shot to Eva.

She waved her palms with an apologetic cringe. "It's nothing. I baited him, is all. Told him I'd rather mingle with the commoners than a mob of noble hypocrites."

Tense as a lion ready to pounce, William glared at Comyn's retreating form. As the Lord of Badenoch was swallowed by the crowd, Wallace let out a heavy exhale, relaxed his grip and regarded her. "Och, lassie, there's never a want for a bit o' excitement when ye're about." He placed his palm in the small of her back and turned his lips to her ear. "But regardless, if we werena celebrating with half of Scotland's nobles, I'd challenge the sputtering hog to a lesson in chivalry."

With a grin, Eva leaned into him as they proceeded toward the path to Selkirk Castle. "Aye?" she teased. "A man as reed-thin as Lord Comyn would give you no sport whatsoever." Her twists of Auld Scots phrases became stronger by the day.

Sir Andrew joined them. "Trouble with the Lord of Badenoch?"

"That man is full of self-importance," said Lady Christina, placing her palm atop her husband's offered elbow—the one not in a sling.

Sir Andrew sighed. "Agreed, but so are over half the gentry in our company."

"Well, he's not worth a second thought." With a sideways glance, Eva grinned at William. "Besides this is a momentous occasion, too important to be filled with misgivings about jealous nobility. Tell me, what has Lord Scott ordered for your celebratory dinner?"

"Anything but swan," said William with a chuckle. "As I recall, 'tis not your favorite."

"Yuck." Eva made a sour face. "It tastes like fishy mutton."

"That it does, though ye use the oddest words, Eva. *Yuck?*" Lady Christina peeked around her husband. "Wherever do ye come up with them?"

William grasped Eva's hand and squeezed. He was the only person in this century who knew the truth about her past and even the fearless warrior still had trouble believing it. He needn't worry, because she had no intension of revealing her secrets to anyone else. Momentarily, she strolled along the wooded path with her friends as if she belonged. "I traveled a great deal with my father. In my experience, I'd say sailors use the most colorful language."

William cringed. "Och, dunna tell me ye'll soon be teaching Lady Murray to talk like a pirate."

The lady shook her finger. "Oh no. Miss Eva must spend a month or two with me and I'll set her to rights."

As they moved toward Selkirk Castle, Eva rather liked the idea of spending time with Christina Murray and learning how to be a proper thirteenth-century lady…until her gut squeezed. *Damn.* Thoughts of the future always had a way of dampening her enthusiasm.

End of Excerpt from IN THE KINGDOM'S NAME

Other Books by Amy Jarecki:

Highland Force Series:

Captured by the Pirate Laird
The Highland Henchman
Beauty and the Barbarian
Return of the Highland Laird (A Highland Force Novella)

Highland Dynasty Series:

Knight in Highland Armor
A Highland Knight's Desire
A Highland Knight to Remember
Highland Knight of Rapture

Pict/Roman Romances:

Rescued by the Celtic Warrior
Celtic Maid

Visit Amy's web site & sign up to receive newsletter updates of new releases and giveaways exclusive to newsletter followers: www.amyjarecki.com
Follow on Facebook
Follow on Twitter

If you enjoyed *Rise of a Legend*, we would be honored if you would consider leaving a review. ~*Thank you!*

About the Author

A descendant of an ancient Lowland clan, Amy adores Scotland. Though she now resides in southwest Utah, she received her MBA from Heriot-Watt University in Edinburgh. Winning multiple writing awards, she found her niche in the genre of Scottish historical romance. Amy loves hearing from her readers and can be contacted through her website at www.amyjarecki.com.